DEN OF WOLVES

DEN OF WOLVES

A BLACKTHORN & GRIM NOVEL

Juliet Marillier

ROC

NEW YORK

ROC
Published by Berkley
An imprint of Penguin Random House LLC
375 Hudson Street, New York, New York 10014

Library of Congress Cataloging-in-Publication Data
Names: Marillier, Juliet, author.
Title: Den of wolves: a Blackthorne & Grim novel / Juliet Marillier.
Description: New York, New York: Roc, 2016. | "A ROC book."
Identifiers: LCCN 2016032088 (print) | LCCN 2016035347 (ebook) |
ISBN 9780451467034 | ISBN 9780698139244 (ebook)
Subjects: | BISAC: FICTION/Fantasy/Historical. | FICTION/Fantasy/Epic. |
FICTION/Romance/Fantasy. | GSAFD: Fantasy fiction. | Historical fiction.
Classification: LCC PR9619.3.M26755 D46 2016 (print) | LCC PR9619.3.M26755
(ebook) | DDC 823/.914—dc23
LC record available at https://lccn.loc.gov/2016032088

Macmillan trade paperback edition / September 2016
Roc hardcover edition / November 2016

Printed in the United States of America
1 3 5 7 9 10 8 6 4 2

Jacket illustration by Arantza Sestayo
Jacket design by Adam Auerbach

For my grandchildren.
May they grow strong as the oak. May they be flexible as the willow.
May they blossom like the hawthorn.

CHARACTER LIST

This list includes some characters who are mentioned by name but don't appear in the story.

At Wolf Glen

Cara:	aged fifteen
Tóla:	her father, landholder at Wolf Glen
Suanach: (soo-a-nakh)	Tóla's wife, Cara's mother (deceased)
Della:	Tóla's sister, Cara's aunt
Alba:	Cara's personal maid
Gormán:	chief forester
Conn:	assistant forester
Bardán: (bar-dawn)	a wild man
Dáire: (dah-reh)	his wife (deceased)

At Winterfalls

Blackthorn:	wise woman and healer
Grim:	her companion
Cass:	Blackthorn's husband (deceased)
Brennan:	Blackthorn's son (deceased)
Oran:	prince of Dalriada
Flidais: (flid-is)	his wife
Aolú: (ay-loo)	their son
Deirdre: (dee-dra)	Flidais's maidservant and companion
Mhairi: (mah-ree)	maidservant
Nuala: (noo-la)	maidservant
Donagan:	Oran's body servant and companion
Aedan:	Oran's steward
Fíona:	Aedan's wife, housekeeper
Brid: (breedj)	cook

Niall:	farmer
Eochu: (okh-oo)	stable master
Eoin: (ohn)	man-at-arms
Fergal:	man-at-arms
Lochlan:	chief man-at-arms
Emer: (eh-ver)	Blackthorn's young assistant
Fraoch: (frech)	village smith, Emer's brother
Scannal:	miller
Clíona:	sheep farmer

At Longwater

Fann:	a local woman
Osgar:	her brother
Ross:	her husband
Ide: (ee-deh)	mother of Fann and Osgar
Luíseach: (lee-sakh)	Ide's sister-in-law
Fedach:	Luíseach's son, aged fifteen
Eibhlín: (ev-leen)	a young woman
Corcrán:	a young man

The Swan Island Men

Ségán: (seh-awn)	leader of the Swan Island men
Cúan (koo-awn)	
Art	
Earc (ark)	
Caolchú (kehl-choo)	
Cionnaola (ki-neh-la)	
Lonán (loh-nawn)	

Others

Master Saran	
Master Bress:	lawmen
Mathuin:	chieftain of Laois
Lorcan:	king of Mide
Cadhan:	chieftain of White Hill, Flidais's father
Branoc:	a baker
Conmael:	a fey nobleman
Brígh: (bree)	
Oisin: (a-*sheen*)	a druid

And Not Forgetting

Ripple:	a well-trained hound
Bramble:	a bad-tempered terrier
Sturdy:	a cart horse
Mercy:	a fine mare
Willow:	Tóla's favorite riding horse

DEN OF WOLVES

1

BARDÁN

He's curled in a ball, shivering, under a piercing white moon.
He'd forgotten how bright the moon was, how its light could go right
through a man, cold in his bones, searching out what was hidden deep.
Go away, he breathes, arms up over his head, knees to his chest, trying
to be invisible. *Leave me alone.* But the light seeks him out, finding a
way through the high canopy of the beeches, through the rough blanket of bracken and fern he's scrambled together, through the rags of his
clothing, right inside him. Into his mind, tangling his thoughts. Into his
heart, probing his wounds. It's been so long. How long has it been? How
long has he been away?

An owl cries, eerie, hollow. In the undergrowth, something screams.
Something dies. *Stop,* he whispers. *Don't.* But nobody's listening. His
words fall into the quiet of the night forest and are lost. He's lost. The
cold moon will kill him before he can find his way. The way back to . . .
to . . .

A fragment comes to him; then it's gone. Another piece, and another.
A story . . . but the meaning slips away before he can grasp it. Shivering
body. Chattering teeth. A man . . . A man building . . . A man making
a house, a strange house . . . He can feel the wood under his hands,

his crooked hands . . . Long ago, so long ago . . . Was there a rhyme for the building, a charm, a spell? Crooked hands. Crooked yew. He makes the words with his lips, but there is no sound. *Blackthorn, ivy and crooked yew.*

He can't remember much. But what he remembers is enough, for now. Enough to keep his heart beating; enough to keep him breathing through the cold night, until morning. The beech tree will shelter him; she will spread her strong arms over him, shutting out the chill eye of the moon. And when the sun rises and the long night is over, he knows where he will go.

2

CARA

The forest knew everything. News passed on a breath of wind, in the call of an owl, in the small pattern of a squirrel's paw prints. The trout in the stream learned it. The lark soaring high above saw it. The knowledge was in the hearts of the trees and in the mysterious rustling of their leaves. It was a deep-down wisdom, as solemn as a druid's prayer.

She never talked about it. Not with Father, not with Aunt Della, not even with Gormán. She'd learned long ago that if she spoke of that great knowledge, people thought she was being foolish or fanciful. That didn't matter. What mattered was saying it to the trees, over and over, so they knew she was their friend and guardian and could hear their slow voices. She spoke to each of them in turn, in a whisper, with her body against the trunk and her cheek pressed to the bark, as if she and the tree shared the same beating heart. Rough oak, smooth willow, furrowed ash, every tree in the wood. *I will protect you. I will guard you. I give you my word.*

The promise wasn't foolish or fanciful. It made perfect sense. One day the holding at Wolf Glen would be hers to watch over. Mother was dead. Father would never marry again. There was nobody else to inherit the house, the farm, the forest. All of it, and all the folk who lived and worked there, would be hers to care for, hers to look after.

Father didn't talk about the future, even now that Cara was in her sixteenth year. But she knew he expected her to marry someday and produce an heir. She let herself dream, sometimes, about what might have been if she had not been a girl and the only child. She could have become a master wood-carver. She could have spent all day making creatures and chests and chairs with fine decoration, toys for children, platters to hold fruit, spindles and cradles and walking staves with owls on them. Or she could have been a forester like Gormán. Gormán had been her friend since almost before she could walk. He had taught her the properties of different woods. Sometimes she would open up her special storage chest and get out the collection of little animals she'd made over the years. She loved them all, from the rabbit she had crafted from pine at six years old to the owl she'd coaxed not long ago from a well-weathered block of oak. The owl had its wings lifted, ready for flight, and when Cara looked at it she imagined spreading wings of her own and flying off over the treetops, wild and free. When she had held each of her little creatures in turn, stroked each, spoken softly to each, she would shut them away in the chest again.

Soon, she knew, Father would start looking for a prospective husband for her. Father and Aunt Della had set their expectations high, hoping for a chieftain's son. But wouldn't that mean she would have to leave Wolf Glen? That could not happen. She would be like a sapling pulled up roughly, roots and all, then shoved into barren ground where it could not thrive. She would turn into a dull shadow of a woman whom nobody could possibly want as a wife. And who would look after the forest if she was not here? Her father loved Wolf Glen as she did, but his love was tinged with a darkness she did not understand.

Some girls were already wed at fifteen. Some were mothers. But that was not possible for her. It was unthinkable. If she married, how would she have time for any of the things that mattered? There would be no time to hear the many voices of the forest, no time to watch the patterns of leaves and light, no time to breathe the crisp air, no time to feel the weight of a fine piece of wood in her hands, seeing in her mind the forms that lay within. What if the husband her father chose for her did not understand these things? What if she tried to talk to him and her words suddenly vanished, the way they did sometimes when she was talking to Father or Aunt Della? The suitor would think her a half-wit, and Father would be furious, and that would make it even more impossible to get words out.

Perhaps she could refuse to wed unless the man loved the same things she loved. Somewhere, surely, there must be at least one other person like her. If she could summon the right words, maybe she could persuade Father to wait awhile. Some women married and had babies when they were quite old, twenty or even five-and-twenty. Her maid Alba had told her so. There was plenty of time. Years.

Or so she thought, up till the day the wild man came to Wolf Glen, and everything changed.

She'd been out by the barn, showing Gormán a drawing she'd made for a carving of a squirrel. He'd promised to look out for the right piece of wood but warned her it might take some time to find it. "Off you go, then," he'd said in his gruff way. "I've my big ax to sharpen, and I don't want you anywhere near while I'm doing it, young lady."

Alba had come to the yard too, but now she was nowhere in sight. One of the farm cats had produced a litter of kittens not long ago, and Cara guessed her maid was in the barn petting them; Alba loved cats. It was a good opportunity to go walking on her own—not far enough to get either Gormán or Alba in trouble, just down to the heartwood house. She could be back before anyone noticed she was gone. There was a rule about wandering off without a companion, and Aunt Della would be unhappy if she found out Cara had broken it. The rule was nonsense. Cara could find her way home from anywhere in the forest, even places where she had never been before. The trees were her friends. What harm could she possibly come to? Perhaps Aunt Della thought her stupid enough to get in the way of an ax like that giant implement Gormán was working on now.

That was just as silly. Gormán had taught her to be careful in the workshop. She knew how tools should be used, how they were kept sharp, how they were protected from rust. She knew how to avoid cutting herself or someone else when she used her wood-carving knives. But she couldn't explain that to Aunt Della. In her aunt's opinion, a young lady should spend her time sewing, spinning, weaving, and learning how to run a household, not messing about with sharp objects and making things that were of no possible use to anyone. Most times, while Cara was still struggling to find the right words, Aunt Della would end the conversation by saying, "Oh, Cara, you're such a child." But that wasn't true. She had her moon-bleeding now, and her body was changing, and that meant, surely, that she was not a child but a woman.

The heartwood house was not much of a house, only an old ruin in a clearing. Each winter it crumbled away a bit more. Although it was not very far from the barn, the pattern of the trees and the rise and fall of the land meant it could barely be seen until a person was almost on top of it. Father had been building it at the time of her mother's death. Once Suanach was gone, work on the house had ceased. It had been left as it was, hardly even a shelter for forest creatures, since it had no roof. In another year or two the last of it would fall and the forest would reclaim the clearing. Cara liked the quiet way the wild things were moving to blanket the broken structure.

When she was little, but old enough to be curious, she'd been full of questions about the heartwood house. In those days she'd had no trouble saying what she wanted to, straight out. She'd been brimming with words. Why was it called that? What was it for? Why couldn't they finish building it? Back then, more of the structure had been standing, and it had been easier to imagine what it might have been like had the work been finished. She had noticed, even then, that there were different kinds of wood in it. She'd wandered through the ruin touching them, looking at the colors and the patterns of them, guessing what they were, until Father had caught her at it and ordered her away from the place, saying it was not safe. He did not answer any of her questions. Indeed, he was so stern and sad that she stopped asking him.

Aunt Della gave all the questions the same response: she had not been living at Wolf Glen while Cara's mother was alive, and when Suanach had died, the heartwood house had been abandoned. So Aunt Della knew nothing at all about it except, she said, that it was a subject best not discussed, and especially not in Tóla's hearing. Cara would be better off putting her excess curiosity into learning her letters and numbers or improving her plain sewing.

Gormán knew the answers, some of them anyway, but even he was reluctant to talk. When she was a little older Cara realized her persistence could have got him into trouble. He could have lost his position in the household and been sent away from Wolf Glen, which had been his home for years. Gormán was a kindly man, and patient with her. Why was it called a heartwood house? That was a name from an old tale. No, he did not know the tale, but a heartwood house was said to be lucky. When Cara had commented with five-year-old bluntness that it had not been very lucky for her mother, since she had died, Gormán had crouched down, taken her hands in his and looked her straight in the eye.

"Cara," he'd said, his voice so soft and sorrowful it made her feel shivery, "don't ever say that to your father. Promise me."

"But why?"

"Because he thinks, if he'd got it finished, she might have . . . because it would make him very, very sad. Promise."

"I promise." She'd hardly understood, back then. "Why didn't he get it finished?"

"Never mind that."

"You could have built it," she'd said.

That had made Gormán smile. "Finding the wood, getting all the pieces ready, maybe. Putting a house together, no. I'm no builder. And this would be quite a tricky sort of house. A very special house." Then, in a different tone, "Want to see a thrush's nest? I spotted one this morning, up in the big oak."

Her mother and the heartwood house and the things she could not ask her father had all been instantly forgotten. A thrush's nest! With eggs in it, or even little baby birds! She was, after all, only five years old.

But the promise she'd made was a deep-down thing, and Cara did remember it. As time passed and she grew up, the heartwood house crumbled away year by year, and Father did not mend it, and never once did she ask him why.

There was a special tree down by the heartwood house. Cara called it the guardian oak. When she was little, it had seemed to her so tall that its topmost branches surely touched the clouds. It had seemed a being of wonder and secrets, full of hiding places, tenanted by all manner of creatures, the seen and the unseen. She'd been a confident climber almost from the time she could walk, and had spent more time than her father and aunt ever imagined up in that tree, safe in the cradle of its great arms, pretending to be a squirrel or a bird or a beetle, peering out through the foliage to see folk about their work, hoping nobody would come looking for her before she was ready to be found. Birds would gather on the branches around her, preening their feathers, making their subtle sounds, taking so little notice of her that she might as well have been part of the tree. Sometimes they would come and perch on her shoulders or in her hair. She used to tell the guardian oak stories, the kind of stories little children make up, and she thought the tree replied in a voice so slow and deep that human ears could not really understand it, though she knew what it was saying: *Ah, yes. Tell me more, small one.* Even now she told the tree her secrets. It was so much easier to talk to trees than to people. People didn't stay quiet and listen, really listen. People interrupted. They fidgeted. You could see from their faces that their thoughts were at least half on something quite different. Aunt Della would be thinking, *How will this strange child ever find a husband?* Father would be lost in some dream of the past, his eyes full of a sorrow his only daughter could not lift. Gormán was a good listener, but even he would have his mind on whatever job he had to start on as soon as Cara had finished her tale.

Fifteen was not too old for climbing trees. If she was quick she could get up to her favorite perch, sit there awhile, and still be back at the barn before Alba grew tired of the kittens. She tucked her hem into her girdle, eyed the distance, then jumped to hang by her hands. Once she had a good grip, she swung her legs up and braced her feet against the trunk. From there it was a simple matter of stretching one arm a bit farther to grab a particular side limb, then hauling herself up to a firm purchase. She climbed higher, up to her lookout, where she could sit comfortably at the junction of trunk and branch and see without being seen. The barn, the stables and the yard, a certain way off, and Gormán working on his big axe. Still no sign of Alba. Farther away, twin rows of lovely beeches leading to Wolf Glen's main dwelling. And nearer at hand . . . She froze. There was a strange man down there, almost directly below her, standing so perfectly still he might have been made of stone. He was wild-looking, filthy, with matted hair halfway down his back, a bristling beard and crazy eyes, and he was staring at the scattered remnants of the heartwood house.

Now perhaps you understand why it is not advisable for a young lady to go wandering about on her own, said Aunt Della in her mind. Though probably this was just some fellow down on his luck, a hapless wanderer who would pass by and never be seen again. As daughter of the house she should climb down, introduce herself, and point the way toward the kitchen, where they'd give him a good meal. And a wash; he was the dirtiest person Cara had seen in her whole life. But she did not climb down, not even when she saw Alba come out of the barn, look around for her, then head directly toward her hiding place. Alba didn't call Cara's name; she could guess where she was, and she understood that drawing attention might get Cara in trouble. Gormán looked up from his work as Alba passed, then went back to it.

The wild man did not move. The heartwood house seemed to hold him spellbound. Should she shout to Alba, warn her? While Alba and Gormán would be able to see the top of the guardian oak, the heartwood house would be invisible from over there; the trick of the land made sure of that. They could not see the man. But if she made a noise, the man would know she was there, and although Alba could run back to Gormán, Cara could not. Not without climbing down and going right past the stranger.

She waited, not moving, as Alba came closer. When the maidservant was almost at the heartwood house, the wild man started, turning his head. He had seen Alba, but she, walking steadily forward, had not seen him.

"Alba!" Cara called. "Go back! Fetch Gormán!"

Alba halted, stared, then turned and fled. And now the wild man's attention was all on Cara. If she had thought herself well concealed, she'd been wrong. He was staring at her as if he wanted to eat her up. In the filthy, neglected ruin of his face, his eyes were burning coals, hungry and desperate. Ice spread through her. Her heart hammered so hard she thought she might lose her balance and come crashing down at his feet. *Gormán's coming,* she told herself, gripping the branch so tightly her fingers hurt. *Gormán's coming and he's big and strong and it will be all right. Just stay up here and don't move.* What if the wild man could climb? *Don't think about it, Cara. Breathe. Wait.*

An endless time, then, while he stared, stock-still, and Cara stared back, thinking that the moment she took her eyes off him he would be up the tree like a squirrel and it would be all over for her. In that time she heard a dog barking somewhere on the farm, and birds moving about in the foliage, and the wind stirring the leaves, and she hoped she could hear the voice of the oak, saying, *You will be safe. You are one of ours.* How could that man keep so still? Nobody could be so still. Could he be one of the fey, a being with magical powers? Cara had never been sure if they were real or just a thing in stories. She'd wanted them to be real, but that wasn't the same. If this man was one, he was unlike any description of fey folk in any tale she'd heard. Weren't they supposed to be elegant and beautiful? This man looked—and smelled—as if he'd been rolling in the midden.

She was shivering. Her fingers didn't want to hold on any longer. Spots danced before her eyes; she went from freezing cold to burning hot. *Don't faint, Cara.* If she fell from this height, the wild man would be the least of her problems.

And then there was another voice: Gormán's. "Cara? Where are you?" He strode into view with Conn behind him. Gormán had the big axe over his shoulder; Conn carried an iron bar.

"Up here," she called, feeling more foolish than frightened now.

The wild man moved, backing away from the oak as if to give her room. Perhaps he really was only a wanderer in need of a good feed and a corner of the barn to sleep in.

"Climb down, Cara." Gormán spoke calmly, but there was a note in his voice that scared her. He had his eye on the stranger, every moment. Even when she jumped down the last bit to land more or less beside him, he did not look at her. "Conn will walk back to the house with you. Do as I ask, please. Conn, make sure Alba has delivered the message. Now go."

Cara risked a quick glance at the wild man, and he made a sound. Perhaps he was trying to talk, but what came out was a grunting, moaning noise, so sad and terrible that tears sprang to her eyes.

"Come, Cara," Conn said. "Quickly."

She turned and followed him. He was walking fast; she had to scurry to keep up. But she still heard what Gormán said, behind her.

"In the name of all the gods. You're alive."

Later that same day, Father sent for her. It would be a lecture on behaving like a lady. If he started that conversation about suitors, perhaps telling her young men of good breeding would not be interested in a person with twigs in her hair and her skirts hitched up to an unseemly height, she'd have only herself to blame. Cara wondered whether he would say anything about the wild man. How was it that Gormán knew him? And where was he now?

She changed into a gown she knew her father liked, in soft wool dyed violet-blue. There was no sign of Alba, so she plaited her own hair and pinned it up as neatly as she could. It was somewhat wild at the best of times, with a tendency to curl when there was the slightest trace of damp. Aunt Della had been known to refer to it as a bird's nest. Cara quite liked the notion of walking around with a clutch of peeping owlets snuggled up there. Her hair was the right color for a nest, being of many shades of brown—lichen, oak bark, pebble, vole, autumn beech. Plaited, the colors blended into an innocuous muddy hue.

"Father?" She tapped on the open door of the council chamber.

"Come in, Cara." He was sitting at his worktable with documents spread out before him. Cara had thought Aunt Della might be with him, but he was alone. "Close the door, if you will."

There was a flask of mead on the table, with a pair of goblets. At his gesture, she poured a small measure for herself, a more generous one for him.

"Well now, Daughter." Father gazed at her as if thinking hard. She could not tell if he was sad—he was often sad—or merely thoughtful.

Cara's stomach felt suddenly odd, as if there were a knot of eels squirming around in there. Should she try to say sorry for what had happened earlier? It wasn't as if she had done anything wrong. All she'd done was take a slight risk. Nobody had been hurt. Yes, she had broken a rule, but . . .

"I know how much you love this place," Father said. "As much as I do, I believe. When your mother died . . ."

It had been a long time ago. Never having known her mother, Cara did not miss her. But Father still grieved her loss. There was something sorrowful about him even when he was at his most commanding.

"Never mind that," he went on, collecting himself. "If I have been critical, sometimes, of your tendency to . . ." He faltered again.

Something was wrong. Something more than her error of judgment. She made those often enough, and usually got no more than a mild reprimand from Aunt Della.

"Your aunt and I have been discussing your future," Father said. "Your welfare. You are nearly sixteen. I believe I have been somewhat selfish. Keeping you up here with me, out of touch with other folk . . . not finding opportunities for you . . . The situation must change. It's for your own good."

Words bubbled up, urgent words. But they lost themselves before her lips and tongue could speak them. All that came out was a desperate little sound, a chirp of panic.

"Within a year or two we'll need to consider a marriage for you. To be honest, that prospect seems hardly possible at this stage. Your aunt and I agree that you are entirely unready for it. To mingle with society, to create and manage a household of her own, a young woman requires a certain modicum of social awareness."

In her mind was an anguished plea: *Don't send me away! Oh, please!* She tried to get the words out, tried so hard she choked and had to gulp down a mouthful of mead.

"You make no comment," Father said gravely. "But I know you can speak when you choose to, Cara. I've heard you talking away to that maid of yours. I've heard you chatting with Gormán. This stubbornness is childish. I don't understand it. Can you not see how distressed your aunt is by your refusal to talk to her? You are not a wild creature but a young lady of good family. Della has given up years of her life to care for you."

She hung her head. He considered her a disappointment. A burden. As if it were her fault her mother had died when Cara was less than a year old. As if her father's grief were her doing. He didn't love her. Couldn't, or he would understand that if she could talk to him, she would say that she loved him more than anything, that he was her family, that she would give everything she had if only she could bring back his smile.

She looked at him again. He gazed back, and she thought she saw in his eyes a reflection of the inadequate daughter that motherless infant had grown up to be. She made her lips form the sound; tried as hard as she could to get it out. "Wh-what . . .?"

"I'm sending you away for a while," he said.

Cara had wondered, hearing old tales, what it felt like when your heart turned cold. Now she knew. It was like being a tiny bird, a robin or wren, and looking up to see a cat two paces away, ready to pounce. "Wh-wh—" Her voice was a thread. "Where?"

"Not far," he said, and her heart unclenched just a little, letting her breathe. Perhaps he meant only a few days' visit somewhere . . . From full moon to half—she could perhaps bear that . . . "I had thought to send you to court for a period," Father went on, "but I believe that would be too much to ask. You will go instead to Prince Oran's household at Winterfalls. As he is now a married man with a child, it will be perfectly proper, and if you apply yourself, you should acquire all the skills your aunt believes you need. You will meet a wider circle there, including some young men of good family."

Winterfalls. Cara had visited the place a few times, as it was on the way to the Dalriadan court. Prince Oran had seemed a reserved sort of man, scholarly and quiet. A little stuffy for a man his age. When Cara had last been there, he had not yet been married. His wife would be a younger version of Aunt Della, all too ready to tell people when they were not meeting her expectations. It would be unbearable. It would be a lonely exile. She wanted to ask how long a while was. She wanted to tell him she could practice her court manners perfectly well at home, since Aunt Della knew all about that sort of thing. She wanted to remind him that she'd done nothing to disgrace him, the time he and she had gone to Cahercorcan for a few days. Perhaps folk had thought her silence impolite; perhaps they had found it odd that she'd spent so much time up on the high walkways looking out to sea, or sitting in the garden on her own. But she had been perfectly well behaved. The worst she had done was occasionally forget to conceal a yawn of boredom. She could say none of this. It was too many words; it was too hard. If she tried, she would cry, and Father hated it when she cried.

A new thought came to her. That wild man, out by the guardian oak—did this sudden decision have something to do with him? "The . . ." she whispered, "the . . . man . . . b-before . . ."

"This is nothing to do with any man." His response was swift; so swift that she thought it might not be true. But he was her father. A father did not lie to his only daughter. "Your aunt and I have been discussing this matter for some time," he added. "It's for your safety. For your future. For the future of Wolf Glen. If you're to marry, you must at the very least learn to stammer out more than a word or two at a time. The sooner you learn to sustain a conversation and to conduct yourself in an appropriate manner, the sooner you can come back to Wolf Glen. That seems to me entirely reasonable."

She pushed down the roiling mass of feelings that threatened to undo her. If she wept or screamed or ran from the room, he would say she had just proved how badly she needed training in ladylike behavior. "H-how . . . how long? And when?"

"Until you have learned what you must learn. I will miss you; I have no desire to lose you for any longer than necessary. But necessary it is. As for when, I will ride to Winterfalls with you tomorrow and see you settled."

Tomorrow. This was a bad dream. Why would he do this to her? Didn't he know it was like wrenching out her heart?

"Your aunt will help you pack," Father said. "Best attend to that now."

"Alba?" she managed. "C-comes too?"

"You won't need Alba. There will be many maidservants at Winterfalls. Mature, responsible maidservants."

"B-b—"

"Go, Cara. Do your packing. Say your farewells. Within a few days you'll be thanking me for this." He regarded her more closely. "Don't look so woeful, Daughter. The world will not turn to ruin just because you are away from Wolf Glen for a season or two." He picked up his cup and took a drink.

A season or two? She sprang to her feet, knocking her own cup over. Mead ran across the worktable, and as she looked about for a cloth, Father snatched the documents clear of the flood. She fished out a clean handkerchief from her pouch and attempted to stem the flow. "I c-c-can't!" Tears were building behind her eyes. "Father, p-please!"

"Leave that, Cara. Let the servants deal with it." Father's tone was suddenly weighed down, burdened with that old sorrow. "My decision is made, and you must learn to live with it."

3

BLACKTHORN

"He's in perfect health, Flidais," I said, watching as Aolú practiced rolling over on the mat beside us. "And very strong for his age. It won't be long before he's taking his first steps."

We were in a comfortable chamber that had been fitted out as a nursery before the little prince's birth last autumn. Flidais's handmaid and companion, Deirdre, was folding linen and putting it away in a chest, but none of the nursemaids was present. Since Aolú's father was the crown prince of Dalriada, the infant had more attendants than any child could possibly need. But Lady Flidais liked to do things her own way. She nursed Aolú herself, when many royal women would have hired a wet nurse. She bathed him and changed his soiled linen. I liked her approach. Which was saying something, since I had little regard for princes and chieftains in general. Power and wealth too often made folk lose their good judgment. It made them cruel and unthinking. I had seen it too many times to count.

"I'm happy to hear that," Flidais said now, shaking a rattle and making the baby gurgle in delight. She was a slight woman, and today, sitting cross-legged on the floor with her dark hair loose over her shoulders, she hardly looked old enough to be a mother. I tried to imagine her at five-and-twenty, with perhaps a whole brood of children around her skirts. I pictured Aolú walking, running, starting to talk. Aolú at the age my son had been when he died. Aolú at the age my son would have been now, if he had lived: a young man of fifteen.

"What's wrong?" Flidais had seen something on my face. A slip. I had forgotten to guard my feelings. Here at Winterfalls nobody knew about my past. Except Grim, of course; but Grim was different.

"Nothing. I should be heading home. Unless there's anyone else here who needs my services." As healer and wise woman for the district of Winterfalls, including the prince's household, I tended to a wide range of ailments and injuries. There was nothing wrong with young Aolú, but Flidais was a new mother and liked to be reassured regularly that he was progressing well.

"No, but . . . Deirdre?"

"Yes, my lady?"

"Will you find Cara and ask her to come and speak with me, please? I'm not sure where she will be."

"Of course, Lady Flidais. It may take me a little while to find her."

"Who is Cara?" I asked as Deirdre went out.

"A girl who's been sent to stay with us. Her father is Tóla of Wolf Glen. You'll know of the place; it's up in the forest to the west. Tóla is a kinsman of Oran's, a rather distant one, but it means that if he asks a favor, we try to say yes."

"Why has he sent his daughter here?"

"I'm not quite sure," Flidais said. "It was all a little odd." She hesitated. "This is in confidence, Blackthorn."

"Of course."

"Tóla's a widower; Cara is his only child. I'd never met the girl before, and Oran hardly knows her. Wolf Glen is only an hour or so away by horseback, but folk don't go there often; the way through the forest is said to be challenging. Tóla and his daughter arrived here without warning. He spoke to Oran, Oran spoke to me, and the next day Tóla was off home again, leaving his daughter behind. We have no idea how long she'll be staying and nor does she. Tóla said something to Oran about introducing the girl to a wider circle and improving her court manners. But that can't be the only reason, surely, or he would have done things in a more appropriate way. A letter first, perhaps, asking if we'd be prepared to have her for a while. And . . . well, as time passes, I find I have very mixed feelings about the situation. It shames me to admit that. The girl is . . . unusual."

"Oh?" I did not ask why. Flidais had got into the habit of talking to me, in private, as if I were her friend and equal. I had to remind myself from time to time that she would one day be queen of Dalriada, and that the affairs of her household were not for me to inquire about. Unless, of course, the query related to someone's state of health, which just possibly this one did. Oran and Flidais had chosen not to have a court physician living at Winterfalls. Most folk of royal lineage would not dream of relying on the services of their local wise woman. They placed a great deal of trust in me.

"Cara's very withdrawn," Flidais said. "She doesn't speak; or, at least, she can manage a word or two, please or thank you, but that's all. Oran tells me her father believes she can talk if she wants to and she's being willful. But we've seen little sign of that."

"How old is this girl?"

"Fifteen. All knees and elbows. As the family is so well connected, and their holding so prosperous, there will doubtless be suitors before long. I can't imagine how Cara will deal with that. She often seems . . . not quite present. When we're working on our sewing or spinning, she sits gazing out the window as if the rest of us don't exist."

"Maybe she's shy. Or homesick. Or both."

"Perhaps that's all it is. The hurried way she was left here—that would upset any girl of her age. And her father asked that she not be allowed to ride back to Wolf Glen, even for a brief visit. I'm sure she'd rather not be here. But I did hope she would warm to us. It's been ten or twelve days now since she arrived, and she's still as edgy as a fox in a trap. None of my maids has managed to get close, and she won't talk to me."

I recalled how uncomfortable I had found my stay in this household. I had felt as out of place as a wrinkled walnut in a bowl of glossy cherries. There hadn't been a moment when I'd been prepared to let my guard drop. It had been exhausting. "She may not be sure where she fits in."

"That's why I thought Deirdre or one of my other handmaids might help. Deirdre's father is chief lawman back at Cloud Hill. Mhairi's father is a landholder of some note, but without the royal connections Cara's father has. They're young women of similar upbringing to Cara's. But we've had no success there. It's impossible to draw the girl out."

"Unusual," I said. "She's at that age when most young women can't stop chattering."

"So, will you speak to her? If there's something wrong, your expert eye may be able to discover what it is."

"I'll try, of course. But if she doesn't talk to you, she's unlikely to unburden herself to me. I'm hardly known for my warmth and tact."

"Ah," said Flidais. "But in this instance, your somewhat blunt approach may be just what is needed. You might surprise her into speaking up."

"Is there anything at all that she likes doing? Is she ever happy?"

Flidais gave a wry smile. "She's calmer out of doors. When we can't find her, the garden is the first place we go searching. Or somewhere out on the farm."

"Doing what?"

"Walking. Riding. Climbing trees. Always on her own."

"Perhaps that's what she's used to at home." Although Cara's father did not sound the type to let his daughter run free.

"Wolf Glen is quite a prosperous holding. They run sheep and cattle, and Tóla sells timber for building. Since Cara is the only child, I suppose it may all be her responsibility one day. He may be after a wealthy husband for her. Someone who can keep it all going when he's no longer there. I can't see Cara as a landholder in her own right. She seems quite unworldly-wise, even for a fifteen-year-old."

"Either way, if Deirdre is not back soon, I'll have to talk to the girl another time. I said I'd go over to Silverlake today to check on a very sick old woman; sick enough that I don't want to leave it until tomorrow."

Flidais was all apologies. "Of course you must go, Blackthorn. Cara can wait."

"She could ride over to Dreamer's Wood to visit us," I suggested, picking up my healer's bag. "Emer is there most mornings. Cara might find it easier to talk to someone closer to her own age." I had promised to teach my young assistant a certain difficult decoction on her next visit. If Grim did not have work that took him elsewhere, I would also fit in a writing lesson for the two of them. That could wait until Cara was gone. Emer might be able to concentrate with an audience, but I was sure the presence of a stranger, even if she was a fifteen-year-old girl, would drive everything Grim had learned right out of his head. And I wanted him to succeed. I wanted it even more than he did.

He'd told me the story now, some of it at least: how he'd once been a novice in a Christian monastery, and how he'd been happy there, and how the Norsemen had come, raiding. How he'd fought and fallen, and how, when he regained consciousness, everything he had loved was gone, including the old scholar who had been teaching him to read. My friend had carried that burden a long time in silence. And now I had picked up where his beloved Brother Galen had left off, which felt curiously like a privilege.

With Emer, things were more straightforward. If she was one day to become a wise woman in her own right, she'd need basic reading and writing to keep a book of her cures and discoveries. She'd need to be able to label her preparations and her raw materials accurately. I was not sure how Grim would use his new skill, once he'd mastered it. He did love tales. If we both worked hard, he could learn to read a simple book in Irish. I should ask Flidais if there was anything suitable in the library at Winterfalls. Both Prince Oran and his wife were scholars. If I'd had any spare time, I would have written something for Grim myself. But another project was consuming my hours of solitude; a perilous, secret project. Maybe the account I was writing would never see the light of day. But I knew, heart-deep, that I must set the words down.

"I'll ask Cara when we find her," Flidais said. "She may not give me an answer, of course. If she does come, I'll send her with an escort;

Oran has promised her father she won't go beyond our walls on her own."

Silverlake was a fair ride, and by the time I got back, dusk was falling. I returned my borrowed horse to Scannal the miller and walked home across the fields, guided by the warm light from our cottage windows, over on the edge of Dreamer's Wood. Our home, Grim's and mine, was far enough from Winterfalls village and the prince's dwelling to afford us some privacy, but not so far that folk could not reach us if they needed our help. Conmael had chosen it well.

Ah, Conmael; my mentor, who was one of the fey. A mysterious stranger, or so I'd thought at the time, who had saved me from execution and released me and Grim from vile imprisonment, but only after I'd promised to adhere to his rules for seven years, gods help me. Those rules were three: I must live here in Dalriada and not go south to seek vengeance against my enemy, Mathuin of Laois; I must say yes to every request for help; and I must use my abilities only for good. To someone who did not know the angry, bitter creature I had become, that might not have sounded so hard. But it was hard. Making Mathuin pay for his crimes, not only against me but against a whole host of wronged innocents, had become the only thing that mattered to me; even more so after a year's incarceration in his cesspit of a lockup. I had struggled to keep my promise. Twice, I had come within a hairbreadth of breaking it, even in the knowledge of the punishment Conmael had threatened. As for saying yes when folk asked me for help, that was not always as simple as it sounded.

We'd had to lie once or twice, Grim and I, or at least to withhold part of the truth, and when the person being deceived was Oran or Flidais, lying did not come easily. They had been good to us, generous and understanding. They had demonstrated that not every person of noble breeding was a heartless piece of scum like Mathuin.

Nobody at Winterfalls knew that Grim and I were escaped felons. Nobody knew about Conmael—most folk did not believe the fey were real anyway, or thought that race had died out long ago. And now we had another secret, an unpalatable one. Last summer we had headed west, with Prince Oran's blessing, to assist a lady with a monster that had taken up residence on her land. An old friend of mine, a man who knew of my past, had accompanied us on that journey. He and his dog. When we had returned with the dog but without the man, we'd had to lie about the reason. To tell the truth would have required us to reveal far more of our story than was safe. So we'd said simply that Flannan had traveled on elsewhere, and that sometime later we had found the dog, Ripple, wandering in the woods, with no sign of her master. If Flannan's remains should be found buried under a tree somewhere between Winterfalls and Bann, who was to say we'd had anything to do with it?

Grim hadn't had much choice. He'd killed Flannan to save my life. The whole episode had been sickening. It had reminded me afresh of how perilous our situation was, for Flannan, whom I had thought a friend and ally, had been sent by Mathuin of Laois to track me down. Even now, Mathuin might be wondering why his errand boy had sent no further word, no pigeon bearing the news that I was safely accounted for. The fact was, although my enemy might now assume that I was dead, he'd possibly want to make quite sure of it. He knew I would not be easily silenced. He knew I'd lay my life on the line to see him brought to justice. And now, because of the messages Flannan had sent him, Mathuin must know where I was, or at least where I'd been. The cold feeling in my gut told me Mathuin wasn't going to leave this alone.

Nearly home. I could smell something cooking, perhaps barley broth. Fresh bread too. Grim was a capable cook and an excellent gardener, and we ate well. My spirits lifted. There had been good things about the day: Aolú's robust health and Flidais's trust, the fact that my tonic seemed to be easing the old woman's rattling cough, and now the welcoming light in the windows. Maybe I was turning soft. Maybe vengeance was beyond me now. But no; that was not true. I only had to think of what I had lost: of my husband and child burning, and Mathuin's men holding me back and laughing as my family died. Of the lost souls in the lockup and the ruined lives of Mathuin's victims. I would see him face justice. I would make that happen if I died doing it.

Ripple barked, inside the cottage. A moment later the door opened and the dog came out to hurl a challenge to all comers. Then the big form of Grim appeared in the doorway and Ripple, quieter now, ran to greet me.

"Long day?" Grim reached to take my bag.

"Long enough. I rode to Silverlake and back. Scannal said he'd seen you earlier."

"Did a few jobs for him in the morning." Grim deposited the bag and went to stir a pot that was bubbling on the fire. "This and that." He gave me a searching look. "You all right?"

"More or less." It was uncomfortable, sometimes, how well he could read me. "Thoughts going round in circles, that's all."

"Anything special?" He set the pot on the flagstones by the hearth, found a ladle and began filling two bowls. A platter of bread and cheese was already on the table. Ripple settled in her favorite spot close to the fire.

"The usual. Flannan. Mathuin. What might happen. If I could find Conmael I'd ask him about it. About the seven years, and whether he might be prepared to compromise. And other things. But I haven't seen him since we came home from Bann. Going out into the wood and wishing he'd appear doesn't do the trick anymore. Either he doesn't want to talk to me, or he's gone away somewhere."

"What other things?" Grim put a bowl of soup in front of me. "Careful—it's hot."

"Smells wonderful. I'd ask him about the past. I'd tell him my theory about how he and I might have met as children, unlikely as it is. Because if I've guessed correctly, that could make him readier to help me. I'd tell him I think five more years is too long to wait for justice. Conmael may be right about my needing all that time to learn self-restraint, much as it galls me to admit it. But I'm not the one who matters. Every day that passes, Mathuin destroys more folk's lives. How can it be right to let that go on for five more years instead of stopping it now?"

Grim dipped his bread in his soup, saying nothing.

"And what about Flannan's wife and children, supposing that story was true? What happens to them when he never comes home? What happens to them if Mathuin finds out I'm still alive? Flannan said they would pay the price if he failed in his mission."

"Sad if what he told you was true," Grim said. "No woman deserves to have that happen. But it could be there never was any wife or children." He chewed on a crust, small eyes thoughtful. "Say you could track his wife down, anyway. What would you say to her? *Sorry, your man was a liar and a killer and we had to make an end of him. Now let us rescue you.* She'd spit in your face."

"I'm not suggesting we do anything. Only . . ." I could not say it. If Flannan had been telling the truth about having a family, and about Mathuin having made their safety the price of his delivering me back to Laois, then that woman and her children might be facing the same fate my little family had faced. They might die in terror as my husband and son had. They might be added to the long list of Mathuin's victims.

"Hard to stand back." Grim wiped out his bowl with a piece of bread. "Not to do anything. Harder than running forward with a big stick in your hand, screaming your head off. But this is something you can't run at. If you do, you get rubbed out. Gone as quick as a snap of the fingers. And Mathuin keeps on doing what he does." When I did not reply, he added, "Hard to choose. Wait, and let the bad things go on. Act, and maybe waste your chance anyway, because the timing's wrong. The best plan in the world can fall apart. Like Flannan with his pigeons. A hawk happens to spot the chance of a meal, and just like that a message falls into the wrong hands. Mine, as it turned out. If it hadn't been for that, he would have got what he wanted, and so would Mathuin. And we'd be . . . somewhere we didn't want to be."

A shiver ran through me, deep down. We'd had some very strange adventures, Grim and I. We'd driven each other half-crazy at times. We'd saved each other's lives more than once. We'd solved some knotty puzzles; we'd dealt with the uncanny and with human evildoers. We'd become used to each other. Only . . . just as there was unfinished business between me and Conmael, so there was unfinished business between Grim and me, something neither of us would put into words, something that had lain between us since Midsummer Eve, when I'd been cursed into a monstrous form, and Grim had—so it seemed—broken the curse by holding me in his arms and letting his tears fall on my face. At the time it hadn't mattered a bit to me how I'd become myself again, only that the hideous experience was over. But the wee folk that lived in the woods around Bann had been hinting for a while that true love's tears would be vital to the success of my mission there. I'd thought they meant the herb that went by that name; had even gathered some and taken it with me. Later on, the wee folk had made it clear they had meant a different kind of tears.

I wasn't sure I believed in true love, the kind of grand, sweeping passion told of in the ancient tales. Oran and Flidais came close. Then there'd been Lady Geiléis of Bann and her bespelled sweetheart. But they were extraordinary. Grim and I were . . . we were ourselves. Friends. Good friends. Companions who slept in the same bedchamber, but not in the same bed. He looked after me, kept me safe, saved me from my own rash impulses, stood by and let me rant and throw things when I needed to. I gave him a home. A purpose. That was the way he saw it. I stayed with him at night so that when the burdens of the past became overwhelming he would not find himself alone in the dark. I valued his hard work, his gentle nature, his strength, his quiet wisdom. But that wasn't true love. I'd loved my husband. We'd been tender toward each other, back in the time before Mathuin, when I'd still been capable of softness. What I felt for Grim was . . . different. Different from anything else.

"Brew?"

I started. While I'd been wrapped in my thoughts, Grim had cleared away the bowls and put the kettle on the fire, all without saying a word.

"Mm."

"Conmael will turn up when he's ready," Grim said. "No point worrying about it."

I wrenched my mind back to our conversation. "Something might have happened to him."

Grim gave me a sideways look. "You planning to go hunting for him in the Otherworld? Might be a bit much, even for you."

"Of course not. I wouldn't know where to start. Only, if he's gone somewhere and isn't coming back, then . . ."

"Might be a sort of test. Maybe he's waiting to see if you rush off south again, soon as you think he's not looking."

"A pox on it!" I thumped my fist on the table, making spoons rattle. "I'm sick of waiting! What am I doing here?"

Grim went on making the brew. The movement of his big hands was measured, careful. After some time, he said, "You want me to answer that?"

"No. I know already what you'll say. Doing good. Helping folk. Just like Conmael told me to. That's one side of the scales—I know. But it can never balance five more years of Mathuin doing what he does."

There was a pause. "Could be," Grim said in a voice that suggested he was treading very carefully, "it's not your job to fix that. Could be it never was."

I made myself wait before speaking. Drew a breath or two. "If everyone took that attitude," I said, "scum like him would rule the world. If we don't stand up for what's right, we're no better than he is."

"You might feel that way," Grim said. "But you're one woman. One woman can't fix every wrong. One woman or one man can't help every soul in trouble. Doesn't matter how much you want to."

"I don't want to fix every wrong. Only this one." I knew even as I spoke that this was no longer true. It had not been for some time. There had been other wrongs, smaller ones maybe, but to the folk involved, as big as life and death. Between us, Grim and I had fixed some of them, or gone a certain way toward doing so. An abused girl; a prince trapped in someone else's lie; a woman with a sick child, on her own and struggling. If I said those were not important, I would be denying the value of a human life. If I said I'd helped them only because my vow to Conmael demanded it, I'd be lying. Which put a new idea into my head. "Maybe Conmael would think I've changed enough by now. Seen the error of my ways. Maybe, if I could find him, it wouldn't be so hard to convince him."

"So you tell him you've changed. He says yes, forget the seven years. And you rush off south again and get yourself killed."

"Even you don't believe in me." In my mind, for some reason, was the look on Flidais's face as she played with baby Aolú. Had I ever been like that, full of hope, lit up by joy? Had my eyes held that same delight as I played with my own son? "A pox on all of it," I muttered, fishing for a handkerchief. What was wrong with me? Where had the brave Blackthorn gone, the one who knew her own mind?

Grim moved to sit beside me on the bench. Put an arm around me. "Not true, and you know it," he said. "Believed in you from the first, when they brought you into that place of Mathuin's. All us poor god-forsaken sods did. That hasn't changed." When I said nothing, he went on, "Have a cry, if you want. You've seen me bawling like a baby. No shame in that."

I wasn't thinking about shame. I was thinking how remarkable it was that something as simple as human touch could lift a person's spirits so quickly. My tears were still falling, but with his arm around my shoulders I felt . . . safe. Safe from my own anger. Safe from my own sorrow. Able to imagine a future like the one Mathuin had ripped away from me. For a moment I closed my eyes and let myself drift. Then I got up, shrugging off Grim's arm, and moved over to the fire, where I pretended to warm my hands. "I'm fine," I said. "Nothing wrong with me." A pity my voice made such a lie of the words. I changed the subject; hauled myself out of deep water. "Flidais is sending a girl here, maybe tomorrow. A young woman who's staying in the prince's house. Wants me to talk sense into her, I think. Will you be here?"

"Got a job on," Grim said. "Big job, up at Wolf Glen. Wanted to talk to you about that."

"Mm-hm?" Wolf Glen. That was where Flidais's girl came from. "Talk away, then."

"Been asked to help with the building up there. Some kind of house or hall, special job. Might take a while; could be right through summer, the fellow said. Good pay. We could put quite a bit by."

I thought of all the reasons Grim would not want to go and stay at Wolf Glen over a whole spring and summer.

"Ride up in the morning, ride back before dark," he said, as if he could read my mind. "Sleep here, work up there. Told the fellow that was the only way I'd do it. Told him any day the weather's not right I won't go."

"And what did he say to that?"

"He said fine by him. Said he'd lend me a horse."

"That's generous." It was generous enough to make me suspicious. Was someone trying to separate us? My mind filled up again with Mathuin, with plots and traps and perilous lies.

"Fellow said he wanted someone who doesn't need telling what to do all the time. And he wanted someone big and strong. Lot of heavy lifting. Fancy thatching to do later on. Said he'd asked around the district and everyone told him I was the man for the job."

"It sounds like he needs a whole team of men."

"Didn't talk about it much. I told him I'd go up there in the morning and have a look. Said I couldn't give him a yes or no till I'd seen it. Be gone most of the day."

"Oh. All right."

"Sure?" He was looking at me rather more closely than I found comfortable.

"I've got Emer coming over, and maybe this girl of Flidais's. It seems an odd coincidence. Flidais's girl is from Wolf Glen. The daughter of the house. She sounds difficult. But she may just be homesick."

"Give her a job to do," Grim said. "Work for her hands. Helps, most times."

"A long day for you," I said, thinking that if he decided to take on this building work, he had a lot of long days ahead. Perhaps more time apart would be good for the two of us. "I'd been thinking of a writing lesson."

"I can catch up after supper."

"If you say so." He'd likely be so tired he'd fall asleep the moment supper was over. Building a house would be hard work. A hall, even harder. On top of that, there'd be an hour's ride each way. "We'll see how it goes, mm?"

4

BARÐÁN

They've given him a shelter. Not in the house. Not in the barn or the outbuildings. But not too far away. That man would leash him if he could, that man he cannot look in the eye, the one whose words sting like a scourge. That man would treat him like a vicious dog. The master. That's what he calls himself. *Master* Tóla. The name sticks in his craw.

Gormán has found him the old hut among the pines, a place where the foresters store bits and pieces. Cleared it out, got him some blankets, a few pots and pans, shown him where the stream is and where he can safely make a fire. As if Bardán knew nothing at all. The past is misty, true. This place, this world feels not quite real, something he's wandered into by mistake, somewhere he doesn't belong. He's been here before, he knows that . . . but the rest . . . Where's it all gone? He remembers the master, and Gormán, and the heartwood house. There was a howling grief; he wanted to plunge a knife into his own belly and cut it out. There was a night of running, running, the trees flashing past like tall ghosts, the monsters closing in, his throat raw with shouting. Running to the end of the world.

The heartwood house is a wreck, too far gone to save. The master has let it go, let it sink back into the earth. A sad ruin. Like himself. But the master wants it built again. Wants him to finish the job he started long ago.

They told him that the day he first came back; the day he saw the girl in the tree. It made him laugh, though the laugh came out as an animal sound, a grunting bray that made them flinch. He showed them his hands, the clawed fingers, the joints stiff and knobby as old juniper.

"We'll get you a helper," the master said. "Someone to do the work. As long as you remember how it's to be made. As long as you can show him how. Can you remember?"

He wanted to say no. He wanted to say he would not do it, would do no work at all. But something in Gormán's eyes, a tiny shake of Gormán's head, warned him. "Maybe." He forced the word out, fought to shape it. He'd been silent a long time. His voice was rusty, like an ax left out in the damp. "If not . . . what?"

The master's eyes turned to ice. His mouth was a thin line. "Be very careful," he said. "It's one thing if you cannot remember how it's done. But if you do remember, and you lie to me about it, the penalty will be severe indeed. Make no doubt of that. You owe me. You failed to complete the job before. That failure brought down a great misfortune upon me and mine. I had not thought you would come back after so long. But here you are, and now you must keep your promise. You will finish the heartwood house. I want it done thoroughly and quickly, everything correct, nothing left out. Now answer the question. Do you remember how?"

If he lied, they would kill him. They would take him out into the forest somewhere and make him vanish. He'd be under the earth, fodder for worms. "I can do it," he said. "Not quick. Can't build with fresh-cut timber."

"We saved the materials." That was Gormán speaking up. "They've been stored in the barn, under cover. Looked after over the years. The bulk of what you'll need is there. Anything else, Conn and I can find for you. You just need to tell us what's still required."

"So you'll do it?" The master, sharp as sharp.

Stupid question. He was hardly going to say no. He nodded. Didn't tell them about the roof, how tricky that would be, near impossible to find what had to go in it. Quick? Hah! Not likely.

"There'll be rules," said the master. "Break them and you'll pay dearly. Keep your distance from the big house. Don't speak to any of my folk save Gormán and Conn. Not one word, you understand? When we find a fellow to help with the building, you'll need to talk to him. But only what's needed to get the job done, no idle gossip. Don't think of going off anywhere. Gormán's to know where you are at all times. Stick to that or you'll be locked up when you're not on the job. I'm half minded to do that anyway, but I'll wait. See how this goes. Understood?"

He made a sound, something close to *yes*. Nodded again, in case it wasn't clear enough. Then they found him this hut and a few bits and pieces, and he tried to settle in. Waited for them to find a helper. So far it hadn't happened, and that was no surprise. Who'd want to come and work on this? Who'd want to work for a man like the master?

Now, lying on his straw pallet in the meager shelter, he remembers Tóla with dark hair, not gray. A smoother face, fewer lines. A straighter back, squarer shoulders. Gormán, too, is older now, but with him it's more of a weathering. Like an oak that broadens and deepens and grows stronger with the storms of winter on winter. Master Tóla has his storm inside. An angry storm, churning away in his vitals, hollowing him out. Was he like that back in the old days? Back when Bardán's hands were strong and straight and nimble-fingered? Back when his world was whole?

The night is cold. The woolen blanket itches his skin; the walls close him in. By moonlight he makes his way outside, digs out a hollow, gathers pine needles, dry and fragrant. He burrows down; covers himself as best he can. Under the trees, under the night sky, he can feel the heartbeat of the forest. Here, he is not quite alone.

5

GRIM

Not sure what I'm getting myself into. Don't want to leave Blackthorn on her own after last night. She's edgy. Stayed awake, staring into the dark. She didn't want to talk. I sat up and kept her company, made a brew or two, waited out the night with her.

I ask her if she wants me to stay home. She says no, quite snappish. Hates to look weak. At least Emer's coming, so she won't be all by herself. That girl too, the one from Wolf Glen.

I'm away early, get a horse from Scannal's, head off up there. Not knowing what to expect. Never been to the place before, but I've heard plenty about the ride. Big forest, a lot of it pine, some of it different trees all mixed up together. Most I know the names of. Some I don't. In the deepest parts the trees are like gnarled old giants. Place is all winding tracks that go back on themselves. Sudden dips, steep hills, rocks where you don't expect them. Patches where you'd go into mud up to your knees if you didn't watch out. Glad I chose Sturdy. Cart horse, not a riding horse, but steady and strong. Good horse for a big man. Ripple runs beside, keeping away from Sturdy's hooves. Likes a run, Ripple does. I'll say one thing for that bastard Flannan, he trained his dog well.

Pretty ride. Woods are all shadows and light. Birds everywhere, all kinds, little peeping things and big ones with slow-beating wings. Creatures scampering around in the trees and in the grass. Place is full of life. Sort of spot where you'd find those wee folk, like the ones we met in Bann. Or even Conmael's kind, the fey folk of the old tales. So much forest here, and it's so tricky, they'd have no trouble hiding if they wanted. I look around for them as I go, but no sign. Not that Conmael gives you a warning before he pops up out of nowhere. Likes seeing folk jump—that's my guess. Wonder if she's right and he really has gone off somewhere. Wonder how it works, that world and our world. How do they fit together? Could be a man walks into a cave and finds himself somewhere he didn't expect. Or takes a swim, dives under the water, comes up and everything's changed. Heard a tale once. Fellow walked into a mushroom circle and got taken off into a fey place, didn't get home for a hundred years. Wife, children, grandchildren all dead and buried. Doesn't bear thinking about.

Ride takes about an hour. I come over a rise and there's Wolf Glen, big stone house, double row of beeches, all grand enough for a prince. Which is funny when you think of it. Prince Oran's house at Winterfalls is more ordinary than this one, and he'll be king someday. Makes me wonder why this fellow would be wanting to build another house. Got a perfectly good one from what I can see.

Someone's been watching out for me, seems like. By the time I get to the courtyard there's a groom waiting to take Sturdy off to the stables and another man telling me to wait. Seems the master of the house is going to show me the job himself. Ripple has a wander around and I wait and wait some more.

Then here's the fellow I spoke to in Winterfalls, Gormán's his name, looking pleased to see me, and another man who I guess from his fine clothes is the master of the house. No smile from him. He looks like a man with a burden.

"Grim," says Gormán. "You're timely. This is Master Tóla. If you'll walk with us, he will explain the job to you."

We walk, and the master of Wolf Glen asks me all sorts of questions, ones I've already answered for Gormán, but never mind. Can I work with stone? Can I work with wood? What building have I done before?

Am I skilled at thatching? Can I work every day until the job's finished even if it runs through till autumn?

It's a yes to most of that. I tell him what I've already told Gormán about not wanting to stay up here overnight but being happy to ride to and fro. And needing one of their horses, because Scannal has to have Sturdy for his cart. Remind him about not coming up when the weather's bad. Can't say about autumn—need to see the job first. What exactly is it he's building?

They show me, up around the far side of the house, past their barn and stables. A ruin of something. Master Tóla wants it rebuilt. A heartwood house, it's called.

I walk all around it. It's biggish. It's three times the size of our cottage, which is the only bit of building I've done more or less on my own, though I've helped with plenty of others. I'm guessing from the wreck of it that the walls were stone at the base. There'd be wooden posts and beams, maybe wattle and mud up top. What's left here is mostly broken stone, rubble, a few rotten old bits of wood.

"Doesn't look too hard," I say. "You'd need a few helpers, though. What is it, a grand hall for councils and the like?" Never heard of a heartwood house.

"The purpose does not matter," says Master Tóla. "The significant part of this, the challenge, is the manner in which it is constructed. For the wooden parts of the house, every kind of timber in the forest must be used."

I don't say a word. Getting used to strange things; must be living with Blackthorn does that.

"There are rules for the laying of the stones; for the fashioning of the posts and beams; for the manner of thatching. Rules that must be adhered to in every particular."

Sounds as if he's fussy. Maybe explains why the job didn't get finished last time. Not sure I'm so keen to do it after all. Though the pay Gormán mentioned is a tidy sum, and I've got plans for how to use it, plans I'm not telling Blackthorn yet.

"These rules," I say, "are they written down somewhere? Be easy to make a mistake. Who's going to be in charge?" Not him, the master, I'm guessing; doesn't look like the kind of man who gets his hands dirty. And not Gormán, who's told me already that he'll only be helping out when he can.

"Ah," says Master Tóla, meaning, I can guess, *This is the bit we decided not to tell you before, in case you said no.* "We have a man here by the name of Bardán. Odd sort of fellow. He's been living wild; forgotten the ways of ordinary folk. But we need his help. Very few men know how to build a heartwood house. Bardán is one of them."

"Mm-hm," I say, waiting for more. Thinking, can't be any odder than the things that have happened to Blackthorn and me since we came north together. Strange stuff follows us wherever we go.

"Before I call him," the master says, "I need to make it clear that your work here will be not only assisting Bardán with the building work, but also keeping him under control." He looks me up and down, while I'm thinking I don't like the sound of that at all.

"I'm no guard," I say, though that's not quite true. I've done guard duty for Prince Oran before. But that's not the same as being someone's minder. I'm thinking of Slammer and Tiny, Mathuin's thugs from the lockup. Thinking I'm never ever going to let myself be like them. "That's not the job I came here for."

"You're a big, strong man," says the master. "You'll earn your pay by doing what Bardán tells you to do on the heartwood house. He'll earn his keep at Wolf Glen by showing you how to do it. There'll be a tidy extra sum for you if you make sure Bardán sticks to the rules we've given him. If you can't agree to that, there is no job."

"Mm-hm," I say again. "And what rules are those?"

They run through them: Bardán is not allowed to talk to anyone but the foresters and me. He's not allowed anywhere near the main house. He has to sleep in a little hut out in the woods. He's not allowed to leave Wolf Glen before the heartwood house is finished. I'm thinking, *I hope you're paying him well*, but I don't say it.

"And you don't talk to him about anything except the building," says Master Tóla. "Understood?"

"Mm-hm. Who was building this before?" They must've had someone who knew all these special rules about a heartwood house, back
then. Not sure how long ago; a while, from the looks of things.

"He was. Bardán. But he left with the job unfinished." It's Gormán
who tells me this; Master Tóla's staring off into nowhere as if he's forgotten me for the moment. "We have most of the wood saved from last
time, in the barn."

"Something from every kind of tree."

"Something from every kind of tree. Even the ones you wouldn't
choose to build with if you had any common sense. But some of the bits
are small. Doesn't matter if they're just tucked in somewhere, as long
as they're all there."

"Sounds odd. Why would you do it like that? Might mean the
place wasn't as strong as it could be. Or as weather-tight."

"Building it the right way brings good fortune," Gormán says.
"But it has to be done just so."

"That's him," says the master, and I see someone coming down
from the forest, over the other side of the ruin. A man who might have
walked right out of an old tale, he's so shaggy and wild and strange. I
wonder for a bit if he's not a man at all but some uncanny thing, a troll
or suchlike. Master Tóla turns back to me. "Will you do it?" Sounding
as if it matters a lot, me saying yes.

"I might talk to him first. Get a better idea of the job."

The master's mouth goes tight. Eyes not so warm now. "Don't take
too long over it. The pay's better than you'll get anywhere else. Use of a
horse, a good one. Freedom to come in and out, provided you don't
gossip about the work down in the settlement. We'd be wanting you to
keep this to yourself, the same as Bardán."

"Is that right?" I say, thinking their bags of silver don't look so tempt-
ing now. Why would they want everything so secret? It's only a house.
Bardán's close now; just on the other side of the ruin. Taking a good look
at me. I give him a nod. "Quick chat, that's all I need. Then I can give you
an answer. If it doesn't suit you to wait, maybe Gormán here can come
down and let you know. Master Tóla," I add, trying to be polite.

"Very well," he says. "Take your time." Thinking, I'm guessing, that if he's too sharp about the rules, I'll change my mind about doing the work. "Gormán, I'll be in my council chamber. Bring Grim down there when he's made up his mind, will you?"

A few things I learn really quick. First, Bardán's not ready with his words. Second, he doesn't want to be here. Doesn't want to do the job. Doesn't say so, not right out, but the look in his eye, the set of his shoulders, the way he talks, all that tells me he's not happy at Wolf Glen. Third, he's going to build the heartwood house anyway.

Me, I'm wishing Gormán would take himself off so I can talk to the wild man without having to watch my words. But Gormán's not going anywhere. If I'm here as Bardán's minder, maybe the forester's my minder, stopping me from asking the wrong questions. Happiest little building team in Erin, we'll be.

I walk around the ruin again, with Bardán next to me and Gormán behind.

"Stones first?" I ask. "How high? How many courses?"

He shows me with his hands; hands that make it clear why he needs a helper for the building. Can't tell how old the man is—could be my age, could be Gormán's, could be anywhere in between. But those hands are crippled. They're stiff and bent; they must hurt. Which means the man laying those stones is going to be me.

"Stone on stone," Bardán says. "Stone on stone on stone." He shows me how high they'll go—about up to his shoulder. "Posts set in. Oak. Ash. Beech."

"Wattle and mud up above?" I ask, and he nods. Danu's mercy. This is a poor, sad wreck of a man. But he was a builder once. Wonder what happened, to twist up those strong hands. "How many couples for the roof?"

"Nine," says Gormán from behind us. "Built steep."

Nine couples! That's a tall place all right. "Thatch, yes?" A man would need a good long ladder. And a head for heights.

Bardán gives a grunt for *yes*.

"Straw?"

Another grunt.

"You got the materials ready for that too?"

"We'll have them by the time you need them," says Gormán. "I doubt you'll be thatching before the end of summer."

Cast my eye over the place again; try to see this heartwood house. I'm thinking Gormán's right. It'll take a long while to put together, even without the special touches. Not sure I want to be coming up here right through spring and summer and maybe into autumn.

"What do you think?" Gormán asks me. "Will you do it?"

I look at the wild man, wondering what his story is. Wondering why they need all the rules. Something wrong here, has to be. "Why not get a whole team in?" I ask. Anyone with any sense would do that. "Doesn't need to be craftsmen, just strong lads who can learn quick and follow orders. Six or seven men, you could be all done by midsummer. Maybe earlier."

"Don't suggest that to Master Tóla," Gormán says. "He wants it done with as few as possible. You, Bardán, and me or Conn to help you when our own work allows. Anything needing more men, we can ask some of our farmworkers to lend a hand. Nobody from outside, except you. Never mind how long it takes. That's the way he wants it done."

"What if that doesn't suit me?" I ask, though I'm starting to get a picture in my head of the thing finished, and it's a pretty sight, standing tall and fine among the big trees. I could do a nice job with the thatching. Make a bit of a garden around the place if there's time.

"Then you don't do the job," Gormán says. "And either way, you don't talk about it when you go home. Understood?"

"Mm-hm." If they don't want me to talk, I won't talk. Except to Blackthorn, but that's different.

"I think you're the right man for this work," Gormán says now. "And I know Master Tóla does too. Folk speak very well of your abilities."

"Just, right through to autumn, that's a long time. Every day." Not used to being away from Blackthorn so much. Could be hard. On the other hand, Blackthorn might like a rest from having me around all the time. And I do get to go home every night. Sleep under our own roof; know she's there, close by.

"The offer of accommodation here at Wolf Glen still stands."

"Suits me better to ride in and out. But thanks."

"The master might be prepared to pay more," Gormán says, "to be sure you'll stay until this is finished. However long it takes."

Dagda's bollocks. Master Tóla must have a lot of silver to throw around. He's already offered me extra for keeping an eye on Bardán.

"Gormán!" There's another man over by the barn, lanky young fellow, red-haired. "Give us a hand here, will you?"

Gormán looks at me, looks at the wild man, hesitates.

"Go on," I say. "I'll just have a bit more of a look. Then I'll come and find you."

I'm guessing Gormán's under orders not to leave me and the wild man on our own. Not until he knows if I'm staying. But he says, "All right. Don't be long," and heads off.

I walk around the ruin one more time. Bardán walks a step or two behind me, like a rough sort of shadow. Doesn't say a word.

"You all right with me doing the job?" I ask after a while. Not up to him, of course. But it sounds like he's the only one who knows how to build this thing. Be happier if he thought I was up to it. Pretty sure there's going to be more to it than they've said so far.

All I get is a grunt and a nod. Then Ripple comes over. She's been exploring everywhere like a dog does, finding new smells. Now she sniffs Bardán's leg. He's got a pretty strong stink about him.

"You like dogs?" I ask. Trying to put him at his ease. Not that anyone would be easy here, with all the rules about not saying this and not saying that. "This one's mine. Ripple, her name is. She'd be coming up with me most days. Long way for her. But she likes a run."

He reaches out to stroke her head with his stiff fingers. I see a flash of teeth in the bristling beard. Maybe a smile, maybe more of a grimace. Gone quick.

I try again. Look around first, though I know there's nobody close enough to hear. "Listen," I say. "This feels a bit odd. Not quite right. You sure you want to build the thing? You sure you want to work for this fellow?" Could get me in trouble. But I'm not working for Master Tóla yet.

Bardán looks right at me. Eyes like an animal's when it's trapped and wants to bolt, but can't.

"No need to be scared," I say, quiet-like. Think, once I've said it, that it could be a lie. No need to be scared of *me*; that's true enough. Can't say the same about Master Tóla or even Gormán, friendly as he is. Can't think how to say what I want to say—that I'm not happy to do the job if this poor sod's being forced into it for some reason. Got a feeling he's not quite right in the head. Reminds me a bit of Dribbles, back in Mathuin's lockup. Never said much, and when he did there wasn't a lot of sense in it.

"Got to finish," Bardán says. "Stone on stone. Wattle and mud. Nine couples. Every tree in the wood."

"For good luck, yes?"

"That's what they say." He smiles again, only this time I know he's not happy; he's angry. "An old tale. The heartwood house."

Seems he can put his words together all right if he tries. Makes me wonder if it might be just that he hasn't talked for a long time. Forgotten how, nearly. Where's he come from? Where's he been? In some place like that hellhole of Mathuin's? "How long since you tackled the job last time?" I ask.

"Can't say."

That's all the answer I'm going to get. The man's all closed up, and no wonder. Morrigan's curse, think how it would be. A builder, a master builder from what they've said, and now he couldn't even tap in a peg. Poor bastard.

"You want me to help, Bardán?"

"Need help," he says. "Got to finish."

"All right," I say. "I'll do it." Surprise myself, because I'd been thinking I'd tell Master Tóla I needed another day to make up my mind. Thinking I'd talk it over with Blackthorn first, things being so odd up here and all. But I look at the wild man's sad face, smell his stinking body in its ragged clothes, and I remember Blackthorn helping a big lump of a man when he was out in the woods, in the dark, in the rain, running from his nightmares. "Grim," I say. "That's my name."

Bardán nods. "Grim."

"I'd better go and have a word with Master Tóla," I say. "Find out what I need to bring with me. Find out about a horse." I look at the ruin again, thinking it'll take a few days just to clear the spot. Hoping they've got the stones set away as well as the wood, because shaping stone for a great big house isn't something I can do on my own.

Down at the main house, I tell Master Tóla I'll do the job. He doesn't look as surprised as he should, seeing as the job is as odd as they come. I tell him I want my payment split into three parts. One to be paid now, or within a day or so, one when we're ready to start on the roof, and the last one when it's all finished. That does surprise him. Surprises even me. Though it shouldn't, since we've been let down before, Blackthorn and me. But I'm not in the habit of telling folk what I want done.

Anyway, he says yes to everything, the horse, the payment, the other things I've asked for. He wants me to give my word, again, about sticking to his rules. Can't see any reason he'd need them, myself. Wolf Glen's on its own, a fair ride from the settlement. Not the sort of place you pop in to say good morning because you happen to be passing. And none of the locals at Winterfalls have talked about these folk, the way they do about Oran and Flidais and their household, or even about people who live in the other settlement, Silverlake. So why all the secrets? I don't ask, though, just tell him I'll keep my mouth shut if that's part of the job. Then I say since I'm here already, I can put in a day's work now. "Make a start on clearing away the old stuff. Getting the site leveled off and ready. Bit of help with lifting the stones would be handy, if you've got a lad free. Since the fellow who's giving the orders can't do that. With his hands and all."

The master smiles. He's got one of those faces that's always a bit sad, though. "I'm glad you are so keen to get started, Grim. Handle the pieces with respect and care; everything is precious."

Could've fooled me. Lot of old crumbling stones and splintered timbers. I don't say that out loud, just nod. "Might take a look at your materials, if I can," I say to Gormán, who's come down with me. "See what's set away. Give me an idea of how long it'll all take."

"I'll lend you Conn for today," Gormán says.

"And Bardán?"

Funny look on Master Tóla's face, like he's swallowed something nasty. "The wild man? He'll have his rules for preparing the site, no doubt, same as for all of it, and you'll need to stick to them. I just hope you can make some sense of his gibberish."

"He's clear enough," I say. "I'll be getting on with it, then."

End of the day, I'm aching all over but happy with what we've done. Conn's as skinny as a bean pod, but he's strong. And not a talker, which suits me. Odd team, but it worked well enough, Bardán watching and telling us how it should be done, Conn and me shifting the stones to the spots where they needed to go. Felt like a jumble at first. But the wild man knew what he wanted. Broken bits in one pile. Bigger pieces stacked alongside the edges of what'll be the new house. Out the back of the barn they've got shaped stones from the old build, piled up neat. And inside the barn, keeping dry, is the wood they saved. Oak, ash, beech, like the wild man said. And more. All sorts. Some of it cut to size, some logs with the bark still on. Makes it easier for me to guess what kind they are. Looking at all that wood, I'm thinking I might have taken on too much. If Bardán knows how it's going to fit together, he must be the best builder in all Erin. Which he could be—who knows? Can't judge a man by how he looks. Or how he talks.

I'm off home then. Riding Sturdy, leading the horse I've been given for getting to and fro. Nice big gray, a mare, name of Mercy, which I like. Gormán's said they'll switch between her and another horse so as not to wear them out. Scannal can stable them for me.

Ride feels shorter on the way home, though I'm tired and so is Ripple, running alongside. Make sure I get out of the woods before dusk falls. Cuts the working day a bit short, but still. Common sense. That forest isn't the sort of place you want to linger in after dark. Could be all sorts of things in there, and I'm not just talking wolves and the like. Glad to get clear of the trees and head over to Scannal's. I drop off the horses, have a word to him. He says he'll look after Mercy, no trouble, and just come and fetch her in the morning. Then I'm off across the fields for home with dusk turning everything to soft shadows. Ready for bed right now, every bit of me worn out. Only supper first would be good. And didn't I promise to do something for Blackthorn?

Good smell of cooking from the cottage, something with meat in it. Ripple pushes past me, forgetting her manners. Blackthorn's been busy. Row of little jars on the shelf, with labels stuck on. Some potion she's made with Emer. I remember what it was I said I'd do. Catch up on the reading and writing lesson I missed. Head's so fuzzy I couldn't tell one letter from another.

"Long day," Blackthorn says, ladling whatever it is into a couple of bowls. Gives me a good look over, as if she doesn't much like what she sees. "Eat up. Go off to bed. Don't bother about anything else." She sets our bowls on the table. Puts a dish down for Ripple.

I eat. Try not to fall asleep between one mouthful and the next. "Good dumplings," I mumble. They are good; made with onions and mutton fat. After, I feel a lot better.

"Got a story for you," says Blackthorn. "If you can stay awake long enough."

"Mm-hm?" Hearth fire's burning. Place is cozy. Ripple's lying across my feet, twitching in her dreams the way a dog does. Miles away from Wolf Glen and the wild man and all the stuff I'm not supposed to talk about. Different worlds, and I know which one I like best. A story would be good. Right way to end the day.

"I'm not going to tell it," Blackthorn says. "Not all of it. You have to help. You read one part, I tell the next part." She takes a wax tablet from the shelf, the one she uses to teach me and Emer our letters. She opens it up on the table, and there's writing in it, not practice letters but whole words. They swim around like little fish; can't make any sense of them.

"Might be a bit tired," I say, wishing I'd been born a clever man. "Can't see it clear."

"That's why I kept it short," says Blackthorn. "Come on, now—one word at a time. Point as you go. Start here." She puts the tablet on the table in front of me, guides my finger to the spot. Words skipping about like finches in a fruit tree, dancing out of reach. "Breathe slowly," she says. "You can do this."

"A . . . a bird . . ." I narrow my eyes, try to catch each word in turn as my finger touches it. "A bird calls. Called."

"Good."

She's right beside me. Her arm against mine. I remember in that place of Mathuin's. Anyone laid so much as a finger on her, she'd lash out. Even after we were free, long after, she'd flinch if anyone reached out to her. Couldn't bear even a friendly clasp of the hand, she was so hurt. And now she's here, so close, not scared anymore.

"Go on, Grim."

"Wake up! Wake up! Summer is here," I read.

"Try this word again." She points.

"Sun . . . sunrise. Sunrise is here."

"Well done. Now my turn. Telling, not reading. It was a fine spring morning and a man was setting off on an adventure . . ."

She's got this all ready for me while I've been away. Tells a bit of the story, about a fellow who goes off fishing and finds a strange creature in a lake. Every so often she stops, and the next part of the story is there on the wax tablet, nice and simple for me to read. Not that it's easy; wouldn't be even if I was properly awake. Wish I was quicker at it. But I get through it, word by word. Creature turns out to be a beautiful woman in half-fishy form, and she tells the fellow he has to give up something he loves if he wants to keep her as his wife.

"My horse," I read. "No, I cannot do it. My dog. No, I cannot do it. What can I give?" I look up at Blackthorn. "Sad ending, is it?"

"It depends," she says, smiling. I like the way a smile changes her face, warms it up. "The ending can be whatever you want."

What can I give? is the last writing on the tablet. "You want me to finish it?"

"If you like."

Harder than I thought. I see in her eyes that it's a sort of test, not only the reading part, but this too. Remember a time, not so long ago, when I finished one of her tales with blood and destruction and sorrow all round. Upset a few folk. Want to get this right. Try to put myself in the fisherman's shoes. Try to think the way a water creature might. Why's she asking him to give something up? Does she want to be in human form? Or is this some kind of bad magic?

"Fisherman thinks, what else is there to give? My freedom; my name; my home. My good health; my strength; my courage. Says to the water creature, *What do you want? Speak without fear. If you would rather be free, I will walk away and never trouble you again.* Costs him a bit to say this. He's a lonely man, and the water creature's beautiful. Fair face, long green hair, all shiny, eyes like forest pools. And the tail of a fish. She can't live on land, can't be his wife without changing. Ah. He sees it now. If she changes, she'll get a good husband. But she'll lose something a lot more precious. If he won't give up his freedom, how can he ask her to give up hers?"

"Oh, very good," Blackthorn murmurs. "Go on."

"Water creature doesn't say anything. Just stretches up to where he's sitting on the bank and plants a kiss on his lips. That kiss goes straight to his heart. Like a flash of lightning deep inside, it is. Then, with a whisk of her tail and a twist of her body, she's back into the water and away. Fisherman gets up, all dazed and dizzy with what's happened. Calls his faithful dog. Takes the rein of his dear old horse. Walks away home. Not thinking, *How foolish I was to let her go.* Not thinking, *I just missed my one chance of happiness.* No, even when he's back home, horse in the stable, dog sleeping by the fire, fresh brew in the pot, he's thinking: *How wonderful. How remarkable. I just saw something I'll remember my whole life.* That night he dreams only good dreams."

Blackthorn says nothing at all. Just nods, then goes to put the kettle on the fire.

"Didn't make you cry, did I?"

"Of course not," she says, wiping her eyes. "Peppermint or chamomile?"

I yawn my way through the brew, too tired to talk now. Time enough to tell her about the heartwood house and the wild man another day. I remember something. "How was that girl? The one from Wolf Glen?"

"Didn't make an appearance," Blackthorn says. "Just as well, really. It meant I could take Emer through all the steps of a decoction and give her a reading lesson and cook supper. Washed a lot of clothes, weeded the vegetable patch."

"Good. You might be needing to do a bit more in the garden, if you can find the time. Looks as if I'll be up at Wolf Glen most days for a while. Big job." Can't stop yawning. Put a hand over my mouth.

"Off to bed," Blackthorn says. "I'll tidy up here. So, early start tomorrow again?"

"Mm. Horse at Scannal's. Tell you all about it later." Too tired to move.

"Come on, big man." She takes me by the arm, gets me over to my bed, helps me lie down. Second-last thought I have is, *Glad I took my boots off.* Last thought is how good it feels when she tucks the blanket over me. Then I'm asleep.

6

She had to get out. Not out riding with Lady Flidais and her attendants, all dressed up and talk, talk, talking along the way, expecting answers Cara could not give, expecting smiles she did not have in her. Not out walking to the settlement, so Lady Flidais could drop in to every cottage and check on someone's welfare. *Out*, away from the prince's holdings, out where only wild things lived, out beyond the trappings and the boundaries of this place where she didn't fit and never would. Out to run, to climb, to hide. To go home. Only she couldn't go. Not home, not out, not anywhere.

There was no point in asking Lady Flidais or any of her women—Deirdre or Nuala or Mhairi—because every single person in the household knew Cara was not allowed beyond the walls without an escort. And escort didn't mean just one of them, it meant a guard as well. What did they think she was, a wayward child of six? It almost made her wish she were a married woman and ruler of her own household. But she didn't wish that. She would not have her own household, not truly, until Father died, and she couldn't bear to think about that. Even while she cursed him for sending her away, she still loved him. He was her family. Why couldn't he live forever?

There was a spot near the stables where, if she screwed up her eyes and concentrated hard, she could almost catch a glimpse of the home forest. The hills rose in the distance, lovely under their green blanket. It looked far away but it wasn't so far. Barely an hour on horseback. She could be there and back on the same day. Why would Father forbid that? And why wouldn't he explain? If she could get there, if she could surprise him by simply turning up, maybe she would find out.

The trouble was, everything at Winterfalls was organized. The riding horses were kept in the stable, where there was always someone keeping an eye on them. When they were let out for exercise or to graze in a field, there were workers nearby, grooms, farmhands, folk going up and down the tracks with carts or barrows or herds of cows. Even if she could take a horse without being noticed, she'd have to pass through one of the gates to get out, and all of them had guards, except for a little one up near a copse of birches. Even there, someone would most likely see her. She might manage to gallop a short distance, but she'd be stopped before she even got to that patch of woodland across the fields. Dreamer's Wood, it was called. Where that wise woman lived, the one she was supposed to go and talk to. It was days and days since Flidais had asked her to ride over there. She was running out of excuses for not going. A wise woman! Some old crone who'd tell her to pull herself together and be thankful for her blessings. Why would Flidais imagine she'd want to unburden herself to someone like that?

It wasn't that Flidais was unkind. She was all right, as ladies went. She was youngish. She meant well. But she didn't know what to do with Cara any more than Aunt Della did. She suggested looking at the books in the prince's library. She invited Cara to sit with her and the other ladies in the mornings, when they all did sewing or spinning together. She didn't mind Cara walking or riding around the home farm, but she always sent someone to tag along with her, Mhairi or Deirdre asking questions, trying to make her talk. And if it was Mhairi, she brought a wretched little dog, the snappiest, most ill-tempered thing Cara had ever met. When she'd tried to make friends it had bitten her finger.

In the evenings they all sat around and listened to folk playing music, or they told stories, or sometimes Prince Oran or Lady Flidais would read from a book of tales. Cara didn't mind the tales. They let her pretend for a while that she was somewhere else. Or that she was someone else, someone who could speak when she needed to, someone who could go where she pleased. Except that when the story was finished and the book was closed, the longing for home came back tenfold, an ache in her chest so strong she thought she might be sick from it.

It was ages since Father had dumped her here without a proper explanation, and he hadn't come to see her, not once. When she told Flidais, yet again, that her stomach hurt and she didn't feel like riding, Flidais said she would send for Mistress Blackthorn, the wise woman. Cara said there was no need; she'd be fine tomorrow. Or the next day.

"Oh, good." Flidais smiled. She was always nice, even when she thought she was being lied to. But Cara wasn't lying. She did feel ill. Being away from home made her heart ache. "Then you will be able to go over and see Mistress Blackthorn at last," Flidais went on. "You'll like her, Cara. She's very—direct."

Cara managed to stammer out a *Yes, my lady*. It was plain there could be no more excuses; she'd have to go and see this wise woman. If Blackthorn was direct, she'd probably ask all kinds of questions, and Cara's words would vanish the way they did when Father got angry, or when Aunt Della lectured her about her inadequacies. She wanted to stand up for herself. She wanted to speak. But when people she loved got cross and cold and unkind, she could feel herself shrinking down, like a creature going into its shell to hide. And when she shrank, the words spun away, out of reach. That was why visiting a wise woman was pointless. Blackthorn wouldn't say the only thing Cara wanted to hear, which was, *You should go home.*

She went to have another look at the side gate. It was done up very securely. Getting out that way would require dismounting, unfastening the gate, leading the horse through, then closing the thing properly behind her if she didn't want to let a flock of sheep out. It did seem odd that there was the one entrance without its own guard, but she guessed anyone who came in this way with ill intent would be stopped before they could get near the house. There were always plenty of guards closer in. Prince Oran was the only son of King Ruairi and would be the next king of Dalriada. And the baby boy would be king after Oran. So it was fair enough for the place to be well protected. Just inconvenient.

There was an old bench under the birches. Cara settled herself there and tried to make a plan. There was no point in getting out only to be stopped within a few miles. If she did that, they'd put her under lock and key so she couldn't try again. Not actual lock and key, but the next nearest thing. They'd have someone shadowing her every waking moment. Even in the privy. So the plan needed to be foolproof. Therefore, no horse. She'd go on foot. Once she made it as far as Dreamer's Wood she'd have a good chance of evading pursuers. She just needed to choose the right time. There was open ground between Dreamer's Wood and the much bigger forest of Wolf Glen, quite a long stretch of it, but she was quick, and she knew how to find hiding places where other folk might miss them. If she was unlucky and someone saw her before she got to Dreamer's Wood, she could say she was going to visit the healer. On her own. Which she'd been told not to do. And she'd only say it if she could actually get the words out.

The voice of common sense spoke up. What would Father think when she turned up on the doorstep? Wouldn't he be angry? Wouldn't he pack her off straight back here, telling her a daughter should obey her father?

She would tell him she loved him. It was true. She would promise to be on her very best behavior, every moment of every day. If he let her come home, she would not go into the forest without Gormán, she would not even go out of the house without a maidservant, she would . . . Only she couldn't. When she was a child, not so very long ago, she'd been able to talk to Father, talk to him properly as she still could to Gormán. But as she grew older, that changed. It became harder to please him; harder to be the daughter he seemed to think she should be. And every time he got angry, even a little bit angry, it got harder to speak. The words just went away. Catching even one or two, saying *Yes, Father* or *No, Father* was like climbing a mountain. Nobody understood that. Everyone thought she was just stubborn. Except for Gormán, and Gormán hadn't done a thing to stop Father from sending her away. And Alba—she'd been able to talk to Alba. But Alba hadn't come here with her, and in her heart she knew Father had dismissed her maidservant for what had happened that day. What *had* happened, exactly? How could it be such a terrible thing to climb a tree and be up there when a stranger passed beneath? But it must have been terrible, somehow. She didn't believe all that talk about court manners and meeting a wider circle. Those couldn't be the only reasons he had sent her away.

Even if she could make the words come out, Father would think her arguments childish. And those promises, the ones about being obedient, would be lies. The forest drew her; it was her true home. The trees and the birds and the great stillness calmed her spirit. Did that mean there was something wrong with her? A girl in a tale might sicken and fade away if she was taken from the forest. A girl in real life, a landholder's only daughter, did not give in to such fancies. At least, not according to Father and Aunt Della. And, kind though Lady Flidais was, it was clear that she and her attendants found Cara odd. Perhaps she really was sick. Perhaps she had some disease of the mind. Or maybe she was under a spell. A charm spoken over her cradle, binding her to Wolf Glen. Maybe an evil spirit had attended her birth, causing her mother to die and Cara to be forever different, a stranger in her own world. Perhaps she really did need to talk to a wise woman. If she could get the words out.

Then Lady Flidais got distracted. A messenger rode in from the south with some kind of bad news. Nobody told Cara what the news was and she didn't ask. But both Flidais and the prince were looking solemn and thoughtful. There were meetings behind closed doors, and people from court, councilors and the like, coming to Winterfalls to talk to Prince Oran. With so many visitors, the grooms were busy and so were the serving people, from Aedan the steward and his wife, Fíona, right down to the scullery maids. Nobody asked Cara about riding over to see the wise woman, or about an escort, or about whether she was still feeling sick. Nobody had time to bother with her, which suited her perfectly.

She chose a day when they were all especially busy. She didn't say a word to anyone, just packed a few things in a little bag and wandered up the hill toward the birches as if she were going for a short walk. And when she judged that there were no eyes on her, she climbed over the gate and slipped away toward Dreamer's Wood.

7

BLACKTHORN

The day was fine, the sun was shining, and I was out in the wood gathering mushrooms. Several kinds grew here, some perfectly edible, others, such as the ones locally known as screamers, very much the opposite. Screamers had plain pinkish caps with a darker blush at the edges, set on sturdy stalks. They looked harmless, even appetizing. But eaten in sufficient quantity, screamers could kill. They would at the very least send a person mad. I had seen folk tear at their own skin until it bled, bash their heads against solid walls, run about blindly, shrieking in terror. Hurt themselves. Hurt other folk. One way or another, a person who ate screamers would never be the same again.

My basket was full. Its contents were entirely edible. I turned for home, my mind on what story I would use for tonight's reading lesson. A flash of color under the trees brought me abruptly back to the here and now.

There was a girl at Dreamer's Pool. A girl *in* Dreamer's Pool, a young woman with her shoes off, paddling in the shallows. The last time anyone had gone in there, they'd been changed forever. The pool was fey. Perilous. Forbidden.

Best not to call out. If I frightened her, she might lose her balance and fall right in, all the quicker to become a fish or a dragonfly or a goat. How could she be so stupid? Everyone knew to keep out of the pool. Everyone . . . I walked down the path toward her, staying as quiet as I could. As soon as she saw me, I would warn her to get out. But in a calm tone, so she wouldn't be startled.

As I came closer, it struck me how still she was, as much a part of the woodland as stone or water or tree. And . . . was that a bird on her finger? Yes, a redpoll perched there with complete confidence, while on the young woman's shoulder, half-concealed by her cloud of wispy brown hair, a yellow-breasted siskin preened its feathers. I sucked in a breath; my steps faltered. Perhaps this was not a foolish human girl who had strayed where she should not, but one of Conmael's folk.

Something alerted her. She turned her head toward me. The redpoll took flight; the siskin darted away. The girl was on the verge of doing the same—I could see it in her eyes. She came quickly out of the pool, keeping her gaze on me as if fearful I might attack.

"I'm sorry if I startled you," I said, walking down to the flat ground beside the water, the only spot where a person could easily venture in. "I must warn you. Dreamer's Pool is not a safe place to go wading or swimming. You should keep out of the water altogether."

She was slipping on her shoes, tugging her hem out of her girdle, thrusting items back into her bag. In a hurry to leave. "Why?" she asked, not looking at me. Her voice was barely more than a whisper.

"If the tales are to be believed, and experience tells me they are, then this pool is full to the brim with magic," I said, thinking maybe I could guess who this was. "It changes things. Man into creature. Creature into woman. And there's no way to reverse it. At least, no way known to humankind." She had hitched the bag onto her back. "But perhaps you are not from these parts," I added. "You may not know the tales. Is your name Cara, by any chance?"

"How . . .?" Her response was as quick as a blade, but faded before she finished it. She might have been daydreaming back there in the water, but now she was on high alert. I did not think she was fey, after all; her features looked human, if unusual. She was tall, willowy, awkward in her movements now she knew she was not alone; a girl who had not yet grown into her woman's body. Her pale skin was dotted with freckles. She had a big mop of wavy hair with many shades of brown in it, and wide, wary hazel eyes, now full of the wish to be somewhere else. She seemed afraid of me. Why would that be? I had tried to speak kindly.

"How do I know your name?" I said. "I know because Lady Flidais told me about you. That's if you are the young woman who's come from Wolf Glen to stay in the prince's house. I am Mistress Blackthorn, the healer."

"Oh." She relaxed a little; unfolded the arms that had been tight around her body. Bobbed her head in a sort of nod.

"Lady Flidais spoke to me about finding you a tonic. Something to help you feel better."

No reply to this. She stood there staring, on the verge of flight. I recalled what Flidais had told me about Cara's reluctance to speak.

"Why not come back to my cottage now and we'll talk about it? It's not far. You do need to be careful in Dreamer's Wood. It may sound odd, but it's true. Nobody goes in the pool. They should have warned you." But then, wasn't she forbidden to ride beyond the prince's walls without an escort? "Do you have anyone with you?"

She shook her head. "I should be going." It was a whisper.

"Going? Where?"

She shrugged. I could not tell if that meant, *I don't know* or *It's none of your business.* But I could guess. She was out alone, against the rules her father had set out to Flidais.

"I think you might be running away. Heading for home, perhaps. On foot. Let's say the prince's folk don't catch up with you. You might get there before dusk. But I doubt that; it's a long walk. And, from what I've heard, a difficult one. You might find yourself out in the forest after dark, which wouldn't be ideal."

Cara stared at me, silent. I couldn't help thinking of a wild creature cornered. What did that make me? A fearsome wolf, a ferocious boar, a monster?

"They will send someone after you very soon," I said. "Probably have done already. If you come with me, back to my cottage, we can sit down together and talk or just have a brew, and when Donagan or whoever it is arrives, you can tell him Lady Flidais suggested you come to see me and you forgot you were meant to take someone with you. Better, surely, than being apprehended and escorted back in disgrace."

"I could get there. I know the way. I just need to reach the forest. Our forest. After that they wouldn't find me."

So she could talk, sometimes at least. "Shall we make a wager?" I asked. "I'm betting that by the time we reach my cottage, we'll be able to see someone from the prince's establishment riding in this direction."

"But that means . . ."

"That you can't go where you were planning to go? Yes, it does. However, when you consult a wise woman, you can expect to do so in private. By the time whoever it is gets here, we'll be sitting indoors by the hearth fire, and he will have to wait for you out in the garden, where he can't possibly hear our confidential discussion." When she still looked as if she might make a run for it—and if she did, there'd be no catching up with her; she had youth and long legs on her side—I added, "Truly. If you try to run now, it can only end in failure. Which would probably make any future attempt much harder. And who knows? I might be able to help."

She came with me. Shoulders drooping, face closed, every part of her heavy with disappointment. As I opened the cottage door, she looked over her shoulder. I followed her gaze. Across the fields came two men on horseback, heading our way.

"As I said." I ushered her inside, closed the door, went to build up the fire.

Cara mumbled something.

"What was that?"

"I said I'm not a child!"

Morrigan save us. Was that the choice, to be silent or to snap like an ill-tempered terrier? Had I been like that at fifteen? I filled the kettle, not looking at her. "What would you prefer," I asked, "to speak with me for a while in private or wait outside for your escort?"

"You'll tell her. Lady Flidais."

"If that's what you think, you don't know much about wise women. Keeping confidences is a necessary part of the work we do. Lady Flidais didn't ask me to report back to her, only to talk to you. If you want to chat about the weather, that's fine. If there's something else on your mind and you want to tell me about it, go ahead. Either way, you have an excuse for being here when they ask. No need to mention you were bolting for home." Not that it had looked that way when I'd first seen her. She had appeared entirely at peace with herself and the world. Had she forgotten, standing in that perilous place, that she was running away?

I got out the jar of dried peppermint leaves and the crock of honey. Two cups. Two spoons. "As for the part about heading off without an escort," I told her, "I'll leave you to work out what to say. Please sit down. You're making me edgy."

Cara seated herself on the bench, bolt upright, her hands clutched together on the table before her. The kettle boiled. I made the brew, filled the cups and sat down opposite her. She didn't say a word.

Horses outside, and men's voices. "What shall I tell them?" I asked, not getting up.

"What you said. Before." And after a moment, "Please."

I went outside, shutting the door behind me, to find Donagan and one of the prince's men-at-arms dismounting. Donagan was one of the few who knew the strange truth about what had befallen Flidais at Dreamer's Pool. He had stood by Prince Oran in times of great difficulty. And he'd been kind to Grim. Courtier though he was, I viewed him as a friend.

"Cara's here, Donagan," I said straight out. "She's safe. But we've just sat down to a brew, and I need to talk to her privately. Can I bring you two a cup?"

"Thank you, Mistress Blackthorn," Donagan said, his crooked smile telling me far more than he was prepared to say. "That is a great relief. Don't bother with the brew. We're happy to wait out here and rest the horses. Is Grim somewhere about?"

"Away on a job. All day." I remembered, just in time, that it might not be wise to mention he was at Wolf Glen. From what Grim had told me, the situation up there was odd and the landholder had placed all kinds of restrictions on what could be said and to whom. Add the fact that the same landholder's daughter was currently in my house and behaving oddly herself, and it seemed best to keep my mouth shut about the whole strange affair.

"In demand," Donagan said.

"In high demand. Word gets around quickly when a man's a good worker."

At first, when I went back inside, I thought Cara had given me the slip, fled out the back door and off into Dreamer's Wood. But no; she was standing in a corner, in the shadows, with something cupped in her hands. She was holding one of Grim's little carvings, a hedgehog done with meticulous care, right down to the suggestion of prickles and an enquiring expression on its beady-eyed features. The girl's wary look was gone; now her face was all wonder and tenderness. For a moment, the beauty in that expression stopped my heart.

"My friend made it," I said. "The one who lives here with me. Grim, his name is."

Cara stroked the little creature with one finger, as gently as if it were alive. "I make things too," she whispered. "At home. I used to."

If I asked too many questions, and there were plenty I could think of, chances were she'd go silent again and we would get nowhere. "I'd enjoy hearing about that," I said. "But only if you want to tell me. Come—let's sit down and finish this brew."

She sat, the hedgehog still in her hands. I sipped my tea and held my tongue. This girl was something of a puzzle. Despite my dislike of complications, she intrigued me.

"I make birds, mostly," she said, not looking at me. "An owl. A raven. A finch. That was the hardest. So small."

"From wood?" It would be unusual for a girl to be taught wood carving. This girl had long-fingered, capable hands; they were more the hands of a craftswoman than a person born to be lady of the house.

"Mm. Only I can't do it at Lady Flidais's house. I couldn't bring my tools." Cara drew a shuddering breath. "Father made me pack and leave in a rush. He wouldn't let me go out to the barn. He wouldn't let me say good-bye." Another breath; she was plucking up courage for something. "Does Grim have tools? Knives and chisels, small ones?"

"He does. But I couldn't let you use them without asking him first. And you'd need to do it here."

"Oh." Her shoulders slumped again.

"I didn't say no. I only said we must ask Grim's permission. You must know how a craftsman values his tools."

"I—I just—"

It really did seem hard for her to shape the words; to get them out at all. But when she spoke she did so clearly enough, despite the mouse-like timidity. Was there someone at home who cut her off every time she tried to speak her mind? Someone who believed young women should be silent and biddable? If that was so, why had she been trying so hard to go back?

"I believe Grim might let you use his wood-carving tools provided you promised to look after them, and provided you were only here at the cottage when I was at home. Or Emer, my assistant—she's a girl from the settlement, a little older than you. I know it's hard for you to talk, Cara. You're doing well."

She gave me a sideways glance. "My words won't come out," she said. "They're in my head, only my mouth won't say them. People ask questions and all I want to do is climb a tree and sit there on my own."

"When I saw you in the wood you weren't in a tree. Or alone."

"But—oh, you mean the birds. Yes, they come."

"Unusual," I said.

"Is it?"

Just how unusual, clearly she had no idea. No point in pressing her on that. I tried to guess what had upset her before. Was it the thought of needing to speak to Grim? Was she afraid of men? "I'll ask Grim about the tools for you," I said. "He's working for someone just now, putting in very long days, so he's only home at night. I should have an answer for you tomorrow, if you'd like to come here again."

"Oh. Yes. Thank you, Mistress Blackthorn." She smiled, and her face lit up again. Only a child, really; at least, not much more than one. What had her father been thinking of, sending her to Winterfalls on her own and expecting her to fit in?

"We'd best not keep Donagan waiting too long," I said. "I have one question for you, and you need not answer it if you don't want to. Also, remember what I said about wise women keeping secrets."

"You want to know why I was running away." She addressed this to the tabletop.

"Something like that. I might also mention that even though I think of Prince Oran and Lady Flidais as friends, I hated staying in their house. Grim and I were there for a while after our cottage burned down. A long story which I won't bore you with now. I felt so out of place I wanted to scream. And Grim found it as hard as I did, only he's better at making friends and talking to folk. You'll have your own reasons for not wanting to be there. I do know, because Lady Flidais told me, that your father wants you to stay at Winterfalls awhile, and not to go home until he's ready to have you back there."

"About the wood carving. Father didn't show me how to do it; Gormán did. My father's chief forester. Father thinks carving isn't a suitable occupation for a young lady."

I busied myself stirring more honey into my tea.

"He doesn't understand," Cara said. "He doesn't know how much it hurts. I can't be away. I should be there."

I sipped my tea. Waited.

"I'm not—" Cara said. "I just—" She set the little hedgehog down on the table and put her head in her hands. "I can't explain. It's too hard. You'll think I'm mad."

"Mad, no. But there is something about you that doesn't add up."

Silence for a few breaths, then, "What?" she asked.

"You're like two different girls, the one who stood quiet in the pool, so quiet that wild birds were unafraid to perch on her, and the girl wound up as tight as a bowstring, ready to run the moment she knew I was there."

Cara gazed at me, big-eyed.

"They are the same girl, of course," I said. "And that intrigues me, Cara. I like a mystery."

She smiled. A watery, sad sort of smile it was this time.

"Come back tomorrow," I said. "Grim can find some wood for you to work with—that's if he says yes about the tools." He would, of course. Grim was generous to a fault. I just hoped Cara knew what she was doing and wouldn't cut off any fingers. "Let the prince's household give you an escort next time. I'd rather not upset Flidais by breaking the rules. I can promise you whoever it is will stay outside. They'll do as I bid them."

"If only Father would *say*," Cara spoke under her breath, more to herself than to me. "He never said how long it was for, only that it might be until next autumn. That's so long! And he didn't tell me why. From one day to the next, everything simply changed. If he'd warned me . . . If he'd explained properly . . . But he just said, *You're going to Winterfalls*, and the next day we rode to the prince's and he left me there. He didn't even let my maid come with me. I think he dismissed her. Father knows, he *knows* I can't live away from Wolf Glen. He knows I get sick if I can't be near the trees. But he just . . ."

I ordered myself not to leap to conclusions; not to judge. "What reasons did your father give for sending you to the prince's house? Flidais said something about court manners." It was not hard to imagine what a trial that would be for a girl who liked standing barefoot in forest pools and communing with birds. If I'd told her the very first thing Flidais had done when she'd arrived in these parts as a new bride had been to strip down to her shift and go swimming in Dreamer's Pool, Cara would not have believed me.

"That's what Father said. Meet a wider circle. Learn how to talk to people. Because I can't, most times. The words get stuck. But I can do the things I'm supposed to. Aunt Della—that's my father's sister who brought me up—has taught me how to dance and sit nicely and make conversation and do embroidery. I don't like any of it, but I can do it if I have to. I don't need practice."

"Have you told Flidais this? She's quite understanding." But young, I thought; not so very many years this girl's senior. No wonder she was struggling.

"I can't," Cara said. "I can't talk to folk. I told you."

A moment's pause; we regarded each other across the table.

"You're different," she said. Her cheeks had turned pink. "Like Gormán. And Alba. Alba's my maid. Was my maid."

Plainly this loss had hurt, and I did not press her for explanations. "What would you rather be doing, instead of dancing and conversation and embroidery?"

"Making things from wood. Walking in the forest. Climbing trees. Telling the trees stories, and listening to theirs." She flushed crimson, pressing her lips together as if to stop further words.

Tread softly, Blackthorn. "Speaking of conversation," I said, refilling her cup, "that's the most interesting thing you've said since we met."

"Really?"

"I wish I had the same ability, Cara. I imagine trees have some very, very old stories to tell. Wise tales. The kind more folk should listen to. Only most people can't hear them." I wanted to ask if she had told her father about this; whether he knew, as her only living parent, what she truly cared about. But I did not ask. From what she had said, and from what she had not said, I suspected her father was one of the folk who made her words dry up before she could get them out. A bully. I hadn't liked the sound of him when Grim had told me what he knew, and now I liked it even less.

"Do you actually mean that?" Cara's voice was little more than a whisper. "Or do you think I'm still a child who makes things up, someone you must be kind to so she doesn't start screaming and throwing things?"

That made me smile. "Grim would like you," I said. "Believe me, I do my own share of screaming and throwing things. As for children making things up, who is to say those things are not real? Perhaps only children can see them. The world is full of wonder. But . . . it's full of danger too, Cara. The bright and beautiful exist alongside the dark and shadowy, the evil and perilous. I know your father has hurt you with this decision. But you should abide by his rules for now. He may have some very good reason for doing what he's done." Secrets; Wolf Glen seemed to be full of them.

Cara bowed her head. What she had expected of me I could not guess, but it was clearly more than this.

"You'd best be going," I said, mindful of the two men waiting. "I'm fairly sure Grim will agree about the tools. But I'd like a promise from you. Please don't make another attempt to get home on your own without coming and talking to me first. I know from experience the dangers of rushing off on impulse, thinking you can make the world better."

Cara mumbled something.

"Promise," I said.

"Can I take this?" She had picked up the little hedgehog again, curling her fingers protectively around it.

I didn't want to give it to her. I wanted to snatch it away, wrap it up in my red kerchief, stow it away in my apron pocket until she was gone. The feeling was so strong it startled me. The words, *It's mine!* were on the tip of my tongue. I took a deep breath; governed my features. "You may borrow it," I said. "Please bring it back when you come to visit me tomorrow. The hedgehog was a gift from my friend. He made it especially for me."

"Oh." She was clutching it as if it were a talisman, as in a way it was; all of Grim's makings had something of a charmed quality. But this was not her talisman.

"You could make your own," I suggested. "Couldn't you?"

"I could try. I've only made birds before." Cara downed the rest of her tea, then rose to her feet. The little hedgehog had vanished into her pocket.

"Farewell until tomorrow, Cara. Come in the morning, when Emer is here. If you bring Deirdre or one of the other ladies, Emer can keep her entertained while we talk. Just one more thing."

"Mm?"

"I don't want to find you in Dreamer's Pool again." Odd how the girl had seemed more at home there than anywhere else. "Please heed my warning about the place. Tomorrow I'll tell you a story about two brothers and a prize boar, and what befell them at that very same pool."

"That sounds like an old tale. Something made up."

"You say that, after what we've just been talking about? Even the most made up of stories has its roots in the truth. That one more so than many. Hear it and you'll never paddle in Dreamer's Pool again. I'll bid you farewell now, and thank you for talking to me."

Cara's smile was like sudden sunlight on her cautious features. "I'm sorry I was rude," she said. "Aunt Della wouldn't like that."

"I don't suppose Aunt Della would be happy about you running away either," I said. "But I won't be telling her, or anyone else, about any of it." Grim excepted; but that was different. "Off you go now. I'll see you in the morning."

8

BARÐÁN

I t's colder here. In that other place, where he was before, it was warm all the time. No need to burrow deep at night. No need for coverings like this rough sack of a blanket Gormán's given him. He slept in a . . . It fades away; he can't catch it in his thoughts. A green thing, like a pea pod . . . Was he smaller when he was there? Shrunk down by sorcery? That place was full of strange things, but he does not think the folk were giants. Did they give him the green bed? The little house in which it hung from the twisted withies of a roof thatched with living plants? Or was that little house only a feverish dream? How long was it, how long has he been away?

He tosses and turns under the inadequate covering. Thinks of the man, Grim, riding home on his big horse, sleeping sound under a cottage roof, by a warm fire. Thinks of Gormán and the young fellow in the foresters' quarters, tucked up snug and safe. And Tóla, *Master* Tóla, in his big grand house, under his fine linen sheets. Tóla the liar. Tóla the thief. Tóla the cheat. Tóla the killer. That smooth-faced man is evil to the core. One thing Bardán knows: he has not returned solely to build the heartwood house. He has other business with Tóla. Something happened here, long ago. Something vile and unjust. Something so wrong it is like a silent scream; like a shadow lying over trees and birds and animals and humankind. That wrong, unresolved, unpunished, has drawn him here. But when he tries to remember, the story fades away.

"Come back! Come back!" He beats his hands against his wretched skull, his head full of ghosts that dance out of sight before he can quite see them. A woman smiling. A hearth fire glowing. His own hands, steady, capable, a craftsman's hands, smoothing a piece of fine beech wood. A smell of good food cooking. Never much to spare, but enough. Enough to make them happy. Someone singing in a low voice. *Oh, hush-a-bye baby, and hush-a-bye lamb* . . .

Dagda's bollocks, it's cold! The dream vanishes, broken to smithereens by his shivering body. *Ask the master for another blanket, you fool,* says one of the voices in his head. *In the morning, ask him. You can't build the heartwood house if you're dead of cold.* But the other voice says, *I asked that man for a favor once. Never again.*

9

GRIM

We're caught, Blackthorn and me. Caught by the promises we've made. Just as well we share our secrets, the two of us, or we'd be in real trouble. The girl, Cara, turned up at last. Not to see Blackthorn the way she was meant to. No, she was running away from the prince's place, heading home on her own. Blackthorn talked some sense into her. But she can't tell Flidais. The things folk say to a wise woman, they're in confidence, so she keeps her mouth shut. About trust, isn't it? If you tell a wise woman you're sick or sad or angry, and the reasons why, you don't expect her to spread it all around the place.

And me? I've made a lot of promises to Master Tóla, who's Cara's father. Don't talk to anyone outside Wolf Glen about the heartwood house, or who's building it, or anything about the work. Don't talk to Bardán about anything *but* the work. Have to keep on reminding myself. Anyone I meet from the settlement, such as Scannal, I just say I'm doing a big building job up at Wolf Glen. Got to tell them something when they ask why I can't shift flour bags or give someone a hand with some stock or help dig a drain. They're used to me being around. Used to me saying yes. I don't say what I'm building. Don't want to tell lies. Not if I don't have to.

We talk about it, Blackthorn and me. Now we've only got that little bit of time between me getting home and me falling asleep. Funny; never used to sleep more than a short stretch at night. Mind too full of bad things. These days, I'm out as soon as my head hits the pillow. When I dream, I dream that rhyme Bardán says while I'm working: *Stone on stone. Stone on stone on stone.* Woke up once, and Blackthorn told me I'd been saying it out loud. Asked me if there was more of the rhyme and where it came from. Think there must be more. Maybe when we get to the wood part of the build, I'll hear it. Something old. Old as the trees.

Question is, should Blackthorn mention the heartwood house? To Cara, I mean. The girl's been coming over to see her every few days. Doesn't talk much. When she does, it's all how unhappy she is and how she wants to go home. I asked Gormán about the girl, why she was at Winterfalls, and he wasn't pleased. Said it was none of my business, and not to speak of her to Tóla or anyone else. But he did have an answer. The master wants her out of the way until the building work's finished. Makes some sense. Girl's got no mother, only that aunt I've seen around the place a couple of times. Tóla doesn't want his daughter there while he's got a couple of rough-looking fellows like Bardán and me working for him. Wants to keep his only child safe, which I understand. Might be a bit that way myself if I had a daughter. But I wouldn't want my daughter unhappy. I wouldn't want her not understanding why. Blackthorn says Cara doesn't know that and it's upsetting her.

Maybe Tóla wants the heartwood house to be a surprise. Pretty big surprise, that'd be. Seems a bit mad. But aren't I planning the same sort of surprise for Blackthorn? Tóla's bags of silver are going to pay for another room in the cottage, somewhere she can spread out all her work things and not be cramped up with our stores and pots and pans and so on. I'm not telling her about that, not yet anyway, so maybe it's fair enough that Tóla's not telling his daughter about the heartwood house. Mind you, I plan to tell Blackthorn before I start building, not after I finish. Make sure she's all right with it. And I'm not sending *her* away.

Cara's using my wood carving tools. Gormán's been teaching her since she was a little thing. That's what she said. No reason why a girl shouldn't be handy with these things. She's making a little bird. I left her a nice piece of pine, easy to work with. Knows what she's doing—I can see that. Strong hands, fine touch. Blackthorn says it keeps the girl happy. Nothing like hard work for driving away the shadows.

Weather's been good. Got four courses of stones in place. Bardán's shown me how to lay them. Need to cut a groove on some of the stones and line them up so the posts can be set in deep. Those have been shaped already, from when they tried to build this before. All stored away in the barn. Corner posts of oak. Different timbers for the ones in between. Beech, pine, elm, larch. Wattle will be ash, hazel, willow. That'll need to be gathered fresh for the job. Crazy sort of house. Crazy or magical, depending on how you look at it. Wonder how many more kinds of trees there are in this forest, and how we're going to know if we've left any of them out. And what happens if we do.

The day we set the posts in place, three of Tóla's farm lads come to help, as well as Gormán and Conn. Nobody talking much. I'll be glad when this job is done, and not just because I'll see more of Blackthorn. I miss the give and take, the jokes and tales the fellows tell when I'm working somewhere else. I miss the good fellowship. Not much of that at Wolf Glen. Meal times, if anyone else is around, Bardán'll move away, crouch down over his rations like a dog that's waiting to have his share snatched off him. Though if it's just me and him and Ripple, he'll talk a bit. Gormán and Conn, they're friendly enough, but they don't chat, not much, and when they do it's to each other, about their work and what needs doing: cutting timber, carting logs, pruning or planting or clearing. Sounds a good life, out of doors, plenty of different jobs. They don't talk about the master, unless it's something about their work. They don't talk about the past and they never mention Cara. Seems like they're keeping to the same sort of rules Tóla's set for us.

When we're on our own, just Bardán and me, I break those rules. Can't help it. Man's sad as sad. In pain too, with those hands. Not going to pry for his story. Seems as if there's something big there, but he can't remember. I keep thinking of Mathuin's lockup and how being in that place jumbled up people's minds. Wasn't just Blackthorn and me who got turned half-crazy, but every one of those poor bastards. Bardán could have been somewhere like that. Someplace he couldn't get out of. Until now. But why would he come here? Nobody's kind to him here. Yes, he's got a roof over his head and they're feeding him. But the rules, the way they look at him as if he's more monster than man, the way they don't talk to him, that's its own sort of prison. It's like the stone walls are still there, and the buckets of slops, and the other things. You just can't see them.

"About your hands," I say one day when we're taking a break. "My friend's a healer. A wise woman, one of the best. Would Master Tóla let her come up here and take a look? Blackthorn might be able to help you. Not to fix them up all new. But she'd have a salve or something that would ease the pain."

"Wouldn't want her at Wolf Glen," he says. "The master. Doesn't want anyone."

I know that, of course. But I like the idea of Blackthorn riding up here with me and Ripple one day, keeping me company on the way. "She could give me a salve to bring for you."

Bardán doesn't say yes or no. Just looks at his hands.

"No harm in trying," I say. "What do you think?"

He shrugs.

"Only," I go on, "it would help if I knew a bit about how they got that way. You're young to have your hands stiffen up like that. If I could tell Blackthorn . . ."

Bardán turns those piercing eyes on me all of a sudden. "Breaking the rules, Grim," he says.

"Doing the right thing," I say, lowering my voice, though I know there's nobody within earshot. Gormán and Conn are out in the forest, and from where I'm standing I can see the track down to the house. "Nobody else needs to know."

"Old," Bardán says. "I think. Maybe . . . old."

Can't make sense of this. "You don't know how old you are?" Could have forgotten, locked up somewhere or forced to do some cruel master's work. Could have forgotten a lot. Or chosen to bury the past, the way I did. Some of mine's well hidden away, even now. But I do know how old I am.

"Don't know how long," he says. "How long I was away. These . . ." He holds up his misshapen hands. "They're old man's hands."

I go over and sit down near him. He's on one big block of stone and I'm on another. Make sure I can still see that path. Last thing I want is to get the poor bastard in trouble for talking to me about the wrong thing.

"Old man's hands, yes," I tell him. "But you've got no white hairs." His hair and beard are a filthy, tangled mess. Give them a good wash, they'd come up oak brown. That's my guess. "And you can stand up straight. Old men get that hunch in the back, you know?" I think about what he said. "Away. Away where, Bardán?" Shouldn't ask. Shouldn't expect him to tell his tale when I don't tell mine. "Forget that, it's none of my business."

He stares into nothing, face like a sad dog's. "Far away," he says after a while. "Another place. Building, building."

Things go quiet for a bit. I get back to work. He watches me. Ripple's hunkered down in the shade, keeping an eye on both of us. I think about how it would feel if you couldn't remember. I wouldn't mind forgetting that place of Mathuin's and the stuff that happened there. Be happy if I didn't dream about it ever again. I bet there's things Blackthorn would like to forget too. But then, if you forget what's bad, cruel, unjust, you might not care anymore about setting things to rights. You might stop standing up against the folk who do evil deeds. And someone's got to.

Then Bardán says, "A hundred years."

"What's that?" Must've heard wrong.

"Gone. Away. A hundred years." Bardán's not looking at me; he's staring off into nothing. Maybe waiting for me to say, *What? A hundred years? You're crazy.*

"Happens in the old tales," I say. "Heard one or two about folk wandering into mushroom circles or the like. Next moment they're somewhere else. The Otherworld. And they can't get back. Mostly the other way, though. Feels to them like they're in that place for a day or two. But when they come back, to this world I mean, all the folk they knew are old or dead and there are strangers living in their house." I take a quick glance at Bardán. He's looking at me hard, as if what I'm saying makes sense to him. Morrigan's curse! Could it be . . .? I was going to say, *Wife, children, all gone,* but I don't. "Could work the other way. Hundred years. Long time." I look at him again. "A man could learn a lot about building in a hundred years. And ruin his hands doing it." Thing is, Blackthorn and me have seen some strange old things; things most folk would say couldn't be true. There's Conmael. Take one look and you know he's fey, even if he hadn't got us out of Mathuin's lockup with some sort of spell. There's Dreamer's Pool, where we saw a dog turn into a woman and a woman turn into a dog. And when we went to Bann there were tiny wee folk and a man-monster and a curse that kept people alive more than *two* hundred years. Which all means I don't jump to the conclusion that Bardán's crazy, even if he can act that way. Learned to build a heartwood house, didn't he? And a heartwood house sounds to be as magical as a house can be. Where would he do that, if not in the Otherworld?

But then, Bardán was the one building the heartwood house the first time. And that was before those years away. So the fey might have taught him how to do it better, but he already knew a lot about it.

"Going to ask you something," I say, looking around again in case anyone's near. "You don't need to answer if you don't want to."

Bardán makes a sound that might mean, *Go ahead, then.*

"Who taught you how to make a heartwood house?"

He doesn't answer. Which is fair enough. I get back to work, wondering. Would hearing some kind of old tale or rhyme be enough for a fellow like him, good at building already, to get the know-how of this? And where would he have heard it?

Long while later, when I'm busy with pegs and string, checking that things are straight, Bardán speaks up. As if I'd only just asked that question.

"My father. He showed me."

Have to think quick, get my head away from the build and back to what we were talking about before. From the look on Bardán's face,

I'm guessing that while I've been pacing around and measuring, he's been remembering something he thought he'd forgotten. That sad face of his, mostly hidden behind the beard and the thatch of hair, has got a different look on it now. Surprise. Almost wonder.

"Your dad, hmm?" I keep it light. "He a builder too?"

A quick smile. He's got a few teeth missing in the front. "Dad," he says, sad and happy both. "A builder, yes."

"He taught you well." Bardán's a wreck of a man, down on his luck and angry too, something simmering away inside him. But he knows his job. He knows it inside out. Makes my heart bleed for him. "Not just the building work," I say. "The . . ." Can't find the words for what I mean. "The knowing of it," I say. "The right doing of it." Want to ask where his father learned to build a heartwood house, but I don't. He doesn't owe me his story.

Time passes. Spring moves on. Stone work's all finished, frame standing nice and strong. Weather stays dry, only a light fall of rain here and there, easy enough to work in. Truth is, I'd like a few days off. Be good to stay home with Blackthorn for a bit. Maybe catch up with a few of the fellows from the settlement. But it's warm and fine, flowers popping up everywhere, birds busy in the woods, new green on the trees. And the way I've agreed to things with Master Tóla, I'll only get time off if it's too wet for work.

Lambing starts, meaning the farm lads will be too busy to give us a hand for a while. Gormán and Conn are busy too, doing their own work out in the forest. Which means most days it's just Bardán and me. Blackthorn's made up a salve for him. When I show him he doesn't seem impressed, but he lets me rub it into his hands anyway.

"She says it'll ease the pain," I tell him. "But you have to remember. First thing in the morning and last thing at night. She says be patient."

Bardán just sits there staring at his hands. Got no faith in it, that's plain.

"Blackthorn knows what she's talking about," I say. "Good at what she does. Doesn't tell folk they'll get better if she knows it can't happen."

"Different," Bardán says. He holds up his hands, a sorry sight. "*They* wouldn't help. How can she?"

Feels like I'm holding my breath. "They?"

"Them. In that place. Where I was. Where they kept me."

"The fey?" Risky, saying that, maybe. Thing is, I'm pretty sure that's what he means. Either he went there, to the Otherworld, or he thinks he went there. Funny about the hands, though. Seems like the kind of thing Conmael could fix in a click of the fingers if he wanted to. Those wee fey folk at Bann, they healed me quick as quick after Flannan stuck his knife in me. Quicker than any human healer ever could.

Bardán shrugs. "Might have been a cure. Who knows? Nobody offered. And I didn't ask. Couldn't."

"Why not, Bardán?"

"I couldn't talk, in that place. I could understand all right. But . . . the words wouldn't come out. Hard to get my tongue around them, even now."

Morrigan's curse! All those years, silent. Among strangers. "Getting clearer every day," I tell him, which is the truth. "Just a matter of practice." Then I ask, "Was it a spell? A charm they put on you, to keep you quiet?"

"You've got a lot of questions."

"No need to answer them. Not if you don't want to. I'm interested, that's all. Never met anyone who's been to the Otherworld and come back again. Only—" I shut my big mouth a bit too late.

"Only who?" Bardán's peering at me with those strange eyes, looking inside my head.

I take a risk. Pretty sure he's not playing games with me. "Only the fey themselves." I think of those little folk up in Bann, kind folk they were, only as high as my knee. I think of Conmael, who's more or less the opposite, though well-meaning in his own way.

"Where?" Bardán asks straight out. "Where is the place, the crossing?" Sounds worried. Sounds as if he's hoping I'll say I don't know.

"Crossing?"

"To that other realm. The—the portal."

Getting in deep now. Deep enough to feel like trouble. "Don't you know where it is?" I look over my shoulder, hoping I won't see Gormán or Conn coming. "Not long since you got back, if I've put the pieces together right. Don't you remember where you came out?"

"It was dark. Cold. Nighttime. I ran and ran. And hid away, buried myself deep. Hid from the moon. Hid from the truth. A sad, bad truth."

My cloak's on the ground; Ripple's lying on it. She shifts when I tell her to. I pick the cloak up, put it around Bardán's shoulders. He's shaking now. I should know not to do that. Wake up what a man wants to keep hidden. Should know better than most. "Sorry," I say. He's put his face in his hands, bowed his head onto his knees. "Only trying to help. Big fool that I am."

Bardán mumbles something. Might be, "It's all right." Then he says, "You're a kind man, Grim. Only . . . I had a friend once. I thought he was a friend. But he . . . he . . ."

"Tell me if you want. Or leave it if you want. Thing is," I go on, thinking maybe he does need to get it out, whatever it is, "I won't pass it on. Not to Tóla, not to Gormán, not to anyone here. Promise. I'm a man who keeps his promises."

"What about back home?" Bardán asks, clutching the blanket around himself. "Wife, family, would you tell them?"

Makes me feel odd, this. Sadder than it should—don't know why. "No wife," I tell him. "No family. Only Blackthorn. My friend. My trusted friend, who I live with. And yes, I might tell her. But that's not the same. Telling her's like telling the other part of me. She'll keep your secrets, same as I will."

"Hmmph," Bardán grunts. "The master wouldn't think much of that."

"Lot of secrets in this place," I say, thinking I'd better get back to work before the master has something else to be unhappy about. "More than a fair share. Pity about that. What the master needs is a team of five or six strong men, working on this job every fine day, and we could get it finished before midsummer, thatching and all."

Bardán watches while I get on to the next job, which is shaping the pegs and wedges that'll hold the crossbeams in place. Not going to get the beams up without a proper team. Not unless Tóla fancies losing a worker when someone drops something heavy on someone else's head. "Have to tell him," I say, "that it can't be done without more men. There's a few lads I know in Winterfalls who would lend a hand for a fair payment."

"Secret," says Bardán. "He'll say no."

"Then he might not get his heartwood house finished. Can't see us doing it on our own without a miracle. Take a look at this, will you? Are you sure holly's all right for these pegs?"

"Holly," Bardán says. "Strong for justice. In the rhyme. Every tree in the wood. That's the way he wants it. *Master* Tóla." The way he says it, it's as bitter as nettle tea. "Making his luck."

"Don't like the man much, do you?" I want to ask what happened, what made that hate fill him up. Seems to me Bardán's a good man deep down, if a bit odd. We're all odd in our own ways. But I don't ask, because a woman's coming up from the house with a tray. This time it's not a serving woman but a lady, the master's sister, Mistress Della. Seen her from a distance before, not close up. Like Tóla, she's a shortish, squarish person. His hair's mostly gray. Hers is mostly fair, and done up in plaits. Rosy cheeks, smiling mouth. Looks pleasant.

"Good day, Mistress," I say, knowing Bardán won't say it for me.

"Good day," says the lady. "Grim, isn't it?" Puts her tray down on a flat stone, shoos Ripple away, gives me a good look over. "I brought you some provisions."

"Thank you," I say. The bread and cheese and onions look good; we get hungry, doing this job. Me more than Bardán, since I'm doing the lifting and cutting and shaping, and he's mostly sitting there telling me how to do it all. My mind's still on how foolish Tóla is not to hire a crew to get this done. Be all finished in two turnings of the moon, and no hurt backs or broken hands or crushed heads along the way. Why's it all so secret?

Mistress Della has said something and I've missed it. "Sorry, what was that? Must be tired; thoughts are far away."

"It's a big job," she says. "But I can see the hall taking shape. You do excellent work, Grim." She glances at Bardán, then turns her eyes away quick. "And you," she adds. Odd. Is she scared of him? They did send Cara away.

I give her a smile. Comely woman, in her own way. Feels good to get a sort of thank you. Tóla's a miser with his praise—just looks the place over and nods, most times. "We're working as hard as we can, Bardán and me." I give Bardán a smile too, but he's staring at the ground, doesn't see it.

"My brother is grateful," Mistress Della says. "He may not be free with his thanks, but never doubt that he values your work."

"Be better if we had a few more helpers," I say, thinking she might be the one to convince Tóla, seeing as she's his sister. "Be finished much sooner. Besides, won't be safe getting the crossbeams up without a proper crew."

She goes a bit pink in the cheeks, and I'm sorry I said it. Not her fault if the master's funny about letting folk know what he's up to. "Nobody would want you to put yourself in danger, Grim. I understand my brother can call in the farmworkers to help, and of course Gormán and Conn . . ."

"Best way to go ahead, if you ask me, is to have the same team here every day. Five or six workers all day, every day, until it's finished. Or at least until we start thatching; I can do that with just a couple of helpers." I glance at Bardán. "Two lads to pass things up and hold things in place and so on, and Bardán to tell me the tricks of the job."

"It's . . ." she starts, then look at Bardán again and stops. "May I speak to you in confidence?"

I want to tell her anything she says to me can be said to him too, but that would be stupid when she might tell me something useful. I get up and follow her down the path a bit, out of Bardán's earshot.

"My brother wants no more outsiders here," Mistress Della says. "Only you, Grim. He . . . He has always set a great deal of faith in . . .

in luck charms and the like. A heartwood house is an idea from an old rhyme. It is said to confer every blessing a person could possibly want for himself and his kin. He was devastated when . . . when the building could not be completed, the first time. Suanach—his wife—died soon after the work was abandoned. He believes that if the house had been finished, her life would have been saved. When the builder came back," she gives Bardán another glance, "my brother saw it as a second chance. A chance to do things properly. There can be no mending the past, of course. But he can secure the future."

I try to think what question to ask. Cara is the future. It doesn't take a scholar to understand that. But Cara hasn't got a mention, though this lady's been more or less a mother to her, from what I've heard. "Doing it properly, doing it right, I understand that," I say. "But not the bit about no outsiders. Especially when getting in a crew would mean doing things quicker and safer. And I don't understand why Master Tóla can't treat his master builder more kindly." Hope that's not too direct for her.

"My brother loathes gossip. He is a very private man. As for the builder . . . there is a sad story attached to him. A story that would bring the strongest man to tears. It justifies my brother's caution a hundred-fold. His rules are made with good reason."

"What story, Mistress Della?"

"I'm not at liberty to share the tale." Her face tightens up; I see her wishing she hadn't said so much. "Please don't mention that we spoke of this. Best that you just do the work, take your payment and keep quiet. It's the way things are done here. Now, I've been keeping you from your meal. What bad manners!"

The conversation's over. No more answers to be had. We walk back to where Bardán and Ripple are waiting. "Thank you, Mistress," I say, and wait for her to move on. I'm not going to start eating with her watching me.

She crouches down to pat the dog. Ripple rubs up against her hand as if the lady's her best friend. "What a fine dog you are," says Mistress Della. "You remind me of my old Dancer, that I had when I was a girl. She was a beautiful thing, long limbs, fine, soft coat . . . It broke my heart when I lost her. You get attached to them." She straightens, looking away from me, gazing over the part-built house to the many greens of the forest. "If he is sometimes a little demanding," she says, "if he seems harsh, remember his loss. It was grievous; he never recovered fully. Now I should go. Enjoy your meal."

When she's gone I sit down, put the tray between Bardán and me, give Ripple her share. Don't say a word. There's a jug of ale as well as the food. I pour a cup for me, a cup for Bardán. I think about what Mistress Della's told me.

Doesn't make a lot of sense. Tóla believed the heartwood house would bring all sorts of luck, good fortune and so on. Bardán ran off before he got it finished. Not long afterward, Tóla's wife died. And he blames Bardán. If Cara was a baby when Mistress Della came to Wolf Glen, it's fifteen years or thereabouts that Bardán's been away. Away in the Otherworld, or someplace he thought was the Otherworld. Only, he's got fey knowledge. And if he learned from his father, that could mean his father was there too. Where else would you learn how to build a heartwood house? It's not only using the different woods. Bardán's telling me all sorts of little things that matter, exactly how the pegs are made and where they go, how many wedges I'll need, how deep to set the poles, what the pitch of the roof is going to be. There'll be more—no doubt of that.

"Seems a pleasant woman," I say. Pleasanter than her brother. Not that it would be hard.

"Come up to check on us." Bardán's eating without looking at his bread and cheese. Staring off into the forest as if half of him's somewhere else. He doesn't ask what she said to me, which is just as well.

"Easier to talk to than Master Tóla." Morrigan's britches, this ale's going down a treat! Didn't know how thirsty I was. "Wary of you, though."

"Wise to be wary. She's that man's sister."

"You hate him, you hate her. Is that what you mean?"

"He . . . he took . . ." All of a sudden, Bardán's right back in his nightmare, whatever it is. "He gave me . . . he made me . . ." Hands shaking so hard he can't hold his cup steady. I take it before he spills ale all over himself.

"All right. It's all right," I tell him, knowing it's not, knowing how it feels when the past comes up and takes over everything, a crashing, crushing wave. "Breathe, Bardán. Breathe slow." I move the tray away, crouch down beside him, put a hand on his shoulder. He might lash out. His eyes are crazy, filled up with all the bad things. Shudders running through his whole body. Know how that feels. "Breathe, friend. In . . . out . . . You're here, with me. Here at Wolf Glen. Doing good work. Making something fine. Breathe slow, Bardán."

I go on like this a while, and he shivers and stares and grinds his teeth, and I'm hoping Gormán might come and help me, but I'm thinking maybe it's better if he doesn't, because Gormán's no more friend to this poor soul than Master Tóla is. Makes me wonder why they want him here, even if he is the only one who knows how to build the heartwood house. Makes me wonder why he stays. Why he thinks he needs to stay. If I was him, I'd be walking off into the forest right now, turning my back on the master and the rest of these folk and making a new life for myself. Only it's never so simple, is it? I should know that.

"Tell you a story," I say. That's what Blackthorn does, sometimes, when the darkness comes back and I'm too crazy or sad to make sense of things. "Give you something different to think about. There was this fellow once, a shepherd he was, went wandering off with his sheep to a field with a big hawthorn growing all by itself in the middle . . ."

Bardán's calming down. Only half listening, maybe, but that doesn't matter. Just needs something instead of those voices from the past, the ones that hide away in your head and sneak out when you don't expect it. I tell him how the shepherd met a beautiful fey woman and fell in love the moment he clapped eyes on her.

"'I will marry you,' the woman said, and Dougal's heart leaped in his chest. 'But,' she went on, and his heart sank a bit, 'first you must climb to the top of the Perilous Crag, find the Red Giant's cave, and bring me back his most precious possession.'

"Now Dougal, being a shepherd, was fleet of foot and good on ledges. He'd fetched more lost sheep back than anyone could count. So he got up the Perilous Crag, all right, and found the Red Giant's cave without much trouble. So far, so good, he thought. Maybe the fellow's out for a walk and I can get this done quick and painless.'"

Bardán's listening. Nodding here and there. I wonder what's best with this story. Get it wrong and he might come unstuck the way I did when Blackthorn started telling that tale about warring clurichauns. Turned me half-crazy for a while. But make it too bland and he'll stop listening, and when you stop listening, the dark things come back into your head.

"Next thing," I say, "the Red Giant came roaring out of the cave. 'Who dares come up my crag? Who dares approach my cave? Don't you know I can snap you in half with my two little fingers?'

"Dougal was scared. Who wouldn't be? But he thought of the beautiful fey woman, and he looked the giant in the eye and said, 'I do know this: you have something precious in your cave and I need to take it away. My whole future depends on it.'

"Now you might be wondering why the giant, big as he was, didn't just reach out a finger and push Dougal over the edge. Easy, it would have been. Only there was a charm over the place, and over the giant's treasure, that the big man himself couldn't lift. A fey charm, a bad one. 'You can't have it,' the giant said, planting his big feet apart and folding his big arms. 'Unless you can guess what it is. Take as many guesses as you want. Only, if you haven't got it right before the sun goes down, off the cliff you go, and there won't be much left of you when you get to the bottom. Who'll look after your sheep then?'"

When Blackthorn was telling it, she stopped there and passed over the wax tablet, and there were the questions for me to read. So I tell it the same way.

"'Is it gold?' 'It is not gold.'

"'Is it silver?' 'It is not silver.'

"So it went on; Dougal guessed all kinds of jewels; he guessed bronze or copper or fine glass. He guessed cattle or sheep. He guessed a fine hunting hound, a swift riding horse, a magic sword. To each the answer was no.

"It was hardly going to be a castle or a fleet of ships or a parcel of land—how could the Red Giant keep any of those in a cave? Even the horse or dog would be tricky. The sun was going down, sinking into the west. A golden light shone on the rocks around the cave mouth; it would soon be dusk, and it would be over the cliff for Dougal."

"Down," murmurs Bardán. "Down, way down." I can see his jaw clenching again; I need to get this finished quick.

"It came to Dougal, a bit late, that he'd been foolish to think a beautiful fey woman was ever going to want to wed him. What was he, after all? An ordinary shepherd, not handsome, not wealthy, not magical in any way. Folk called him kind. They called him dependable. They called him a good friend in time of need. But he was hardly the husband for a woman lovelier than springtime and more graceful than a swallow. Maybe he should say this to the Red Giant."

"A good husband," Bardán says, surprising me. "Kind, dependable. That was what she wanted."

I'm about to tell the next part when I see Gormán coming over from the barn. "We've got company," I say, finishing my ale and setting the cup on the tray. "Tell you the rest tomorrow."

"Full of theories," Bardán said. "Everyone in the village. She'd fly off one night and leave him on his own. She'd abandon her child. She'd turn the milk sour and curse the cattle so they dropped dead calves. But she didn't. He was a good husband, and she was a good wife. She was the one got them out of that place. Why would she want to go back?"

I'm trying to warn him to shut up, hold his tongue, but he keeps on talking, telling a story that's a bit like the other one but not the same, and now Gormán's here, not looking pleased at all.

"A word of warning," he says. "Break the rules and you'll be out of a job," he nods in my direction, "and you," he looks at Bardán, "will be in all kinds of trouble."

I don't like this. Don't like it one bit. "Lose the two of us," I say, keeping it quiet-like, "and the master won't get his heartwood house built. Thought he wanted it finished, every part just so. Taking a break, telling a tale or two, what could be wrong with that?"

Gormán looks a bit discomfited. "A tale? Depends what it is. Best if you keep your minds on the job. That's what he wants."

"Been meaning to talk to you anyway," I say, thinking this is an opportunity. "I know Master Tóla doesn't want the whole district knowing about this. But it doesn't make sense to keep working with only Bardán and me and a bit of help here and there. We'll be putting the crossbeams up soon. Can't do it without a crew. I know you and Conn and the farm lads can't leave your work for a longish stretch. We'll need to get in some fellows from Winterfalls settlement. Give me a few days' warning and I can get you six good workers."

"He didn't agree to that when you suggested it before," says Gormán. "And he won't now."

"No wonder it never got finished, first time around," I say.

"First time around, we had a crew," Gormán says. "If Bardán here hadn't run off in the middle of the job, the house would have been built years ago."

"Ran off. Fell down," murmurs Bardán. "Way down. Down into the dark. No way back . . ."

"So, will you ask him?" I keep an eye on the wild man. Hoping he won't fall back into his nightmare. He was starting to come good when I was telling the story. "The master? Ask him if we can have a few fellows from the settlement to help. We can tell them not to talk about the job when they get back home." Soon as I've said this, I think it wouldn't work, not with the hour's ride each way. They'd have to come up to Wolf Glen and stay till the job's done, and Master Tóla was never going to agree to that.

"I can ask," says Gormán.

I hear what he's not saying. *But it's pointless. He doesn't like strangers at Wolf Glen.* Sounds like Master Tóla's his own worst enemy. "Tell him it's not safe to put the beams up without a proper crew. Doesn't matter how much silver he's offering. A good man doesn't put his workers at risk." I think of an argument Master Tóla might listen to. "Heartwood house is supposed to be lucky, isn't it? How lucky will it be if some poor sod's died in the making of it, all because the master had his own way of doing things?"

Gormán nods. "He won't have workers from Winterfalls here," he says. "But I'll tell him what you said."

"Good. And now we'll get back to work, Bardán and me." I take a breath, and then I say, "You and Conn. Been working together a while?"

"A while, yes."

"Don't you tell tales and sing songs, help you through a job?"

Gormán smiles. "Neither of us has the gift of a good singing voice. Not that it matters when you're out in the forest. The birds don't judge."

"So, that's all we were doing, Bardán and me. No harm in it." Thing is, I don't like the way they treat the wild man, as if he's some kind of mad beast, not a man at all. Doesn't matter what that sad and terrible tale is, the one Mistress Della was talking about. Nobody deserves to be treated so badly. I've seen the wretched little hut he sleeps in. I spend all day working next to his smell, which is the smell of a man who hasn't had a hot bath for a long, long time. I take home a few extra fleas and creepy-crawlies every night, thanks to Bardán. Be easy enough to house him in the barn, some dry straw, a few good blankets, a proper roof over his head. Or in the foresters' quarters, next door. But no. Nobody wants him near. Only they don't want him too far either. Because he's got the magic to finish the heartwood house.

Gormán takes himself off, and I get back to work. Morrigan's britches, even carrying one of those roof beams over from the barn would take four fit men. How does Tóla think we're going to haul them up? By magic?

"Stone on stone," says Bardán. "Stone on stone on stone."

10

BLACKTHORN

For a long time I'd been best alone. Not that I greatly loved my own company; I lost patience with myself almost as quickly as I did with other people. But I needed quiet, solitude, time to think things through. Time to stop myself from acting like an impulsive fool who thought she could solve the world's injustices all by herself.

After the vile ordeal of Mathuin's lockup, I'd acquired Grim as a traveling companion, not wanting him, not choosing him, but bound to let him tag along because of Conmael's poxy rules. And now I was so used to having the big man around that when he was off doing his long days on the heartwood house, I couldn't help missing him. It felt as if part of me was absent.

Not that I was alone much now, even with Grim at Wolf Glen. Most days Emer was with me, capable Emer, concocting various cures, giving the cottage a sweep-out, bringing in water from the well, even when I reminded her she was a healer in training, not a servant. And now there was Cara, whose measure I did not yet have, not fully. She'd taken to coming over from the prince's house in the mornings, duly escorted, and hanging about the cottage until someone came to collect her. The attraction was not myself or Emer, but Grim's wood-carving tools. She used them every morning. I wished Tóla could see her work and recognize her rare skill.

She couldn't carve all day, and I saw a virtue in keeping her busy, since she was forbidden to do what she most longed to do: go home. "If you're going to be here with us," I'd said to her once it became apparent that she meant to continue these daylong visits, "I want you usefully occupied. Find a job and keep out of our way while we're working. Emer knows how to handle poisonous plants. You don't. And while Emer is my student and assistant, you have no such arrangement with me. I don't imagine your father wants you to become a wise woman."

She surprised me, as we got to know each other better, by proving quite capable at a variety of domestic tasks. I was less surprised when her speech began to flow easily in my presence. I was beginning to think fear lay at the heart of her problem. Not the kind of fear a person feels when confronted by a charging bull—I could imagine Cara shinning up a tree to escape—but a terror of getting things wrong, especially if her mistakes offended those she loved. Her father in particular. If I was right, that man had a lot to answer for.

Time passed, the season advanced, and a rich crop of unwanted plants sprang up in Grim's usually well-tended vegetable patch. One warm day Emer went off into the wood to gather herbs, and Cara and I settled to weeding. We worked in companionable silence for a while, enjoying the sun.

The garden began to look more like its old, tidy self; Grim would be pleased. With the advancing spring, the days were lengthening. There should still be light enough for him to see it when he came home.

A peeping sound made me turn my head toward Cara. Crouched beside the garden bed, she had a bird on each shoulder, one on her head, and four or five others close by, helping themselves to worms as her weeding efforts uncovered them. There were no birds on my side of the garden. I watched, fascinated, not daring to speak lest I scare them away.

Somewhere in Dreamer's Wood, someone screamed. The birds took instant flight. Cara and I scrambled to our feet.

"Emer," said Cara. "Quick!"

"No." I grabbed her arm, holding her back. "Wait." We stood still, listening. No more screams. But a man's shout, cut off abruptly, and the sound of someone moving through the woods. There was only a moment to weigh it up. Emer was strong and sensible. She was wiser than her years. I had to put Cara first. She was in my care, and she was fifteen years old. "Come back inside," I whispered. "Do as I say."

Out there, it had gone quiet. I hustled Cara into the cottage. "Stay here and keep silent." I grabbed the knife I used for cutting up joints of meat and stuck it in my belt. "No rushing to the rescue, understand?"

"But—"

"Flidais is expecting me to keep you safe. Stay inside until I come back. This may be nothing."

"All right." Cara's voice sounded tight. We both knew Emer was not a screaming kind of person.

I went back out, shutting the door behind me. Stopped to listen. Cattle exchanging remarks in the nearby field. Birds in the wood. And below that, a man's voice, speaking calmly, and Emer saying something in her turn.

They came into sight before I reached the edge of the wood. Emer was pale but composed. She had her herb basket over her arm. Walking with her was a young man. A somewhat unusual-looking young man. His garments were those of an ordinary traveler, but his features were graven with a striking pattern, a clever tracery of lines that gave the suggestion of a hunting hound. He had two sheathed knives at his belt. My grip tightened on my own knife, though nothing in Emer's manner suggested danger. This would have been an excellent time for Grim to put in an appearance. But Grim was miles away at Wolf Glen, and so was Ripple, whose protective presence would have been welcome.

As they came closer I saw that the fellow had on a leather breast piece under his short cloak and protective bands around his forearms. Warrior garb.

"It's all right," Emer said as they reached me. She set her basket by her feet. "This man is Cúan." The name matched the skillfully executed tattoo. *Young hound.* "There was a—some kind of disagreement—but it's over now. Cúan, this is Mistress Blackthorn, whom I told you about."

"Good day, Mistress," the warrior said, giving me a polite nod. "Might I have a word?"

"A disagreement," I said. "Between whom?" Whatever it was had frightened Emer. She might be calm and composed, but her eyes told me a different story.

"Nothing you need concern yourself with," the man said. "It's over now. I'm sorry the young lady was troubled. She was not involved in what occurred."

A woefully inadequate explanation. I held his gaze, waiting for more.

"We were riding to Winterfalls, to Prince Oran's establishment. My companions have gone ahead. I thought it best to make sure Emer came safely home. And I have a question or two for you."

Emer was shivering now. She needed a restorative brew. Behind me, the cottage door creaked open. No surprise. Cara was not fond of rules, even those designed for her own benefit. "You'd better come in," I said. Why this man would want to speak to me, I couldn't imagine. "I'll make a brew."

The young man waited while I made tea and Cara set out some bread and honey. With Cúan present the room seemed suddenly too small. Emer sat by the fire, saying nothing.

I poured the brew. Cara passed around the platter. "It seems you're not going to tell us anything further about what happened just now, Cúan," I said eventually. "What was it you wanted to ask?"

"You might tell me whom you have seen passing along that track in recent times. The track through Dreamer's Wood. Carters, farmers, folk taking pigs out to forage . . . it would seem a convenient way for all of those. But few enter the wood; is that correct?" Whatever he saw on my face, and perhaps also on Emer's, seemed to give him pause. "You wonder why I would ask such a thing," he went on, flashing a charming smile that didn't fool me for a moment. "It may reassure you to know that I am heading for Winterfalls at the invitation of Prince Oran. My companions also."

"Then you can ask Prince Oran about the road and the wood," I said, not caring that I sounded sharp. "He knows as much as I do."

"Not quite as much, surely. You live here, right on the edge of Dreamer's Wood. The prince's dwelling is some distance away across the fields. Your answers are the ones that interest me."

"Forgive me," I said, "but I have absolutely no idea who you are or why you would want me to divulge anything at all to you. A more effective approach might have been to visit me with the pretext of an aching belly or a sprained ankle, and just happen to fall into conversation about the oddities of Dreamer's Wood. Anyone from the local settlement could tell you the place has given rise to many strange tales over the years. They would say it is not wise to enter the water of Dreamer's Pool. Walking or riding along the track is fine, but taking too long about it might be inadvisable. As for who has passed this way in recent times, the local folk generally go by the more direct route, using the main track. People seldom bring their stock through the wood. Emer and I gather herbs there frequently, but the nature of our calling means we are safe provided we take no ill-considered action."

"Such as what?"

"Forgive me, but unless you are a druid, I cannot understand how that can interest you in the least."

"Jumping into Dreamer's Pool for a swim." Emer spoke up, sounding more like her usual self. "Cutting herbs without saying the correct words of thanks. Harvesting poisonous mushrooms, unless it's for a remedy of some kind. Harming creatures."

"And you . . .?" Cúan turned his delightful smile on Cara, who dropped her gaze immediately.

"This young lady is visiting me for the day. She lives in the prince's household."

He seemed to be waiting for more.

"You haven't told us why you're asking questions," I said. "And being less than subtle about it."

"If I had some nefarious intent, Mistress Blackthorn, I would be a great deal more subtle, I assure you. There was some trouble earlier. An altercation. It's been dealt with, so you have no need for further concern. But it's useful if I can be as fully informed as possible."

"You're saying there was someone in the wood who shouldn't have been there?"

"It's been dealt with, Mistress Blackthorn."

There was no choice but to accept this at face value. Neither Cara nor Emer knew anything of my past or Grim's. Nor, indeed, did anyone at Winterfalls. They did not understand how any stranger asking questions might be one of Mathuin's spies, come to seek us out and silence us. They did not understand that any disturbance brought back the familiar terror. This young man had a way with him. But Flannan had been a charming man too. Not only charming, but an old friend of mine. I would not be trapped like that again.

"You live here with Mistress Blackthorn?" He addressed this to Emer.

I opened my mouth to say, *Mind your own business*, but Emer was quicker. "I live in Winterfalls settlement."

"Emer is my assistant." I made my tone suitably quelling.

Cúan's gaze moved from one side of the cottage to the other, taking in the two shelf beds, both neatly made up with blankets and pillows. He did not ask the obvious question, and I did not offer any information. When Emer seemed about to speak again, my frown silenced her.

"You come from the island."

We all turned to look at Cara; this was the first time she had spoken since Cúan's arrival. The flat statement rendered the young man momentarily silent.

"What island, Cara?" I asked.

"In the north. The warrior island. They all have the . . ." She gestured to indicate the facial tattooing. "Serpent, bird, wolf, salmon and so on. I've seen you. Not *you*," she added, flicking her gaze over Cúan and away as if he were of as little interest as a fly on the wall. "But some of the others."

"Where was this?" He was keeping his tone friendly, but I'd seen the way his eyes sharpened.

"By the lake. At Wolf Glen. Gormán was selling them logs. For building."

I asked what seemed the safest question. "What lake is that, Cara?"

"Longwater," Cara said. "To the west. You can't get timber in and out on this side; the track is too narrow. And tricky. That's what people say."

Now that she had started talking, I feared she would blurt out something best kept to ourselves. We knew nothing about this man. Good manners did not make him a friend.

"What do *you* say?" Cúan asked, before I could speak a word.

Cara gave him a shy, sweet smile. It brought a different look to his face, a softer one. Just as well he'd be on his way soon; that was a complication I could do without.

"The forest is my friend," Cara whispered, looking down at her feet. "The paths lead me where I need to go."

"Then you are blessed indeed," said Cúan with gentle courtesy. "Mistress Blackthorn, it's past time I departed." He rose to his feet. A tall man; though not as tall as Grim. Few were. "Thank you for your hospitality, and my apologies to you, Emer. You were so quiet, we did not know you were in the wood."

"It was nothing," Emer said.

"All the same. If I may, I will come past in a few days and make sure you are quite recovered."

"So you'll be staying in the district awhile?" I opened the door, wanting him gone.

"I can't say," Cúan said. "Good day to you all, and my apologies once more." It seemed he had no horse with him; he headed off down the garden pathway, then took a track across the fields toward the prince's residence.

"I hope he doesn't mind cattle," said Emer. "There's a long-horned bull in the next field over, and the spring being what it is, he's feeling the need to protect his ladies."

"What happened, Emer?" I asked, watching the golden-haired figure as he walked away with easy strides. "Why did you scream?"

"There was some kind of—of scuffle, not a fight exactly, but—I
heard a grunt and a gasp and saw someone moving around under the
trees and someone else running, with a knife in his hand. That's when I
screamed. They were really close, as if they might come down the bank
right onto me. But they didn't, because Cúan appeared and blocked my
view. He took a while asking me who I was and where I lived, and telling me everything was all right and there was nothing to worry about.
By the time he moved aside there was nothing to see. Then he politely
offered to escort me back here, and that was that."

"He didn't ask you about who I was or where I came from, or anything like that?" I tried to sound calm, as if this question was of little
importance.

"I said you were the local healer and that I was your assistant. He
asked if he could have a word with you. All very correct."

"Mm-hm. Cara, tell us some more about this island. Are you saying
there's a whole community of warriors there, all with animal names?"
It sounded more old tale than reality. On the other hand, I knew from
experience how closely interwoven the two could be.

"Gormán sells them logs," Cara said. "He takes them to the lake
shore on the ox cart. There's a settlement where they load the barges." A
pause. "I'm not supposed to go over to that side of the forest. But Gormán
let me go with him once or twice when Father was away. Just so I would
stop pestering him about it. That was what he said. That's where I saw
the men with the . . ." She made the gesture again, suggesting a facial
marking. "Don't ever tell my father. Gormán would get in trouble."

There was a whole story behind this. It was sounding more curious
all the time. "If I ever have the opportunity to speak to your father," I
told her, "I'll make sure I don't mention it. Why wouldn't he want you
visiting this lake and the settlement there? If you stand to inherit Wolf
Glen someday, surely you should be learning all about the place and
the work." If she'd been a boy, she would already have been helping her
father run things.

"It's to keep me safe. Because he loves me. That's what he says."

"Is this island in the lake? With its complement of warriors?"

"No, it's much further away. Off the north coast," said Emer, surprising me. I'd never heard of the place before, and I'd assumed she hadn't either. "A sea island with a deep water anchorage. It's called Swan Island."

"Populated by tattooed warriors who might have walked right out of some tale of Cú Chulainn."

"There's a school of warcraft there," Emer went on. "Fraoch told me about it." Fraoch the smith was Emer's brother, notable for his skill on the bodhrán, and for being the only man in Winterfalls who approached Grim's height and breadth. "Leaders send their men-at-arms there to learn . . . I'm not sure exactly what. Skills they can't be taught at home, I suppose."

"Secret skills? Such as a druid or wise woman might teach?"

Emer grinned. "Not quite the same. But yes, secret skills. At a guess, things like spying and getting through locked doors and killing someone with your bare hands."

"Morrigan save us. Who's in charge of this establishment?"

"I don't know, Mistress Blackthorn. It's been there a long time. I'll ask Fraoch if you like."

"No need for that. I do wonder why Cúan and his companions are here, and what actually happened in the wood. But I don't want to seem unduly interested. Let's just wait and see." Another thought occurred to me. "This island. How far is it from Cahercorcan? Would the king know about it?"

"I think it's quite close, within a few miles."

"Oh." So all sorts of people would know of it. Including Grim, most likely. We had stayed at court for some time. He had many friends among the men-at-arms, both in that royal household and the one at Winterfalls. "I wonder why I haven't heard of the place before."

"It's what Emer said," put in Cara. "Secret knowledge, like the things you teach her. Say Prince Oran wanted his men taught those other skills, spying or getting into places through locked doors—he wouldn't want everyone to know about it, would he? The same for any leader who sent his men over there to be trained."

Cara sometimes surprised me like this. Her manner was often vague and distant, as if she were not quite in the same world as the rest of us. Yet she would come out with a statement that showed she had not only been listening, but listening attentively.

"That still doesn't explain what they were doing in Dreamer's Wood. But never mind that now. Emer, we should do some writing. Cara can help you." I'd been surprised to find that the girl was capable at reading, writing and numbers, thanks to the tutelage of her aunt.

We worked through the lesson, the three of us. Emer was diligent, as always. Cara kept looking out the window, distracted by every bird that flew past. And I was less than a perfect teacher, for my thoughts kept going to Mathuin, and to the man he had sent to track me down before, and to Cúan with his lovely blue eyes and disarming manner. The most courteous, the most guileless-seeming of folk may carry a hidden blade, ready to strike.

It was only midafternoon when I told the two girls we were finished work for the day. We wouldn't wait for Cara's escort to arrive, but would walk over to Winterfalls together. It seemed a good opportunity to ask Flidais if she knew anything about the Swan Island men. I had seen less of her than usual recently. There was some kind of problem in the south, where her family lived. Nobody seemed prepared to say much about it, but I sensed it was serious. Both Flidais and Oran seemed preoccupied.

Not for the first time, I wished I could tell them the whole truth: who I really was, why it was so vital that I bring Mathuin of Laois to justice and what was preventing me from acting now. The reason why, even on the sunniest and most peaceful of days, part of me was full of dread. But I could not tell. They trusted me. They trusted me with their little son, the apple of their eyes. I was an escaped prisoner, scarred and damaged almost beyond repair. Maybe they would forgive me for being less than truthful up till now. Maybe they would understand that I had reasons for being bitter and angry. I did not believe for a moment that they would hand me over to Mathuin, who had threatened Flidais's father. But they might no longer want me as their local healer. And that would mean losing the cottage, and losing the community, and being on the road again. And if I lost those things, Grim would lose them too. The truth could be perilous.

As it happened, there was no chance to talk to anyone but Deirdre, who came to the door of the prince's establishment to shepherd Cara inside. The household was in a flurry of preparation. Oran had been called to court for an urgent council, and Flidais was going with him, along with baby Aolú and various attendants. They would be heading off first thing in the morning and might be away some while. Deirdre did not know who would be at the council. But she told me there had been more bad news from the south. Flidais's parents had left Laigin and sought refuge at the court of Mide. There had been an attack on their holdings with many slain, and Lord Cadhan and his wife had been lucky to escape with their lives. Their territory was now in the hands of Mathuin of Laois.

11

BARDÁN

F alling asleep, shivering with cold, he tells himself the story. It's not yet clear to him, not all of it, but what he can remember soothes his hurts. It takes him back, far back, to the time when he was a boy of five or six. His father showing him how to smooth a block of beech wood, stroke by careful stroke. Patient, so patient. His mother close by, in a gown of willow green, her hair spilling over her shoulders, the sun turning its brown to gold. The song she sings, so familiar that he feels it still, running in his veins, sounding in the depths of him. *Every birdling in the wood . . .*

His father grew up in that other realm. They stole him out of the cradle and left a changeling in his place, a wretched, wailing creature with a head like a turnip and beady, knowing eyes. Once they stole, twice they stole, stole them right away . . . Where else could his father have learned the making of a heartwood house, but in the realm of the fey? Down, down, deep, deep down . . . They brought him up as their own. They taught him. They made him theirs, or tried to. But he did not belong in that other place; could never truly belong.

In the fey realm he lived and grew and became a young man. And his eyes lit on a young woman who was neither fey nor human, but half and half. Trapped in that other world, like him. The young man fell in love; so did the young woman. Discovered, they fled, hand in hand. She found the way out. She led him from the deep realm and into the light.

The fey were angered, for this was never meant to be. The young man was to stay there, to work, to use his skills in the service of the fey. Why else would they have nurtured him from a babe and taught him all he knew? They had raised him; they had trained him. He owed them. As for the young woman, the fey considered her one of their own. But it was too late. Both were gone. They were safe in the human world. Or so they believed.

When you stole from the fey there was always a price to pay, and that price could be high indeed. But those two, Bardán's father and mother, did not think of that when they ran out together, making their escape. That was the way they saw it, an escape from servitude. To the fey it was theft. The young woman had been theirs, and the young man had not only turned his back on them, he had stolen her. At first, the fey left the two alone. That did not mean all was happy ever after. Inevitably, there would come a demand for restitution.

Bardán rocks to and fro in his meager shelter, thinking of the good, trying to shut out the bad. They'd been young when they'd left that place, the two of them. His father sixteen, barely a man. His mother even younger. But they had been strong of heart, and staunch in their love for each other. So his father had worked as a builder, and his mother had taken in mending here and there, though folk thought the two of them too odd to befriend. In time their only child had been born. Little Bardán. They had raised him simply, according to their means, but with kindness. There had been no more children, and his mother had died when Bardán was ten or eleven years old. It was not a violent death, but a slow decline over a long, chill winter. In the end she could no longer draw breath.

The local folk would not have her in the village plot. They could not trust a man who had lived in that other realm—never mind that it was through no fault of his own—and still less a woman who might have sprung from anywhere at all. Bardán's father buried her himself, not far from their little house on the edge of the forest. He spoke words over her grave, and young Bardán, standing beside him, hummed the song she had loved. The song she had sung to her little boy, her only child, from the day he was born:

Starling, woodcock, owl on wing
Nightjar, chiffchaff, bunting sing
Goldcrest, warbler, thrush and jay
Redpoll, siskin darting by
Golden feather, scarlet, white
Bright as summer, dark as night
Weave a charm for luck and good
Every birdling in the wood
Feather bright and feather fine
None shall harm this child of mine.

It was an odd song. Back then, Bardán had not thought about what it meant. He had only known that it made him feel calm and happy and safe. It had told him he was loved.

And now, now that the boy who wept long and hard over his mother's grave is a man himself, now that his father, too, is gone, Bardán understands. The song is about give and take. It is about keeping the balance. Look after the wood, and the wood looks after you. Respect all that dwell in the wood: the birds in the trees, the fish in the streams, the creatures that run and walk and creep on the land. The trees, every kind. And the fey . . . but there the meaning blurs. *Respect the fey and they won't play tricks. Leave a bowl of bread and milk on the doorstep at night. Tie offerings in the hawthorn. Build your house just right.* That is what it should mean. But it isn't so, can't be, or why would the fey have stolen a baby and left that turnip child in his place? Had his grandparents failed to respect the laws of the wood? He'd asked his father this, but his father would not talk about them, the parents whose hearts had been broken on that long-ago day, the parents who had been dead and gone by the time their true son came back home with his unusual bride.

"Once they stole, twice they stole, stole them right away," Bardán murmurs, looking out through the broken door of his shelter, where moonlight gleams faintly on the pale limbs of a willow. From where he lies he cannot see the moon itself, and that is good. Hidden here, in the dark, he feels safer. On his own, out of the way, in the quiet. Only he wishes Grim were here. He likes Grim's stories, though he was glad the one about the Red Giant never got finished. A story like that couldn't have a happy ending. *Once they stole, twice they stole* . . . Why can't he get that out of his head?

Somewhere out there, in the dark woods under the cold moon, is the place where he went down in the earth. The place where he fell and fell and didn't come back again for a hundred years. Or what felt like a hundred years, only when he came back, that man he loathed and feared was still here, but older. So it can't have been so long. Was it long enough for *them*? When he found a way out did they simply let him go, his father's debt at last acquitted? Was the price of his father's error Bardán's sanity? His mind is a muddle, his thinking disordered. His body is a shambles too, but that is his own doing. A penance imposed by himself. He will not bathe in hot water, will not cut his hair, will not come fully back to his own world until he finds . . . Until he finds . . .

There is a sticking point, a door in his mind that simply will not open. Something happened. Something dire and terrible, something back then, before he fell down and down and ended up in another place entirely. He was running through the woods, through the night, running and running, running to get away, running from the monsters, and then he fell, and he hit his head, broke his teeth, and when he woke up he was in that place and he couldn't remember what had come before. Couldn't remember anything. Only, when the fey had patched him up and fed him and given him something that made him sleep for two days and two nights, he did remember how to build. He remembered the skills his father had taught him. And they set him to work. Years and years of work. Years and years of silence. At first he couldn't talk. His lip was split, his jaw was not right, his teeth were smashed. And by the time they were healed as well as they ever would be, he'd got out of the way of speaking, and he never quite got back into it, down there.

While he worked, the past came back to him. Not all at once. Just bits, snippets, half thoughts. The master. The wretched heartwood house. Gormán, who'd once seemed a friend. And, later, the story of his parents, who were never quite part of Longwater settlement. Who were always thought of as different. His father, whom the fey blamed for fleeing, and blamed twice over for stealing his mother away. His parents' escape had condemned their son to those years of servitude. And yet, he treasures the memory of them. He holds it dear.

It's a puzzle. There are pieces missing and he doesn't know where to start looking. His father's gone. His mother's gone. He's out of that fey place, and wild horses couldn't drag him back in. The master won't talk. Gormán won't talk. Conn's too young to know anything. One thing Bardán understands. He can't leave Wolf Glen. Because the only part he's sure about, the only part that's certain, is that he must finish the heartwood house. He knows how it should be done in every particular. He knows the consequences of making even the slightest error, knows them in ways Master Tóla could never understand. Grim might understand. Grim likes tales, and he's open to the strange and uncanny. But though there are things he might tell Grim, this one is his own, most carefully guarded secret. His plan. His vengeance.

12

GRIM

Season's been unusually dry, just a light shower or two. Long run of good working days. Been wondering when we'd get some solid rain. It comes at last, pelting down, one day when I'm halfway home. Riding through the forest, I keep dryish, but going across the open fields, I get wet through. Ripple's a sorry sight, head drooping, tail down, plodding along at Mercy's heels. Mercy just keeps going, steady as steady. Can't say I'm keen to ride her to Scannal's and walk back, which is what I do most nights. Be good to get warm again first, have a word with Blackthorn and a bite of supper. Worst of the downpour might have passed by then. Doubt it, though. My bet is, it'll be wet again tomorrow and I won't be going up to Wolf Glen.

That's good and bad. I'd love a day off, to tell the truth. Get time for a proper talk with Blackthorn, watch her working, do a few jobs around the house. Maybe meet Cara at last. Cook supper so Blackthorn doesn't need to. All good. Truth is, though, even one day off and I'd be worrying about Bardán. What'll he do with himself if I'm not there? Huddle in that useless little shelter, getting colder and damper and sadder all the time? One thing's sure—the master won't be inviting him in for a hot supper and a night's rest in a proper bed. Gormán might soften. Give him a corner in the barn. Funny, how I keep thinking the wild man won't be all right without me there to keep an eye on him. Foolish. But I do think that. Feels like right now I'm the only friend Bardán's got.

My mind's on home, the glow of the fire, the smell of supper cooking, Blackthorn saying, *Get those wet things off, big man. You're dripping all over the floor.* I ride around the path that skirts the wood. Ripple sees home and gets her heart back all of a sudden. Sprints ahead.

"Well done, Mercy," I tell the horse, giving her a pat on the shoulder. "Give you a rest and a rub down, eh, before I take you over to Scannal's?"

I come closer. Dusk's falling now, but there's no light from inside the cottage. No smoke from the chimney. Door closed against the rain, which is fair enough. But she'd have the lamp lit. Always does, so I can see my way home. Ripple's at the door, barking to be let in, but nobody's opening up.

I get off Mercy's back, lead her in under the eaves, tether her where it's dryish. Heart hammering now, which is foolish. She'll have been called to someone ailing or to a childbed. Had to leave in a hurry. Maybe she's left me a message. Something simple that I can read for myself. "All right, girl," I tell Ripple. "Quiet now." I open the door. Hands clumsy with cold, shaking on the latch.

Nobody home. Fire's out. Been out a while, no glow under the ash blanket. No sign of supper, not even the makings of it. Must have been an urgent call. It happens. It's the nature of the job. *Shut it,* I say to my stupid thoughts. They're busy telling me all the bad things this could be. She's alone somewhere out in the rain with a broken leg. She's rushed off south to find Mathuin of Laois. Again. Only this time she's gone too far to be stopped. She's decided she wants to be on her own. Doesn't want me around, getting in the way, needing her too much. If I lose her, I can't go on. Not even now, when I've started to sort myself out.

I make myself breathe slowly. Weigh it up. A cold, wet horse, no fire, not much fodder for Mercy. A wet ride over the fields to Scannal's. But there's a warm stable and a good feed there. Mercy's carried me for an hour in the rain already. And she's not my horse. Also, someone at Scannal's might know where Blackthorn's gone. If they don't, I'll go to the settlement, drop in at the smith's, ask Emer. Only thing is, if Blackthorn gets home while I'm out, she'll be the one coming in to a dark house, no fire, no supper. Be happier if I could get the place warm and bright for her.

Make up your mind, Grim. Don't stand there dripping all over the floor. "Right," I say to Ripple. "You're staying here. Then at least she knows we're back." I find an old cloth and rub the worst of the wet out of Ripple's fur. There's flint and tinder and a good stack of dry wood. I always make sure of that. I set a fire on the hearth, get it burning well, put on a couple of big logs that'll last a while. Do it careful; don't want them falling out and setting the house on fire while I'm gone. I light the oil lamp. She's left the wax tablet on the table, the one she uses to teach us our letters. I look for a message, but all it says is: *What bird are you? I am a crow.* Which I'm guessing is the start of whatever she wanted me to read for her. The start of something she didn't get finished.

Don't think about it, Grim, I tell myself. But I can't help it. In my thoughts there's someone knocking on the door, and Blackthorn opening it because it might be a person in trouble. Only it's not one of the locals with a sick child or a wife giving birth or a friend with a sprained ankle; it's Mathuin's henchmen come to take her away.

"Bad news from the south," says Scannal. He takes hold of Mercy's bridle to lead her into his stable. "I heard it in the settlement. Something about Lady Flidais's parents and an attack. The prince is off to court first thing tomorrow—that's what they're saying."

"An attack." Thoughts working fast, too fast. "Who by?"

"I don't know much about it," Scannal says. "One of the local chieftains in those parts, some fellow who's always stirring up trouble. Bad business."

"Seen anything of Blackthorn today? She wasn't home when I got there. Not sure where she'd be in all this rain."

Scannal shakes his head. "I haven't seen her. Maybe in the settlement?"

"I'll head over there now. Won't be needing a horse tomorrow unless this clears quicker than I think it will. Hardly building weather."

"Go carefully," he says. Which is good advice, since the light's fading fast and the rain's coming down in sheets. Couldn't be wetter if I tried. And it's turned chilly. Hope Blackthorn's inside somewhere, waiting for a break in the weather. But deep down, I know something's wrong.

Walk to the settlement, boots all mud, heart going too fast, mind full of stories with bad endings. *Stupid*, I tell myself. *Healers get called away all hours of the day and night. What are you expecting, that she's going to be there with a lamp lit and your supper ready on the table every time you come home? This is Blackthorn, not a village wife.* Thing is, though, our life, hers and mine, has got a surprise around every corner, and a lot of them are bad ones.

Next stop is the smithy, where there are lights shining and folk moving about. Knock on the door. Fraoch comes out, takes one look at me and asks me in for mulled ale and a bite to eat. But I'm too worried to say yes, good though their supper smells. Emer comes out with her hair done up in a kerchief and her apron on. Tells me Blackthorn walked over with her and the girl, Cara, in the afternoon, and Emer hasn't seen either of them since. Emer thinks Blackthorn was going back home to make up some salves.

Hard to ask the right questions. Hard not to rush off blind, start searching everywhere. Almost dark. "Scannal told me there's some kind of trouble for the prince," I say.

"That's right," says Fraoch. "An attack at Cloud Hill, in the south. Where Lady Flidais comes from. Some fellow's marched in with a big body of men-at-arms and taken over her father's holdings. That's what folk are saying, anyway. Sounds bad. The king's called a council and Prince Oran's heading off to court in the morning. Taking a fair number of folk with him. You sure you won't come in and get dry, Grim? You look like a drowned rat. An oversized drowned rat."

"Thanks, no. Bit worried about Blackthorn." Mathuin. Who else? His land's right next to Cloud Hill. She'd have heard the news when she dropped Cara at the prince's, wouldn't she? What would she do? I try to think the way Blackthorn would think; never easy. First choice: go home, lock the door, make up the fire and start working on something tricky, a potion of some sort. Try to keep her mind off Mathuin with hard work.

I know she didn't do that. Second choice: something foolish. Let those thoughts turn her a bit crazy, the way they've done before. Grab a cloak and head off in the rain, south toward Laois, knowing she'll never be able to get on with her life until that man's been punished. She might have done that a year ago. More or less did do it. But now? Only if this has scared her half out of her wits. Third choice: go and talk to the prince and Lady Flidais; find out more about what's going on. Maybe tell them the truth about us and Mathuin, in case it could be helpful. Only she wouldn't do that without talking to me first. Would she?

"She might be still at the prince's house," I say.

"Why don't you come in and dry off," says Fraoch, "and I'll walk over there and ask? It won't take long." Looking at me as if he thinks I might drop in a heap any moment.

"No, I'll go," I say. "But thanks."

I get to Prince Oran's house. Rain still bucketing down. Guards are trying to keep dry and watch out for trouble at the same time. I get a stroke of luck—one of the guards is Eoin, the other one's Garalt, and I know both of them well. Which means I don't need to waste time explaining myself, except to ask if Blackthorn's there. Garalt opens the gate and calls another guard. That man heads off to find out for me.

"Heard there was an attack," I say, thinking I may as well find out more if I can. "In the south. You heading off with the prince in the morning?" I remember that Eoin came from Cloud Hill with Lady Flidais, when she came north to marry the prince. Garalt's a Winterfalls man.

"The fellows who are going are packing up right now," Garalt says. "Lochlan and a team of others; I'm head guard while Lochlan's gone. Prince Oran wants enough of us here to defend the place if we have to. Can't see that happening; we've had peace for so long. And this conflict's a long way to the south."

"Things can change fast." Now that I've stopped walking, I feel how cold I am, block of ice on a pair of numb legs. I stamp my feet a bit. Hope someone comes out with news while I can still walk. "This attack in the south. Was it Mathuin of Laois?"

"Who else?" Eoin's voice is like winter. "Big party of men-at-arms moved in under cover of night, surprised Lord Cadhan's guards. Place was awash with blood, the messenger said. Good men fallen, brave men. Friends of mine. There's been an itch in my sword arm since I heard that news. A powerful wish to ride to Laois and spill some blood in my turn. That's how all the fellows are feeling, all of us that came from there with Lady Flidais."

"What happened to Lord Cadhan and his wife?" I want news of Blackthorn, but I need this news too.

"They're safe. Got out by a secret way, underground. Cadhan didn't want to go; wanted to stand and fight. His wife persuaded him to leave. Curdles my guts to think of it." He bows his head.

"I'm sorry," I say. There are no words big enough for this sort of thing. We stand there a bit, the three of us not saying anything, until a woman comes out of the house, wrapped in a cloak. My heart leaps, thinking it's her and she's safe. But no, this woman is taller. It's Deirdre.

"Blackthorn's not here, Grim," she says. "She brought Cara back a long while ago, then left. She did ask me if she could have a word with Lady Flidais, but my lady doesn't want to see anyone at present. The household's been turned upside down since this news came from Cloud Hill."

Her eyes are red; she's been crying. I remember that she comes from Cloud Hill too.

"Hope you didn't lose anyone close," I say.

"We don't know yet. Not all the names. That's the worst part, not knowing."

"I'm sorry," I say again, though that's never enough. "Will you be going to court, Deirdre?"

"Lady Flidais wants me to go with her, yes."

"Good luck with it, then. You'd better get in out of the rain."

That's when Donagan, the prince's man and a friend of mine, comes up behind her. "Grim! You look freezing, man. Come in if you want, dry off and warm up."

"Thanks, but no. Looking for Blackthorn. If she's not here, I'd best go and look somewhere else."

He knows how worried I am; that's plain on his face. "She'll have found shelter with someone, surely," he says. "When you do find her, could you pass on a message from Lady Flidais?"

I nod. Try not to show I'm shivering.

Donagan moves me away from the two guards. Lowers his voice. "It's the girl. Master Tóla's daughter, Cara. Lady Flidais says she's not sure how long she and the prince will be away, and she wants Blackthorn to keep an eye on Cara while she's gone. Maybe come over here to stay for a bit, if she can manage that. Seems Blackthorn's got a knack with the girl that nobody else has."

First thing that pops into my head is: why can't Cara go back to Wolf Glen? That's what I'd ask if I didn't already know the answer. So all I say is, "I'll pass the message on." Thinking how tangled up things get when folk start telling lies. "When I find Blackthorn." *If* I find her. "Safe journey." Before I turn to go, I see Donagan put his arm around Deirdre's shoulders. She gives him a sad sort of smile. Kind folk, the two of them. If bad things didn't happen to kind folk, it'd be a better world.

I go round the settlement, getting wetter and colder with every step. She's nowhere to be found. Couple of folk saw her in the afternoon with Emer and Cara, but not after. It's like she's vanished. I remember something. Wish I hadn't. About going to the Otherworld to find Conmael. Joke, wasn't it? That's what I thought. Now I'm wondering. And while I'm wondering, my feet are carrying me back home. Might be wrong. Hope I'm wrong. She could be out on one of the farms or over in Silverlake. She wouldn't thank me for making a fuss, getting half the settlement out searching in the wet, if it turned out she was busy delivering a baby or sitting by some old fellow's deathbed.

It rains. I keep walking. Out of the settlement, along the farm track past Scannal's. The bull's a darker patch in his dark field, just standing there. Can't see far ahead, but that light in the cottage window's a welcome sight. Stupid voice in my head's talking again. *She doesn't belong to you, Bonehead. You're not her keeper. If she wants to go off and get herself killed, that's her business.*

"Shut it!" I say out loud, hitting myself on the head. Voice just keeps on. *You know what your problem is? You care too much. She wouldn't like that.*

By the time I get to the door I'm in quite a state. Ripple's barking, but nobody opens the door. I know before I go in that Blackthorn isn't there.

House is warm. Makes me dizzy. Have to sit down before I fall down. Dagda's bollocks! Weak excuse for a man! On the bench now, everything swirling around. Ripple lays her head on my knee, looks up at me like she knows how I feel. "It's all right, girl," I tell her. "She'll be home soon."

I sit there a while. See things in the flames that I don't want to see. Glad the dog's with me. She's dried off now, hair all silky under my fingers. I think of Blackthorn when she was turned into a monster, skin scaly, mouth crammed with teeth, trying to talk to me and only groans coming out. How I held her in my arms and cried over her. Promised I'd stay by her if it took two hundred years. They talk about folk having their hearts broken. When she came back to herself I felt my heart mend, all the pieces coming together again. Stronger because it was broken before. Odd, that.

After a bit I get up, take off my wet things and hang them up out back, put on dry ones. Set the kettle on the fire for a brew. Find some bits and pieces and make a supper of sorts, halfway between a gruel and a soup. It'll be hot, at least. Get out a flask of mead, some cups. Feed Ripple. House is as cozy as I can make it. I'm tired enough to fall asleep right now. One more thing to do. If it's foolish, so be it. Feels like it might help bring her home.

I get out the wax tablet again. Read it aloud: "What bird are you? I am a crow." Know already what I want to write, and it's not what Blackthorn would have asked for: *What bird are you? I am an owl,* and so on. It's something a lot harder. For me, anyway. So I write, or do my best to write:

Who is this woman?
Her hair is red as flame

Her eyes are wise as an owl's
Her hands are strong as a warrior's
They are gentle as a mother's
All fight on the outside
All goodness within
She walks her own path
Her name is Blackthorn.

Takes me a while. Get up to put wood on the fire a couple of times, stir the pot, shift the kettle to one side, think of the next part. Spelling won't be right. Never mind that. Nobody's going to read it but me. When I'm done I go over it a couple of times, listening to the wind howling outside and the rain still bucketing down. Wonder if what I'm doing is a sort of spell. That'd be a joke. She's the wise woman. I'm just the big lump of a hanger-on, not a speck of magic in me. Wish there was some. I'd use it to keep her safe even when she's far away and I can't bring her back.

Quick as a flash, Ripple's up and at the door, ears pricked, body tight, listening. Then barking so loud it hurts my ears. I slam the cover shut on the wax tablet, no time to rub over what I've written. Let this not be someone with bad news. Let it be her. Let it be her.

I open up. The wind bellows into the house, bringing rain with it. And there she is on the doorstep, cloak clutched around her, hair in rat-tails, face ghost white, eyes hollow. Far from all right. But home. She's home.

I get her inside, push the door shut and shove the bolt across, tell Ripple to quiet down. Blackthorn just stands there, water running off her clothes onto the floor. Think I can hear her teeth chattering.

"Fire," I say. "Sit." Steer her over to the bench and sit her down. Pour a cup of mead and put it in her hand. "Drink."

She drinks, chokes, drinks again. "Morrigan's curse," she mutters. "I could do with some of Father Tomas's brew right now. But on second thoughts, maybe not."

Father Tomas's brew nearly got both of us killed when that traitor

Flannan ambushed us by night. Doesn't do to sleep too sound. Your enemy can creep up on you. "Get you some dry clothes?" I ask.

"Please. Don't bother with the screen, you can just turn your back." Her voice is shaky. "You were home before the rain?"

"Got dampish." I look in the storage chest, take out a gown, a shawl, a shift for underneath, some stockings. Lay everything on her bed. I find a big cloth for drying. "Ready when you are." Wondering if I can rub out what I wrote on the wax tablet while she's busy getting changed. But no; she's sure to see and ask me what it is. So I just move the tablet to the shelf and start setting supper out, making sure I don't look at her. We've got good at that over the time we've lived close. We saw each other unclothed, shamed and hurt, time after time in that place of Mathuin's. Means we're more careful than most to show each other courtesy now.

I find some bread I didn't spot before, put it on the table with the bowls of broth and the mead cups. Take my time about it.

"That looks good, Grim." She's dressed now, taking her wet things out back to hang up.

"Let me do that—"

Too late—she's already gone. Soon after, she's back. "*Dampish*, you said." She comes to sit at the table. "You were soaked through. Your stuff's still dripping everywhere."

"Went looking for you. After I dropped Mercy off." I sit opposite her; Ripple settles by my feet. Bit more color in Blackthorn's cheeks. Hands steadier. Hope she'll tell me where she's been and why she was looking like a ghost. Don't ask, though. Her and me, we've got our own way of doing these things. "I know about the raid at Cloud Hill. Spoke to some folk over at Winterfalls. Donagan. Deirdre. Eoin."

"Tell me." Darkness back in her eyes. Voice wobbly again.

"Eat that while I do. Need something warm in your belly."

"Tell me, Grim. I know Cloud Hill was overrun. I know Flidais's parents are in Mide."

"Can't tell you much more than that." I share what I know, which isn't a lot. "Plenty of folk upset. All them who came from those parts with Flidais. No news of who died and who survived. They've got families there, friends, comrades."

She says nothing at all. Spoon halfway to her mouth, forgotten what she's doing, staring into space.

"Lady?" I say it soft, put my hand on her arm. She starts, drops the spoon. Broth splashes onto the table. "Nothing we can do right now. Have your supper."

"Someone has to do something," she mutters. "How much more can that man get away with? He just takes what he wants, and folk let him push them down in the mud. This is—this is—"

"One mouthful at a time. Want me to feed you?"

"I'm not an infant!" she snaps, and starts eating again, which was what I hoped she might do. "You didn't ask where I was before."

I break up the bread, pass her a share, keep my big trap shut.

"I was here. Not in the house. In Dreamer's Wood. Wandering about at first. Angry. Too angry to stay inside. I would have done some damage. It wasn't just the news about Cloud Hill that had upset me. There was a—an episode here earlier, something odd. I'm not even sure what happened, but Emer saw some kind of fight in Dreamer's Wood, and a fellow brought her back here and started asking me questions."

"A fellow? What fellow?"

"A fighting man with tattoos on his face. From someplace called Swan Island. Very polite. Said he and his friends were heading for Prince Oran's, at the prince's invitation. But Dreamer's Wood was out of their way. So I had Mathuin on my mind even before I took Cara back over to the prince's. Why would fighting men be skulking around in the wood? Why would they want to know anything about me? It felt like Flannan and his lies all over again. And then, hearing what Mathuin had done at Cloud Hill—I was angry. Disgusted with myself for being so helpless. So useless. Furious with Conmael for making me come all the way to Dalriada and for making me promise not to go back. I tried to think it through. Made myself go through the possibilities. And then . . ."

"Then what? Go on, eat that bread while you tell me."

"I tried to summon Conmael. Tried as many different ways as I could think of. But he didn't come. And . . . No, you don't want to hear this."

"I could guess." Hope I'm wrong, though. "Talked about the Otherworld, didn't we? A while back? How, if Conmael wouldn't put in an appearance, you might go looking for him there?"

"You were the one who thought up that ridiculous idea." She's not meeting my eye.

"Didn't think you'd try it, or I wouldn't have said it."

"I didn't try it, exactly. I spent a lot of time just standing by Dreamer's Pool, wondering if Conmael passes through some kind of portal every time he comes to our world, and whether that doorway is a physical one. Often he just . . . appears. Out of thin air. That's what it looks like, anyway. I walked around the wood, and the rain got heavier, and I peered down some cracks in the rocks and some hollows under trees and tried to convince myself I could actually find a way in. And . . . I tried some other tricks. Hearth magic. Chanting. Telling stories. The more I did, the more useless I felt. I hate that. It muddies my thinking. For a bit there, I'd half convinced myself Dreamer's Pool might *be* the portal."

This shocks me more than anything else she's said. "Morrigan's curse! You wouldn't do it, would you? Jump in there and get turned into an ant or something?"

"An ant," she says, giving me a funny look. "When you put it like that, it seems an even stupider idea than it was that night when *you* nearly jumped in."

"Mm." I think a bit about what she's told me. "Those men, the Swan Island men. They could be telling the truth. About Prince Oran calling them in. From what I've heard, they're choosy about who they work for. Can't see them doing Mathuin's business."

"So you know about them?"

"Not much. Heard a mention here and there. They're dangerous all right. But not known for hurting women. The fellow did bring Emer home."

We're both quiet for a bit. Listen to the rain pelting down out there. Wind howling.

"Good night for a story," I say, to get her mind off other things. Then I wish I hadn't. Don't want her looking at the wax tablet. Not before I've rubbed out my little bit of foolishness. "That fellow I'm working with, Bardán, he's got a story that would make the hairs on your neck prickle, or I think he has. Only he can't come out with all of it, or won't. Says his father taught him to build. But the way he talks, it's like he was in some other world, and not just for a bit. For years and years. Makes me wonder about those doorways. Portals. Bardán talks about going down. Falling. I've wondered if that's what he means. A cave that leads to the Otherworld."

"You think that's where he got his remarkable gift for building, not from his father?"

"Polished it, maybe. He told me part of a story about folk escaping from the fey world. Could have been his own story—that's if he brought a wife back with him. Could have been his father's story. The fellow was switched for a changeling, as a babe. Raised in that place. Met a girl who was half fey, half human. She found the way out. They got away together. The more I think about it, the more I think it was his dad's story. If he grew up there, didn't leave until he was a young man, he could have learned all sorts of fey building tricks and taught them to his son. No wonder Bardán knows how to make a heartwood house."

"A changeling." The firelight's on Blackthorn's face, flickering. She's got that thinking look. Hair curling in wisps as it dries out. Like little flames. "I can't help wondering if that's the key to getting Conmael back," she says. "Or to understanding why he *isn't* coming back. I never told you, did I? The whole story about Cully, and my theory about why Conmael rescued us from prison."

"Tell me."

"It was a long time ago, when I was a child of ten or so. In the south, at a place called Brocc's Wood. I'd been sent to live there with a wise woman who'd agreed to take me as her student. I got on all right with the other children, though they were wary of me, and with good reason. But they treated me with respect, because their parents trusted Holly—that was my mentor's name. There was a woman who lived on the very edge of the village, a woman with a child but no husband. She was never looked on as part of the community. Folk told stories about her, how she'd lie with any man for a loaf of bread or a jug of ale, how she'd been thrown out by her husband for her slatternly ways, how she didn't even know who her son's father was. It was cruel. Even at that age I saw how unjust it was, since she and her son had only come to the village a couple of years before I did and nobody really knew much about her. It was all invention. But she was a poor soul, too beaten-down and sad to stand up for herself.

"The boy, Cully, was a year or so younger than I. He was an odd-looking lad with long, spindly limbs, pale skin, big eyes, and a nervous way about him. People called him the changeling. They didn't mean he really was a fey child. They meant he was different; he didn't belong. Cully had no friends. The other children shunned him as their parents did his mother.

"That disturbed me. When I got the chance, I talked to him. Told him stories. Taught him some games, just little things we could play with sticks and stones. We weren't friends, exactly. I didn't have time for friends, what with Holly's lessons and gathering herbs and helping around the house—Holly was quite old and had sore joints, so a lot of the cooking and cleaning fell to me. But I didn't see why Cully should be taunted and bullied and shamed."

I can see that boy, funny little thing he is, all by himself under a tree, watching while the others run after a ball. Them in the sun, him in shadow. "Go on," I say.

"There was one time when I caught the others red-handed, abusing him," Blackthorn says. "Calling him names, worse ones than changeling. Calling him bastard, saying his father was a murderer or a madman or a demon. Saying foul things about his mother that they must have learned from their own mothers and fathers. Things they probably didn't even know the meaning of. And Cully just standing there in the middle of their circle, white as a sheet, letting it all rain down on him. I marched in and told them what I thought. Shamed them with their own cruelty. Said if I caught them at it again, I'd turn the lot of them into toads. I wasn't sure I could really do that, but they must have believed I could. They never teased him again. And if they told their parents what I'd threatened, I never heard a thing about it."

"Could be the parents didn't fancy being toads either."

"Anyway," says Blackthorn, "in time I moved on. Left Brocc's Wood. Never did find out what happened to Cully. Only . . . I've wondered if it could have been him. Conmael. A real changeling. A fey child brought up as a human boy. A boy who was always out of place in this world. A boy who repaid my small act of kindness, years later, by saving my life. Though he did put conditions on it. As if he saw, even when we were children, that my anger could all too easily boil over and make me lose my good judgment." She gets up to fetch dried herbs for a brew. "What do you think, Grim? It seems a mad theory. The favor Conmael did for you and me was huge. It changed our lives forever. And what I did for Cully was such a little thing. Besides, you know what Conmael is like. Tall. Imposing. Handsome. Every bit a nobleman and obviously fey. A different creature from that awkward, frightened boy."

"What do I think? I think the only way you'll know is if you ask him straight out."

"Which I can't do."

"You could be right about him. The world's full of strange things. Stuff that doesn't make sense until you really think about it. Happenings like the ones in the old tales." I fetch out two clean cups. She drops the herbs in, tops them up with hot water. Fine smell. I'm guessing chamomile, lavender, pinch of something I can't put a name to. "Take Bardán. There we are, building this house for Master Tóla, and Bardán keeps singing bits of old songs, muttering bits of old rhymes. No sense to it. Only, deep down, I'm thinking it all links up. Meaning something bigger than what's in the words. Only I can't understand it. Can't work out how the pieces go together. Makes me wish I was a clever man."

Blackthorn gives me a look I've seen before, often enough. "You have a great talent for putting the pieces together, Grim. I've seen you demonstrate it over and over. Now, tell me, does this rain mean you'll be home for a while?"

"If it keeps on like this, yes. Not much I can do up there in a downpour. Only . . ."

"Only what?"

"Bit worried about Bardán. They're not kind to the fellow. If I'm there, I can keep an eye on him."

"Like me with Cully."

"Don't think there's anything fey about Bardán."

"There would be," Blackthorn says, "if that tale was his father's. About being switched at birth, and then being led out of the Otherworld by a girl who was half fey and half human. That girl would be Bardán's mother, if she and his father stayed together. So he'd have fey blood. That could be what gives him his unusual knack as a builder. That and his father's teaching. Does he look fey? Part fey?"

I'm ready to say no, but I stop to think. "Can't tell. Bardán's wild-looking. Tangle of hair and beard and leaves and dirt. Doesn't wash, doesn't shave, doesn't change his clothes. Not that I've seen. And doesn't want to."

"Doesn't want to? Why not?"

"Offered to cut his hair for him once or twice and he said no. Asked Gormán why they don't let the man wash and shave, and Gormán said it's Bardán's own choice not to. Odd. If he'd clean himself up, maybe they'd give him somewhere better to sleep."

"That's like an old tale," Blackthorn murmurs. "A sort of curse. *Don't wash or cut your hair or nails for seven years, and you can have your sweetheart back.* Or, *if you would win the treasure, let not so much as one drop of water touch your skin from Imbolc to Lughnasad.*"

"Hope the treasure wasn't a woman," I said. "The fellow would be a bit stinky after all that time. She might thank him for his patience but say no, thanks."

"She might enjoy giving him the long-postponed bath."

"If you could smell Bardán, you wouldn't say that." I think about the wild man in his rickety hut, with the rain pouring down and the wind blowing fit to lift the roof off. "Don't understand why they hate him so much. I know he walked off and left the heartwood house half-built. But that might not have been his fault. Sounds like he fell into that other place, the fey place, by accident. And he came back, didn't he? Came back to finish the job. Which they want him to do. So why treat him like he's dirt?" I remember something. "Forgot to tell you. Lady Flidais asked if you can keep a special eye on the girl while she's away. Donagan said."

"Cara? She's here most days anyway. I don't know how I can keep more of an eye on her than I'm doing already."

"Lady Flidais said you could go over there and stay for a bit, if you wanted. Easier to watch over the girl. And . . ."

"And what? You know how much I'd hate that."

"Be safer. With this trouble in the south. Plenty of guards, even with the prince taking a big escort."

"With what's happened at Cloud Hill, I'd have thought it was an appropriate time for Master Tóla to fetch his daughter back home," Blackthorn says. "But he won't know about Oran and Flidais going away. Not unless someone's ridden up there today with the news, and that seems unlikely in this rain. Besides, you would have met them on your way down."

"I can tell him what's happened when I do go back. Won't be tomorrow. My guess is it'll stay wet a few days. About the girl. Want me to make myself scarce if she comes over here? Could be hard not to let slip I've been working for her father."

"If she comes, and if she asks, just tell her the truth. I take it Tóla has no idea you live with the local wise woman. And since he hasn't visited his daughter since she first came to Winterfalls, he won't know that Cara's decided she'd rather spend her time with Emer and me than with Flidais and her ladies."

"Only thing is, if I tell her about the heartwood house and Tóla finds out, I could lose the job. And then there'd be nobody to watch over Bardán."

"Who's Tóla going to find to replace you?" Blackthorn gives me a smile. "Nobody else could do what you're doing. Sounds like you're building the whole thing almost single-handed. If the man has any wits, he'll recognize that." She gets up. "Time for bed. I'm tired enough to sleep soundly even with Mathuin marching around in my head."

Turns out she's wrong. She falls asleep quick enough, but she tosses and turns with bad dreams. Mutters and curses and once or twice shouts out, all without waking up. Covers on the floor. Pillow awry. Don't want to wake her if I don't have to. I get up, kneel by her bed, put the blanket back over her. Her face is all wet with tears. I dab them away with a corner of the blanket. Settle myself on the floor beside her. Wrap both my hands around one of hers. Hum a bit of that tune I've heard Bardán singing: *Every birdling in the wood* . . . When she's quiet, when her breath's not a sob anymore but peaceful, I rest my head on the bed next to her. Folk are easy hurt, no doubt about that. Easy wounded. Easy broken. There's poor Bardán, and that boy Cully and his mother. There's young Blackthorn, sent away from home when she was only ten. Wish I could mend them. Wish I could mend them all.

13

Cara loved the rain, loved the many feelings of it on her skin. Rain could be soft, like a mother's touch. It could be as hard as a punishing whip. It could be as warm as a sunny morning or cold enough to set ice in your bones. Walking in the woods in a rainstorm, she could feel the trees breathing deep, stretching their roots into the damp soil, reaching out their leaves to catch the wet. She could feel how thirsty they were, and she rejoiced with them, letting the rain soak her to the skin and turn her hair into a mad, tangled mop. She would take off her shoes and slosh through the mud, and not care at all about the woeful state of her skirt. That was the kind of thing Aunt Della would say: *woeful state*. It was the kind of thing the servants at Winterfalls might mutter to one another, just loud enough for her to overhear.

Blackthorn wouldn't say it. Blackthorn would tell her to put her shoes by the fire to dry out, and give her a cloth to wrap around her hair, and suggest it might be a good idea to tuck up her skirt next time she went paddling in mud puddles. She wouldn't tell Cara to hang up her own cloak; she'd just expect it. And if Blackthorn was too busy to listen, she'd say so straight out. But she'd promise to find time later, and she'd keep the promise.

Today the rain was coming down in sheets and the fields between Winterfalls and Dreamer's Wood were dotted with little lakes. And Prince Oran's household was bustling with activity, with the prince and Lady Flidais about to head off for court, some folk going with them, some folk staying home to look after the house and the farm, lots of guards on duty, more than usual, as if a war far to the south might come all the way here, which was just silly. Nobody noticed when Cara put on her cloak and headed out along one of the farm tracks. There were good climbing trees up the rise; she knew most of them now. This old yew was a friend, ready to accept her hands and feet on its massive twisted trunk, welcoming her with its many spots to sit and think. Secret spots. The yew was full of surprises. She took off her shoes and climbed barefoot to a high perch. "Thank you," she whispered, laying her cheek against the yew's trunk.

On a fine day you could get a wide view from here. Today the rain veiled everything. She could make out Dreamer's Wood, a darker haze, and the water lying on the fields, and cattle huddling under the little groves that dotted the landscape, hazel, willow, apple. The settlement lay beyond the walls of the prince's establishment, a scatter of cottages around the more substantial forms of the smithy, the weaver's, the baker's, the brewer's. The mill stood by itself in farmland. Within the prince's walls, closer at hand, grooms were leading a steady stream of horses from stables to gate. Men-at-arms, dressed for a journey, rode their own horses down to the courtyard. She narrowed her eyes. Was that the man who'd been at the cottage yesterday, the one with the dog tattoo? Cúan, hound, that was his name. But no. This was a different man, darker, and the facial marking was different too, with a strong, sharp line emphasizing an already beaklike nose. This one was marked like a bird of some kind, maybe a hawk. She'd never seen him at Winterfalls before. But he wasn't sneaking around like the other one; he was riding openly with the prince's guards. Going to court with them, it looked like. She'd mention it to Blackthorn. Only it looked as if nobody would be bothered to escort her over to the cottage today. They were all too busy.

"It's an opportunity," Cara said to the ancient yew. "I could walk out that gate and over to Dreamer's Wood, and instead of visiting Blackthorn, I could simply keep going all the way to Wolf Glen. I could do it; I know I could. And when I got there I wouldn't even need to let Father see me. I could stay under the trees until I was right near the barn, and I could just slip in and visit Gormán and Conn. I could ask Gormán to tell me the truth. Why Father doesn't want me there. What's going on. It would be easy. Nobody would even miss me. Mhairi's not going to care. And who else is there?" Donagan was going to court with the prince. Deirdre and Nuala were going with Lady Flidais. The nursemaids were going to look after the little boy. That did leave quite a few folk at Winterfalls, but none of them had shown much interest in Cara. Most of them saw her only at meals, or occasionally in passing. Anyway, they'd be tired and out of sorts after all the fuss. She could do it. She should do it. Her father hadn't come to visit her once. Not once.

She watched as the stream of horses and riders slowed to a trickle and stopped. She watched as the rain eased slightly and a hint of watery sunlight brightened the cloudy sky. In her mind, she heard Blackthorn's voice. *Don't act unwisely, Cara. Think it through.* Hadn't she promised she wouldn't try to run away again, at least not without telling Blackthorn first?

She didn't want to think it through. Her feet needed to go. They itched to walk, to stride, to run for home. It was Blackthorn's fault, and practical, cautious Emer's, that her mind filled up with all the reasons not to go. Getting there and back on foot would take up most of the day. She might get Gormán in trouble. Her father's guards might see her, and then Father would be angry and do something even worse than making her stay at Winterfalls. Send her to court, for instance, where there wouldn't even be Blackthorn and Emer and Dreamer's Wood. Anyway, the truth was that soon enough someone at Winterfalls, probably Mhairi with her wretched, yappy little dog, would notice she wasn't anywhere to be found. And then there'd be a stupid fuss, and they'd ask Blackthorn, and Blackthorn would guess where she'd gone.

"A pox on it," Cara muttered, closing her eyes and resting her forehead against the tree. "A pox on being sensible. I'm going home and I'm not letting anyone stop me."

14

BARÒÁN

Wet. Wet and cold. The floor of his hut is a quagmire. His bedding is clammy. The wind pokes chill fingers through every crack in the place. Him, a master builder? Hah! Can't even mend the holes in this miserable hovel. Fingers don't work. Hands don't work. Useless cripple. His father's years of patient training, wasted. That lost time among the Others, that crushing, silent time, all for nothing. What in God's name is the point of this? Or is the point that there's no point, no ending, only the dark and the cold and the stone of dread deep in the belly?

In the dark, trembling and wretched, he can't stop thinking of that story, the tale Grim was telling him, about the Red Giant. Never finished it. Had to be a sad story. Had to be. But he wanted the ending now. Needed the tale to finish.

"Is it gold?" he whispers. "No, it is not gold. Is it silver? No, it is not silver, nor jewels, nor land nor animals nor a fleet of ships nor a kingdom. It is a treasure far more precious than any of these. It is . . . it is . . ."

The answer is in him somewhere, deep down, hidden away. He knows it's there, if only he could find it, if only he could fight a way through this fog in his mind. Not just the answer to the Red Giant's question. But the last piece of the puzzle. The missing part of him.

Dawn breaks at last. His legs won't bend. His arms ache. Sitting up half kills him. There'll be no making a fire out there; the rain's still coming down and the wood is soaked. And Grim won't be coming. It's too wet for him to work. Without Grim, the day stretches ahead long and empty and hopeless. Nobody to listen. Nobody to hear. Nobody to tell tales and pass the time of day with him over a meal. He did not know how much he had missed those things until Grim brought them back.

Up, wretch, he tells himself. *Or have you sunk so low that you'll piss in your bed for fear of the world outside the door?* He forces himself to stand. His joints are an old man's this morning. A hundred years old. *Out,* he orders himself.

It's a matter of pride to walk a certain distance from his hut, rain or no rain, before he empties his bladder. There's a privy down by the barn, but he's not allowed to use that any more than he can go in and sleep warm next to the animals or cook himself a hot meal over the little hearth Gormán and Conn use, in their quarters. How the master must despise him! Though not as much as he loathes Tóla.

The rain hammers down with furious intent. It floods over the roof of the hut and pours off, a relentless waterfall. The track to the barn has become a rushing stream. Every bird in the forest must be hiding away, seeking shelter in the dark recesses of the trees. Perhaps they call out. Perhaps they cry, *No more, no more! Our small ones are drowning in the nest!* But their voices are lost in the roar of the deluge.

Back in the hut, he considers his damp pallet. He could huddle there, wrap his arms around himself, squeeze his eyes shut and wait out the endless time until—until what? Until the rain stops? Until Grim comes back? Until the heartwood house is finished and he can leave this place forever?

"Until I find what he took from me," Bardán mutters, wondering where the thought came from. Realizing, a moment later, that he was thinking of the Red Giant and the unfinished tale. "Until I find my treasure."

Grim told him once that when you felt sad or angry or hopeless, a story could help. A story could lead you into a different world for a while. It might be a world where a foolish youngest son could turn into a brave and clever hero, or a beaten woman could end up as a wise leader of folk. And when the story was ended and that world was gone, you still had the idea of it inside you. Like a flame that didn't go out even when the bad things rattled and swirled and screamed, and worse, oh, much worse, when they whispered and goaded and tormented.

He could tell a tale now. That's what Grim would say he should do. He tries to imagine Grim here in the hut, sitting by him, solid and strong. Grim's not a handsome man. But he has truth and kindness in his gaze, and a steady pair of hands. He's told Grim his father's story, the part he knows, the part he remembers. It's a tale as strange as anything you could make up. But true; sad and true. After his father and mother came out of that place, the Otherworld he supposes it was, they were happy after their fashion. His father had a deft touch with wood, so precise and clever that folk called it uncanny. But they paid for his work all the same, and there was always food on the table. They did not live in the settlement of Longwater, but in the forest above it, on the western side of Wolf Glen. Bardán's father built the cottage. Snug and warm it was, not like this wretched place. Bardán's mother made it cozy, the walls hung with her embroideries of strange and wondrous things: ships sailing to far islands surrounded by long-toothed sea creatures; a man with wings, flying over a great settlement of flat-roofed houses, and tiny folk in red gazing up and waving. And birds, always birds. She dyed the wool herself, finding the materials in the forest, making colors there were no names for, rich, remarkable hues. Bardán had loved those pictures. What had happened to them? Where had they gone?

He sees the image again, as when he told Grim the tale. Himself and his father, side by side at his mother's grave. His father ashen-faced, silent, robbed of words. The emptiness in his own heart, as if all the joy and laughter had been ripped out of him. Her soft voice echoing through his mind, singing his song, the lullaby he had heard every night since he was too small to remember. *None shall harm this child of mine . . .* Ten-year-old Bardán hummed the tune, there by the turned-over soil and the sad bunch of wildflowers they'd laid on it, and suddenly there were tears streaming down his father's cheeks, and a great sob came out of him, a sound so terrible that Bardán's heart flinched as if a knife had gone into it. His father sank to his knees, hands over his face. Young Bardán wanted to comfort him, but he stood frozen, hardly able to think. And in the woods all around, the birds broke out in song. *So, she is gone,* they seemed to say. *She loved us, and she is gone.*

That day is still clear and bright in Bardán's memory, though so much else has faded away. The day of mourning. The day of loss. His father digging the grave. Carrying her out of the house, cradled in his arms. Laying her to rest, wrapped in a fine blanket of her own weaving. Filling in the grave. Covering her up. The earth on her face, on her closed eyes, on her white, white skin.

"Bardán? Got food for you." Gormán's there, banging on the door of the hut.

Bardán pushes the door open a crack. It's light outside, or as light as it can be with the rain still pissing down and the sun barely up.

"Open up, will you? I'm getting wet."

Bardán opens the door further, takes the covered bowl Gormán's holding.

"No work today," Gormán says. "Grim won't be coming in this weather. You want to warm up later, come down by the barn and I'll find you some dry firewood. Get you another blanket."

Gormán's a mystery. Seems like he could be a kind man if he wanted to. Makes Bardán wonder what hold Tóla's got over the fellow, to have him doing the master's bidding even when it means being cruel and unreasonable. Wasn't Gormán once his friend? Or as close to a friend as anybody got? Now, when he looks at the man, he sees someone he can't trust. "Thanks," he mutters, not wanting to accept the unusual favor, but knowing he'd be a fool not to.

"No wandering off," Gormán cautions. "Don't think Grim not being here makes any difference to the rules. You're either here, or you're down by the barn, or you're in between. Nowhere else, understand? I'm too busy to keep an eye on you all day." He's off without waiting for an answer.

Where would he go? Everything depends on following the wretched rules. Everything depends on finishing the heartwood house.

But then, today he's not building. Can't, because with Grim gone, he has no hands. So it makes no difference where he goes or what he does. And since Gormán can't watch him all day, who's to know if he goes walking in the rain when he's finished this meager breakfast? If he shuts the door of his hovel behind him, they'll think he's inside sleeping, or weeping, or going quietly madder than he is already. That's if they bother thinking anything at all. A man's allowed to visit his mother's grave, isn't he? And his father's, right beside it. A loss almost beyond bearing, that was. If it hadn't been for Dáire . . .

The memory hits him like a great wave. A groan comes up from deep in his belly. He can't stop, doesn't stop till his lungs are bursting and he has to suck in air. Dáire, oh gods, his best friend, his love, his wife . . . How could he have forgotten her? The sweet, funny slip of a thing who, of all the folk in Longwater, was the only one who'd stop and talk to him, the only one who'd smile and laugh with him, the only one who knew he was a man with a man's hopes and needs and feelings. Dáire who had stood by him through the terrible grief of his father's passing. When they'd wanted to wed, she had argued the case with her parents, pointing out that Bardán was a capable craftsman with his own house and plenty of work, and was well able to provide for her. What matter who his parents had been, as long as he was a good man and loved her? So they were wed, and tasted happiness for a while. Too short a while, before she too was gone.

His throat is choked with grief. His eyes are pouring tears. His nose is running down into his beard. This is like losing her all over again. *Get up,* he orders himself. *Go there. Go there now. Tell them you still love them. Tell them you still miss them. Tell them you were lost and could not come for a long time, oh so long.* But maybe by now the graves are lost too, lost in the long grass and the brambles and the passing of time. Is the little house still there, and the bright hangings on the walls? What became of it when he—when they—

He shudders. Some bird of ill omen hovers above him; he feels its dark wings. The last doorway is still closed. Locked against him. The last secret still lies hidden. But Dáire . . . All those years in the other realm, and when he came home, she was gone from his thoughts, gone as if she had never been. That is a betrayal that surely even a sweet soul like hers could never forgive.

"I'm sorry," he whispers as he finds his old cloak, his worn and cracked boots, a length of wool to wrap around his head and neck. Everything damp; never mind that. "My wife, my love, from the bottom of my heart I'm sorry." He opens the door a crack. Looks out through the rain, down toward the barn, up along the track, all about. No sign of Gormán or Conn. No sign of anyone. If they have any sense, they'll be indoors eating their breakfast by a warm fire.

He steps outside, shuts the door behind him, and walks off into the forest. Fear jangles his bones and whips his heart to a gallop. What if he goes too close to the place where it happened? What if he falls? What if the nightmare repeats itself and he's trapped in that other realm all over again? But Bardán has already paid his father's debt to the fey. What was that long time of work and silence, if not recompense for the wrong they said his father did them?

Be careful, he tells himself as he passes along tracks only birds and animals and fey folk can find. *No caves, no hollows, no dark corners. Watch out for odd groups of trees. Keep one foot on the ground. No mushroom circles, no rings of stones. Watch out for knotted grasses and lines scratched in bark and piles of white pebbles. Keep moving. Be back before supper time.*

Once he is far enough away from Tóla's house, he hums under his breath as he walks, and in his mind he is a small child, lying on the bed by an open window. A shaft of sunlight touching his mother's embroideries on the walls, and a little breeze stirring them to odd life. A man riding a white horse. A woman playing the harp. A dog chasing a ball. Had there been a dog? Outside, the sound of his father's saw, cutting wood. Closer at hand, his mother singing. *Feather bright and feather fine, none shall harm this child of mine.*

15

BLACKTHORN

The episode with Cúan had unnerved me. The news of Mathuin had left me shaken and furious. I stamped about, starting a task and leaving it half finished to pick up another, and generally getting in my own way as well as Grim's. Waiting for him to tell me to calm down and stop being stupid, which he didn't do. Instead, during a lull in the rain, he went outside with Ripple at his heels to chop more wood and stack it under cover. Not a word of reproach. I found myself wishing he would be angry, and hating myself for it.

When Cara was in one of her fidgety moods, which was quite often, I would tell her to choose one task and keep at it until she finished. Following my own good advice, I decided to prepare a reading lesson. I opened the wax tablet, ready to write. Found myself reading instead. Found myself writing something in my turn. Closed the tablet and put it away. A change of plan. No reading lesson; instead I would make a brew, set out a platter of bread and cheese and be honest with Grim about what was bothering me. I might get only one day before the rain cleared and he had to be back at Wolf Glen. It would be foolish to waste even a moment of that time.

"Brew?" I stood in the doorway, watching as Grim straightened and wiped the sweat from his brow. There was enough wood there to keep my hearth fire burning for many days. Until the weather warmed with the first breath of summer.

"Sounds good. I'll just put the ax away safe." His smile told me he knew I was making an effort, and was glad of it.

When we were sitting at the table, cups in hands, he said, "Worried, aren't you? About Mathuin and this attack?"

"I didn't sleep very well. As you know." I'd woken from a nightmare to find him sitting on the floor beside my bed, holding my hand. I thought I could remember telling him sharply to go back to bed and leave me to fight my own demons. Then lying awake while he made a brew and brought me a cup. "Sorry I snarled at you. Last night. I was half asleep. Still in the nightmare."

"Got a suggestion," Grim said.

"Mm?"

"For today. Even if the rain keeps up. We could walk over to Winterfalls, to the prince's house, and talk to a few folk. See if anyone knows any more about the whole thing, Cloud Hill and all. Maybe set your mind at rest a bit."

I found myself reluctant to say yes. Which was stupid, because I did want to go; I did want to find out everything I could. If there was anything I could do, anything at all, to help bring Mathuin to justice, then I was bound to do it. Only . . . I had so much looked forward to this day, a whole day with Grim and me both at home, a day when neither of us had to rush about doing anyone else's business.

"Only if you want to, of course," Grim said. His voice was soft; his eyes were full of understanding.

"I want to and I don't want to—that's the truth. But if we don't go, I'll be wound up tight all day and no use to anyone."

"We'll go, then. Soon as we've finished this. Rain's not too heavy; should get there quick. Talk to a few of the fellows, see who knows what. Might be home in time to get a few things done. Could be the weather will clear and I'll be back off up to Wolf Glen in the morning."

"Mm." My thoughts were a jumble. The sooner he finished this odd building job, the sooner he'd be back home again. But right now I was filled with a need for him to stay, not to go to Wolf Glen anymore, to be here where I could see him and hear him and argue with him whenever I wanted to. Which was beyond stupid. I began to wish I had not written anything on the wax tablet. But I couldn't erase it now, in full view. As for the remarkable words he had written there, maybe they proved that he was braver than I was, setting his feelings down for me to see. Or more foolish. Allow someone to become too dear to you and you give your enemy a weapon more deadly than the sharpest sword, more lethal than the strongest poison. I knew that all too well, and Grim knew it too. Time enough, when Mathuin was dealt with, to recognize what there was between him and me. If there was anything more than a close friendship. I shouldn't have written those words. It was too soon. "Yes, we'll go," I said. "Grim, what can they do? The king and Prince Oran? Laois is so far away, much too far for King Ruairi to retaliate with force, even supposing he wanted to. He'd have to take his men across Ulaid and Mide and into Laigin to reach Mathuin's territory, and Mathuin's known to have a strong personal army. I'm no expert in these things, but even I can see that would stir up even more trouble. It could draw in other leaders, perhaps against their will. Would Lorcan of Mide be prepared to fight alongside Ruairi?"

"Folk say Lorcan's a peacemaker," Grim said. "Sounds like he's offered a safe place for Flidais's parents and whoever got out with them. That might be as far as it goes."

"He's a kinsman of Oran's father."

"If he jumps into the conflict with his own fighters, the whole thing gets bigger and bloodier. Nobody would want that."

"If Mathuin isn't stopped, it'll get bigger and bloodier anyway. Morrigan's curse, will that foul wretch be allowed to trample on folk all over Erin?"

"Thing is," Grim said, "it's got bigger than us now. You want to stop him. I want to stop him. Any of those poor sods who were in his cesspit of a prison and managed to survive want the same thing. Same for all the ordinary folk he hurt. But what he's done now, it's a big step more. And maybe it's for kings and chieftains to fix it, not the likes of us."

"First you say the kings and chieftains won't want a war. Then you say it's up to them to do something. That doesn't make sense. Come on. If we're going, we should go now before the rain starts again."

I banked up the fire. Then, cloaked against the weather, we set off on the path across the fields to the prince's house, with Ripple beside us. The bull was under the trees with his cows and did not bother to approach. The sky was heavy with clouds; there would be more rain soon. Our boots gained a rich coating of mud. Small lakes filled each hollow, and ducks swam there. The air was chill.

"Could be," remarked Grim, "there's another way out."

"Another way out of what?"

"The problem. Getting rid of a tyrant without a war."

"Oh. Well, yes. I could think of a couple. But not ways I can imagine King Ruairi using. Even less Lorcan, if he's the peacemaker folk say he is. Assassination. Just about impossible in Mathuin's case, I'd think, since he goes about surrounded by retainers and is quick to stifle any dissent. Magic. That's not going to happen. What do the fey care if a human tyrant runs rampant? If Conmael cared, he wouldn't have stopped me from speaking up when I had the chance."

Grim made no comment on this.

"Yes, I know. Mathuin planned to silence me before I got the chance to say another word. And yes, Conmael saved my life. And yours. But he doesn't care about bringing Mathuin to justice, or he wouldn't have forbidden me to do anything about it, would he?"

"Just didn't want you rushing in before it was the right time. Didn't want you getting yourself killed. For nothing, most like. That would be a waste."

"I know that. But when is the right time? And why isn't Conmael here so I can ask him about these things?"

"Can't answer that," said Grim. "Maybe he's waiting for the right time to put in an appearance. And maybe what's wanted isn't force but cleverness."

We were nearly at the gates to the prince's stronghold when a man came riding toward us from the settlement, forcing his horse to a pace that was downright dangerous in the wet. He hauled the animal to a halt and slid down next to us.

"Mistress Blackthorn! You need to come, quick!"

"Slow down." Grim's deep voice, calm and sure. "Take a breath or two. Now, what is it?"

The fellow gasped out his message. A woman in labor—it had gone on too long, the babe was stuck, the woman was getting weaker, she'd expected to deliver safely without a midwife but something must be wrong, he'd ridden all the way to find me, I had to come now, now—

"All right, take it slowly," I said. "Where is this woman? How far?"

"Longwater. In the settlement there." The messenger was white-faced and shaking, shock setting in now he had found me. "You take the main road west; then there's a track along the river. I'll ride back with you, show you where to go."

"How long is the ride? I'll need to borrow a horse." If she was already fading when the young man left there, chances were she would be dead before I reached her. And I didn't have my healer's bag with me.

"On the western side of Wolf Glen, isn't it?" said Grim. "Be well over an hour."

"Not if you go the back way," said the messenger. "Takes only half the time. But we should be leaving now."

"If you're coming with us, you need a fresh horse. That one's not up to it." Grim's tone was blunt. "Best to borrow three fresh mounts, leave your horse here for a rest. I'll knock on the prince's door and ask Eochu."

"Thank you, Grim. Be as quick as you can. And I'm going to need my healer's bag."

"I'll ride back and get it. Catch you up on the way."

Grim had friends in the prince's household, and this stood us in good stead now. We were soon riding west on borrowed mounts, Grim having made a quick trip home for the bag and caught up with remarkable speed.

The messenger's name was Osgar, and the woman in labor was his sister, Fann. As we rode along I offered calm words. But I would not lie to him about her chances. It might already be too late to turn the babe if it was awkwardly placed. The lengthy labor might have weakened the child so much it would not survive. The cord might be around its neck. The mother's heart might give out. I did not tell Osgar those things, merely that I would do my very best, but that I could not give him an iron-strong promise that both mother and baby would survive. Did she have other children? No, this was the first. How old was Fann? Over thirty; she had married late. I did not tell him that an older woman faced a higher risk, especially with her first child.

"I'll do everything I can for her, Osgar," I said. "Believe me."

Eventually the road was met by a well-made side track, broad enough for carts and the like. It ran alongside a stream, now swollen by the rain to a small river. We must have crossed it on our journey to Bann last summer, when we'd continued west on the main track. My mind had been on other things, and I remembered little of that ride. Gods, it felt so long ago. At the junction there stood a way-marker: rough letters carved onto a slab of stone.

"Longwater," read Grim without a moment's hesitation. Which just went to show that with good teaching and the right attitude, a man can very quickly learn his letters. Even a man who has always believed himself stupid.

"Is this the way up to the lake, Osgar?" I asked. "Where they bring timber in and out?"

"That's right, Mistress Blackthorn. Quick way to Longwater settlement. The other way, by the master's house, that's far longer. Most folk keep clear of it."

"Oh?" It seemed a good idea to keep him talking about anything other than his sister and the difficult task ahead. I knew already that the local people were wary of the forest track, though Grim never seemed to have any trouble with it.

"Forest's tricky," Osgar said. "Got those paths that keep changing, you know? All ups and downs, slipping and sliding, trees that move about and make you lose your way. Or so folk say."

"That does sound rather frightening."

"Something not right about the place." Osgar's tone was quieter now. He glanced over his shoulder as if someone might be following, listening in. "Wolf Glen. Ill-luck place. That's what folk say. I heard he's building that house again. The house that's meant to make things come right. For the future, that is. Can't undo the past. His wife died, you know. The master's wife. Suanach, her name was. Died before her child was a year old. Broke the master's heart. He hasn't been right since. That's what I heard. Never go up there myself."

Grim didn't say a word. Of course, he was forbidden to speak about the heartwood house to outsiders. But I wasn't. "What house? Is it something magic?"

"I don't know much about it, Mistress Blackthorn. Only, first time they tried to build it, the fellow that was doing the work ran off with the place half finished, and nobody else knew how to do it. Then the lady died, and the master blamed the builder. This house, it's made very special. Brings good fortune if it's done right. My auntie told me the story. She lived there for a bit once. At Wolf Glen, in the big house. Wet nurse for the infant. Had enough milk for her own boy and the girl as well. Long while ago. My cousin's a young man of fifteen now. Sixteen next autumn and thinks himself all grown-up."

Oh, my treacherous thoughts, suddenly full of my Brennan as he might be now, a fine young man of just that age, with my red hair and his father's steady gray eyes. What might he have become, but for Mathuin?

"Is that the settlement up ahead?" asked Grim.

The terrain opened up and the lake came into sight, a slender body of water with forested hills behind. There was a scattering of houses along the shore, neat, well-kept dwellings, each with a garden patch. House cows grazed in a walled field. A bigger building stood close to the water, perhaps a storehouse, and beside it was a jetty at which two barges were moored. I saw a spot where carts might be drawn up, and a fenced enclosure with horse troughs. Neither man nor beast was in sight today, though we had been lucky with the weather. The rain had eased to a patchy drizzle.

"The house is along the end," Osgar said, pointing ahead. "This way."

After that I was so busy I had no chance to think about Mathuin or Wolf Glen or anything else except the task at hand. Folk came out to meet us well before we reached the woman's house. Many hands were ready to help us down and lead the horses to shelter. I suggested to Grim that he go off with the men to share some ale at Osgar's house next door and wait for news, and that he take Ripple with him. I didn't need to add that his job was to keep them calm, quiet and out of the way. Then I went in.

One look told me I needed to act quickly or I would lose both Fann and her unborn child. There were several women tending to her, and they'd been doing a good job, or as good a job as untrained helpers could. The hut was warm; a girl was keeping an eye on the fire, on which a pot of water bubbled. They'd been burning lavender and rosemary.

"I'm Blackthorn, the healer," I said, rolling up my sleeves. "Someone make a brew. For yourselves, not for Fann. And have something to eat, all of you. I'll need you alert and strong."

"I'm Fann's mother." An older woman, her hair showing threads of silver, came up next to me as the others busied themselves. She looked wrung out, but was holding her voice steady. "My name is Ide. We're so grateful you were prepared to come all this way, Mistress Blackthorn."

"Be glad that Osgar rode to fetch me; a pity it wasn't earlier. Never mind—we'll do our best. Tell me how this has gone so far. When did her pains start?"

"Just after supper last night. But not strong until the middle of the night, and it was well after sun-up when she felt the need to push." Ide lowered her voice, turning away from her daughter. "It was hard. Very hard. She tired herself out. Now she can't push anymore. And the pains have died away."

Danu save us. "This is her first child?"

"That's right. Ross, that's Fann's husband, works on the barges, loading and unloading."

As she spoke I examined Fann; felt the tightly distended belly, noted the slow pulse, the pallid skin slick with sweat, the eyes that did not quite seem to see me. I attempted a reassuring smile. "Good work, Fann—you're doing well. Someone pass me my bag, will you?"

One of the women brought it over and I got out the finely shaped wooden instrument Grim had made for me. "I use this to listen to what's happening in there," I said, knowing from experience that folk found the process frightening if they did not understand. I put one end of the instrument against the taut skin of Fann's belly and set my ear to the other. "Everyone quiet now."

All the women went still. I could hear the rain coming down again outside, but within the house it was as if even the spiders in the corners and the mice in the walls were waiting for the reassurance of life.

"Good," I said after a little, aiming for a briskly competent tone. I hoped I had not imagined that faint sound, a tiny, tentative drumbeat. "We need to get this baby out as quickly as we can. He—or she— seems to be the right way around. But we need to get things moving along. Now, I can smell that someone here knows their herbs. Do you have calamint? In particular, the kind with small grayish flowers? And ordinary garden thyme?"

"Thyme, yes," Ide said. "But not the calamint; I didn't think we'd be needing it. Curse me for a fool!"

"Can it be gathered close by?"

Fann groaned, moving her head from side to side.

"Not in the garden here. Up on the edge of the woods there may be a plant or two. If I'd thought earlier . . ."

"Someone must run up there and gather it. Now. Someone who can find the right thing straightaway. I'd go myself, but I need to stay with her." I prayed that this would not come to a choice between mother and infant. I had never had to cut a child from the womb, but I had seen it done when a woman would have died anyway, and it was a brutal, bloody business.

There was silence in the room, save for Fann's breathing.

"Does anyone know exactly where the plant grows? We must make up a tea to get labor started again. A very strong infusion. I need the herbs right now. Or as soon as you can possibly get them." I promised myself I would never again let the supply of dried calamint in my healer's bag run out. Never. Though the fact was, the fresh herb was far more effective.

"Up by the old hut," Ide said. "Where that strange woman used to have her garden—you remember, the one folk said was fey?" She glanced at the others. "If there's calamint anywhere, it's there. Only," she said, looking at me, "it's all overgrown. Turned to wilderness long ago. The son buried his whole family close by the place. Father, mother, wife. Folk have given it a wide berth ever since."

The others were avoiding my eye. It seemed that even with their friend at risk of her life, nobody was going to volunteer.

"I can't run," Ide said. "My joints are too stiff. And I'm the only one likely to find the right plant in all the weeds around the old hut. Apart from yourself, Mistress Blackthorn."

"Can someone take you on horseback?" Morrigan save us, did they plan to wait until Fann expired right before their eyes?

"Not all the way there. It's off the track. Too steep for horses."

There was only one answer. "Start making a tea with fresh thyme," I said. "Strong. See if you can get Fann sitting up, or even walking around if she can manage that. Keep on sponging her face. Let her sip warm water. I'll be back in a moment." Grim was not a wise woman or a druid. But he was a gardener. And he could run.

16

GRIM

Quicker to ride up as close as I can to this hut and run the last bit. Hoping I can find the plant she needs. From the sound of it, if there was a garden once, there isn't anymore. Osgar gets me a horse, asks if I want someone to come with me and I say no. I can see nobody wants to do it. An old man points out where the place is, a bit downhill from two massive beeches, no missing them.

"There used to be a path," says the old man. "When the builder fellow lived there. Bardán, his name was. It'll be a bit grown over; he's been gone years and years. But you can see where to head off the main track. Post still standing, though the sign's gone. You can tie up the horse there."

Bardán. Morrigan's britches! As if I didn't already have too much to think about. No time to ask questions now. I tell Ripple to stay with the others; no need for her to get wet and tired all over again. Then I get on the horse and head off. Try to put my thoughts straight while I'm riding up to the forest. First thing, calamint. Remind myself what it looks like. Pick the wrong herb and this woman could die because of me. Baby too. Got to be quick, got to get it right. Second thing, Blackthorn. I rushed back to the cottage for her bag, saw the writing tablet on the shelf, thought, good, this is my chance to rub out those words I wrote. Only, when I opened up the tablet my words were gone. Something else was written there. Written by her. Hurry or no hurry, nothing was going to stop me reading it.

Who is this man?
Strength in his hands
Truth in his eyes
Love in his heart
Honor in his spirit
His name is Grim.

Just as well she wasn't there when I read that. Filled me up with feelings. Blushing all over my big ugly face. Tears in my eyes. Couldn't believe she'd written that about me. Me, Bonehead, that was. She must've liked what I wrote, or she'd never have done that. Didn't have time to sit and look at it then, but I made sure I remembered it, every word. Struggled with *honor* for a bit, first time I read it, but I worked it out. Brother Galen would've been proud of me.

Still thinking about it now. What it might mean. If I'm being foolish to think it might mean what I'd like it to mean. Wishing Mathuin was dead and buried so she could stop worrying and maybe let herself have time for . . . Nah. *Doesn't pay to get ahead of yourself, Bonehead.* Let yourself dream too deep, and sure as sure the next thing will be a nasty wake-up, bucket of slops in the face like in the lockup. So I go on to the third thing that's in my mind. Bardán. The wild man. Bardán the builder, who used to live in this hut I'm heading for. Not so far from Tóla's house at all, only on the other side of the wood. If what those folk were saying is true, Bardán had a mother and father and a wife, and they're all buried up there. Danu save us. No wonder the man's half crazy. Loses his whole family, then ends up in the Otherworld for years and years. And some time in the middle of that he was building the heartwood house and stopped with the place half finished. Must be folk in these parts who know more about all that, what happened to him, the bits he still can't remember. But that can wait. The herbs can't.

Doesn't take long to get there. I tie the horse to the post and head in on foot. Not much of a path left; that fellow was right about nobody coming this way anymore. Only not quite right, because when I get to the old hut, someone's there before me.

I stop dead in my tracks. Bardán. Bardán, who's not allowed to leave Wolf Glen. Bardán, all the way over here, sitting on the broken steps outside the hut. Face all tears. Something in his hands, an old cloth of some kind.

"Grim," he whispers, and gets to his feet. Ready to run, is my guess. Looking as wild as he did the day I first saw him.

"It's all right," I say, quiet-like. Thinking of trying to catch a dog or a horse that's spooked. Thinking how slow and careful you have to be, not to send them bolting in panic. "I haven't come to look for you. I need to pick some herbs—calamint—for Blackthorn. My friend, you know, the healer. Woman down in Longwater giving birth, or trying to. Need to find the plant in a hurry." Cast my eye over what might have been a garden, long ago. Remains of a drystone wall, something that could have been a path. Stuff growing everywhere, all under and over and tangled through itself. Maybe there's calamint there, but finding it's going to take time. And that's what I haven't got.

Behind Bardán, the door to the hut's open. Place looks like a nice shelter for spiders and birds and field mice, not much more. But it had been a home once. Bits and pieces of furniture still in there, a bed, a table, one or two crocks and cups. Like he just walked off and left the lot, all those years ago. And nobody's come near since.

Want to ask him what he's doing here, and doesn't he know he'll be in big trouble with Tóla. But there's no time. "Could you help?" I ask instead. "The calamint. Need it in a hurry. Don't know where to start looking."

Bardán's not hearing me. Tears still coming fast. "*Every birdling in the wood,*" he murmurs. "*Feather bright and feather fine . . .*"

He's in no fit state to help. He's the one who needs help, but I've got to find this herb and go, quick as I can. There's wormwood by the old wall, breaking free of the long grass. Yarrow. Lavender. Row of spiky thistles on guard. I head over there, squat down, start pulling out grass, hunting for calamint. Fresh green leaves, smallish; strong smell when you crush them. Gray flowers. What if that woman dies, and the child, all because I'm not up to the job Blackthorn's trusted me with?

"Woman," says Bardán, making me jump. He's right behind me. Didn't hear him move. "What woman?"

"The one in labor? Fann, her name is. Her man works on the barges." All the time I keep hunting through the grass and weeds. "Brother called Osgar. He's the one came to get us. Me and Blackthorn." Why can't I find what I want? "Must've been your garden once," I say. "Herbs, flowers, vegetables for your family."

"I helped him," Bardán said. "Dad. Made the rows straight. Like a builder. He showed me. Mama sat on the steps and sewed her pictures. Singing, always singing. *Feather bright and feather fine, none—*" He stops, just like that. Like there's a wall there, stopping him from saying the next bit, whatever it is. "See?" he says instead, and holds out the rag he's been clutching. "She made this."

Seems like nothing much. But I remember Blackthorn's red kerchief and how that ended up being a lot more than it looked like. So I take the thing from Bardán's hands and spread it out. Full of holes, fraying away, faded and tired. But beautiful; like a lovely dream. Finest thing I've seen in a long while. Before it got old this was a picture of birds done in bright wools. A piece you'd be proud of if you were the maker. Big enough to hang on the wall; pretty enough to fill up the little house with happiness. All different sorts of birds on it, perfect down to the last feather. Small, big, in between, from a little snippet of a wren to a swan with its wings spread wide. You wouldn't think an ordinary woman like Bardán's mother could make such a thing. For work like that you'd need a touch of the uncanny in your hands. But then, if that story he told was the true tale of his parents, she *was* part fey. His mother. Ran away from the Otherworld in company with a boy who was switched for a changeling.

"The last one," Bardán says, stroking the embroidery with a crooked finger. "Fading away."

"Someone with clever hands could mend this," I tell him. Wish I could comfort the fellow, but this is a deep-down grief. Those tears, they're not over his mother's embroidery, or not only that. He's crying for the past, for the lost, for what couldn't be. Know that feeling well. Know how it eats out your insides, so kind words don't help anymore. "There's one or two of the women at Winterfalls, Lady Flidais's hand-maids, who do fine work like this."

Bardán snatches the ragged cloth from me, holds it to his chest like it's a treasure. Which, in a way, it is.

"It's all right." Keep my voice soft; try not to rush things. "I wouldn't take it from you. Bardán, I need the herb. Calamint. If you can remember where it is, please help me."

"Kind," Bardán says, coming out from wherever he was for long enough to see me properly. "Grim. Kind. Over there, at the corner."

And there it is, half hidden under a giant comfrey plant. Surprised it's been getting enough sun. There're enough fresh leaves on it for a brew. Hope so, anyway. I bend to pick, and there's Blackthorn's voice in my head: *Take what you need, but leave enough—make sure you don't kill the plant. Remember to say thank you.*

"Thank you," I say under my breath. "You might save a life today. Two lives. Owe you a big debt." I'm not sure if I'm thanking the plant, or some sort of force that helps things grow, or maybe a god. Or God. Been thinking about him a lot since I was at St. Olcan's.

Got to rush back. "I have to go, Bardán," I tell him. "If I don't get these leaves down there quick enough, that woman could die." Leaving him here by himself feels wrong. I know he'll be in big trouble with Tóla for going away. Even though today wouldn't have been a workday, and even if he's only visiting his old house. Don't like the thought of him facing up to the master on his own. "I can come back in a bit, if you—"

He's got his head in his hands. Shoulders shaking. The bit of cloth over his knees, where he sits on the steps. "The blood," he sobs. "So much blood . . . They didn't come. They wouldn't come . . . And she . . . she was so white, white as snow, and all the red . . ."

He's weeping so hard I can hardly make out the words. Morrigan's curse, I can't walk off and leave him like this. "Who, Bardán?"

"Dáire. My Dáire. Here, here, I'll show you." He drops the embroidery on the steps. Takes my arm, leads me around the path and up behind the hut to a spot I can tell straight off is a grave. Everywhere else is overgrown. But this patch has been weeded today, from the looks of it. Pile of long grass and bits and pieces to one side. All freshly pulled. Must've been a hard job with his hands the way they are. What's left is the remains of the grass and a few daisies popping their little heads up here and there. And three stones. Names carved into them, two I can't read for the moss and the wearing away. Third one starts with a D. *Dáire,* I'm thinking. The others I can guess, since I've heard the story down in Longwater, or part of it anyway.

"Your mother and father?"

Bardán manages a nod. "And . . ." He kneels by Dáire's grave marker, bows his head. Voice comes out sort of strangled. Seeing the past like he's right back in it—that's my guess. Back in the worst of it. "So much blood. How could there be so much? And the little face, the little eyes . . . She never even . . . she never . . ."

"Dáire . . . your wife?" Hard to think of the wild man as married, settled, plying the trade his father taught him. Sounds as if she died in childbirth. Poor sod lost wife and infant both. No wonder he's a bit wrong in the head.

Bardán nods. "Wanted to show you."

"I'm sorry. Hard for you. Very hard." Explains a lot. Though not everything. "Bardán, I have to go back to Longwater. I have to go right now. But I'll come up later, when Blackthorn's finished down there. Walk you over to Tóla's, if you want. The master won't be happy you've left the place and neither will Gormán. Be easier for you if I come too." Soon as I've said it I have second thoughts. If he headed off now, he'd be back there much sooner. Rain still coming down on and off. Could be nobody's noticed he's not there. Might all be indoors, keeping dry.

He could slip back in, no trouble. And it could take a long time for this child to be born. Even if it's quick, there's things that could go wrong. Badly wrong. Blackthorn might need me for a while. Most of the day, even. "If you don't want to wait for me, just go," I tell him. "I can't tell you how long I'll be. Will you be all right here?" Stupid question. This man will never be all right again. Lost too much. Doesn't mean I should stop helping him, though. Poor sod.

"Go," Bardán says. "Go quick. Save them."

17

Women came in and out of the cottage, bringing food and drink, making sure there was firewood and fresh water and anything else I asked for. Men wandered up to the door from time to time, wanting to ask questions but not quite prepared to put them into words. In the end, I told them to go next door and stay there or I'd be tempted to turn the lot of them into newts. It had been a long, long time since I had said such a thing.

Grim gave the men jobs to keep them occupied. Both Osgar and Fann's husband, Ross, were among those gathered in the next-door house. I sent one of the women over to let them know we'd given Fann the draft and were anticipating that things might speed up now, and she reported back that on Grim's instructions the men were busy stacking firewood under cover, drawing water from the well, and cooking batches of flat-cakes. Grim and I knew from experience the disastrous results that might come from drinking mead on an empty stomach, especially if a person was already upset or tired. Once or twice we heard them singing over there.

"How can they do that at a time like this?" said one of the women. "When Fann's in here . . .?"

Dying, I thought but did not say. The draft had been a strong infusion of thyme and calamint. I had added a drop or two of a tincture made from a particular fungus, a substance I was loath to use except in the most extreme of cases, as it came close to administering a poison. I kept a tiny vial of it in my healer's bag. I had not expected to be using it. But I'd weighed up the risk against the probability that if I could not get Fann's labor started again, I would have to cut the baby free or lose both of them anyway. Now we were waiting; waiting for the draft to work.

"That's not a drinking song or the like," I said. "It's a fine old song about a man who went off to seek his fortune and ended up seeing all kinds of wonders. A song to put heart in a person." I could imagine who had suggested it. I could hear his voice among the others. He didn't sing at home. But we'd sung in Mathuin's prison, all of us, raising our cracked and broken voices in defiance of the rules, as if pretending to have hope might make that hope reality. We'd sung the night that poor soul died under torture; sung him to his last merciful sleep. Hope. Hope fought hard to stay alive. Even when you thought it was beaten to nothing, burned to ashes, drowned deep, still it flickered away, waiting to be found again.

Fann coughed. Moaned. She'd been lying flat on the bed, but now she was moving about, struggling. "Aah," she groaned. "It hurts! Oh, gods!" There was a tone in her voice that I recognized. Our chance, our one chance, was almost here.

I put my arm behind Fann's shoulders and lifted her to sit upright. "More pillows," I ordered. "Wedge them behind her back—that's it. Now, Fann, listen to me. Soon I'll need you to push again. The draft you took will help the baby come, but you have to help too. So when I say push, you push as long and hard as you can, even if you're so tired you can't even think straight. And when I say stop, you stop pushing and let us do the work. If you breathe like this," I demonstrated the short shallow breathing that helps a woman not to expel the baby too quickly, lest the cord strangle it before it has the chance to draw its first breath, "it will be easier to hold back. These pains will be strong. Think about your baby. Your son or daughter. Be brave for your child." I hated those words, even as I knew I had to speak them. Fann wasn't going to manage this if I told her the truth: *You're almost too exhausted to push, chances are the baby will be born dead, there's a possibility the draft will kill you, and if you don't succeed in getting the child out, you'll both die anyway, unless I use my knife to save the infant at your expense. But do your best.* Hope. You had to have hope, or what was the point of anything?

I wished men were allowed in the birthing chamber. Grim's quiet strength would have steadied me. Now that Fann was in full labor again—perhaps I was the only one who knew how lucky we were to have achieved that—none of us had any time to run over with news for the men. From time to time their voices came to us, like something from another world, singing songs of heroism and courage and magical happenings. Always songs that ended in triumph: the treasure found, the lovers reunited, the battle won, the enemy vanquished. I hoped Fann could hear them.

I lost all sense of time. The day was measured only by the spasms in Fann's body, the color of her skin, the speed of her pulse, the shadows around her eyes. I dabbed a tincture of certain spices on her neck and added a few drops to the fire. A pungent smell filled the chamber, setting us all sneezing. Fann sneezed too, then wiped her eyes and kept on pushing.

Ide drew me aside while two of the others took their turn supporting Fann.

"Mistress Blackthorn. How much longer before you . . .? What if she . . .? I can't make myself say it." Her face was gray with weariness and with the knowledge of what might come.

"This is our last chance for the child to be born naturally. Either she does it now or we'll face a very difficult choice."

Ide nodded. "Gods help us. Would you . . .?"

Would I use the knife? Not while Fann lived—that was certain. "She can do it," I said. "Your daughter is a strong woman, Ide. Like her mother. Come—let's help her."

A healer does not lie. But sometimes she does hold back from complete honesty—when the truth would cause needless hurt; when it would make the innocent feel guilty; when it might stop a person from doing their best to save a life. I was glad that Fann did not prove my statements false. She was strong, all right. I came to realize, as she gave the last of her strength to the work in hand, that she would have got that baby out if it killed her. But, gods be thanked, in time the child was born, a tiny boy whose cries were like the call of some fledgling bird fallen from its nest, and Fann rested her head on the pillows with the look of a woman whose job is done, and done well. Everyone was weeping with relief. Yes, even me. Ide tied the cord and cut it. I gave Fann another draft to help her expel the afterbirth cleanly. The other women dealt with bloody cloths and the other debris of birth. The child, still making those little sounds, was wrapped in a very small blanket and placed in his mother's arms. Over there, the men were still singing.

"One of you go and tell them," I said, noting with interest that the chamber seemed to be moving around me and realizing I was almost too tired to do what must still be done. "Ross can come to the door, and Osgar. But not a whole crowd of men, and they're not coming inside." Fann might be calm and smiling, but her ordeal had come close to breaking her. What she really needed was a good long sleep. I hoped the boy would not be too weak to suckle.

I needed to sit down. Now, before I fainted. I needed to stop remembering my own son's birth, and how Cass had come in and held my hand afterward, and how he'd told me I was the best woman in the world, or at least in his world, and never more so than right then. How he'd whispered in his new son's ear that he'd keep Brennan safe until the day he died. Which was exactly what Cass had done. For they had died together, on the same day, with Cass crouched over our son, trying to shield him from the flames. It was filling up my mind. The smells of that day, the terrible sounds, the rage and grief and hopelessness . . .

"Mistress Blackthorn!" Ide was motioning for me to sit down on a bench. "You're white as a sheet. You've been on your feet too long. Here . . . Eibhlín, some ale for Mistress Blackthorn, quickly."

The girl brought ale and I sipped it while the baby's father and uncle came to the door, holding sacks over their heads against the rain, and Ide took the child over to show them. Ross spoke to his wife across the chamber, his face aglow with delight. Fann managed a smile and a few words. Later on, when I was more confident her bleeding would stay under control, we'd let him come in and sit with her awhile. I'd taken quite a risk with that first draft. I'd have to watch her until I could be sure there were no adverse effects.

Ide sent the men away, gave the baby back to his mother, cast a firm eye over me. I forestalled her question. "I'll be fine in a moment. Really."

"You worried me for a bit, Mistress. Looked like you'd seen a ghost."

"I believe all will be well now," I said in a murmur, not wanting Fann to hear. "But there's always the possibility of complications. I'm sure you understand that. We need to watch both of them. The child is small. He'll probably need to be coaxed to feed."

"Will you stay for the night?" Ide asked. "I know you must be busy, folk needing you and so on, but if you could, we'd be so grateful. And your friend, of course."

The prospect of the ride home was not appealing. It was late in the day and I was dog-tired, more tired than I had any right to be, since it was Fann who'd been doing the hard work. It would be sensible to stay anyway. If I was here until morning, I could reassure myself that Fann was recovering well and the baby feeding before I left them. "That is a kind offer. Thank you, and I'd welcome it."

"I think you saved my daughter's life," Ide said quietly. "For that, you'll have friends in Longwater forever, Mistress Blackthorn."

"It's what I do," I said, and thought immediately how churlish that sounded. "I'm glad to be of service."

The afterbirth was taken away to be buried under a special tree when the weather cleared. An old ritual and a good one. I wondered if the spreading hawthorn still grew in the garden of that burned-out house in the village where Cass and I had settled. That tree would have many tales to tell, happy, sad, tender, joyful, cruel and tragic. I would never know. I would never go back there.

A tap at the door. It was Grim, with Ripple at his heels. I went out to talk with him, under the eaves of the house.

"All's well here," I said. "But they'll both need watching for a while. Ide has suggested we stay overnight."

"Tired, mm?" Grim reached out as if to brush a strand of hair from my face, but drew his fingers away without touching me. "Sad too."

Tears pricked my eyes. I wanted nothing more than to lean on him, shut my eyes and will the rest of the world away for a while. What in the name of Danu was wrong with me? I'd delivered dozens of infants without turning to mush. "A few memories coming back," I said. "Nothing to bother yourself about. But I do want to stay, just to make sure she'll be all right. If the weather clears and you have to work, you could get to Wolf Glen from here easily enough, couldn't you?" I hoped it would go on raining. We hadn't had our day together yet. Not Fann's fault; she could hardly be expected to time her child's arrival to suit us. But I'd been looking forward to that day. Foolish woman.

"Thing is," Grim said, and there was a note of apology in his voice, "I don't think I can. Stay, that is. Met Bardán before. Up at that hut where the herbs were growing. Seems like that was his house, a long time ago."

"What was he doing there?" My heart had gone down to my boots. I ordered myself sharply not to be so silly. "I thought you said they kept him on a short leash."

"That's the problem. If he doesn't get back to Wolf Glen soon, he'll be in trouble. Told him I'd go back when you didn't need me anymore. Walk over there with him. If I'm around, they might go easier on the poor sod. He's in no fit state to be on his own. Been weeding around his wife's grave. Funny, I didn't even know there was a wife until today. Her and his parents, all buried up there. Don't think he'd been to the house since he came back from the Otherworld. If that's where he was, all those missing years."

I swallowed several things I wanted to say, all of them selfish and wrong. "You'd better go, then. I can cope here. And if I don't want to ride home on my own in the morning, I'll ask Osgar or one of the others to come with me."

"You sure?" Grim had a little frown on his brow. His eyes told me how easily he saw beneath my surface. "I can stay, if you want. Bardán's a grown man. He walked over here; I daresay he can walk back. May even have headed off without me, seeing as the light's fading."

"I'll be fine. You should go." I drew a breath, trying to make it steady and quiet. "Grim."

"Mm?"

"Thank you for looking after the men. Ross must have been beside himself with worry."

"All smiles now," Grim said. "But yes, he was a bit of a mess for a while there. Easy to understand. I'd be the same if . . ."

"Yes, well, you'd better be getting on," I said, turning so he couldn't see my face. "If it rains again tomorrow, maybe you can come home in the morning."

"Maybe. Maybe not. Depends what happens with Bardán. And I've got business with Master Tóla. A proposition. Might get the job done quicker than we expected. That's if he'll listen to me."

"Go safely," I said. Drat these tears! "I hope it works out well."

"Make sure you get a good sleep," said Grim. "And do ask one of the fellows to ride back with you. Best not go on your own."

"I can look after myself."

"All the same. I can leave Ripple with you, if you want."

One glance at Ripple was enough to tell me what the dog would think of that arrangement. "She wants to go with you. I'll manage, Grim. Now, I'd best get back in."

"Be safe, Lady." He said this so softly I almost didn't catch it.

I couldn't find it in me to reprimand him for using that name, the one he'd invented for me in the lockup; the one he wasn't supposed to use anymore. Instead I looked at him over my shoulder and attempted a smile. Hoped he couldn't see the tears. "You too, big man."

18

CARA

It was meant to be. The rain, the distractions at the prince's house, and then, when she passed by Dreamer's Wood, the fact that Blackthorn's cottage door was shut and there was no smoke from the fire, meaning the wise woman was not home. Then, the fields between Dreamer's Wood and the bigger forest of Wolf Glen lying empty and quiet under the rain, save for a few miserable-looking sheep huddled under the trees and a scatter of ducks trying out the newly formed ponds. A crow kept pace as she moved quickly over the open area. The bird would fly a short distance, then land on a stretch of drystone wall or a convenient post to shake the damp from its feathers and wait for Cara to catch up.

Once she was safely in the shelter of the Wolf Glen forest, she tried to work out what she would say to her father. That was if she didn't decide to see Gormán, then leave. Father would be upset with her. She knew the look he'd have on his face, sad, reproachful, most likely angry as well. Holding it all in check, the way he did. But wouldn't he be glad to see her, too? He loved her. Even when he was at his sternest, he loved her. Even when he sent her away with no proper explanation. She knew it as she knew the sun followed the moon across the sky.

She mustn't weep or shout or lose her temper. That would only make things worse. He would tell her, yet again, that she was a child and needed to be taught how to conduct herself. So, no tears, no babbling out her woes, no rushing to throw her arms around him, even if that was what she most wanted to do.

"I must make a case," she said to the crow, which had alighted on the pale bough of a young birch and was holding a large moth in its beak. "Set things out calmly, point by point. Explain that I'm perfectly capable, or I wouldn't have been able to walk all the way home through the forest on my own. Tell him it's not Lady Flidais's fault I left Winterfalls without anyone noticing—she could hardly be expected to watch over me when they'd all been called to court. And it's not Blackthorn's fault, since I wasn't at her house today. Or Mhairi's, because I made sure she wouldn't find me."

The crow gulped down the moth. Its bright eye seemed to say, *So far, so good, my friend. And then what?*

"Then I'll tell him that if he wants me to act like a grown woman, he should start treating me as one. And that means explaining properly. Trusting me with the truth, whatever it is."

Since the bird had finished its meal, she walked on. After a moment she felt a sudden jolt as the crow landed on her shoulder. Just as well she had on her thick shawl as well as the cloak. She could hear the bird thinking. Or maybe that was the trees. *All very well. All very measured. But you know what will happen, Cara. You'll step up before your father and open your mouth, and the words won't come.*

"I can talk to Blackthorn," Cara muttered, swishing at some long grass with a stick and thinking how hateful the truth could be. "I can talk to Emer. I can talk to lots of people now."

One look into your father's sad eyes and you will be struck dumb, as always. What you have done cannot please him, no matter how you disguise it. It can do nothing but make him sadder. Turn around and go back. It is not yet too late.

"Stop it!" she snapped. The crow lifted its wings, startled, then furled them again. "I'm not listening. I have to do this. I have to know."

You cannot talk to Lady Flidais or Prince Oran. You cannot talk to Mhairi and the others, beyond a few words.

"I can talk to Gormán. And I will. I'll find him first, before I see my father or Aunt Della. If Gormán says I should go home, I'll go. After I get him to tell me what's happening up there."

What if Gormán says it is none of your concern?

"He won't. Gormán is my friend."

The way was mostly uphill, and being off the main track meant a lot of scrambling over rocks and hauling herself up by exposed tree roots. Her boots were thick with mud. Everything she had on was wet. That was no more than she had expected; she knew the forest in all its moods. The crow came and went, finding shelter where it could. Rain dripped and trickled and ran from the foliage. The paths were treacherous.

"Look on the bright side," Cara said to the crow. "This should bring up a few juicy worms." It might have been a good idea to bring some food with her. That was what Father and Aunt Della would think, anyway. They wouldn't believe she could gather enough food in the forest to keep her going, any more than they believed she could find her way home from any part of Wolf Glen, even the deepest and most remote areas of the woodland. The thought of that seemed to frighten her father. Mention it, and she'd surely be dispatched back to Winterfalls, or even sent off to court, without the chance to say a word more. If she could say any words at all. If she did not become that other Cara, the one who stammered and struggled and eventually lost her voice altogether. Why was it that she could talk to some folk and not to others? Why was it that the person before whom she became most helpless, the one who most quickly turned her mute, was the one she cared about most in all the world?

"I can remember talking to him, you know," she told the crow as they headed up a rise under old oaks. Here, the dense canopy held off the worst of the rain, and it became easier to draw breath. "When I was little. Aunt Della would take me in to see him every evening before supper, and I would sit on his knee, and we would tell each other what we had been doing that day. I'd show him my crooked embroidery and my untidy writing, and he would praise me for trying my best. And he would tell me about selling a load of pine or buying a new stud bull. I wanted to ask him about Mother. What she looked like, the things she enjoyed doing, how she died. Only I didn't. I knew it would make him cry."

The crow made a derisive comment.

"I don't know what happened. Or why. But the older I grew, the harder it became to talk to him. Or to almost anyone. Like a spell, a curse, that stole away the words. He'd ask a question and when I opened my mouth to answer, there'd be nothing. Nothing at all. He thought I was doing it on purpose. Playing a trick; being troublesome. So did Aunt Della. I think he still believes that, or why would he think going to Winterfalls would cure me?"

"*Kraaa.*" The crow flew down to the forest floor and began to claw up the sodden debris, hunting out some morsel.

"I could always talk to Alba. I wonder where Alba is? If she'd come to Winterfalls with me, I would have had one friend there, at least."

"*Kraaa.*"

"All right, all right. I know. It's all nonsense. Even you don't believe in me."

Everything went still for a moment. As if an uncanny voice had spoken without making a sound. As if an unseen hand had stirred the troubled pot of her life and said, "Ah!" Then, with a rush and flurry of wings, there came a goldcrest to perch on her shoulder and a tiny, bright wren to settle in her hair. The crow came up to her feet, fixing her with its perceptive eye. *We believe in you. You are one of ours. Now, shall we be getting on?*

She'd meant to go straight there by the quickest route she could find. There was no using the main track. Even in this weather there might be folk coming out and in, farmhands or messengers. But she'd intended to find the most direct way for a person on foot, a person who was wood-wise and could make speed even where the trees grew close and the undergrowth was dense and the ground was full of sudden drops and difficult rises. Allowing for the need to cross streams swollen by the spring rain, she'd calculated that she would reach the house and barn at around midday.

What led her astray she did not know. The rain eased; the way should have become simpler, quicker. But after that still moment, the moment of magic, the forest seemed full of strange shadows. Cara knew the place was tricky; there were countless tales of folk being lost, of carts going off the track and getting stuck, of travelers hearing eldritch sounds or spotting things that could not possibly be there. Wolf Glen's own workers came to and fro without difficulty, as if the place had accepted them. It was outsiders who had trouble. That was why people used the other way, to the west, through Longwater. Though folk didn't like that path either. They only visited Wolf Glen if they really had to.

Cara found herself hesitating; needing to stop and check the terrain ahead; needing to fix markers such as a particular tree or stony outcrop to be sure she was on track. Something was wrong. She always knew the way; she knew it inside, deep down, without needing to think about it. Had she wandered into some fey place, some place of danger, without being aware of it? She knew the signs to watch for: mushroom circles, piled-up stones, woven grasses, odd things hanging from low branches. She had seen none of these. But here, in a clearing surrounded by graceful pale birches, she felt the pull of something perilous. "I'm heading home," Cara whispered to whatever might be there, invisible, watching and listening. "Home."

The crow flew up and away. A cry broke the quiet of the clearing, the voice of something small, lost, hurt. A wordless call for help.

Her gut tightened; her skin prickled. She opened her mouth to call, *Don't worry; I'm coming*, but no—best go quietly, looking out for danger. Where had that little voice come from? Surely down there, where the rocks formed a sort of mound almost like one of those old cairns, the ones with chambers where perhaps, long ago, dead warriors had been laid to rest. Thornbushes had almost covered it, a fierce barrier.

No wonder the little creature was stuck. What if it had some horrible injury? What if she couldn't free it? Mistress Blackthorn would know what to do. But Mistress Blackthorn wasn't there.

The thorns were thick and strong. Cara had her good knife at her belt, but she would not blunt it, cutting a way through, unless there was a need for that. She would risk calling out.

"Who's there? I can help you!"

She waited for perhaps the count of ten. Then, faintly, came the small cry again. No words; but, undoubtedly, *Help!* From the cairn, yes; but not near the spot where an entry would be. From somewhere deeper down.

"*Kraaa!*" The crow was up in the birches somewhere, and its call was a stark warning. *Don't. Don't go there.*

"I can look, at least," muttered Cara. "I can't just walk past and do nothing."

In the end she did use the knife. The thorns were easier to cut than she'd expected. Quite quickly she cleared them away from what did indeed prove to be an entrance, a narrow opening between the stones that seemed to lead to a cave. Or maybe a tunnel. Common sense, along with her knowledge of old tales, said go no farther. Caves and tunnels were like mushroom circles: alive with the possibility of danger. Even a person with no belief in the uncanny would think twice about entering a doorway like this, all shadow inside. Especially if nobody knew where that person was, and the doorway was far from any dwelling of humankind.

"*Kraaa!*"

"Hello?" Cara called, peering into the dark space. "Are you there?" Stupid, really. That little voice had been a creature's, not a human child's.

It came again, weaker, more desperate. In pain. Alone. In the dark. *Help! Help me!*

It should be safe to go a little way in, at least. Far enough to catch a glimpse of what lay ahead, but not so far that she lost sight of the forest outside. Without a candle or lantern, she would be foolish to go right in. But the small voice had not seemed very far away. Perhaps she could reach the hurt one and bring it out to safety.

Cara bent her head and stepped into the passage. Inside, the roof was higher than the doorway had suggested; she could stand almost upright. But the way was narrow. Her body blocked most of the light, making it impossible to see ahead.

"Where are you?" she called, and took a step forward, and another. No reply. She put her foot out for the third step, but the ground was not there. She fell into the dark.

19

I weigh it up, walk or ride back to Wolf Glen. Quicker to ride, only Bardán most likely can't, with his hands. Too hard for him to go up behind me. Walking's slow, but from what Osgar and the others have said, if we go quickly, we'll get there before dark. Sounds like the way in's a lot shorter from this end. Had to tell them about Bardán being up at the hut and working at Wolf Glen with me, or it would have looked odd, me heading off into the forest. Didn't want to give offense, seeing as they'd offered a bed for the night. So I broke one of Master Tóla's rules. More than one, if you count asking the fellows if any of them would be free to come and help, supposing there might be a building job on offer.

None of them knew Bardán was back. Not one. Thought he was gone forever, left the district or dead. They had heard Tóla was building the heartwood house again. They were interested all right, but nobody wanted to talk about it. And when I told them about Bardán they went quiet. Sounds like his wife was a local girl. But nobody wants to talk about him or her or any of it. Some kind of secret there, a big one, hanging over the whole place. And over the wild man most of all.

I'll say one thing for him—he knows his way around the forest. And he can cover ground faster than you'd think. Bardán doesn't fancy the main track, the one carts come up and down with lengths of pine for building. The fellows at Longwater said most of the timber ends up on Swan Island. I've heard of the place. School of warcraft over there, like something from an old tale. Mysterious. No wonder they need a wood supply. Place would be too windy for much to grow. Only a few trees, and they'd be all bent and twisted. Like a man getting beaten every day, and no escape from it. But alive. Hanging on.

A bit like Bardán. Lost his family, sounds like he lost a baby too, lost the good use of his hands. Lost any friends he had in Longwater, from the way the men were talking. Or maybe he never had them. But if his wife was a local girl, that doesn't make much sense. There's a lot about the man that doesn't make sense. Why did he go back to work for Tóla, after everything? Why's he coming with me now?

Can't ask. The man's still upset, though at least he's stopped weeping. Walking along beside me and Ripple, wrapped up in his own thoughts. Points the way from time to time, knows exactly where he's going. I was expecting to be leading him, but it's the other way round.

When I got back to the hut, he was waiting for me on the steps. Door was shut on the sad inside of the little house. He'd said his goodbyes to the dead. No sign of that rag of embroidery. He got up and came with me, and he didn't say a word about Tóla or what might happen when we got there. Only asked about the baby down at Longwater, if it had been born safely, if the woman was all right, if Blackthorn was all right. I said yes to all three and thanked him for waiting. He just nodded. When I add it up, seems to me he might know Fann and Ross and a few of those other folk down there. Not the youngest, but the ones around my age or Blackthorn's or older. I don't ask. Don't want to set him off again.

But while we're walking, something's bothering me. Thing is, Bardán's a lot like me. He's a man carrying a weight from the past, a burden that's sucking the life out of him, making him angry and crazy and sad. That was me, not so long ago. Me before I met Blackthorn. Me before I went to Bann and let some of that madness out before it ate me up. If those monks at St. Olcan's hadn't helped me, I'd still be that way. But they did help. Still got that dark stuff inside me—doesn't go away so easy—but the pieces of me have started to fit back together. Started to mend. Bardán's far from mending. And with Tóla and Gormán hanging over him with orders and rules and threats, he's going to stay broken a long while. Seems like it might be my job to help him. Reach out a hand to him the way Brother Fergal and Brother Ríordán and the others did to me. See him as a whole man, a real man, the way Blackthorn did when she kept me from going mad in the lockup. When she invited me to her campfire. When she pulled me back from the brink. Like the good Samaritan, from the Bible. Brother Galen read me that story long ago. You don't walk on past. Doesn't matter if I believe in God anymore. Still got to do the right thing. Only, not so easy, because Blackthorn needs me too. I saw that before. She wasn't only tired out from what she had to do today—she was sad deep down.

Makes me feel like one half of me's pulling east, other half's hauling west. Ripping me in half. Want to be in two places at once. Can't happen. Thing is, though, I know Blackthorn's strong. I know she'll cope without me. Bardán, he's a different matter. Needs me over there to speak up for him. Talk to Tóla for him. Can't say I'm looking forward to it, but I'll do it. No choice. Anyway, it's time someone stood up to that man. He's a bully.

"Not that way!" Bardán's sharp, calling me onto what looks like a tricky path, narrow and wandering.

"You sure?"

"Keep your eyes open," Bardán says. "Look there, see? Forbidden. Go down that way and you might wander forever."

I look where he's looking. Between two trees there's a silvery mesh of spiderweb. All right, I might not want to walk straight into that, but *forbidden*'s a strong word. Then I spot something. Half-hidden in the shadows beneath the web, there's a big knot, tricky sort of thing, woven from long grass. If that's not the work of little fey fingers, I'm a clurichaun. Seen that sort of craft before, the tiny baskets they carry, every bit just so. "The fey," I say, glancing at Bardán. "A warning."

"Eyes open," he says again. "Won't let them trick me twice over. Never going to that place again."

Asking seems like opening a box of trouble. But then, I have to deal with Tóla for him. "Was that what happened when you went there?" I try to sound as if I don't care much one way or the other. "You missed a warning sign?"

"Hah!" It's halfway between a cough and a laugh, bitter as gall. "No time to look, no time for signs, no time for anything. Running, running. Falling. Down, down . . . Gone . . ."

"What were you running from, Bardán?" I say it quiet. Gentle. If he doesn't want to say, I won't push him.

No answer from the wild man. He walks on, and I walk on, and the shadows get longer. Looks like I'm going to be sleeping the night at Wolf Glen. Hope Gormán will give me a spot in the foresters' quarters. Hope Blackthorn's going to be all right at Longwater. Chances are I won't see her now until tomorrow night.

"Tell me," says Bardán, still walking.

"Tell you what?" Thought it was me who'd asked a question.

"The story. The Red Giant. What happens next?"

Morrigan's curse! Where did that come from? "Can't remember where we got to," I say, though I can, even though it's a while since I started telling him the tale. Fact is, I don't want to tell him the rest. The story's too sad.

"Tell it, Grim."

"Where were we up to, then?" With luck he won't remember.

"The shepherd. Dougal. Nearly sunset. Guessing all the things that might be the Red Giant's most precious possession. If he didn't guess in time, he'd be thrown off the cliff. If he did guess, he'd get the treasure and take it home and marry the beautiful fey woman."

He's remembered every little thing. "It's a sad story," I say. "A sad, sad story."

"Tell me!" Sounds like he's going to leap up and throttle me if I don't. Sounds like he's so desperate to hear it, he might do anything.

"It's only a tale."

I hear him sucking in a big breath. Maybe not going to kill me after all. Not that he could. But he might do a bit of damage. "Grim, tell me."

"Sun was just about down, sky had that sort of smudgy look," I say, wishing he hadn't pushed me into this. Wondering if I should change the end of the story. But that would feel wrong. A kind of insult, as if he was a child, too young to hear the truth. "Dougal was nearly out of time. Wondering if he could bolt for it before the giant pushed him off the cliff. Once he was on the narrow path down, the sheep track, he should be safe. Getting there was the tricky bit.

"'Well?' bellowed the Red Giant. 'Run out of answers, have you?'

"Then came a little sound from inside the giant's cave, like a whimper or a wail, not much of a thing at all, but Dougal heard it. 'A baby,' he said without thinking. 'Of course, the most precious thing is a baby.' Then, a bit too late, he did think. Started to get an idea of what this would mean, for him, for the beautiful fey woman, and most of all for the Red Giant. 'Listen,' he began. But the Red Giant wasn't listening. He'd gone into the cave and now he came out with his face all blotched with tears and his baby in his arms. A giant baby, of course. No tidy wee bundle, but a big, bulky thing the size of a full-grown sheep. Wailing its head off. 'Listen,' said Dougal again, 'I—'

"He was going to say, *I can't take your child. Forget the whole thing.* But, with a great sob, the giant laid the child down gently at the shepherd's feet. 'Oh, my wee one,' he murmured. 'Oh, my heart's dearie.' Then he turned and took two great strides forward, and before Dougal could get another word out, the Red Giant leaped off the clifftop. Like thunder, the noise of it was. Rocks crashed down all about him. In far-off places, folk remarked, *That must be quite a storm.* The sound of his landing was terrible to hear. 'Oh gods,' muttered Dougal. 'What have I done?'

"The giant baby screamed and sobbed and hiccupped. Nobody left to tend to it. Only Dougal. So he picked it up—no trouble for him; he'd been hefting injured animals for years—and found a way down the cliff path, holding the infant's face against his shoulder. Didn't want it to catch sight of its father's broken body down below. The cliff path wasn't easy. Chunks and splinters of rock everywhere, broken off by the terrible fall. The giant baby thrashed about, beating at Dougal with its hands. Dougal's heart was heavy. The kindest and fairest bride in all the world wasn't worth a loss like this. The person who'd laid this charm or spell on the Red Giant had been cruel. Bitter cruel."

Bardán stops in his tracks, so sudden I nearly walk into him.

"Cruel," he mutters. "Oh, cruel . . . Once they stole, twice they stole . . . His heart was broken, torn to shreds . . . How could a man live after such a blow? So he ran, and he fell, down, down . . ."

He's back in the past. Got this mixed up with his own story somehow. "There's a bit more," I say. "Want me to tell the end?"

He walks on, silent now.

Seems best to finish the tale. The ending can't make up for the terrible wrong. You can't undo a thing like that. But it puts some goodness back into the story. "Dougal took the giant baby home. The beautiful fey woman took one look at it and shrank back in disgust. '*That* is the Red Giant's treasure?' she said, eyeing the red-faced, bawling infant. 'My treasure now,' said Dougal. He thought about the curse laid on the Red Giant, binding him to give his child away to the first man who guessed the nature of the prize. His reward for taking the baby was the hand in marriage of this lovely, mysterious lady. A bride more beautiful and noble than a poor, simple shepherd was ever likely to find. 'It's all right,' he told the lady. 'You don't have to marry me. I'd be too busy, with the baby and all, to give you the time you deserved. So I release you from the spell. If that's what it was.'

"The lady took herself off straightaway. And Dougal? He'd always been a good shepherd, and he kept on being one, looking after his flocks, earning a living, keeping himself to himself. Only he wasn't alone anymore. He had his baby to look after. When the boy was small, Dougal cooked his supper and sang him lullabies and told him the names of all the sheep. He made the lad a sheepskin coat and wooly slippers. When the giant boy was older, and as tall as Dougal, they tended the sheep together. The giant boy grew tall enough to mend the roof without a ladder. He grew tall enough to pick the fruit from the highest boughs of the apple tree. He grew so tall that he and Dougal had to build a bigger house. Local folk were wary of the boy. Thing was, though, it was handy having such a big lad living among them. He scared away thieves and raiders and bad folk of all kinds. Even the wolves were afraid of him. Which was odd, since he was a gentle soul, the kind of boy who'd move a beetle or spider from the path so it didn't get stepped on.

"When the giant boy was sixteen years old and Dougal was getting a few gray hairs, the shepherd told his big son the truth. About the lad's real father, the curse, the terrible thing Dougal had made happen because he had wanted a lovely fey bride. The two of them went to the cliff to see the place where the Red Giant had fallen in a great shower of stones, and they wept there together. The mound was green now. Blanket of mosses and creepers and little flowering things had grown up to cover it. Dougal said a prayer. He said how sorry he was, and he told the Red Giant he'd done his best to be a good father. He said he knew he could never be as good as his son's real father, his first father, the one who'd loved him more than life itself. He said that never a day passed when he didn't think about what he'd done and wish that he hadn't done it. Though, he said, from that sorrow he'd got the best son in all Erin. The giant boy patted Dougal on the shoulder, and picked him up for a hug, and said he forgave him. Then they walked home together. But after that, most days, the giant boy came to his father's grave to sit awhile and talk to him, to tell him about the sheep and the weather and what was going on in the village. Or he would sit there without a word, knowing how lucky he'd been to have two fathers who loved him more than anything in the world." I glance at Bardán. "And that's the end of the story."

Bardán's not talking. Looks like he's in some kind of trance. Walking on, staring straight ahead, face like a mask.

"You all right?"

Nothing. I can't think what to say, so I walk after him, wondering if he's going to explode, let it all out at once, whatever it is he's got trapped in his head. Know that feeling well, things building up, getting bigger and bigger until your mind can't hold them anymore. "You can talk to me," I say. "If you want. Anytime you want. But you know that already."

"Build," Bardán says, and his voice is all cracked and choked like it was when he first came out of the forest. "Build the house. Heartwood house . . ."

"Won't be doing much building today," I say, wondering why he'd bring this up now. Talking to him's like working on a puzzle. Sometimes he talks like everyone else, makes quite a long speech. Sometimes it's a word here, a word there, and a lot of silence. Only it feels like there's words in the silence, strong ones. "Be too dark by the time we get there."

"Tomorrow," says Bardán. "Dry day. Build."

Can't even think about building. Fact is, I'm tired. Got to walk the rest of the way to Tóla's. Then find the master and get him to listen. Tell him what's happened; tell him a few things he should be more interested in. He's ready enough with his bags of silver. Seems willing to pay a lot to get things just the way he wants. Been thinking about that more than I really want to, some idea niggling away at me, can't quite catch it. Wish Blackthorn was here with me. She'd know what it was. Good at puzzles, Blackthorn. Clever. Hope she's all right down there. Hope that woman, Fann, is doing well. And the baby. Danu's mercy, why did I let Bardán make me tell that story? Didn't only make him sad; made me sad too. Fact is, I want to go home. I want out of all this. I'd like to be sitting in the cottage, her and me and Ripple, who's padding along beside me all wet and tired. I'd like to feel the hearth fire and hear the kettle bubbling and see Blackthorn smiling over some silly joke. Ripple snoring by the fire, full belly, resting safe. Wonder if Bardán's life was like that for a bit, in that hut in the woods. Him and his wife. Little garden outside. House cozy and clean, those embroidered cloths hanging on the walls, maybe a jug with flowers, maybe a dog of their own. Good craftsman, back then, he must have been. He would have had enough work to keep them well, even if folk did think he was odd. Then he lost them. That would be a thing you'd never get over. Never. You'd want to die. Like the Red Giant. Only . . . that's what happened to Blackthorn. And she didn't choose to go that way.

"Grim?"

I jump. Been in another place for a bit, didn't expect Bardán to speak. "Mm?"

"You all right?"

"I'm all right, friend. Bit worried about Blackthorn, that's all. She had a long day. Would have liked to be there tonight, make sure she gets a rest, keep her company. She'll be fine without me. I know that. But still."

A silence. Then he says, "Lucky. Blackthorn, she's lucky. To have such a friend."

I can't help smiling at that. "Nah," I tell him. "I'm the one who's lucky. I'd be dead if not for her. I'd be rubbish, like I was before. I'd be nothing. I was broken all to pieces and she put me back together."

"You love her." Not asking, telling.

I'm opening my mouth to say it's not like that with her and me, never has been. We're friends—that's all. But I don't say it, because I'm thinking of those words she wrote for me, and the ones I wrote for her. She wrote, *Love in his heart*. Could mean love of all things, the love Jesus talks about in the scriptures. Could mean the love a man feels for a woman. Or something even deeper and bigger, that's got both kinds of love in it. She knows. She knows about true love's tears and what broke the curse, when she was turned into a monster and I held her and cried over her and said I'd stay by her for two hundred years if that was what it took. "She's got things to do before she can think about all that," I say instead. "A mission. Something I can't talk about."

"That's wrongheaded," says Bardán. "Hold fast to family. It's the most precious thing in the world. Wife, husband, child. Lose that and you're broken all over again. Smashed to pieces, like the Red Giant. This time, no mending. Only . . ."

"Only what?" Now I'm wishing even harder that I'd stayed in Longwater. The wild man's set my belly churning with worries.

But Bardán only shakes his head. Mutters something to himself, something not meant for my ears. We walk on. Light's fading fast. I'm wondering if we'll get there before it's dark. Birds are flying back into the shelter of the woods, chirrups and coos and twitters all around. Then we come out onto the main track again, and ahead of us are the barn and the outbuildings and a bit farther off Master Tóla's great house and the double row of beeches. Lights. A lot of lights. Folk moving around, saddling horses, setting flaming torches in sockets against the walls. Something happening, something big. Every worker Tóla's got must be out there.

Ripple stays by me, tired out but watching for danger. Bardán keeps behind us, which is what I've told him to do. Want to make sure I talk to Tóla before he does. Got my words worked out—just need to stick to them and not get angry. Not let the red rise up and get the better of me. Calm. Capable. Pretend I'm somebody else. Conmael, for instance. That would make me smile if I wasn't so jittery about the whole thing.

"Why don't you slip back to your quarters?" I whisper to Bardán. With all this going on, whatever it is, he's got a chance of getting there without being seen.

"What about you?"

"I'm going to have a word with Master Tóla," I tell him. It's looking like that plan might not be so easy to put into action. Didn't expect the whole place to be full of folk milling about. Something's happened. Can't think what. "You head off to your quarters and lie low. I'll do your explaining for you."

But there's no time for that. Two fellows come running up to us and after them comes Gormán. Before I can say a word the two grab hold of Bardán, one on each side. And now here's Master Tóla in his good clothes, looking white as a sheet, striding up toward us. Got a look on his face like his worst nightmare's just popped up in front of him.

"You!" he shouts, sounding like he could kill. It's not me he's heading for; it's Bardán. Who can't move because those two fellows are holding him tight.

I step forward, into Tóla's path. Need to stay calm. The fellows who are holding Bardán aren't thugs—they're a couple of Tóla's farmworkers, both known to me. "No reason to lay hands on him," I say, looking at the master, who glares back at me. "He's come back of his own accord. Can't a man have a day off when it rains?"

Tóla ignores me. "You!" he barks again, stepping sideways so he can see Bardán. "Where have you been? What have you done?"

Bardán makes a hissing sound. Turns my blood cold, it's so full of hate. Tóla steps past me, too quick, takes hold of the wild man's shoulders and shakes him hard. I'm a hairbreadth from grabbing the master and doing a bit of my own damage. But I don't. Lay hands on him and I'll get myself thrown off the place or worse. And then Bardán will be all on his own.

"No need for violence, Master Tóla," I say. "Bardán here's done nothing you or me or Gormán wouldn't do on a day off. Most of the time he's been with me."

It's like Tóla suddenly sees me. "Why are you here? Explain what you're doing on my property at night! Why are you in company with him?"

Gormán clears his throat.

Tóla speaks again, not so loud. But wound up tight; something's happened, something more than Bardán wandering off without permission. "Over here," he says, and takes my arm, moving me away from Bardán and his keepers. Drops his voice quieter. "My daughter is missing. Fifteen years old and out there somewhere on her own. Gone from Winterfalls since morning. And he's been unaccounted for all day." Meaning Bardán, though why he'd have anything to do with a missing girl, I can't imagine. "All day," Tóla goes on. "All day it's taken them to get a message to me, curse them. You say he's been with you. You know the rules. You know he's not to leave the place."

The man's beside himself with worry. I don't like Master Tóla, never have. But right now I feel sorry for him.

"I can tell you everything I did all day," I say. "Starting with what I ate for breakfast. Or I can help you look for the girl. Help you organize a search. Either way, time's passing."

"What about *him*?" Tóla snaps. Bardán's still standing there with those two holding him. Chances are he can hear every word, even though the master moved me away.

"He means no harm," I say. "Take him over to the barn, find him a safe spot, keep a watch on him if that's the way you want it. But don't hurt him. He's got nothing to tell you about a missing girl. I give you my word. I've been with him most of the day."

Gormán's talking to the two fellows, pointing over to the barn, getting ready to move the wild man.

"Grim!" Bardán's voice is more like its old self. He sounds scared. "No!"

"Go easy on him, will you?" I say to Gormán. "He needs kindness, not a beating." I look over at the wild man. "I'll come and see you when I'm done here," I tell him. "Promise."

Gormán jerks his head toward the barn and the two fellows take Bardán away. Then it's just the three of us standing there, Gormán, Tóla and me in the dark, with folk still busy all around the place, lights flickering in the rain, though it's slackened off now. Good thing. It's not going to be a comfortable bed tonight. It's going to be a long, cold search in the woods. This girl was unhappy at Winterfalls, wasn't she? That's what Blackthorn said. Missed the forest here at Wolf Glen, wanted to come home. Loved trees. And birds; birds came and perched on her, all different ones together, like magic. Wish I'd seen that. But the girl was never at the cottage same time as me. Never saw her in the flesh.

"Your daughter who's missing," I say to the master. "You mean Cara? The girl who was staying at Winterfalls?"

It's like a jolt goes through Tóla's body. "How do you know my daughter's name?" he roars.

Morrigan's britches, this man makes things hard for himself. "Can't help knowing it," I say. "Young Cara's been visiting Blackthorn most days. That's Mistress Blackthorn the healer, who shares a cottage with me. Cara's happier there than at the prince's house. That's what Blackthorn tells me."

"You were ordered not to gossip. Not to talk about your work here."

Lots of things I could say. *While you're ranting about this, your daughter's still out there somewhere*, or, *No wonder Cara ran away, with you for a father.* Or, *If you'd bothered to visit the girl even once, you'd have known she wasn't happy.* "But Blackthorn wasn't ordered to keep quiet about who might have dropped in to see her," I say. "Lady Flidais suggested Cara went over there. Thought it would be good for the girl, seeing as she was unsettled."

Tóla's on the brink of another outburst.

"I'll help you search," I say. "My guess is she'd be trying to get home. She did that once already, only Blackthorn stopped her."

"How—never mind. The messenger said she might have been missing since this morning. Even with the rain, even on foot, she would have been here by now."

"If she stuck to the main path, yes," put in Gormán. "But Cara wouldn't do that. She'd be wanting to get here without anyone seeing her. Not wanting to be stopped."

"Gods!" says Tóla. "She could be anywhere! How could they just let her wander off? A royal household with so many guards? It's beyond belief! I thought she would be safe there."

Gormán makes a little sound, but does not speak.

"Would have been busy this morning," I say. "The prince and his lady were heading off to court. A council, called at short notice. Would have been a good time to slip away quietly."

"Cara is wood-wise," Gormán says. "Swift as a wild creature. Adept at hiding. Master Tóla, if anyone could find a way safely through the forest, she could."

A man comes up, one of the household retainers, with a pack on his back and a staff in his hand. "Master Tóla, we're almost ready. Just waiting for your instructions."

"Get everyone together in the stable yard. I'll be there shortly."

"Yes, Master Tóla."

He's got hold of himself now. Working hard to stay calm. "You still haven't answered my questions," he says, tight-jawed. "Where was Bardán? Why did the two of you come back together? You said he couldn't be involved. How do you know that? Have you been with him all day, every moment? Why aren't you down in Winterfalls?"

Keep calm, Grim. "Thought I would be in Winterfalls. Too wet to work; day off." I told him, clear as I could: the woman in labor in Longwater, the herbs, running into Bardán at his old house, walking back with him when it was all over. "There's a whole lot of folk can vouch for me being at Longwater most of the day, and I can vouch for Bardán. Listen. If you need me to help search, I'm happy to do it. Only I want you to treat him fair. He's not bad—he's only addled in the wits. Needed time to think about his family, shed a few tears. No harm done. Treat him well, he'll work better for you. Find him a warm spot to sleep, better cover, a good meal or two. A kind word."

"It's not for you to instruct me in the accommodation of workers," Tóla snaps. "You're in my employ the same as they are."

"Not quite the same," I say, holding on to my temper. "Don't think you're paying Bardán, are you? And I'm here by choice, making myself useful. If I decide I don't like the conditions, mine or anyone else's, I'll take my tools and my services somewhere else. I'll hand back your silver, all but what I've earned already with my labor. If you want me building your heartwood house, you look after the workers a bit better."

They're both gaping at me. Think I might have said a bit too much. Meanwhile, there's this girl, and it's dark. Tóla's right about one thing: it would have been good if the folks at Winterfalls hadn't taken all day to let him know she was gone.

"Best time to talk about this is after," I say. "After we've found your daughter. You'll be worried half out of your mind. Sounds like your men are waiting for orders."

"You can help, yes. We need every man we can get," Tóla says. "But I'm not finished with you. It sounds like Bardán's not the only one who's been breaking rules. Talking out of turn. I don't want the whole district knowing my business. I made that very clear indeed."

"Master Tóla," says Gormán. "Grim's right—they're waiting. From what he said, he's only talked to this Blackthorn. And it sounds as if she's been a friend to Cara."

The way Gormán talks about the girl, you can tell he's fond of her. As if she were his own daughter, almost. And Tóla listens to him more than he listens to other folk. "Very well," says the master. Notices Ripple, who's been sitting quietly, waiting. "Can your dog track?" he asks.

"Not sure how she'd go in the dark." I don't tell him Ripple's only been with me since last summer. Or that she was trained by someone else. "Have to take her on a long rope or risk losing her."

"Get him a rope, Gormán."

Everyone's gathered by the barn. Tóla raps out instructions. There's a search on at Winterfalls too, since that's where Cara must have started off. But the messenger that brought the news thought she'd be trying to walk home, and that's what Tóla thinks too. Must be feeling guilty. You would, wouldn't you? Blackthorn said he hadn't gone down to see her even once.

The master sends four men off along the track toward Longwater. Four more down the track toward Winterfalls. Three to check the area to the south, but not to go too deep into the forest.

"And you," he says last, looking at me and Ripple, "see if the dog can pick up a scent. Della!"

I haven't noticed Mistress Della standing there quietly in the shadows, but now she comes forward with a garment, perhaps a shift, and passes it to me. I bend down and let Ripple have a sniff. Can't tell if the dog knows what it's all about or not. "Might start down on the Winterfalls side," I say. "Only not on the main track, if what Gormán said before is right. Sounds like Cara would stay off paths where she might meet folk." I look at Mistress Della. "Might be best if I take this with me." She nods, and I tuck the shift or whatever it is into my belt.

"Gormán will go with you," says Tóla. "My sister and I will stay here and wait for news. Cara may somehow make her way home without encountering any of the searchers. I want to be here if . . . Keep your lights burning and go carefully once you're off the main paths."

I want to ask about Bardán, where they've put him, whether he's somewhere warm and comfortable, but I can't. Gormán brings back a coil of rope. He hands it to me and I tie one end to Ripple's collar. He fetches a lantern, the kind that burns oil. Be safer than the torches some of the fellows are carrying; I don't fancy walking in among the trees with one of those. It's dark as dark now. Moonlight hasn't got a hope of breaking through those clouds. At least the rain's stopped. For now. I think of the girl out there somewhere. Wood-wise this Cara may be, but it's no night for anyone to be on their own in the forest. Chilly enough to freeze your bones.

"We'll have hot soup ready when you get back," says Mistress Della. Sounds as if she's been crying. "Go safe, all of you."

We're off, then, Gormán and me and Ripple. For the first bit we walk with the fellows who are checking the main Winterfalls track, the way I'd ride if I was going home. After a while we part company. The other men go on in the direction of the settlement, and Gormán and I head off along a side way, snaking into the woods.

"You know the girl," I say. "If she wanted to get home quick but not be spotted, which way would she choose? What paths does she know?" Seems to me that on such a wet day, Cara wouldn't have wanted to be dawdling in the woods admiring the scenery.

"Cara knows all the paths," Gormán says. "She knows her way to every corner of Wolf Glen. She's never been lost, not even once." He speaks proudly; I'm guessing he was the one who taught her to find her way. "She must have had an accident," he says. "Hurt herself. Or had some other mishap." He doesn't say she might have fallen victim to some evil bastard, and I don't either. No need to put it into words. Every man who's out looking for the girl must have that in the back of his mind. "Or she didn't head up here at all. Could she be at your house? Would your friend be back there by now?"

"Our house would be one of the first places the folk from Winterfalls looked. Seeing as Cara goes over to visit Blackthorn most days. Place will be empty. Blackthorn's staying the night in Longwater, and I'm here." What do I know about Cara? She's different. Doesn't talk much. Likes birds. Knows trees. Clever with her hands. I've seen the little creatures she's been making. She keeps them on a shelf in our cottage, alongside the ones I've made. Chooses one to take back to the prince's house every night, like it's to keep her company. Brings it back next morning and puts it on the shelf with the others. Still a bit of a child, even if she is a young lady of fifteen.

We head on along the track, such as it is. It's slow. Ground's boggy, lantern light stops us from breaking our legs but not much more. All feeling like a waste of time and effort. Me, I'm trying not to think of Cara lying out there cold and dead under the trees, or drowned in a flooded stream, or worse. We walk on and on, slogging through the mud, hauling ourselves up a few steep rises, losing the path and finding it again. I'm thinking how long it is since Ripple was fed.

"Go carefully around here," Gormán says. "Hidden dips, hollows, some of them deep. Easy to fall."

Straightaway I'm remembering the wild man, lost in his nightmare. *Running, running. Falling. Down, down . . . Gone . . .*

"Got something to ask you."

"Go on, then."

"Bardán. Saw him at his old house today. Weeping over his family, over their graves. Seems like he had a good life once. An ordinary life. But he's broken now. Not right in the head. I know he went away. When he was building the house the first time. I know he was away years."

"Master Tóla doesn't make rules for no reason," Gormán says. "Careful there, the bank's crumbling. Step a bit to the right. Use the rocks."

I don't like the idea that's come into my head, don't like it at all. "Bardán talked a bit about that time, when he ran away. That time when he disappeared with the house half built. Don't think he meant to tell. It just came spilling out. Said he was running. Then falling." I make myself take a slow breath, not easy when I'm stumbling over rocks and slipping in the mud, trying to keep up with Ripple, who's pulling on the rope now.

"Mm-hm," says Gormán.

"You know how folk don't like the track up here, the one from Winterfalls. You'll have heard the tales they tell about the place. Wondering if . . . wondering if there might be a . . . portal. An entry. Could be in the ground, down deep."

Gormán's quiet a good while. I know he knows what I mean. But when he speaks he says, "A portal to where?"

"Somewhere a man might learn how to make a heartwood house."

"His father taught him." Gormán answers quick, like he hasn't taken time to think. Like he's had this answer all ready for when someone asked. Then he does think, and he stops walking like he's been hit. "You're saying—"

"I'm saying if there's someplace where folk can fall a long way, so far they're out of one world and into another, that's a place where we should be looking. Finding Cara's more important than keeping Master Tóla's secrets. Even he'd say that. Wouldn't he?"

Light from the lantern's not good, wavering, flickering. Hope the oil doesn't run out. But I can see Gormán's gone white. "There is a place," he says. "Whether I can find it in the dark, I don't know. Surely she wouldn't . . . Cara knows to stay away from the signs. She understands . . ." He's said more than he wanted to already. Told me something he didn't mean to. "I think your dog's picked up a scent," he says.

Looks like she has. Pulling on the rope, trying to haul me down the hill. No way to know if it's Cara's scent or some creature Ripple wants for her supper.

"Follow her," Gormán says. "But take care. Morrigan's curse, I don't know if I want you to be right or wrong. I just pray she's safe. If he loses her too, he'll go out of his mind."

I let Ripple lead the way down a steep bank. Gormán follows. If Cara's come to grief, Tóla's going to blame Bardán, same as he did when his wife died. He's going to say it's the wild man's fault for being slow with the build and not getting the heartwood house finished. Mine too, probably, since I'm the one doing the work. He'll shut out anything that doesn't fit the theory. Like him refusing to get a crew in to do the work quicker. He'll blame anyone except himself. That man's full up with hate. Could be that hate comes from being afraid. Not afraid of Bardán so much, but afraid of bad things happening. Misfortune, like his wife dying while Cara was still a baby. One thing I know, and it makes my belly churn. If his daughter dies, Tóla will lay the blame squarely on us.

20

It was a long, long fall. Time enough for her to think, *When I land I'll die.* And a bit later, *If the landing doesn't kill me, I'll be so broken I'll die anyway.* And then, *Why is it so far? No cave is as deep as this.* And at the end, *It's not a cave. It's—*

She was down. Sore, but not broken. In the dark, on her own. In her mind Aunt Della was saying, *Girls who insist on ignoring perfectly sensible rules are sure to find themselves in trouble.* And her father . . . her father would be beside himself with worry. Even if this was his fault, at least partly. If he hadn't sent her away, if he hadn't left her at Winterfalls and never come to visit, if he hadn't refused to explain . . . But she was the one who'd run off without telling anyone. She was the one who hadn't been prepared to wait.

And now here she was, in some shadowy place deep underground, too far down to climb out of, too dark to make a way through, and nobody knew where she was, nobody at all. Not even Blackthorn. Who was ever going to think of looking for her here? She had nothing useful with her except a small, sharp knife. She was hardly going to cut foot- and handholds in the solid rock, then climb out of what had felt like the deepest well in the whole world.

"This way," someone said in the darkness, making her heart leap in fright. "Warm fire, pretty lights, a feast just for you. Friends, music, dancing."

Cara made herself still. She made herself as still as a frozen pond; as still as a caterpillar in a cocoon, waiting for its moment of transformation; as still as the deep roots of an oak. *Don't hear me,* she willed whoever it was. *Don't hear me breathing.*

The voice came again. "Cold out there. And getting colder. Damp. Long walk. Rest weary feet."

There were tales. Gormán told them sometimes. And Mistress Blackthorn told them. There were those stories Prince Oran and Lady Flidais read after supper, full of all kinds of oddities, including fey folk of different sizes and shapes. Some were dangerous, monstrous, giants or trolls or dragons. Some were little and friendly, needing nothing more than that bowl of milk and crust of bread on the back step. But all of them were tricky. And someone who lived so deep underground that the place couldn't be a cave was surely dangerous. Even if that someone had a sweet voice and a nice manner about him. Or her. She couldn't guess which.

"Don't be shy, Bird Girl," it said now, coaxing. "We're friendly folk. And you're not exactly rich in friends, are you? Come through here where it's warm and safe, and you'll have companions enough to last you a lifetime. Aren't you hungry? Thirsty? Tired out and a little sad? Let us look after you."

There was one story about a girl who went out in the woods and met a fey being, a wispy thing with gossamer wings, and the being offered the girl a tiny cake with a flower on top. She took only one bite. That bite meant the girl could never, ever go back to the human world. She could never see her family again, her mother, her father, her little brothers. She had to stay in the Otherworld for the rest of her life. Cara kept her mouth firmly shut. In the darkness of underground, she could feel the thunderous beat of her own heart.

She was hungry; far hungrier than she should have been, considering she had only walked part of the way to Wolf Glen before she made the mistake with that hole in the rocks or whatever it was. But she had drunk from streams along the way and she had a full water skin slung over her shoulder. Odd that the skin had not split open when she fell. But then, she had landed softly, even though the ground beneath her feet was hard-packed earth.

"Cara!" The way it called her name was like music, almost. Like the chime of a strange bell. "Oh, Cara!" Then a peal of laughter, as if this were some kind of game, no more than an amusement.

You won't make me move, she thought. *You won't make me speak. I'll wait you out.* How long would it be before anyone realized she was missing? How long before anyone started looking? How long could she stand in one spot, in utter darkness, without growing faint? If she so much as reached for the water skin, they'd come rushing in. She knew it, and she'd never, ever be able to go home to Wolf Glen.

Odd, how soon she lost a sense of time passing. The voice kept on, wheedling, coaxing, cajoling. She held her silence. Her back was aching. Had she stood here for an hour, two hours? Or was time playing cruel tricks? Her nose itched, but she dared not lift a hand to touch it. Her mouth was so dry; she was longing for a drink. And as if it knew exactly what was in her mind, the voice whispered, "Fresh water in a little shining jug. Clear as a mountain stream. Wouldn't you like some? And fruit such as you've never seen in your whole life, round and red and full of sweet juices. Crisp to the teeth, delicious on the tongue. Cheeses, oh, such cheeses, golden and salty and flavorsome! Soft wheaten bread to eat them with. Such a meal, and all ready for you, Bird Girl. Why would you stand there in the dark, muzzy head, aching body, thirsty mouth, empty belly? Why, oh why? Who will come for you? Who will find you? How will you call for help? You have no voice."

Stop it. Just stop it. What would Mistress Blackthorn do? To start with, Blackthorn would never be in this situation; she was much too sensible. She wouldn't rush off on a whim and not tell anybody where she was going. But if this did happen to her, Blackthorn would know what to do now. Cara tried to think what the wise woman might suggest. She hadn't talked about the fey much, apart from telling those old tales. But Cara had heard her and Emer talking about magic, not the fey kind, changing people into animals or appearing in a puff of smoke, but what Blackthorn called natural magic, which was something to do with using what was already there. Cara had liked the sound of that. Knowing rain was near, for instance, and using the right words to make it come sooner or hold off until later. Making the fire on the hearth flare up suddenly or setting the candles flickering if you needed a distraction. That sort of thing. She probably hadn't been meant to hear that; it had sounded like secret wise woman learning. But she'd been sitting on the front steps working on her squirrel carving, and they had probably forgotten her.

So, use what was already here. All very well if she could see anything at all. Not impossible even in total darkness, provided she could move around and feel things. But if twitching a muscle or whispering a word might give her away, what was she supposed to do? *Stand still,* she told herself. *Breathe. Wait. The answer will come.*

"I know a secret," chimed the little voice, sing-song, teasing. "I bet you can't guess it."

Cara stood quiet. This was nonsense. She'd be a fool if she let it trouble her. *Be still. Wait.*

"I know a secret. It's about your father."

Stop it. Be quiet. She moved, then; stuck her fingers in her ears. Her arms hurt when she lifted them. And she needed to piss, but there was no privy down here. Imagine being rescued with your skirt all wet and smelly. Imagine being taken to the Otherworld like that; think of the mockery.

"I know a secret. I know what he's building!" the little voice announced.

Tell me. Tell me now. Cara clenched her teeth. Even with her ears stopped she could hear the taunting voice. No friend at all. The kindly words, the promises of comfort were lies. She had to find a way out.

"Your father's a liar, a liar, a liar! And you're a pretender, pretender, pretender!" It had become a song.

Tears came to Cara's eyes. This wasn't fair. It was cruel. Her father was a good man. Even if he was sometimes strict, even if he made her do things she didn't want to do, he loved her and wanted the best for her. He never acted without good reason. Of course he wasn't a liar.

"Your whole life is a lie, Cara. It was a lie from the moment you were born."

Cara's heart went cold. This was a different voice, fey like the other, but much deeper and far, far more frightening. It scared her so much that words came out despite her best efforts. "Don't say that! You don't know anything!" It was a whisper; for the space of a breath she hoped the owner of that voice had not heard.

"I speak the truth." If a wolf could speak in words, its voice would be like this: dark, wild, full of trickery. "Ask your father why he is building his heartwood house again. Ask him why he needs protection. Who is the enemy? Who is the threat? Or does the danger come from within?"

"You're talking in riddles," Cara whispered, unable to let this pass. "First you try to tempt me with promises; then you accuse my father. What do you want?"

"Ah." The tone changed again, softening, sweetening. "Only for you to take a step, and another, and a third. Only for you to look in the mirror. Only for you to be where you belong, Bird Girl." This voice was pure honey; it was the loveliest song of a lark high in the sky; it was the softness of down on the breast of a dove. It was sunlight and rippling water and the sigh of wind in the leaves. A person would need a heart of stone to resist such a voice.

Blackthorn. Remember what Blackthorn said. Use what is already there. But what was here, far underground? Earth. Rock. Little blind things that lived in the dark. Spiders, crawling insects. Creatures that lived among deep roots. Ah! Maybe there was help here after all.

She moved, stretching out her arms. Voices came suddenly, closer than before; there was a note of greedy anticipation in them that terrified her. She took four paces away from where they seemed to be and her hands encountered a rough stone wall. She edged along it sideways. Opened her mind to the deep, slow voice of a tree. *Where are you?*

"Cara! Oh, Cara! This way, pretty one!" One of them was calling, the others giggling, whispering, moving about as if ready to reach out and grab her the moment she came close enough.

Where are you? One cautious step, two, three, and it was under her hand, tough, fibrous, as old as time—the root of an oak. Cara closed her fingers around it; rested her brow against it. Heard, sure and steady, the ancient voice within. *Be safe, Daughter. You are one of ours.*

And not long after there came another voice, not a tree voice sounding only in her mind, but a human voice, a man's, calling her name. "Cara! Cara, where are you?" Up the top. Up in her own world. A stranger's voice.

She shaped the words she wanted. *Here! I'm down here!* But when she tried to call, they would not come out. All she could manage was a whisper. "Help! I'm here! Help!"

"Cara! Are you down there somewhere?"

This voice she knew. Tears flooded her eyes. *Here! I'm down here!* Why wouldn't her voice work, even for Gormán? Had those fey folk put a fell charm on her even while she held the roots of the oak?

You are safe. Hold on. Wait, Daughter, only wait.

She waited, gripping the oak root, willing Gormán to know, somehow, that she was here.

"Cara!" That was the other man. And now there was a dog barking. Perhaps she had not fallen so very far after all.

"Here," she whispered. "I'm here." Oh, gods, what if they gave up and went away, all because she couldn't call like any normal person would be able to? What if they never came back?

A sudden clamor from up there. Birds, cawing, screaming, flapping about. With it, a startled shout. "Morrigan's britches!" After that she could hear them talking, Gormán and the other man, though she could not make out what they were saying.

"Cara!" Gormán called from the top. "Don't be afraid. One of us will climb down to you."

Relief flooded through her. They knew. They knew she was here.

But shouldn't there be light from up there, if they were close enough to call and be heard? Could it already be night? She heard the whisper of a rope snaking down until its end touched the earthen floor of the cavern. Her lifeline. One of the men would come down, and somehow they'd get her back up, maybe with the rope tied around her waist, and then—

"*Kraaa.*" The crow swooped down the shaft to land on her shoulder, sudden and heavy. A warning, clear and urgent. *Move. Now. Quick.* And another sound, a hissing, a muttering, a movement across the dark space. Whatever they were, they had lost patience. They were coming for her.

Cara let go of the oak root, turned, stumbled forward with arms outstretched, found and seized the rope. The crow flew upward, and as the cavern filled with strange sounds, growling, baying, scampering, whistling, she began to haul herself up after it. No time to think. No time to be afraid. Only breathe and climb. Hand over hand; leg twisted through the rope. Strange fingers reached up to rip at her skirt, to claw at her leg, to pull at her shoes. A sound of feet trampling the earthen floor, many feet. A smell of bodies crowded into the space, musky and choking. Their voices raised in a din of shouting, screeching, taunting. She hauled again, and now she was out of their reach. The crow screamed, for a moment drowning their mockery. Cara climbed.

From the top, now, came the calls of other birds; it sounded as if there was a whole flock of them waiting for her. It became lighter. Not daylight, but an unsteady flickering. Her arms were burning with effort. Every part of her hurt. But she was nearly there. Gormán's face was as white as a ghost's as he leaned over the opening.

"Careful, Gormán," Cara called, and her voice came out with no trouble this time, just like anyone else's. A bit breathless, that was all. "Step back from the edge."

Then she was close enough for him to reach her and help her up the last bit onto the level ground at the top. Her legs would hardly hold her. Her arms ached so much she couldn't bear to move them. Her palms felt as if they'd been scorched. The other man was saying, "Move right away from the drop. Out into the open." A big man. A very big man, with a gray dog beside him. He was undoing the rope, which had been tied around a massive stone. Coiling it neatly and putting it over his shoulder. "The plan was that we'd come down for you," he said mildly. "Didn't expect you to do all the work yourself."

Gormán drew her away, out into the clearing. The big man picked up the lantern and followed. The light caught his face, a plain, honest sort of face, looking surprised and smiling at the same time.

"Thank all the gods you're safe, Cara." Gormán's voice was shaking. Big, strong Gormán who had an answer to every problem. "Why didn't you call out and let us know you were there? If it hadn't been for those birds we might never have found you!"

It was nighttime. She must have been down there for hours and hours. Standing in the dark, not moving. No wonder she felt strange. Where were the birds now? The forest was quiet.

"Are you hurt? What happened?"

"Time enough for that later." The other man's voice was quiet, deep, calm. By his side stood the gray dog, as steadfast as its master.

"This is Grim," Gormán said. "There's quite a search on for you. A lot of folk out."

"Mistress Blackthorn's Grim," Cara said, thinking she would have known this without being told his name. Mistress Blackthorn didn't talk about her friend much, but she had said enough for it to be quite plain who this was. A tall, broad man, bigger than anyone else in the district. Kind. Strong. Calm. Good at whatever he did. A man with big hands, who'd made that delicate little hedgehog.

"That's me, and this is Ripple. Best get you home, mm?" He waited a moment, then said, "Good bit of climbing, that. Strong and steady. Well done."

His kindness brought tears to her eyes. "There were—there were things, folk—" No, she couldn't talk about what was down there, not even to Gormán. Not even to this man who was like Blackthorn, a person she knew straightaway was trustworthy. "I couldn't wait for you to come down."

"Home," said Gormán. "Your father is distraught, and there are people out looking for you all over the forest. Can you walk on your own?"

Silly question. Hadn't she just climbed that rope all by herself? "Of course," Cara said as her knees buckled under her and the forest turned to a swirling darkness and then to nothing.

21

Good result. Girl seems all right. No bones broken though she's worn herself out. Can't tell us what happened to her. Or doesn't want to. Not for me to ask anyway. This Cara, she's not a big girl like Emer—she's thin as a young willow. But strong. Can't believe she shinned up that rope so quick. That'd be quite a trick for anyone. Though Blackthorn did say the girl liked climbing trees. Sounds like there was something down there that gave her a fright. Can't help thinking of Bardán and how he fell down into the Otherworld and couldn't get back for years and years. Can't help wondering if it's the same spot. Oddest thing was those birds coming, all kinds together, just when we were going to give up and go looking somewhere else. And Gormán knowing straightaway why they were flying around screeching and flapping their wings in our faces. *She's down there*, he said. *Cara's down there*. And she was.

I carry Cara back toward the house. Gormán brings the lantern. Ripple's off the rope, padding along quietly beside us. When we get to the main track, Gormán calls out, "She's safe! We've got her!" in case any of the other searchers are close. Cara comes out of her faint when he yells, asks to be put on her feet. Goes off to relieve herself behind a tree. When she gets back we give her some water.

"They kept saying . . ." She sounds like she's only half with us, and half still down that hole. "They kept saying drink, eat, aren't you thirsty . . . promising all sorts of things . . . and they said . . ." Her voice fades away.

"Never mind that." Gormán sounds as if he doesn't want to know. If I was him, I'd be asking who said, and what did they say. Fey folk of some kind, I bet. Who else is going to be in a place like that? And if it's the same ones that made Bardán stay and work and ruin his hands, they're not the nice kind. Not like the wee folk of Bann at all, and not like Conmael either. Funny, I could wish that fellow was here right now so I could ask him about this. He'd know who they are and what they're up to. Not that he ever comes to talk to me. Or hardly ever. Blackthorn's the one he's interested in. I just happened to get saved when she did. In the right place at the right time, you might say. Though how Mathuin's lockup could be the right place for anything is hard to believe. Senseless cruelty's about it. Ruined men. Lost hope.

"Grim?"

Gormán's asked me something and I haven't heard a word. "What was that?"

"We should move on. Put Master Tóla out of his misery. Cara says she can walk."

She tries for a while, holding on to Gormán's arm, but she's soon tired. "Sorry," she says. "My legs feel like jelly."

I pick her up again. She's a lightweight, like Blackthorn. Taller, though. Not so easy to carry.

"Sorry," she says again.

"No trouble."

Pretty soon she falls asleep. Limp as a doll, head on my shoulder. Wonder when she fell down there, how long she was on her own in the dark. Or not on her own, but with something else there, whispering who knows what in her ear.

"She sleeping?" Gormán asks.

"Like a babe. Lucky escape."

"Listen," says Gormán, quiet-like. "Don't say anything about those birds. What they did. To Tóla, I mean. He's touchy about these things."

"What things?"

"Anything out of the common run. Anything folk might think was magical. Fey. Upsets him. Scares him."

"You're asking me to tell a lie."

"I'm asking you not to blurt out every little detail about what happened. Cara's safe. She's not hurt. She'll be home very soon. She'll tell him her own version of why she was wandering about in the woods. I'll tell him where we found her and how she got herself out when she heard us. I'll tell him it was thanks to you and your dog that we did find her, which is the truth. No need to say any more."

"Mm-hm." This is odd. It's all odd. "Won't Cara tell him about the birds anyway? And perhaps about whatever it was that was talking to her in the bottom of that hole that might be the same one Bardán fell down a long while ago?"

"Why would it be the same?" He's quick with this. Edgy. Talking the way Master Tóla talks. "What's Bardán been telling you?"

"Not a lot. Might be the same spot. Might not be. Why is it we're not telling the master all this?"

"Can't you just do as you're asked to, Grim?"

"I could. I could follow orders and never ask a single question. Only, I'm sorry for the wild man. You know I don't think he's being treated fair. And I'm going to have a word with the master about it. I've told him so. What if it's all linked up, Bardán falling into the Otherworld and getting trapped there and Cara nearly doing the same?"

"That's nonsense. Why would you think it was the same?"

"Didn't you hear? About someone down there talking to her, making promises, offering things? Sounds like someone wanting her to go right in, don't you think? Trap her the way they trapped Bardán."

"Shh, keep your voice down. You'll wake her. Grim, this is not your concern. Just do the job you came to do and forget about everything else, will you? There are good reasons for keeping Bardán away from other folk. There are good reasons for Tóla not wanting everyone in the district knowing the story. About the heartwood house, I mean. And there are good reasons for Cara staying at Winterfalls and not coming home until the building is done. A word of warning. Speak to Tóla about the wild man if you will. Argue for better conditions. But don't talk to the master about Cara, beyond saying you're glad we found her. She's his girl; his only child. He loves her above the rarest jewel in the world. His worst nightmare is some harm coming to her. He'd do just about anything to keep her safe. Do you understand?"

I think of Cara climbing up that rope. Are we talking about some completely different girl now? Besides, if Tóla loves his daughter so much, why is he making her stay at Winterfalls when she hates it there? Wouldn't he want her at home where he could see her every day? A man who's as ready as Tóla is with his bags of silver needn't worry about safety. He could hire a whole team of bodyguards for her. Wolf Glen might not be the easiest place to work, but there's folk will take any job if you pay them well enough.

"You must have known Cara as long as anyone," I say as the lights from Tóla's house come in sight. Torches burning, showing the way home. "Since the day she was born, I'm guessing."

"Not quite so long," Gormán says. "But since she was very small, yes. Cara wasn't born at Wolf Glen. Her mother went away to stay with kinsfolk. Took time to recover." He takes a look at the sleeping girl, cradled in my arms. "Cara was easy to love," he says, a smile in his voice. I'm thinking, not for the first time, that this would be a good sort of man, the kind anyone would want for a friend, if he wasn't—what, exactly? Something's holding that good man in check a lot of the time, stopping him from speaking out, binding him to Tóla's rules. "I can remember the look on her little face the day they came back here, her and Suanach," he says. "Took her first steps that day, trying to go after some chickens. Big, beaming smile, more gaps than teeth. Apple of everyone's eye. Still is."

"Sad that she lost her mother so early."

"It was, and for Master Tóla most of all. Another reason why he's touchy about his daughter's safety. Please watch what you say to him.

It's been good having you here, doing the work. Wouldn't want to have to find a replacement."

"That a threat?" I keep my tone light.

"A caution. Go lightly. If Cara wants to tell her father there were voices down in that hole, then I'm not going to stop her. But if she doesn't tell him, best that you don't say anything about that. What you heard her say, I mean. Tóla fears the uncanny above all things. He believes the heartwood house is the answer to those fears. If we hadn't found Cara . . . if she'd come to harm . . ."

"I've worked that out," I say. "You can be sure I won't blurt out anything that's going to get Bardán into any more trouble. If it gets me in trouble, so be it. I can handle it."

Cara starts to stir again, so the talk's over. Up ahead someone's spotted us, me with the girl in my arms. And someone must have run to tell the master, because before we get to his grand house, there he is, running toward us like any ordinary father who's just got his daughter back when he didn't know if he ever would. I put her down, she staggers into his arms, Tóla wraps her in a big hug. Tears running down his cheeks. Mistress Della's crying and laughing at the same time. Cara looks asleep on her feet. Nobody says much for a bit; then Tóla lets his daughter go and Mistress Della takes charge. Puts an arm around the girl and leads her away toward the house.

Tóla doesn't go with them. Turns to Gormán and me. "You found her, the two of you? Where was she? What happened?"

"Fell down a deep hole," I say, taking care with my words. "Not hurt, beyond a bruise or two. But she was stuck. No way out. Down there a while. Far off the nearest track. Ripple picked up the trail, led us to the spot. We called out, she called back. Let down a rope and she climbed up. All by herself. Tired out—who wouldn't be? But unharmed. That's about the size of it, Master Tóla."

Tóla glances at Gormán, who just nods. Doesn't say I got it wrong about Cara calling out, which was the only lie in my story. Sounds like she lost her voice for a bit. Something Blackthorn's told me happens to the girl quite often. Didn't think of it when we were searching.

"I owe the two of you a great debt," Tóla says. "And I thank you from the bottom of my heart. We're all weary. I'll speak with you again in the morning. Grim, you will stay here tonight, of course. Gormán, you'll find a spare bed for Grim in your quarters?"

"Plenty of room," says Gormán. Makes me wonder again why they don't put Bardán in there, if there's so much space. Wonder where they did end up putting him. All very well for Tóla to be full of thank yous now. I haven't forgotten he shook a man who was unarmed and held fast. Tomorrow I'll be asking a few questions. Asking for a few changes. And if Master Tóla doesn't like that, he can find himself a new builder.

22

Cold. Everything aching. Rope around his wrists, rope around his ankles. Why? What crime has he committed? The master's in charge here, in charge of every little thing. Except one. Except the heartwood house. He just needs to live long enough to get it done. He just needs to survive the cold and the damp and the blows. And the sadness. The cottage all crumbling away, the graves neglected, the lovely embroidered picture, the last one his mother ever made, worn away to rags and tatters. Gone, all gone. And . . . and . . . There is a sorrow harder than those. A sadness fit to wrench the very heart from a man's body. A grief deeper than the deepest grave, darker than the most shadowy corner of the forest. A loss beyond all others.

Did Tóla say something about a missing girl? Bardán remembers the day he came back to Wolf Glen; the day he looked at the ruin of the heartwood house and saw in his mind how he would build it again. The day he saw a girl up in the big oak. A girl who looked like someone he once knew, long ago. But when he asked, Tóla said, "There's no girl here."

"It was a lie," the wild man mutters to himself, struggling to move his aching limbs, wondering where Grim has gone. Grim, with his kind face and his sharp knife that could cut these bonds in an instant. "There was a girl. A baby girl. Where did she go?" Memory hits him, as cold as the winter sea, and on a sobbing breath he whispers, "Where is she? Where is my daughter?" But he's down deep again, in some dark cellar, and there's nobody to hear.

23

Wemhave our bowl of soup in the kitchen of the big house. Then head over to the barn to sleep. They're well set up there, Gormán and Conn: proper shelf beds, a good hearth, plenty of room. Enough beds for three more men, if they wanted to fit them in.

Conn's been out searching with one of the other teams, so he comes in with us. Fire's been banked up, just needs a stir and a log or two. Conn finds a water bowl for Ripple, who's got a meaty bone in her jaws. Carried it all the way from the kitchen. Given to her by Mistress Della, no less. Gormán looks in a chest, gets out blankets for me. "You can have that bed," he says, pointing. "Conn, find that good mead, will you? A cup before we sleep wouldn't go amiss."

"Where's Bardán?" I ask.

Nobody says anything right away. Been hoping I'd forget to ask—that's my guess. Conn fiddles around with the bottle and cups for a bit. Then Gormán says, "Bardán's to be locked up at night from now on. We can't use his old quarters anymore; not secure. Tóla's orders."

And? I think, but I hold back from saying it. Get on the wrong side of Gormán and he'll stop telling me anything at all. When it comes to it, I'm just a hired man here. Need to tread careful or I'll be gone and

Bardán will be on his own. "So where have you put him?" Trying not to let it show that I'm angry. There's room for all of us in here, the two of them, Bardán and me, and a bed left over. He could've been warm and dry all this time.

"Root cellar," Gormán says. "Other end of the barn, down below. It's dry. He's got bedding."

"Show me."

"He'll be asleep by now."

"Show me, Gormán." Didn't think I looked so fierce, but Ripple growls deep down, like she'd attack if I gave the order, and Gormán takes a step back.

"If you insist," he says. "Not much to see. Through here. Mind your head."

The foresters' quarters, where we've been, are down one end of the barn. Shut off from the rest by a wall. The other part's bigger. A few cows in there, shuffling around and making sleepy mooing sounds. Smell of straw and dung. Gormán's brought the lantern. There are shadows moving around on the rafters, eyes catching the light up there, an owl tearing at something in its claws.

"Down here," Gormán says. We're near the far end. And there's a trapdoor in the barn floor, with a handhold cut into it.

"You're joking." He's not joking. Red rage boils inside me. I'm a hairbreadth from picking the man up and shaking some sense into him. Or worse. I want to go on shaking until I kill him. *Breathe deep, Grim.* "Open it up."

He creaks the thing open. Pitch-dark down there. My head's full of Mathuin's lockup, the dark, the screams, the beatings, the stench, the days that went on and on and on. The endless nights. Heart's beating fit to split my chest open. Skin's gone cold and clammy all over. Blackthorn tied up by the wrists. Slammer doing unspeakable things. I bashed myself near senseless that day, trying to break down the bars of my cell. Couldn't get out. Couldn't help her. *Breathe.* "Give me the lantern."

There are steps down, six or seven of them. Tight space; if I go down, I'll block out most of the light. I put the lantern on the edge of the trapdoor and go down anyway. The wild man's not asleep. I can hear him crying. The red rage turns to something darker. It turns black as night and cold as the grave. It's not Gormán I want to kill; he's a weak man carrying out orders. The one I want to punish is the master.

"Bardán? You all right, brother?" Stupid question.

"Grim?" It comes out on a choking sob. I know what he's feeling. Same thing Blackthorn and I felt at night, in that place, when one of us was falling apart with the burden of everything, and the other one said out of the dark, "I'm here."

"Where are you, man? Can't see you."

He moves; wriggles into the narrow strip of light. Can't move far, though, because he's lying on the floor, tied at the wrists and ankles. The smell tells me he's wet himself. Gormán didn't lie about giving him bedding, but it's in a heap and he can't get it back over himself. Place is cold enough to freeze your bollocks off. Fine for storing vegetables. No spot to put a man.

"Grim," he whispers. "Where's my daughter? What have they done with my girl?"

He must've been dreaming, the sort of nightmares a man has when he's hurt and cold and trussed up in the dark. Only half with me. "Don't worry about that," I say. "I'm going to cut those ropes. Hold steady, will you?"

"What do you think you're doing?" That's Gormán from the top of the steps. "Master Tóla said—"

"I don't give a rat's arse what Master Tóla said." My knife makes short work of the bonds. Ropes have marked Bardán's skin. Morrigan's curse, the man stinks. Never mind that. He'll be feeling numb. Could be hard getting him up those steps. Need two of us. "Give me a hand, will you?"

"You can't do this, Grim."

"Just watch me."

In the end Gormán does help. Must know that if I get stuck halfway up with the wild man on my back, he'll be the one who has to explain to Tóla. Wonder how many other poor sods the master's thrown down here when they got in his road. I'm just glad I don't have to put Bardán over my shoulder and squeeze my way out. I half push, half lift him up the steps in front of me. Gormán hauls him out the top. Strong fellow, Gormán. A forester would be.

"Right," I say when we're all out and the trapdoor's shut. "I know you're not happy. Never mind that. I'll explain to Tóla in the morning. I'll tell him it was all my doing and none of yours. Now, I want this man properly fed. Given fresh clothes. A proper bed. And not tied up."

"He's a danger to himself," Gormán says. "And to everyone else. He has to be tied up."

"Not while I'm here." I know when I say this that I'm binding myself to something I don't really want to do. Something that's going to make my life difficult for a while. Can't see any choice. Bardán's not safe in this den of wolves. Never will be. "I'll take responsibility for him. I'll give my word that he'll keep out of trouble."

"He can't sleep in with us," Gormán says. "Smell would keep us awake all night."

I don't suggest a bath. Pretty sure Bardán would say no to that. Anyway, it's late and we're all worn-out. "We'll sleep next to the cows, him and me," I say. "Bit of straw to lie on, blanket each—no trouble." I know one thing: I'm not leaving him to sleep with the animals while I'm in one of those cozy beds next door. Anyway, they wouldn't agree to that. Makes me wonder what they think he'll do.

"I'll be reporting this to Master Tóla first thing in the morning," Gormán says. "You're likely to find yourself out of a job."

"Not sure I want this one," I say, though it's only half true. "Not after what I've seen today."

Gormán doesn't comment on that. Sees the sense in giving me what I want, for now anyway. Means we can all get some sleep. Probably thinks Tóla will throw me out first thing in the morning. Even if Ripple and I did help find his daughter.

Young Conn's a bit surprised when we all appear at the door to the quarters. Does as he's told, though. I take Bardán out to the privy. Wonder if I'll be having to do that every time from now on. By the time we get back, Gormán's looked out some old clean clothes that more or less fit, and Conn's warmed up some food. They let Bardán eat it by their fire. But only because I'm standing there with a look on my face that stops them from saying he's too smelly, he's too strange, he's too wild. Conn gives me a cup of mead, which I drink. Offer Bardán a share but he shakes his head. Only wants water. Then him and me take ourselves off into the part with the animals, and the door shuts, and we bed down in the pile of straw. Ripple circles a few times, then settles with a sound like a sigh. I've slept in a lot worse places than this. Don't lie down till I'm sure Bardán's got his blankets over him. He's still muttering about his daughter, his baby, his little girl. Don't want to start talking about that, not now. His wife died in childbirth, didn't she? That's what he seemed to be saying up at the hut. Lost the two of them. Must've heard Tóla talking, or the others, about Cara being missing, and it all got mixed up in his head, brought back the past, only twisted round so it was somehow not Tóla's daughter but his girl who was lost. Now's not the time to try untangling it. Not the place either, here in the dark with the cows all sleepy and the night half gone already.

Rain's coming down outside again. Hope Blackthorn's getting a good sleep down at Longwater. Hope Fann's still well, and the new little one. And the father, Ross. Not that he did any of the hard work. How would that feel, holding your baby son in your arms for the first time ever? That'd be like sunshine and springtime and smiles and every good thing you could think of all in one. But frightening too. Because that baby's coming into a world with folk like Mathuin of Laois in it. And Slammer. And Master Tóla, who can't see a real man under a coating of dirt and sorrow and madness. A man would need to be brave to be a father.

I lie there listening to the rain and thinking about things. Bardán mutters to himself about his daughter—where is she, what have they done with her, they've stolen her and so on. Doesn't seem to expect an answer, so I don't say anything much. Only, "It's all right," and "Try to sleep now," and so on. After a bit he goes quiet and I think he's dropped off. But no. He starts to sing, under his breath. Heard this song before, bits of it, while he's watching me work. Only now I listen properly, and he sings the whole thing through.

Starling, woodcock, owl on wing
Nightjar, chiffchaff, bunting sing
Goldcrest, warbler, thrush and jay
Redpoll, siskin darting by
Golden feather, scarlet, white
Bright as summer, dark as night
Weave a charm for luck and good
Every birdling in the wood
Feather bright and feather fine
None shall harm this child of mine.

Bardán's voice is not the best, and he's hardly singing above a whisper. But I hear something in that broken sound. I hear a father singing to a baby, singing her to sleep. I hear a man who's still got something soft and tender in him, even when he's been beaten down and worn away to a ruin. There's power in those words too. Like a charm. Like magic. Wish I could write them down, so I'd remember them all. Blackthorn would like to hear that song.

My thoughts take a sideways slip, and I'm seeing too far ahead. Seeing something in the world of *might be*, the world of *after Mathuin*. Not good. Start those foolish dreams and I'll be over the cliff before you can say Red Giant. And there's things to do here.

Bardán's asleep. Breathing slow, curled up under his blanket. Ripple's wriggled over next to him, keeping him warm. But me? I'm wide-awake, staring up into the dark, listening to the cows, thinking how I never slept at night when I was in Mathuin's lockup, or when I was on the road with Blackthorn, or when we were at court. Always on alert. Couldn't help it. Used to snatch a catnap when I could, during the day. Managed to do my work. When I first started building the heartwood house, riding to and fro and so on, that changed. Got so tired, I was hard put to stay awake long enough to eat supper.

Now here I am, heart racing, jumping every time the timbers of the barn creak and groan in the wind. A bird cries out in the woods, and I'm in that place of Mathuin's, hearing Blackthorn bite back a scream, hearing

Dribbles sobbing, *Stop it. Don't hurt me—please, please!* A cracking sound—the wind, I know it's only the wind—and I'm hearing a whip on naked flesh, and worse things, and I'm shaking the bars, bashing my head against them. Got to get out. Got to save her. Got to stop this—

"Grim."

Bardán's voice snaps me back to the barn, the straw, the quiet sounds. Rain falling. Cows breathing. Oh, shit. That was real. It was too real. "Sorry," I mutter. "Was I shouting?" Can't have been, or Gormán would have been through that door quick smart.

"Hitting yourself in the head," says the wild man.

"Shit. Sorry." Great help I'm going to be if I let that old stuff start eating me up again. "Might stay awake a bit," I say. "You sleep."

"You all right?"

I would be, if Blackthorn was here. But she's in Longwater, and tomorrow night she'll be back home, and I don't think I will be. I don't think I can be, now, until the heartwood house is all finished. "Just need to stay awake a bit. Might do some exercises, warm myself up. You sleep, brother. I'll watch over you."

There's a long quiet then. I get up, start some bending and stretching, know I'll have to do what I used to do in the lockup, keep myself so busy the bad things can't find space to squeeze in. Harder with Blackthorn not here. But I can do it. I have to. Keep going till it's light again. Then face up to Tóla.

I'm standing on my hands in the dark, counting up to twenty, when Bardán speaks again.

"Never had a brother," he says, quiet-like. There's a sort of wonder in his voice. After a bit he says, "You're a good man, Grim. The best. Be safe till morning."

Morning comes. Bardán's still sleeping, curled up with his fist against his mouth like a child. I get up without waking him. Take Ripple out through the sleeping quarters. Gormán's stirring; Conn is just a mound of blankets. I open the door and there's a couple of fellows on their way up the hill, heading in our direction.

Seems the master's thought of everything. The two tell us he's sent them to make sure Bardán doesn't get up to anything he shouldn't. And Master Tóla wants to see Gormán and me, straightaway. Which is before we've even had breakfast. I put Ripple back in with Bardán and tell her to stay. Best I can do, for now.

When we get down to the house, we find out why Tóla's in a hurry. He calls us into his council room and shuts the door. Looks like he's had about as much sleep as I've had, which is more or less none. Looks old and tired and sad. Can't find it in myself to be sorry for the man, though.

"I don't have much time to spare," he says when Gormán and me are sitting down. "I'll be leaving shortly to take my daughter back to Winterfalls." He doesn't give us a chance to comment. Which is just as well, since I'm remembering what Blackthorn said about the girl wanting to come home. Thinking about her trying to do it on her own and falling down that hole and having to wait a long time to be found. Remembering her throwing herself into her father's arms, and him with tears on his cheeks. And now he's sending her away again. After one night under her own roof. Makes no sense at all.

"I owe you both thanks for finding Cara and bringing her home safely," he says. "You'll be receiving an extra payment in recognition of that service. That my daughter was able to leave Winterfalls unnoticed makes it clear that the arrangements there are inadequate. There must also be an improvement in the speed with which they get messages to me. I'll speak to Prince Oran's folk when I'm down there. We can't have any repetition of what just happened." Not a scrap of softness in his voice. He could be stone. How did a man like him manage to father Cara? That girl's like a creature from an old story, a tree nymph or something. The kind of girl the shepherd or farmer's son or builder ends up not marrying because he knows she's too fine for him. Or too different.

"My gratitude does not entirely outweigh my concern about your behavior yesterday, Grim." Tóla's got cold eyes. Hard eyes. Those eyes could bore a hole right through your heart. "You were very ready to take Bardán's part. You suggested we had ill-treated the fellow in some way. You indicated that you might withdraw your labor if we did not make changes. I remind you of several facts. One, you are working for me. Two, you are extremely well paid. Three, you agreed to do the job. I don't recall anything in our arrangement about your making your own terms and conditions and doing the same for your fellow worker."

"What I said. Last night. Yes, it was a good payment. I've earned some of it up to now. I'll repay the rest if we can't work things out."

Tóla's mouth goes tight. Me, I'm wondering why Gormán hasn't spoken up, told his master about me getting Bardán out of that cellar, cutting his bonds, changing the sleeping arrangements and all. Not a word. "It's not a matter of working anything out," the master says. "You do the job my way or not at all. I would be sorry to see you go. But I can't have Bardán going off where and when he pleases, telling his mad tales to half the folk of the district. We'd never get the place built. And yesterday's episode tells me we need it done soon."

Morrigan's curse. Gormán was right about him. He really believes the old tale about the heartwood house, whatever it is. He believes it was fate or a curse or suchlike that put his daughter in danger. Anything bad that happens to Cara before we get the thing finished, he'll blame us for. Same as he blamed Bardán for his wife dying.

"Master Tóla," I say, working as hard as I can to sound polite, though I detest the man and everything he stands for, "you know I said before, once or twice, about getting a few more men in to help. Do the job well. Do it quickly. I know you're not keen. But there are some fellows down at Longwater could handle the work if I was there to help them do it right. And Bardán to tell us all how it fits together."

"Fellows." He's icy now. Doesn't like me breaking his rules. Not one bit. "What fellows?"

"I got talking to some of the lads earlier, while the women down there were birthing the babe. Asked around—didn't tell them what the job was, exactly, just that it'd be a good stretch of solid work for them, with a fair payment. Sounds like there'd be a crew of six if you wanted them."

"You told them. You spread this about when I specifically said, no gossip. I cannot believe this. I trusted you, Grim."

Deep breath. "You can still trust me," I say. "I didn't say anything beyond what I just told you. And those folk don't gossip. Nobody said a word about you or your daughter or anything you might or might not be building."

"That's all very well," says Tóla. "But what about him? The wild man? You get a crew up here and he'll be spinning his tales to every last one of them, telling them all manner of lies. I can't believe those wild stories won't get out somehow. He would poison folk's minds against me. I can't keep him tied up and locked in day and night. He has to be able to direct the building."

That's where Gormán sort of clears his throat. Giving me the chance to get in first. "Thing is," I say, "Gormán and I had a little chat about that last night. We've moved Bardán out of that cellar and into the main bit of the barn—"

Tóla opens his mouth to let out something angry, but I put a hand up.

"Let me finish, will you? I know you don't want him out and about. But he has to be out to help me build. And if I lose the job, you'll still need him to help whoever takes over. If it's going to be me doing it, it'll be me keeping an eye on Bardán. Wasn't that always part of our agreement? So it still will be, but it'll be on my terms, or I'm off right now and not coming to Wolf Glen ever again. I'll be giving back your silver and going my own way." Hoping Tóla hasn't guessed I won't leave Bardán on his own unless there's no other choice at all. Don't want another burden to carry. Leaving him would be a heavy one.

"You're not the man I thought you were," says Tóla. Can't for the life of me tell if he thinks this is a good thing or a bad thing. Could be some of both.

"I know you're in a hurry. So here are my terms. I take responsibility for Bardán, make sure he stays at Wolf Glen. He doesn't tell tales out of turn. He does the job. He doesn't hurt anyone, himself included. You agree to the crew coming in every day until we get to the thatching stage. Couple of men to stay on and help me with that as long as I need them. You pay them a fair rate for their work. I get paid what I've been promised. And Bardán sleeps where he did last night, in the barn with warm bedding. He uses the privy like everyone else. Gets clean clothes when he needs them. A good pair of boots. Same meals as us. And no being put in the root cellar, no being tied up, no being struck or beaten or shouted at. The dog and me together make sure he keeps his side of it."

Tóla doesn't say a word. Neither does Gormán. Me, I'm glad that speech is over. Doesn't come easy to me, laying things down like I was in charge. Rather be given a job and just get on with it.

"You surprise me," Tóla says in the end.

"You think a workingman can't understand justice?" This is out before I can stop it.

He gives a thin sort of smile. "Justice," he says. "There's no justice in this. You don't know that man's story. If you did, you wouldn't be so ready to help him."

Does he mean he's going to tell me? "He was talking about his daughter," I say. Tóla's face changes, quick as a snap of the fingers. Becomes that wolf face, on edge, ready to spring. Feel like I have to go on anyway, now I've taken one step into whatever this is. "Kept saying, *Where is she? Where's my girl?* Like he knew young Cara was missing, and got her mixed up with his own child. Only he's got no family left that I know of. All buried there above Longwater. Mother, father, wife and newborn. He was weeping over their graves. When I ran across him, I mean. Too upset to be left on his own. That was why I came back with him. But I wondered. *My daughter is missing,* he said."

Tóla looks at Gormán. Gormán looks at Tóla. A lot passing between them. One thing's plain to me without any words. They're asking each other, *Do we tell him?*

"If you're staying on to do the work," Tóla says, "and if you must have workers from Longwater here to get it finished, you'll need to know why we don't want that man spreading his mad stories all around. It's essential that you keep him quiet. Quiet night and day. If I agree to what you're proposing, there'll be no going home at the end of the day's work, for you at least. You'll be sleeping at Wolf Glen, watching over Bardán. Keeping him in order. Without that, I'm having none of it."

Pretty sure he was going to say this. Been waiting for it, hollow feeling in my belly. "What about rain days?"

"You'll stay here. If that requires an additional payment, I'll consider it. But you'll be on my premises from now until the day the heartwood house is finished." Tóla gives me a narrow look, sizing me up. Am I as strong-minded as I seem to be or am I just pretending? That's my guess as to what that look means. "If you can't agree to that, I'll find someone else to do the work," he goes on. "And if I believe that person cannot keep Bardán under adequate control, I won't hesitate to tie him up, use the root cellar or employ any other method I choose to ensure my household's safety."

The devious bastard. Clever too. Knows how to read a man. Knows how to find the one thing that'll make a man do what he wants. "Let's hear this tale first," I say, trying not to bunch up my fists. "About Bardán's daughter. If there was a daughter."

A knock at the door.

"What is it?" Tóla barks. I remember that he said he didn't have much time. Taking Cara away more or less as soon as she got here. Wonder when Blackthorn will get home. It'll be a cold hearth waiting for her.

A servant opens the door a crack. "Everything's ready, Master Tóla."

"Yes, very well," Tóla says. "I'll be there shortly. Ask Mistress Della to arrange some food for these men, will you? And a fresh jug of ale."

The servant vanishes. The door shuts without a sound.

"Bardán. Mm. I took him on, the first time, mostly to do the man a favor. Yes, I knew he was a master builder. And everyone knew he was odd, as his father had been before him. There were all kinds of stories attached to the family. Folk said the father had learned his skills in the Otherworld; that nobody could be so good a builder without some kind of fey knowledge. He was supposed to have spent his childhood there. That was the tale."

"How was it a favor?" I ask. "Seeing as you needed him to build your heartwood house. Wasn't Bardán the only one with the know-how?"

"He was the only one. But unreliable. Up and down in his moods.

One day eaten up with anger, the next curled up in a corner weeping. Don't know that I would have taken him on, other things being equal. No certainty of getting the work out of him."

I don't ask a question this time, though I've got plenty.

"What happened was this." Gormán speaks up at last. "Bardán appeared on the doorstep with a little, tiny baby in his arms. His wife was dead—she was a local girl, from Longwater, so we knew of them. He'd had a goat for a bit, kept the child alive on his own, but he couldn't cope anymore. Asked for help. Said he'd work for his keep and his daughter's. We asked why the child couldn't go to her mother's kinsfolk who lived not far off. But Bardán didn't want that. Said if he handed her over, they'd steal her away, not let him near her. Could have been true. The folk over at Longwater thought him odd. He *was* odd. They might have thought the child would be better off growing up in her grand-mother's household."

"Bardán was her father," I can't help saying. No wonder the wild man was sad or angry most of the time. Who wouldn't be? Wife newly in the grave, tiny babe to look after, folk turning their backs on him. Poor sod.

"I took them in," said Tóla. "Bardán to live at Wolf Glen and build the heartwood house. His daughter to be looked after in my house-hold. That was before Cara came along. My wife was a warmhearted woman, generous and kind. She arranged everything for the child. And for some time it all went as planned. Bardán was moody, stubborn, difficult. But he worked hard and he knew what he was doing. The lit-tle girl thrived under the good care of our folk."

Something bad's coming—it's on his face and in his voice. Some-thing so bad that Tóla doesn't say it himself. He gives Gormán a nod instead.

"He got the heartwood house half built," Gormán says. "Quicker than anyone expected. Not all on his own, of course. There were a cou-ple of older foresters working here then, and they helped find the differ-ent woods and lent a hand with the heavy lifting. And some of the farm lads shared the work. We got a couple of fellows in to cut the stone. All the same, Bardán did a remarkable job. Used to come down here and see his daughter at the end of the day, when work was all done. Went on building right through the autumn. And then . . . Well, something went wrong in his mind. And he did something bad. Something so bad you wouldn't believe it."

All of a sudden I'm not wanting to hear this story anymore. Thoughts have jumped ahead to what this could be, and I don't like it. But I have to listen. I'm the one who started all this. "Go on," I say.

"He'd been muttering all day about the child, crazy things, old rhymes and the like. Came down to the house after dark, told the man at the door he was going to sing his daughter a lullaby. The fool let him in. Bardán snatched the child from her cradle while the nursemaid was still half asleep and ran off into the forest with her. He was out of sight before anyone could stop him. And he knew his way around the woods, even in the dark. Impossible to track. Though we tried."

Morrigan's curse! No wonder Tóla was so strung up when his daughter went missing. No wonder he sent the whole household out after her. I ask another question I don't want the answer to. "Did you find them?"

Another knock on the door. The sound makes me jump, I've been so caught up in the story. A serving woman comes in with a tray, sets it on the table, goes out.

"Eat," says Tóla. "I don't imagine you've had breakfast, either of you."

Not long ago I was hungry. Not sure I am anymore. Gormán passes me bread and cold mutton. I hold it in my hand, not eating, waiting for the story.

"We never found him." Tóla's voice is like a bell now, the kind that rings when someone's died, deep and sad. "But we found her, after two days' searching. The child—Brígh, her name was. Out in the woods, lying dead and cold where he'd left her half hidden in the roots of an oak. I didn't want to bring her little body back home where my wife would see it, or the child's kinsfolk in Longwater. The corpse was . . . disfigured. It had been mauled by some wild creature. The damage had been inflicted after death, we believed. That was scant mercy. We buried her close by the spot where we found her."

Holy Mother of God! That's the saddest thing I ever heard. Only, if it was me, if it was my kin, I'd want to see the body even if it had been torn to shreds. I'd want to hold what was left of the little one. Cradle her close and weep tears over her. I'd want to lay her in the ground with my own hands. Got tears in my eyes now, just thinking about it. Blackthorn would be the same. *Was* the same, long ago when her son died with his father crouched over him, trying to shield him from the flames. She saw that with her own eyes. Saw them die. Saw them dead. Don't know if she ever got to bury little Brennan or her man Cass. I know there wasn't much left of them but ash and bone. She'd have touched that ash and bone the same way she touched her living husband and her precious son.

"Grim?"

Done it again, gone off into the past and forgotten where I am. "Thanks," I say, taking the ale cup Gormán's holding out to me. Mind full of questions. What did they tell Tóla's wife when they got home? What did they tell those kinsfolk? Wouldn't most people expect the little girl to be buried down in Longwater? Can't ask. I don't know what to think. Tóla might tell me barefaced lies. But Gormán wouldn't make up something like this. One thing I do know. I'm not going to feel the same about Bardán ever again.

Yet another knock.

"Wait!" snarls Tóla, and the knocking stops. "I have to go," he says. "I don't want my daughter here a moment longer than is strictly necessary. I'll be back later today. And whether or not we have an agreement, Grim, I want Bardán kept out of sight until Cara and I are well away. When he came back, you understand, his mind was in even more disorder than it had once been. He'd forgotten the circumstances of his departure from Wolf Glen. Forgotten all about his child, his wife, his life before. He couldn't tell us where he'd been all those years. We had believed him dead. There had been no word of him, no trace. No message. But there he was, back among us and expecting to rebuild the heartwood house. I'd never found anyone else who knew how to do it. So I said yes. I want it done, and that means I must have him at Wolf Glen. And keeping him, keeping him safely, depends on everyone here working together. Every man doing his part."

This story should make me want to walk away. Turn my back on the lot of them. "I'll stay, Master Tóla," I tell him.

"I'm pleased to hear that, Grim. We have a bargain, then. And now I must be off." He heads for the door. "You may remain here and finish your breakfast. Make sure you close the door on the way out, and call a servant to take the dishes back to the kitchen."

"Just one thing." Something's bothering me. "I need to get word to Blackthorn. About where I am and why I won't be home. She'll worry." Feels a bit awkward. Can't ask Tóla to be my messenger boy. "Your daughter. Cara." I try not to catch Gormán's eye. He did tell me not to talk about the girl. "She sees a lot of Blackthorn, from what I've heard. Could she maybe pass the word on? Let Blackthorn know I've promised to stay up here till the job's done?"

"The arrangements for my daughter will be changing." Tóla speaks with his hand on the door and his back to me. "But as I will be at the prince's residence, I can request that a message be passed on. Didn't you say the wise woman is at Longwater today?" Showing he has been listening.

"She'd be going home this morning," I say, "if all's well with the mother and child."

"Mm-hm. I'll speak to you when I return, Gormán." And he's gone.

Poor Cara. That's what I'm thinking. She'll be an unhappy young woman. What's he going to do—ask for her to be locked up, same as Bardán? Does he think the wild man's going to snatch Cara away same as he did his own daughter? Merciful gods. What a mess.

"Sort of story you wouldn't believe," says Gormán. "Too strange to be true. That's what folk would say."

"Mm."

"We never talked to him about it. When he came back. And he didn't say a word. So this, now, the talk about his daughter being missing, it could be his memory coming back, only mixed up with what's happened. With Cara, I mean."

"Could be."

"Not much we can do about it either way," Gormán says, like he's washing his hands of the whole sorry tale. "Eat up. Better food here than you're likely to get with Conn doing the cooking. Then you can start sorting out some bedding, making a better arrangement for yourself and the wild man. Looks like we're stuck with you." Funny thing is, after everything—Tóla shaking Bardán, Bardán being tied up and thrown down in that cellar, Gormán going along with Tóla's orders—now he's sounding almost happy.

24

BLACKTHORN

The ride tired me more than it should have done. The persistent rain did nothing to improve my mood. Osgar came with me, leading the horses we had borrowed from the prince's household. At the gates of Oran's establishment we found someone to take the animals in. Since I didn't fancy riding up behind Osgar the rest of the way, I took my leave of him then, promising to return to Longwater in a couple of days. He went off to see a friend in the settlement and I walked the rest of the way home across the fields, getting steadily wetter and crosser.

I should have been happy. Fann's baby had been delivered safely. Both mother and son were well enough to be left in the care of Ide and the other local women for now. I'd been farewelled with thanks and smiles and a bag of coppers that I could not refuse without causing offense. It was made plain to me that the entire populace of Longwater considered itself to be in my debt and would continue to do so more or less forever. There would certainly be further requests for my services as a healer. That made three settlements I'd be looking after, in addition to Prince Oran's household and the folk on the scattered farms around the district. Plenty to do. Plenty to take my mind off Mathuin of Laois and what action might be taken against him with or without my being part of it. Plenty to divert me from the question of Conmael and why he had decided to disappear just when I needed him.

But right now I was a mass of contradictory feelings, none of them related to the good work I had done at Longwater. Strongest of all was the longing to be home, with a warm fire on the hearth and the one person there whom I could really talk to. Only he wasn't home. I'd seen from halfway across the field path that the place was empty. No smoke from the chimney. No welcome barking from Ripple. The cottage looked forlorn under the rain, its door closed, its shutters pulled to. No large figure appearing to stand in the doorway, ready to welcome me. He'd chosen to stay up at Wolf Glen even though it was still too wet for building.

So, said a particularly savage inner voice, *you get a day on your own. A day when you can be as prickly and cantankerous as you want. It's not as if there's nothing to do. You can start by making a fire and getting the place tidied up. If nobody comes knocking in search of your help, you can take the opportunity to make some notes in your book, brew some cures, catch up on sleep. He'll be home by supper time. Since when were you the kind of woman who needed a man in the house to make her happy?*

I did those things. The fire, the cleaning up, the cooking, the notes. Firstly, notes about the childbirth in Longwater and the exact proportions of the rather perilous draft I had made Fann drink. I would go through that with Emer next time she came. I did not expect her today; we had an agreement about very wet weather. At the back of my notebook I made some other, more secret notes, pertaining to Mathuin of Laois. I hid the book away, made a brew—often a good way of bringing Grim home—and stood by the window with the shutters open, sipping my drink and telling myself I was not watching out for him.

My moon-bleeding had started. That helped explain my touchy mood; the two often went together. For a long time, season after season, I had bled little and irregularly or not at all. I had wondered if fate's blows had beaten out of me the capacity to conceive another child. For a while I had thought that would be a good thing. How could such a wretched, bitter creature ever be a proper mother? Now, a part of me was glad my body still held that possibility. Hard to accept, that gladness. It didn't make much sense. Hadn't I sworn to myself, after the heartbreak of losing Brennan, that I would never have another child? Hadn't I sworn I would never love anyone again, since doing so would be like nailing my heart up on the wall and inviting folk to throw knives into it? Just as well, after all, that Grim wasn't home. I might say something I would quickly regret. Just as well he hadn't had the chance to see those words I'd written on the wax tablet. I would erase them now. As for what he had written for me, he would never know I'd copied every word onto a blank page of my notebook. His verse lay between a drawing of mistletoe and a set of instructions for brewing mead. Grim would not look there. He knew a wise woman's book was private.

Someone was riding across the fields from the settlement. A man in a hooded cloak. Two others coming behind. Not Prince Oran's men, or I'd see his colors. Nobody I recognized from Winterfalls settlement or anywhere else nearby. The Swan Island men again, with their wretched questions? A pox on them! I left the window, put my cup down on the table, hugged my shawl around my shoulders. Why did I feel so cold? Why did the shadow of Mathuin hang over any stranger who knocked on my door? *Go away*, I willed them. *Go somewhere else and leave me alone.* Which was foolish. Hadn't I been cursing Grim not long ago for doing precisely that?

I heard them stop out front, dismount, exchange a few words. I contemplated pretending I was not at home. If I stood where I was and kept completely quiet, maybe they would simply leave. Or maybe they wouldn't, seeing as the fire was burning and the lamp was lit and there was a pungent smell of freshly chopped onions.

Someone knocked. In my mind, Mathuin himself stood on my doorstep with a long knife in his hand. Not ready to plunge it in my heart; such a man would not deliver the merciful gift of a quick death. No, he'd want to draw things out as long as possible. Not only to punish me, but to enjoy the process every step of the way. In the end, of course, he would finish me. I simply had too much to tell.

I picked up the iron poker. Gripped it, weighed it, considered how I would use it. I opened the door.

A man stood there, cloaked against the rain. "Are you Mistress Blackthorn the healer?" he asked, not bothering with pleasantries.

The other two waited at a distance, with the three horses. It looked as if they weren't planning to stop long.

"Who's asking?"

"Master Tóla of Wolf Glen wants a word with you. If you're Blackthorn."

I swallowed what came first to my lips: *Can't Master Tóla speak for himself?* "I am Blackthorn," I said. Not the Swan Island men. Not Prince Oran's retainers. And not Mathuin's henchmen. I saw, now, that this was a master and two servants. One servant had knocked on the door. The other was holding the horses' reins. And the third man, the one whose clothing was of better cloth, whose boots were less worn, whose tight jaw and cold eyes were unpromising, must be Tóla himself. Cara's father. I wouldn't have guessed; he looked nothing like her. What could he want with me?

"If you're looking for Cara," I said, "she's not here today."

The well-dressed man stepped forward and indicated with a sharp gesture that the other two were to move back.

"Mistress Blackthorn," he said, sounding incredulous, "am I to understand from those words that you have not yet heard that Cara was missing for most of yesterday, and was only found after an extensive search that went late into the night?"

My jaw dropped. "I was in Longwater," I said. "I had no idea—is Cara all right? Is she safe?" It was making a horrible kind of sense to me now. A rainy day, most of Prince Oran's household off at court, Grim and me both away. A perfect opportunity for Cara to bolt for home, or so she must have thought. "Where did she go?" Cara always swore she could find her way home from anywhere in the forest, and I had no reason to disbelieve her. "Where was she found?"

"That is not your concern."

I met Master Tóla's antagonistic stare as calmly as I could, trying not to take an instant dislike to the man. He had the air of a person who felt himself entitled to make rules for other folk, and to insist those rules be complied with. Flidais had told me he was distantly related to King Ruairi, which made him Oran's kinsman too, and hers by marriage. But he was neither prince nor chieftain, only a landholder who happened to be rather wealthy. Maybe he thought I'd be easily intimidated.

"Cara is a friend of mine," I said. "It's natural for friends to inquire about each other's welfare. She's young. She's been unhappy at Winter-falls. I imagine she was trying to get to Wolf Glen." Grim must have been part of the search; it explained, in part, why he had not come home.

"My daughter's behavior can be somewhat erratic." Tóla had low-ered his voice. "In many ways Cara is still a child. Mistress Blackthorn, it would be more appropriate for this conversation to take place behind closed doors." He glanced over at his companions.

"I prefer it to take place out here." I did not want this man in my house. Something about him, that air of entitlement perhaps, reminded me of Mathuin. He set my teeth on edge. "Don't worry, I'll keep my voice down. So, Cara was missing, she's been found and she's safely back home. What was it you needed to ask me about?"

He looked as if he wanted to slap me. "I had thought to question you about how she managed to walk away from the prince's establish-ment unchecked. And about the long delay in informing me that she was unaccounted for. I've been led to believe that my daughter has been spending a great deal of time over here with you. That was hardly what I intended when I sent her to Winterfalls to stay. But as you were not here when she wandered off, in this particular instance you bear no responsibility for her behavior. I did know you had been in Longwater. Your friend Grim apprised me of that fact."

"I see. I should make it clear to you, Master Tóla, that Cara is always escorted by a guard when she visits me, and usually by a female compan-ion as well. When she comes here she occupies herself with various use-ful tasks. There is often another young woman, my assistant, with us. All perfectly appropriate. Cara is not the kind of girl who is content to while away the day with fine needlework and gossip." I waited a moment, then added, "Was that what you were hoping she would learn to do?"

His cheeks flushed red. "That's offensive, Mistress Blackthorn. I'm at your door to ask for your help, not listen to your sly insults. I want what is best for my daughter. I'm well aware that being among other folk is difficult for Cara. If she has made a friend of you, I would not lightly sever that tie. She will need it more than ever now."

There was a silence while I worked this out. I put it together with the fact that, on the day after Cara had been missing and then found, when it was still raining hard enough to make travel difficult and uncomfortable, if not impossible, her father was at Winterfalls with his guards and apparently heading back toward Wolf Glen. Without Cara. Why would she need my friendship more than ever if she was exactly where she wanted to be, back home at last?

"Are you telling me you've left her at Prince Oran's house again?" My dismay and disapproval must have been all too obvious.

"Your manner is not only blunt; it is discourteous," Tóla said. "Perhaps you learned that from your friend. The two of you are quick to speak out. You are all too ready to pass judgment on your betters."

Could he mean Grim? A man of very few words at the best of times? As for *betters*, I would restrain myself from making comment on that ill-chosen word. If I were Cara, I'd be running away from Wolf Glen, not to it. But I wouldn't be doing the girl any favors if I made an enemy of her father. "Let me say it again, then, in terms less likely to offend. Is Cara back at Prince Oran's house, Master Tóla? Will she be staying there for some time?"

"I brought her down this morning. She will be staying indefinitely. Since neither Prince Oran nor his wife is there at present, I was able to speak only to the steward and one of Lady Flidais's attendants. I made my position clear. There must be further restrictions on Cara's movements. I cannot have her returning unannounced to Wolf Glen. Not until a . . . a certain project is completed." He narrowed his eyes at me. "Has Grim spoken to you of the work he is doing for me?"

Ah. Best tread carefully. "Not much. I know it's a big building job.

Stone, wood, thatching. Something that will keep him busy a while."
After a bit I added, "And it's well paid."

Tóla nodded. It seemed I had given the right sort of answer. "I will
be plain with you, Mistress Blackthorn. My daughter cannot return
home until the building job you mention is finished. I have certain rather
rough workers—I do not refer to Grim, you understand, but to others—
whose services I require, and who must be housed at Wolf Glen. It
would be inappropriate, even dangerous, for a young woman of Cara's
age and—sensitivity—to be there at the same time they are. That means
a long stay at Winterfalls for her."

He waited, perhaps for me to ask questions. I had plenty: why
couldn't Cara's aunt keep an eye on her? Why couldn't she be restricted
to the house and kitchen garden or similar while the workers were there?
And anyway, wasn't there only one rough worker at Wolf Glen—the
wild man, Bardán? According to Grim, Tóla had stubbornly refused to
hire extra men for the job even though it was obviously too much for
two. Wasn't it rather unfair, not to say inappropriate, for Tóla to expect
the prince and Lady Flidais to accommodate his daughter under such
odd circumstances, especially in view of the crisis in the south?

I said none of this. Revealing that I knew anything more would get
Grim into trouble. "I understand," I said. "I hope it will still be possible
for Cara to visit me sometimes. With an appropriate escort, of course.
You know—of course you must know how difficult she finds it to speak
out among folk. Here in the cottage, with me and Emer—the young
woman I mentioned—Cara has no problem finding words. It's good for
her to be able to speak freely."

"You judge me," Tóla said, wintry. "Once more you point out my
failings as a father."

That shocked me. "Believe me, I do not make judgments so quickly."
Remembering my first impression of the man, I wondered if that was
quite true. "That would be most unwise. I'm saying only that Cara
needs friends, and that she has friends here. I could have a word with
her about the inadvisability of running away again, if you believe that
would be helpful."

"Thank you, Mistress Blackthorn. I believe . . . I believe I overesti-mated what Cara would be able to cope with. She is . . . in many ways . . ."

"A child, as you said before? She may appear so sometimes. I think perhaps she is not so much childlike as . . . unworldly."

His head went up sharply. "What do you mean?"

"Unused to mingling with folk. Unable to pretend. A little too hon-est for certain company. No more than that." What had got him so wound up all of a sudden? "Those things are part of your daughter's charm, Master Tóla. She is still very young. If you were to ask my advice, I would say, don't push her too hard. Don't test her beyond what she is ready for."

"That is none of your concern."

"Then I will say no more on the matter. Was there something you needed to ask me? Some reason you knocked on my door, beyond wanting to blame me for your daughter running away?"

We stared at each other for a little. His lips were held tight over what were most likely angry words. I wished I was better at thinking before I spoke.

"I shouldn't—"

"Believe me—"

We spoke together, fell silent together. Then Tóla said, "Believe me, I act with only one thing in mind: Cara's welfare. My daughter is very dear to me, Mistress Blackthorn. Dearer than anything in the world. Her mother was devoted to her. When my wife was on her deathbed, I promised her I would keep Cara safe. I will hold to that promise all my life, and if my actions offend some, so be it."

When he spoke like that, from the heart, it became possible to feel a small amount of sympathy for the man. His love for Cara sounded deep and sincere. It didn't make him any less of an arrogant bully. "Your wife died when Cara was a baby, didn't she?"

"Cara was just under a year old when I lost Suanach, yes. My daughter does not remember her mother at all. But that loss has left its mark on her. Her wildness of character, her . . . her oddities of speech and behavior must be largely down to growing up without her mother to guide and shape her development."

It was not for me to point out that the aunt, who had been there since early days according to Grim's account, should have been entirely capable of taking the role of mother, especially if the child had been too small at the time of that loss to remember her real mother for long. In a well-to-do household like Tóla's there would have been any number of maidservants willing to help with a baby girl.

Something was nagging at my mind, something that did not quite fit. Something about babies, children, folk helping . . .

"I've explained to Cara, this time, why I need her to stay away from home," Tóla said. "There is no need to keep that from her when you see her. I am happy for her to visit you here. Or, if you have the opportunity, for you to visit her at Prince Oran's stronghold. I had thought to consult you in your capacity as a . . ." He hesitated.

"Healer?"

"As a healer, yes." He was evidently more comfortable with that term than wise woman. Grim had told me what great faith Tóla placed in the protective qualities of the heartwood house. How he feared the consequences if the place was not completed. Hadn't he blamed Bardán's defection for the death of his wife? So, he was superstitious. Deeply so. Believed in the power of the uncanny. But was afraid of it too, or he would not have shied away from calling me what I was—not only a worker with herbs and potions, a mender of broken bones and a helper to the ailing, but also a practitioner of what might be called hearth magic: minor spells and charms, a slight adjustment of what already existed, a little playing with the nature of things.

"Do you require my services for yourself or for your daughter, Master Tóla?"

"For myself—no, most certainly not." The notion seemed to shock him. "With Cara—if you could watch over her . . . If there were a . . . something protective . . . something she could carry with her . . ."

"A charm, you mean?"

The man was struggling for words, out of his depth. Not wanting to acknowledge the existence of such things, not openly at least. He was a mass of contradictions. And I was getting cold, standing outside in meager shelter.

"I could make something, yes. I'll need to give it some thought. Ideally such an item would contain a contribution from each of those closest to the wearer. Cara herself might be asked to identify those people. Perhaps there is a garment or small item that belonged to her mother. Something from you. Something from anyone else she is fond of. She and I might make the charm together." I thought of Grim's little wooden hedgehog. In the cottage, right behind us, there were several animals Cara herself had carved, each of them full of its own natural power. Created with love and good intent. Crafted with a knowledge of trees and the gifts they gave us. It came to me that Cara could already make her own magic.

"We'd best be moving on." Tóla brought the conversation to an abrupt halt, gesturing to his servants. "If you could go ahead with that, I would be grateful. And I will pay, of course. I don't want this discussed openly, Mistress Blackthorn, or spread abroad. That goes without saying."

I gave him a sort of half nod. Grim and I had already gone far beyond Tóla's restrictions on the sharing of information and I was certain we would again when I saw him next.

The three men were mounting their horses.

"Master Tóla?"

From the saddle, already impatient to be gone, he looked down at me.

"I had thought Grim might be home today," I said, already feeling foolish. "With the heavy rain, I mean."

"Ah," said Tóla. "I almost forgot. Grim asked for a message to be passed on. He'll be accommodated at Wolf Glen from now until the end of the job. The work is taking too long. The new arrangement will ensure the building progresses more quickly. The daily ride to and fro was impractical from the first."

I felt as if I'd been punched in the belly. I had no breath. No words.

"I'll bid you good day, Mistress Blackthorn, and thank you for your help." Without waiting for the reply I was unable to voice, he turned and rode away with his two men following.

"What about rain days?" I whispered. "Can he still come home on those?"

But nobody heard. And it wouldn't have made a difference anyway. I knew in my sad, stupid, ridiculous heart that Grim would be away on rain days too. How dare that man ask me for a charm of protection when he was taking away my own protector, my sanity, my other half . . .

Your what? The inner voice chimed in. *Stop this right now. You're not some silly, pathetic soul; you're a fighter. You're the one who stands up for other folk when they're too scared to speak out for themselves. Don't you dare shed tears. Put on your cloak, go over to Winterfalls and see Cara. Talk to folk and find out what's going on with Mathuin. Don't sit around feeling sorry for yourself. Do something.*

The cloak, the walk, I managed just fine. The tears, not quite so well.

25

He'd left her at Winterfalls *again*. And this time people hadn't even pretended they were pleased to have her there. Mhairi had lifted her brows and tightened her lips. Aedan the steward had been perfectly polite, but had seemed to have his mind on other things. It hadn't helped that Father had blamed them, blamed the entire household, for not noticing she'd run away until quite late in the day. She'd got them all in trouble. For nothing. Her plan had been a disaster. Father hadn't wanted to listen to her, even though she'd done her very best to find the words and get them out. He wasn't interested in why she had done it. He just wanted to get rid of her again, even though in the nighttime, when Gormán and Grim had brought her home, he had hugged her and wept over her and told her he loved her. By morning that softness was gone, and she found herself mute again. He hadn't even let her go to the barn to say good-bye to Gormán and to thank Grim.

Then there was the other thing, the thing that had happened after she fell down that hole. An accident, people had said. But it wasn't an accident. A tiny voice had led her in, made her take one step too many. She hadn't even tried to tell Father about that. She might have said something when they'd hauled her out of the hole, something only

Gormán or Grim would have heard. She'd been dazed and exhausted, not watching her words. She didn't think she'd told about the truly scary part, when those things had swarmed toward her as she climbed the rope, tearing her skirt with their claws. She'd lived that over and over last night in her dreams. Those tales that pictured the Otherworld as a place of delectable treats, of flowery meadows and pretty beings with gossamer wings, had it all wrong. If it hadn't been for the birds . . .

"Cara?"

She flinched. Mhairi was at the door. And the cross little dog. Cara could hear its claws tap-tapping along the floor. She'd thought she would be safe in the prince's library. With Prince Oran and Lady Flidais both away, who else would be in here?

"Mistress Blackthorn's here to see you," Mhairi said. "Come, Bramble! No dogs in the library." The sound of the door closing.

"So, you're back." Mistress Blackthorn's voice was a little strange. She sounded as if she had a cold. But at least she didn't talk as if Cara were a wayward child. Nor was she all soft sympathy and foolishness like some of them: *Oh, you poor thing, lost in the woods all by yourself,* as if she were weak and useless.

"I'm back." Cara lifted her head from her folded arms and looked at her visitor. Blackthorn's eyes were red. Her face looked puffy. "Are you all right, Mistress Blackthorn?"

The healer came to sit opposite Cara at the long worktable. "Why wouldn't I be?" she retorted. "You're the one who's been in trouble, or so I'm led to believe. I knew nothing about it until your father came knocking on my door not long ago."

"Oh."

"I was in Longwater most of yesterday and all last night. I didn't get home until this morning. I missed the whole thing." Blackthorn's expression softened a little. "I'm glad you're safe, Cara."

"Mm. It didn't work, though. He brought me straight back. As you see. And I'm not allowed to go outside without Mhairi *and* a guard."

"I'd tell you I'm sorry, but it sounds as if he has his reasons. Perhaps good ones. May I ask you a question?"

Cara nodded. She could imagine what it might be: *Why did you do it when you'd promised me you wouldn't? Where did you go, all that time? Didn't you say you never got lost in the home forest?* But Blackthorn didn't ask any of those.

"Did you see Grim?"

Cara nodded.

"Was he . . . No, never mind."

"Grim and Gormán found me. At least, the dog found me, Grim's dog, and then they rescued me. With a rope."

"A rope! Where were you? What happened?"

Cara had not thought she would tell all of it to anyone. Her father and Aunt Della had heard the part about falling down a deep hole and being trapped, and about climbing the rope to get out. But she hadn't told them about the things down there, the voices, what they'd offered and the other things they'd said. *Your whole life is a lie.* How could she tell Father that? But she wanted to tell Blackthorn. Blackthorn would know what to do. She might even know what those things were.

"If I tell you what happened, will you promise not to say I was dreaming or making things up?"

"You know me, Cara. You shouldn't need to ask me that."

"Sorry." Her voice had shrunk down; the words were retreating down her throat, hiding away.

"Don't be sorry. Just tell the story. Take your time." Blackthorn fished in her pouch, brought something out. "Borrow this. Hold it while you're talking—it might help. Not a charm exactly, but at the very least good luck. Remember that Grim made it, and Grim loves truth."

The little hedgehog. Cara wrapped her fingers around it. The oak warmed up in her hand. "I spoke to him," she whispered. "Grim, I mean. Just for a bit. When they got me out. I could talk to him."

Blackthorn smiled, but didn't say anything. She didn't tell Cara to hurry up and get on with it, simply sat quietly waiting.

So Cara told the story. All of it, from being up in the yew and deciding to make a run for it, to this morning, when her father had brought her back to Winterfalls and left her, just like last time. All of it, including falling down the hole and being stuck there with those things tormenting her. *Your whole life is a lie. It was a lie from the moment you were born.* And something about the heartwood house, why he was building it. *Your father's a liar. You're a pretender.* She told about holding on to the oak roots and knowing the tree would protect her for long enough to get out. And then the rescue.

"I can't tell Father any of that part," she said. "What happened down there, I mean. I can't tell anyone but you, Mistress Blackthorn. What could those folk have meant about a lie? I don't understand."

"Nor do I, Cara." Blackthorn had a different look in her eye now, as if she were trying to work something out. "I wish I did."

"Father did explain some things. About the men doing the building and why I can't stay there. It made sense while he was saying it, sort of. Him wanting to keep me safe, and not liking me to be up there while the builders are working. He said he'd promised my mother he'd never let anything bad happen to me."

"Mm-hm. He told me that too."

"Only I've been thinking about it. He's got Gormán there. Gormán's big and strong and Father knows he'd protect me against anything. And now there's Grim too. Even bigger and stronger. What sort of builders is he getting, trolls or giants?"

Blackthorn grinned. Cara felt like smiling back, only her mouth wasn't quite ready to do it yet. "I was wondering," she said, "if that wild man is one of them."

Blackthorn didn't answer straightaway. She seemed to be thinking. Then she said, "What wild man, Cara?"

"I told you. Didn't I? The day before Father sent me away the first time, I saw a wild man looking at the heartwood house. And then looking at me. Gormán made me go straight back to the house—the big house, I mean. I wondered if that had something to do with Father not wanting me at Wolf Glen. If that man stayed, if he was working for Father . . . I don't know. I'm just guessing. Did Grim say anything about who was doing the building?"

"Not much," Blackthorn said. "Your father put some rules on what could be said and what couldn't. Unusually strict rules."

"Mistress Blackthorn?"

"Mm?"

"Those were Otherworld beings, weren't they? Those voices down at the bottom of the hole?"

"I don't see what else they could have been, since I doubt very much that the whole thing existed only in your mind. Though you're right: if you told most folk this tale, that is exactly the explanation they would offer. Not because they don't believe in the uncanny, but because they are afraid of it. As it seems your father is."

"No, he isn't! Father's not afraid of anything!"

"Stop and think for a moment, Cara. Why else is he so determined to build the heartwood house? Why is it so very important to him that it be finished quickly and completely? Why would he—" Blackthorn stopped herself. "Never mind that."

"Why would he what?"

"It doesn't matter."

"Tell me! I'm tired of folk holding things back! I thought you, of all people, would be honest with me."

"You are quick to defend your father from criticism, despite his unreasonable treatment of you. I do have some more to tell, but if I go ahead, it could make him angry. Not with you. With Grim, for betraying a secret. And with me, for passing it on."

"Something about the wild man."

"Something about him, yes. He has a name: Bardán."

"Bardán. Go on."

"This story does not show your father in a good light, Cara. I'm telling you in confidence, as Grim told me. And I would ask that you hear me out calmly."

"All right."

Mistress Blackthorn told how the wild man, Bardán, had been hired to build the heartwood house the first time. How he was the only person who knew how to do it. According to what Grim had heard, Bardán had been taught the skills by his father who, if rumor was to be believed, had grown up in the Otherworld and become a craftsman of almost uncanny talents. He'd fallen in love with a half-fey woman and the two of them had escaped that realm together. They'd had a son, and that was Bardán.

It was possible, Blackthorn said, that the fey held a grudge against him and his. They might have felt they were owed something in exchange for those two going free.

What had happened next, Blackthorn did not know. But it seemed Bardán had begun building the heartwood house, then gone away abruptly with the job half-finished. There was an old tale that said a heartwood house conferred a whole range of blessings, as long as it was built the right way. If not, it seemed the opposite might happen. Father had been angry.

"How long ago was that?" Cara asked, while a trickle of ice went down her spine. "Before or after my mother died?"

"I must assume it was before," Blackthorn said. "I have heard that Master Tóla believed she might have survived if the heartwood house had been finished when he intended. If the builder had not suddenly downed tools and gone away."

"But—" No, she could not say it. Would her father, so strong, such a leader, let superstition get the better of his good judgment?

"It seems he came back. Bardán, I mean. Many years later. That day, when you saw him looking at the heartwood house and your father decided to send you away, was probably the first time Bardán had set eyes on the place in years. Where he'd been, why he went off and why he came back, I could only guess at. Grim knows more than I do, and he has a theory. But it's only conjecture. What is fact, Cara, is that your father needs Bardán there to tell Grim how to build the heartwood house—Bardán can't do the work himself as he has crippled hands now. But your father doesn't trust him at all. I would say he fears Bardán, if I didn't think it might spark an angry denial from you. I imagine it hurts to discover that your father is not the perfect man you have always believed him to be. The fact is, Tóla has been treating Bardán poorly. Unfairly. Sometimes cruelly."

"He wouldn't—"

"Grim has seen it. And Grim doesn't lie."

Tears stung Cara's eyes. She brushed them away, furious with herself, with her father, with Blackthorn for saying this, with the way everything had gone awry since the day that man, Bardán, had appeared at Wolf Glen. Why did he have to come back and turn everything upside down? It wasn't fair.

"I've found," Blackthorn said quietly, "that when I'm really angry, a brew helps. I might ask Fíona to send us something. And food with it. It feels like a long time since breakfast."

"How can that do any good?" The words came out in a ferocious undertone, and Cara felt ashamed. "I'm sorry, Mistress Blackthorn. It's just—it's just—"

Blackthorn went over to the door, stuck her head out, spoke to someone, came back in. "I'm not making light of your distress, Cara. The brew's as much for me as for you. Your father's just given me the news that Grim will be staying up there night and day until the building's finished, and that upset me more than I'd have expected."

"Oh." How odd. Blackthorn was such a strong person, so confident and sure of herself. And old—more than thirty, Cara guessed. People of that age didn't have tender feelings. Especially people like Blackthorn. Most folk were a bit scared of the wise woman. Everyone treated her with respect. It was hard to think of her being upset over a man. If that was what she meant. "I can come over to Dreamer's Wood and keep you company," she said. "So you won't be on your own. Maybe they'd let me stay over there." That would be so much better than being cooped up here. They weren't letting her go anywhere outside on her own.

"Most unlikely, I'm afraid," Blackthorn said. "I understand your father's set new limits on your freedom. He did say he was happy for you to visit me. But I'm sure he'd want you safely within these walls at night." She went quiet for a bit, then said, "I didn't get the chance to speak to Lady Flidais before she left. But she left me a message. An invitation to come and stay here for a while. She had in mind that I might be company for you, I think. Or that my presence might deter you from trying to run away." She grimaced.

"Or that *you* might be safer," Cara said. "They have those other guards here now—did you know? Those men with the . . ." She waved a hand around her face.

"They do? Men from Swan Island?"

"Them, yes. I've seen four of them today already. Standing watch with the ordinary guards or patrolling the boundaries."

Blackthorn had gone ashen white. She was not behaving like herself today at all.

"It's probably nothing much," Cara said. "It's just because some of the prince's guards have gone to court."

"What? Oh. Yes, I suppose so." Blackthorn sounded shaken.

There was a knock at the door, and a maidservant came in with a tray. A jug of something, two cups, a small platter of honey cakes. Since Blackthorn didn't seem to have seen the woman, Cara said, "Thank you. Please put it on the table." There was probably a rule about valuable books and sticky fingers, but nobody had said anything, and she had enough common sense to keep the two apart. She realized she had just spoken aloud to a stranger and managed to make herself understood.

The maidservant went out. Cara poured what proved to be ale, passed Blackthorn a cake, considered what came next. She had hoped for an explanation of those strange voices; some wise guidance, maybe, for dealing with her father and the odd story of the heartwood house. But Blackthorn was just sitting there. She'd taken one bite of her food and one drink from her cup, and she hadn't said anything for ages. And she was shivering. It was as if there was a storm all around her, but nobody else could see it.

Cara got up. Took off her shawl, walked around the table and draped it over Blackthorn's shoulders. "Something's wrong," she said. "You can tell me, if it'll help."

Blackthorn gave a kind of snorting sound. Cara could hear words in that sound: *You, help me? How could you help? You're only a child.*

It was like a slap in the face. A slap, and feeling the ground wobble under her feet at the same time. Cara wished she could roll up like a hedgehog, behind her defensive prickles, and forget the rest of the world. Nobody listened to her. Not even Blackthorn. Nobody cared. She didn't fit at home and she didn't fit here. She was a . . . In her mind, the voices chanted their cruel ditty. *You're a pretender, pretender, pretender.*

"Cara?"

Her lips closed themselves together. Her words sank down deep.

"Cara, I wasn't laughing at you. I respect your offer of help. But there's a lot of my story that you don't know; things almost nobody knows. Things that are too dark and evil to tell anyone, let alone a young woman like yourself. I'm ill-tempered and out of sorts today, and I'm sorry. Even at good times I'm not the kindest and gentlest of folk. You know that already."

It was possible to nod. To take a sip of the ale. Not to speak; not yet.

"I'll consider moving over here for a bit," Blackthorn said. "I don't enjoy living among a lot of folk, but I can do my work from this household, and if one of the farm cottages is empty, I'll ask Aedan if I can have that. I draw the line at sleeping in the women's quarters. You could stay with me or here in the main house. Provided Aedan agrees. I imagine he and Fíona are in charge of all the arrangements until the prince gets home."

"Yes," Cara managed. Her voice came out as a croak, but that was better than nothing. She took another mouthful of ale, thinking up the right words for a question she had to ask. "Mistress Blackthorn?"

"Mm?"

"I'm sure there's something more going on. Not just what Father said, about the men doing the building. Something complicated. Something old." She waited for Blackthorn to snort again, or laugh, or dismiss the idea.

"Go on," Blackthorn said.

"Only I can't do anything about it. Not if I'm stuck here. But—Mistress Blackthorn—those voices I heard in that underground place . . . whatever those creatures were, they seemed to know all sorts of things. It's as if they've been watching for ages, years and years. Not just all my life, but before that. Maybe not only watching but . . . meddling."

"I can only agree with you," Blackthorn said. She was eating her cake now; a good sign, Cara thought. "But even if you were still at Wolf Glen, you'd be ill advised to search for them again. They sound like a particularly unpleasant branch of the fey. Malign, almost. But since, as you say, you're going to be stuck in this house for a while, there is one thing you could do."

"What?"

Blackthorn waved a hand at the shelves of books and manuscripts that lined the library walls. "The prince and Lady Flidais are very fond of old tales. I have wondered if, somewhere in this collection, there might be a version of the heartwood house story. I would be interested to see it, and I imagine you would too. So there's a challenge for you. Search through any likely volume or manuscript and see if you can find it." Blackthorn smiled. She was almost back to herself. It was amazing how much better that made Cara feel. "Rather a daunting task, in view of how large the collection is," Blackthorn went on. "But more to your taste, I imagine, than spending your mornings embroidering with Mhairi. And as I have some writing work of my own to do, I could keep you company."

"I suppose I could do it." It sounded pretty tedious, just leafing through all those books. But she did want to know the heartwood house story. What if it was the key to everything? Hadn't those voices said, *I know what he's building,* as if that were somehow important? And spending her mornings in the library would mean she didn't need to talk to anyone except Mistress Blackthorn. That was worth a little boredom. "All right, I'll try."

"Of course," Blackthorn said, "it's possible you could go through every book and manuscript in the place and still not find the story. A pity we don't have a druid handy. When they are training, they learn just about every tale there is, and they never forget them." She rose to her feet. "Now, if I'm to move over here, I'd best go and have a word with a few folk. Find out about a cottage. Let Emer know what I'm doing. Bring some things across and lock up at home. Send word to Grim, if I can work out how. I'll have to go back to Longwater in a day or two. Maybe one of the men there could take a message."

"I'll start looking for books of old tales," Cara said. "I suppose some of them might be in Latin. I don't know very much Latin."

"We may be able to work it out between us. If not, we'll have to wait for Oran and Flidais. And I imagine their minds will be on other matters."

"What— Oh, you mean Lady Flidais's family and that man who's overrun their land."

"I mean that, yes. Cara, be mindful of one thing. You may find the story. It may unlock the puzzle. But knowing the truth doesn't always put everything right. Truth can hurt like a knife in the belly. So be very sure you want to do this."

"I'm sure," Cara said. "I know my father's not a liar and I'm going to prove it."

Blackthorn was staring at her now.

"Why are you looking at me like that?"

"You're different today," Blackthorn said. "Not hiding away any-more. Sure of yourself."

"I'm trying to be more like you," said Cara.

26

GRIM

T hings change quick now the master's seen sense. Matter of ten days or so and we've got our crew on the job. Five men, all from Longwater or close by. None of them builders, but all of them strong and fit. Willing to turn their hands to whatever needs doing. Weather's turned sunny, spirits are up, Gormán and Conn get a chance to go back to their own work and leave the heartwood house to me and my helpers. Ripple's happy. Job of builder's dog suits her. The fellows like having her there. Plenty of pats and morsels of food.

And there's Bardán. The crew are going home at night, coming in every day. Bardán's staying where he is, in Tóla's barn, and that means so am I. Promised to keep an eye on him day and night, so that's what I'm doing, best I can. Been hoping he'd stop going on about his daughter, his baby girl, where is she and so on. But since he heard Tóla talking the night Cara went missing, he keeps on coming back to that. And even though it's nonsense, just his mind mixing things up, the way he says it makes me deep-down sad. Wonder if they tried to tell him what happened, when he first came back. How could you do it? *You stole your own baby and ran off into the woods and left her, and she died cold and hungry and scared.* You couldn't say it to him. Losing his memory's a mercy. If he did remember, how could he live with himself?

When he says it on the job—*Where's my daughter?*—the other fellows take no notice. Or they tell him to shut it. Or they start singing to drown out his voice. But Bardán talks about his daughter at night too. Sings that rhyme, or other ones like it, about the birds, and nothing harming his child. Asks me over and over what happened to her. I say things like, *I wasn't here* or *I don't know.* Makes me think about telling lies. Makes me wonder if it's better to tell the truth even if it'll hurt someone. Even if it'll destroy them. Thing is, if nobody tells him, he might hear it by accident, someone saying, *Do you know what that man did?* That'd be even crueler.

Time passes; summer's coming. We get the roof beams in place. Make the framework for the thatch, nine courses, like it says in the story. And I get my second bag of silver from Master Tóla, which comes as a surprise even though I've earned it fair and square. Couple of the fellows work on the top part of the walls, the wattle and mud. Tóla hasn't asked for shelf beds or a hearth or anything else useful inside the heartwood house. Bit of a wasted effort if nobody's going to use the place for anything. I don't say that out loud. Nor do the Longwater men. Quiet bunch. Except when they're singing. Can't help wondering if Tóla's paid them off. Handed out a few silver pieces for folk not to talk about Bardán or himself or the heartwood house or his daughter. Those houses down at Longwater, they're well looked after. And the folk have got riding horses, as well as carts and suchlike. Didn't notice anyone wearing clothing with patches, or worn-out boots, or shawls with holes in. Makes me wonder how much they're paid for taking stuff up and down the lake. I don't ask, though. How could I, without sounding nosy? But they must know about Bardán. About him taking his baby daughter over to Wolf Glen with him all those years ago and what happened to her. His wife was a local girl. She and Bardán lived near that settlement. But not a word. Not even when he mutters about his daughter in their hearing.

We're still sleeping in with the animals, him and me. Made it a bit more comfortable, proper straw mattresses, floor swept clean down our end. Cleared a bench for our stuff and put up a couple of pegs to hang things from. Conn cooks for all of us. Now the weather's better, we go outside to eat, couple of benches and a table. Means they've got no reason to complain about Bardán's stink. Told him I'd give him a shave and cut his hair anytime he wants. Get him warm water for a wash. He said, *Not yet*.

Missing Blackthorn. A lot. Worrying about her, which is stupid. I know she can look after herself. Know she's probably glad to get me out of her way for a while. But I worry anyway. Got word from one of the Longwater men that she's moved over to the prince's house, so she's not all on her own. Doesn't make me feel better, though. Every time I make a brew I want to put a cup out for her. Like that might make her come walking up out of nowhere, saying, *How are you, big man?* Almost wish one of us would do himself an injury, give me an excuse to go and fetch her.

I'm not sleeping much, between the wild man's muttering, my own stupid thoughts going round and round, cows shuffling and mooing. In the night I do exercises. Bardán doesn't complain. Sleeps through it or lies there looking at me but not seeing me. There's a high window, up where the owl roosts. Open to the sky. That's how I know if Bardán's awake or not. His eyes give back the moonlight.

By morning I'm always tired. Mostly I know what needs doing, so I tell the crew and we all get on with it. Sometimes we're starting something new and we have to wait for Bardán to explain. He tells about the fiddly bits, the bits I can guess are part of the heartwood house story. Little wedges here and there. Those wattle-and-mud walls, up above the stone part. All needing to be done exactly by the rules. Seventeen wattles side to side, five-and-twenty bottom to top. Why? Who knows. But make one mistake and the luck drains right out of the place. That's what Bardán says. Nobody tells him it's rubbish. Nobody says it's making the build three times as hard as it should be. They just get on with the work.

The master comes up every day to have a look. If I spot him in time,

I get Bardán out of the way. Can't be sure I'd keep my temper if he hurt the wild man again. Day comes when I need to ask Tóla about the thatch.

"Fellows have done a good job," I say. "Be ready to start thatching well before you were planning. You should be looking for someone who's got the straw now and wants to sell it. Someone who had more than they needed for the winter. And kept it dry. Can't have anything moldy."

"How long?" Tóla asks.

I cast my eye over the place. Couple of men up ladders, working on the roof timbers. Two doing the fiddly stuff with the wattles. Bardán out of sight, since I told him to go inside until I called him. Looks like Ripple's gone too. One man's inside the heartwood house doing some measurements. "Ten days at the most," I tell the master. Feeling proud of a job well-done and surprised we've managed it so quick. "I know a lot of folk around the district. Done work for most of the farmers. If you want, I can ride around and find out for you." And I could visit Blackthorn. We could have a brew and a catch-up. I could tell her about Bardán and ask what she thinks. Though I don't need to ask, really. She'd say everyone deserves to be told the truth. Even if it's painful.

"You're needed here," Tóla says. Which I thought he would. "You know why. But you can give me some names and I'll send someone out."

I tell him to start with a sheep farmer named Cliona, and if she can't help, to ask her for more names, anyone who grows oats or rye. He lifts his brows a bit but doesn't say, *A woman?* the way some folk might. If he'd heard Cliona stand up for herself at Prince Oran's council, on the matter of whose dogs were worrying a neighbor's sheep, he'd know she's a straight talker with plenty of common sense. I suggest Prince Oran's home farm, something Cliona might not think of. Talk to Niall, who's the farmer there. He'll know who grows what around the district. And talk to Scannal the miller, about who he buys his grain from.

Not going to be quick, even if they do find what's needed. Takes a fair bit of straw to thatch a roof the size of this one. They'd have to bundle it, load it on a cart and haul it up here. Track through the forest would be pretty well impossible. Means they'd have to bring it the other way, through Longwater. Could take a while. Morrigan's curse, I can't wait till this job's over. Daytime's all right, working with the crew. Nights are wearing me out, messing up my head.

There's a question in there, and I don't want to think about the answer. When we've finished this, got the heartwood house built and thatched and all done, everything in its right place, what happens to Bardán? Does he get his pay like the rest of us and head off home? Does he walk away into the forest and vanish? Or does he hang about Wolf Glen muttering his rhymes and singing his songs and asking about his daughter, the one he killed but doesn't know it? What'll Tóla do to him when I'm gone?

It's night. I'm lying on my straw mattress, under my blanket. Done my exercises over and over till every part of me aches. Head full of rubbish, worries and memories and snippets I've heard. We're so close to the end, crew won't be needed at all soon, only one or two men to help me with the thatching. Sometimes I've thought the job would never get finished. Now it feels like it's gone almost too quick. Been almost too easy. What I'm thinking of most is the times Bardán's done that odd laugh, like he's got a secret. Like there's something important about this and he's the only one who knows it. Put that together with how much he and Tóla hate each other and you've got trouble.

Can't ask him straight out. Got to go into it another way.

"You awake?"

"Mm-hm."

"Just thinking. We'll be thatching soon. Is that as tricky as the rest of the build?"

"Tricky enough."

"Wanted to ask something. When I'm doing a whole roof myself, I like finishing off with some creatures for the top. Weave them out of straw, tie them on tight." I was proud of those animals I made for the scriptorium at St. Olcan's. Though two of them ended up with a bit of a fey finish. "Last time, for a monastery, I did salmon, dove, raven and fox. Up here, maybe some birds." I'm thinking of those birds that came when Cara was down in that dark place. That was odd. It was odd enough to make a man think something uncanny was in play. "Crow, owl, couple of others. What do you think?"

"You won't need those," Bardán says.

Odd way to put it. "More a case of liking than needing," I say. "Ever seen a roof done that way? The creatures look nice up there. Gives a sort of rightness to the place. And . . . well, it feels like good luck."

I think he's not going to answer. I think he may have dropped off to sleep. Then I hear a kind of low chuckling. Makes the hairs on my neck stand on end. That laugh, the secret laugh.

"Forget I asked," I say.

"Got to be done by the rules, Grim. Every part by the rules."

"So what are the rules for the thatch? Apart from needing to be straw." Hoping it's not something that'll make the job stretch out into autumn after all. Hoping it'll be quick and simple.

"Never mind that," Bardán says. "Wait till the master's got his straw; then I'll tell you." He laughs again, and someone, Gormán or Conn, calls out, "Shut it!" from next door.

"Thing is," I say, "I don't want to wait and then find out it's a job that's too hard for one thatcher and a couple of helpers, or a job that'll take all year. Better if you can tell me about it now."

Silence. He's not going to oblige. Then he says, "Grim?" Not laughing now. All serious.

"What?"

"Where's my daughter? My little Brígh, my lovely one? Where did she go?"

Morrigan's curse. My guts tell me the time for *I don't know* is over. Never heard him say his daughter's name before. "You know I wasn't here then. When you came to work for Tóla the first time. So all I know is what they told me. Tóla and Gormán."

"What? What?" He's up in a flash, crouching down by my pallet, trying to grab me, only he can't with his crooked hands. I sit up, take hold of his arms, wish I was somewhere else.

"Calm down. It's only a story. But it's a sad story. Bad news. I'll tell it if you want, but you won't like it."

"What?" His whole body's tight.

"Sit down, then."

He sits where he is, right next to me.

"There's no good way to break the news, brother. They told me your daughter died. Long ago, when she was only a baby."

There's a heartbeat of quiet; then he says, "No." It's a deep, sad sound, sad enough to bring tears to the eyes. Like an animal in pain. "No," he says again, "no. She can't be dead. My Brígh, my baby . . ."

Me, I've got the Red Giant story in my head again. A sorrowful tale. But this one's worse by far. The Red Giant story's got a good future in it, for some at least. This one's got no hope at all. You can't say to a broken man, *Go out. Make a new life. Find a new woman. Father another child.* Things aren't so easy. What about Blackthorn, her terrible story? No, I mustn't think of that. Can't let myself.

"How could it be?" Bardán says. Voice a wisp now, faint as faint. "How could my girl be dead? I was running, running. In the night. Then falling down, down . . . But she . . . she was safe. She was! She was! Safe and sound. Snug and peaceful, all wrapped up."

I see it in my mind. The wild man running through the woods. Why, I don't know, but running away from something. Could be a master who beat him—who knows? Could be his wife's death had caught up with him, torn his heart, scrambled his thoughts. She wasn't long gone then. Running to a place like that one Cara fell into, not an ordinary hole in the ground but an uncanny spot. A doorway. And I'm wondering. Wondering if, when a man's scared half out of his wits, he might put his baby somewhere he thinks will be safe, or at least safer than staying with him. Planning to come back and get her later. Or hoping someone will find her in time. Or, if a man's running so hard he can't think straight, he might trip and drop what he's carrying and not even notice. Just keep on running until he falls into another world. Is that possible? Wish I could ask Blackthorn.

"Tell me," Bardán says. Voice like a knife now, wanting blood. "Tell me what happened to her."

"That night when you left Wolf Glen," I say, trying to pick the right words, "they said you took her with you. Your baby, who was being looked after in Tóla's household. They said you went running off into the woods with her. They went searching straightaway. Couldn't find you. Couldn't find her. Searched for two days. No trace of you. But they found your daughter and—I'm sorry, brother, but she was dead."

He bows over, puts his head in his hands. No words now, but he lets out a groan, a sound that ties my guts in a knot. Someone hammers on the wall and yells, "Be quiet!"

Can't even get up and make a brew, which is what I do at home when Blackthorn can't sleep or has a nightmare. Have to go through the foresters' quarters to do that. A pox on this place!

"Where?" whispers Bardán. "Where did they find her?"

"Out in the woods, under an oak tree." I put a hand on his shoulder. He's shaking with sobs. "It would've been cold."

"Wrapped up," he whispers. "Wrapped up snug and warm. Safe. She was safe. It's a lie. It's all a lie."

"You've been away a long time. In a strange place. They didn't treat you kindly there. And when you first came back you didn't remember any of that story."

"They're lying! She's not dead—she can't be! They stole her, Grim. Stole her once, stole her twice, stole her right away . . ."

I get an odd feeling. An uncomfortable feeling. What he's saying is nonsense. He's lost in his old songs and rhymes. But I can't help thinking, *What if . . .*

"Do you mean the fey, Bardán?" But no, it can't be that, a human child snatched and a changeling left in its place. There's no changeling in this story. There'd have been nobody to leave it with. Bardán's wife was already dead. And that was the night he fell into the Otherworld. Anyway, it wasn't only Tóla who gave me that story of finding the baby girl's body, it was Gormán too. They can't both be lying, can they? It's some old tale, surely, that Bardán's mixed up with his own story. Or he's not ready to admit what happened even to himself. Seen that before. When a man's done something so bad, he tells himself it never happened. Tells himself over and over till he believes it.

"I didn't leave her," whispers Bardán. "I wouldn't leave her. I love her. My little one, my dear one, my last sunshine."

And here am I, all out of words. Because the way he says this, it sounds like deep-down truth.

"Help me, Grim," he says. "Help me find my girl."

27

BLACKTHORN

When I'd suggested that Cara look for the heartwood house story, I'd had two motives. The first was to keep her occupied. Maybe she'd find the tale and maybe she wouldn't. Maybe it would be helpful in explaining what had happened at Wolf Glen and maybe it would provide no insights at all. But while she was searching, she wouldn't be brooding over her father's treatment of her, and she wouldn't be hatching yet another plot to run away.

Then there was my own task. Prince Oran's library housed an extensive collection of books and manuscripts, many of them quite precious. And it had an adjoining chamber set up as a scriptorium, with a glazed east-facing window and several writing desks. Shelves held a supply of quills, inks and good parchment. The household did not have its own scribe. Flidais did whatever writing was required for domestic arrangements—lists of supplies and so on—and both she and Oran wrote their own letters. They wrote poetry too. Flidais had told me so. But I imagined that was set away somewhere private. Fíona, wife of Aedan the steward, cleaned the library herself. The place was spotless. And at present, with Oran and Flidais both away, we were the only people using it. It was a perfect opportunity for me to complete the statement I'd been scrawling in my notebook, then make a fair copy. Cara worked in the main part of the library. I worked in the scriptorium. If she had questions, I did my best to answer them. If she needed help with a Latin translation, we worked on it together. I only had to tell her once that my own work was private; after that, she was careful not to look at it.

Writing the document felt like putting my heart's blood down on the page. Every sentence hurt; every word brought back the painful past. But I had to do it. Now that Mathuin had shown his hand against Flidais's family, I felt compelled to record everything I knew about his crimes. I felt as if time might be running out.

We made a decision to work only in the mornings, since my duties as healer continued and I often had to travel some distance to visit folk. Fann and her baby in Longwater, for instance, were still under my care. Nor did I intend Emer's progress with her reading and writing or her training as a healer to be halted by this diversion. Every few days she joined us in the library to labor over her letters for an hour or so. Poor Grim. By the time he came home he would be far behind her. A pox on Tóla! Didn't the man understand folk's need to see one other occasionally, to reassure themselves that their loved ones were alive and well? No building work could be so important that a person needed to give day and night to it. I told myself Grim's absence meant the job would be done more quickly, allowing him to be home sooner. I missed him so much it was like a physical ache. Which was exactly what Cara had said, once, about how being away from Wolf Glen made her feel. And Cara was fifteen years old. I ordered myself to grow up and stop being foolish.

I had doubted Cara's ability to concentrate on a task that would keep her indoors, seated at a table, for hours at a time. But she surprised me, working out a system to ensure she did not miss anything and maintaining a careful record of her progress. Washing her hands before she handled the books. Keeping our morning refreshments well away from anything precious. Staying quiet unless she really needed to ask me something. Not that it was easy for her. When our morning's work was done, she would rush off outside as if set free from a prison cell. Not that she was free, exactly. Her father's rules meant she could go no farther than Flidais's small private garden without both a handmaid and a guard in attendance. This arrangement was inconvenient for the household and irksome for Cara herself. Fíona confided in me that nobody had forgotten the tongue-lashing Tóla had delivered after his daughter went missing.

As for Oran and Flidais and their retainers, they remained at court. Still. I wished someone would tell me what was going on, but I could not ask. Start showing too much curiosity about Mathuin of Laois and I would reveal I had a special interest in that subject. I would make myself vulnerable. Folk would start asking *me* questions.

Surely the king's council must be over by now. Had they decided to take action against Mathuin? They must do something. He'd committed an act of gross hostility against Lord Cadhan, Flidais's father. He'd seized Cadhan's land and killed many of his retainers. He'd driven Cadhan and his wife out. No leader worth his salt was going to say, *Oh, how unfortunate. But there's nothing we can do about it now.*

The question was, what could they do? Laois was far away and Mathuin's forces were formidable. The High King would not want war on his doorstep. Not even a petty war. This kind of thing was like a fire in dry grass. It started small, a flickering flame. If not quickly dealt with, it could grow into a huge blaze, spreading to destroy more and more ground. An attempt to topple Mathuin by force of arms seemed unlikely.

So why were those men from Swan Island here? There were more of them now, each with a different animal marking and a name to match. Cúan, Art, Earc. Hound, bear, salmon. Ségán, hawk. Caolchú, another hound. Cionnaola, wolf-head. Perhaps, when each joined the warrior band, he chose a name to suit his own appearance or his character. Cionnaola had long twists of gray-black hair and features that were almost noble—a prominent, straight nose and piercing dark eyes. Lonán—blackbird—was a stocky, dark-skinned man with a clever face. And so it went on.

The official story was that they'd been hired to supplement the household guard while Oran and his entourage were away. That was believable. But why so many? These were hard men, highly trained and ruthless. I could see it in their eyes and in the way they moved and in the weaponry they carried. Their nice manners—and they all proved to be like Cúan, courteous almost to a fault—could not disguise the fact that these were no ordinary men-at-arms.

While I worked on my document, Cara read story after story and rhyme after rhyme. So far she'd found nothing about a heartwood house. I asked Aedan whether the druid, Oisin, was expected to visit Winterfalls anytime soon, and was told that Oisin came and went when he chose, which I knew already. Time passed and I grew more and more ill-tempered. I wished I had not promised to keep an eye on Cara. I wished I had never heard of Wolf Glen or Master Tóla or his poxy heartwood house. As for those so-called guards walking around the place, every time one of them said good day or gave me a polite smile, I thought of Mathuin's henchmen coming to take me away. My dreams were full of unspeakable things.

"Mistress Blackthorn?"

I started in fright, dropping my quill. Cara was standing right by my desk. I whipped a spare sheet of parchment over my work, even though the ink was still wet.

"You look terrible," Cara said, blunt as always. "You should get up and walk around for a while. That's what you're always telling me."

I felt weak and dizzy. My mind was half in the nightmare past. "I'm fine," I said. "Forget about me. Do your own work." I tried to stand up, but my knees refused to cooperate. My neck ached. How long had I been sitting here?

"You look sick. Shall I fetch someone?"

"No! I don't want anyone!" Only Grim, to make a brew and sit with me while we drank it, and wait until I was ready before he spoke. Morrigan's curse, the big man had put up with a lot from me since the day we'd escaped the lockup.

"It's time to stop anyway," Cara said. "Let's go outside. I'll show you my favorite tree." She flashed a smile. "If you come with me, I won't need Mhairi."

"I must put this away first."

She busied herself with tidying away her own work, while I chose a new hiding place for my secret account. Now that it ran to many sheets of parchment, I could not conceal it in the pouch at my belt as I had done with the notebook. Since the cottage where Cara and I were housed could not be securely locked up, it seemed to me that the safest place to hide this document was among other documents. The testament against Mathuin resided between the pages of a different book every night. I chose volumes I thought an unexpected visitor, even a scholarly one such as Oisin the druid, would not be inclined to examine. This time I slipped it into a weighty volume with a worn, cracked cover. The book was in a tongue so foreign that the letters themselves had unfamiliar shapes. There was no making sense of it. As I closed the pages over my work, I whispered words of protection.

Cara's favorite tree was a magnificent old yew standing on a rise. The trunk was massive, the bark a furrowed landscape of nooks and crannies.

"The best thinking place is up there," Cara said, pointing to some spot entirely concealed by heavy branches and foliage. "But you needn't try to climb up. It might be too much for you. At your age, I mean."

I swallowed an oath. "I might need some help for the first bit," I said, eyeing the distance.

Cara grinned. "I'll get up first, and then I can help you."

Not long after, the two of us were sitting side by side, high above Prince Oran's farmlands. I could see why Cara liked being up in trees so much. This was a whole world, away from annoying handmaids and their snappy dogs, away from mysterious tattooed men, away from thoughts of old enemies and how they might strike again when least expected. The actual climbing I hadn't enjoyed quite so much, though I'd been impressed by Cara's strength as she'd helped me up. Her air of fragility was deceptive.

From up here I could see our cottage, stone gray against the many greens of Dreamer's Wood. Farther away lay the great dark mass of the

Wolf Glen forest. No wonder Cara loved this perch. She could see nearly all the way home.

"I promised your father some time ago that I'd do something for you," I said, "and I haven't done it yet."

"What?"

"He asked me to make you a protective talisman. Something to carry with you. I told him I'd need a piece of cloth from one of your mother's garments, if there are any, and something of his too. I thought he'd be back down to visit you and would bring them." There had been no sign of Tóla since he'd left his daughter at Winterfalls for the second time. As fathers went, I considered him a pretty poor one, for all his protestations that he loved his daughter. He might be a landholder and busy, but he was the only father Cara had. And he'd known how unhappy she was to be sent away.

I became aware of how long Cara had been silent. When I glanced at her, she was leaning against the yew's trunk with her eyes closed. Not asleep; not so quickly. I waited.

"You could go up to Wolf Glen and ask him," she said eventually, opening her eyes and lifting her head. "It would be a perfect excuse. You could find out how things are going with the heartwood house. And you could visit Grim."

"Your father would be angry. He'd think I was being a busybody."

"Not if you reminded him about the talisman and needing the things. Aunt Della would find them for you."

"He might be angry that I've left it so long to remind him. Left you unprotected, as he would see it. He certainly would be if he knew what really happened the night you were missing."

Cara went pale. "Don't tell him! Not about those voices! He'd shut me away forever if he knew. Make me go to a nunnery or something."

"I wouldn't dream of telling."

"Anyway," Cara said, "I'm not unprotected. Not now. I made my own talisman." She tugged at a cord around her neck and drew out from under her gown a bunch of feathers tied together with a length of green silk cord, the latter perhaps obtained from Mhairi's embroidery supplies.

The thing was beautiful. I could feel the good magic in it without the need to touch. She had chosen only small feathers, so the talisman would lie flat against her chest, invisible beneath her clothing. The cord was elaborately knotted around them; I was fairly sure the knots themselves held a protective power. "That's remarkable," I said. "Where did the feathers come from?"

"Gifts," Cara said simply. "Some I find; some the birds bring to me. There are nine here. Nightjar, chiffchaff, bunting, goldcrest, warbler, thrush, jay, redpoll and siskin." She touched each gently as she reeled off the names.

My skin prickled. There was something odd about that list. Where had I heard it before—in an old rhyme?

"This should keep me perfectly safe. Even if I do fall down into a place like that again. Birds saved me. And birds will protect me. So really there's no need for you to make anything. But I thought you might like to visit Wolf Glen. I know I can't go. But he never said you couldn't."

28

GRIM

At first I think she's only a dream. Been wanting to see her so bad, missing her so much, I've imagined this over and over. In the dream I look up and there she is, coming along the path from the big house. Red scarf on her head, red hair under it, basket over her arm. Not smiling or frowning, just looking at me like she knows me better than I do myself.

So when it happens I can't believe it's real. We're having a break, me and Bardán sitting on the big stones near the heartwood house, the other fellows over by the barn. Someone's made a brew, which is welcome. Platter of bread with fresh butter, brought over by Mistress Della, even more welcome. The lady didn't stay to chat this time.

The ghost that's Blackthorn casts her eye over the heartwood house, then over Bardán and me. "Got a spare cup, big man?" she asks. Then smiles. Next thing, Ripple comes running from where she's been with the crew, barking her head off. Blackthorn says, "Down!" Ripple sits and Blackthorn gives her a pat.

I'm on my feet, heart hammering. She's here. She's real. Know what I want to do, which is run forward and wrap my arms around her and never let go. But there's Bardán. Also, she might curse and slap me in the face. "You're here," I say like a stupid fool.

Bardán gets up too. Blackthorn's giving him a long look, the kind that means she's thinking hard. "You must be Bardán," she says. "I'm Grim's friend, Blackthorn the healer. I hope the salve helped your hands." She looks back at me. "It's good to see you," she says. "Been a while. I can't stay long."

There's all sorts of things to ask. Why is she here? Why hasn't Tóla come rushing out and ordered her to go home? What about Cara?

"Brew?" I ask.

She smiles wider. "Thought you'd never ask."

I scrape together some of my wits. "Bardán, ask one of the men to bring another cup, will you? Say I've got a visitor." The Longwater fellows mind their manners around the wild man. They know they'll answer to me otherwise. "Tell them there's no need to rush back to work."

Bardán goes and we're on our own, though probably not for long. I look at Blackthorn. She looks at me.

"I've missed you, big man."

I nod. Still looking. Remembering those words I wrote for her. And the ones she wrote for me. "You come on horseback?"

"Mm-hm. Eochu found me a placid mare. I've left her down by the big house. Grim, we'd better talk now, before anyone else comes. I don't imagine Master Tóla's going to leave me up here unsupervised for long; he seems keen to know every little thing that goes on in this place."

So she's come to Wolf Glen to see Tóla. "You here to report on Cara?"

"You might invite me to sit down."

"Sit. Please." I wave a hand at the stone Bardán's been sitting on.

"I'm joking, Grim," she says as she sits down. "Or trying to. If I don't, I might disgrace myself and shed tears."

"Tears? Why?"

"Why do you think?" She reaches over and takes my hand. I can feel myself filling up with happiness. "You're blushing," she says.

"Better than crying."

"Look at us," Blackthorn says. She's going to say something else, but one of the fellows comes over from the barn with a steaming cup in his hand. Passes it to her, smiles, introduces himself.

"Mistress Blackthorn? I'm Corcrán, from Longwater. I was there the day you helped birth Fann's boy."

She greets him, has a little talk about Fann and how she's faring—well, it seems—and all I can think about is precious time being wasted, our time, hers and mine. In a bit Corcrán takes himself off, and we sit a while without speaking. Don't know what she's thinking. She did say she'd missed me. But she let go of my hand as soon as Corcrán came.

"I had some business with Tóla," she says. "I needed to collect some items for Cara. He's forbidden her to leave Winterfalls until your building job is finished. He couldn't really pack me straight off home the way he did her, especially as I told him I was riding on to Long-water."

"Fair way," I say. "You'll be tired. On your own."

"You know I can look after myself. But I wish you were home, and that is no joke. Not that I'll be there myself until Oran and Flidais get back from court. I've promised to stay with Cara. And she's . . ." Blackthorn looks around as if she's worried someone might hear. The fellows are still having their brew over by the barn; I can hear them talking, laughing.

"She's what?"

"She's going through all the books in Oran's library, looking for the story of the heartwood house. My idea, not hers, and maybe it wasn't such a good one. Grim, about that night when you rescued her—did she tell you . . ." She stops again. Drops her voice to a murmur. "Did she tell you about the voices she heard down in that place? Did she say anything about birds?"

"Had a crow with her when she climbed up. And other birds flying around. Odd. Daytime birds. Should have been asleep at that hour. About voices . . ." I think back. "She said something about being offered things. Someone trying to make her stay. Or go further in. Wasn't making much sense at the time."

"She told me. A secret. But you need to know." Blackthorn's whispering now. Keeps looking over her shoulder. "Fey voices, all the time she was down there, trying to coax her in. And when she wouldn't do what they wanted, they started tormenting her. Saying her father was a liar. Saying her life had been a lie since the day she was born. Cara thinks it may be tied up with the heartwood house story. That if she finds it, it might explain everything. Only . . ."

"Drink your brew. You look like you're seeing ghosts."

She takes a mouthful. "I was the one who started Cara looking. Only the more I think about it, the more I think this may be one of those times when it's better that the truth never comes out."

"There's a sad story about the first time. First time it was being built, I mean." I tell her about Bardán and his baby girl. Tell her the terrible thing that happened, the tale Tóla and Gormán told me. "He says she didn't die. Couldn't have. All wrapped up warm and safe. Keeps telling me that. The way he says it, it sounds like the truth. Wondering now if I was lied to earlier. Bardán asked me to help him find her, you know. His daughter. I feel sorry for him, whatever he's done. Poor sod never had a chance. Down that hole and off to the Otherworld for fifteen years. Came out crippled and crazy."

"Morrigan's curse," breathes Blackthorn. Thinking, most likely, the same thing I'm thinking. Only it's impossible. "There's a few ways you could tell that story and I don't like any of them. The one that's supposed to be true is as bad as the others."

"Thing is," I say, "once folk have made up their minds that a man's lost his wits, it doesn't matter what he says. Doesn't matter what tale he tells—truth, lies, something in between. Folk don't listen. Doesn't make a difference how loud he shouts, or how clever his words are. Nobody hears."

"Danu's mercy," mutters Blackthorn, staring at me. "You're saying Bardán might have been telling the truth all the time? Or trying to?"

I think of those rhymes, the scraps of old lore the wild man mutters over and over. "*Once they stole, twice they stole, stole them right away*. That's one of his rhymes. Stole *them*. There's one stolen child we know about, and that's Bardán's father. But who's the other one?"

We're quiet for a bit, thinking.

"Maybe that story about Bardán taking the child isn't true at all." I picture him out in the woods, running, running. With his baby girl in his arms. Never mind what happened next, dropping her or leaving her, murder or horrible accident or something uncanny. What I want to know is, why was he running? When they told me the story, they didn't say anything about that. Just that he took his daughter and left. Why would he do that? Good job, place to stay, folk to look after the baby— he'd have been crazy to walk away. And he wasn't crazy, not back then, or he wouldn't have been able to build the heartwood house. Not long before, he'd been a man with work and his own house and family.

"One part of it has to be true," says Blackthorn, glancing around again to make sure nobody can hear. "That his daughter died. They found her body. They buried her. They told the kinsfolk."

We look at each other again.

"Only got their word for it," I say. "Tóla's and Gormán's. The kinsfolk never saw the body. They made sure of that."

"Stole her right away," murmurs Blackthorn. "Made her disappear. How convenient that Bardán fell down that hole. No asking awkward questions from there."

"Mm-hm."

"I want to ask you something."

"Be quick, then. Fellows are on the way back over."

"You know what I'm thinking. The same thing you're thinking. A possibility neither of us have put into words because, if it's true, it's going to turn a lot of folk's lives upside down."

"What's the question?" I ask, but I know what it is.

Blackthorn's whispering now. "Whose daughter is Cara, really?"

"She might take after her mother," I say.

"She's surely nothing like Tóla," Blackthorn says. "I wonder if Sua-nach was a woman who could hear the voices of trees. I wonder if birds used to come and perch on her uninvited. I wonder if a crow ever came to her rescue."

"Can't see Tóla marrying a woman like that. For a bully of a man, he's mightily scared of the uncanny."

"Mm. Bardán, on the other hand, had a mother who was half-fey."

"You're saying . . . ?" She's saying what I've been thinking, only I can't see how it could be.

"I'm not sure what I'm saying yet. Most likely something that shouldn't be spoken of here. Grim, what is that rhyme you told me parts of, the one about the birds? It was one of Bardán's, wasn't it?"

"Every birdling in the wood?"

"That's it. Do you know all of it?"

"Heard him sing it all. Can't remember every part, though. Something about feathers. It's a charm to keep a child safe."

"Could we ask him?"

Bardán's coming back, the other fellows behind. And we can't ask, because Gormán appears from the other direction, carrying a bundle of hazel rods I've been wanting for the thatching.

"Cara made herself a talisman, with feathers." Blackthorn talks fast, in a murmur. "Nine different kinds. She went through the list, starling, woodcock, owl—"

"Mistress Blackthorn?" Gormán says, cutting her off. "My name is Gormán. I'm the head forester here. I'm heading over to Longwater now, so I'll escort you. One of the lads is fetching your horse."

I see her wanting to say, *No, thank you; I'm fine on my own,* then deciding not to. Though if she thinks she'll get anything useful out of Gormán, she's dreaming. Me, I'm happy she won't be doing the ride on her own. That would make her cross, if she knew. Gormán must have been down at the house, talking to Tóla. I bet the master asked him to make sure she didn't stay too long.

Lots of things I want to say to her, but I can't, not with him right there and the others close by now, within earshot. *Be safe. Come back soon. I miss you.* And more. Can't say any of it. Just wasted all that time talking about wretched Bardán and Cara and the whole sorry mess.

"I'd better go," she says. "I have a few folk to see in Longwater, not only Fann." Which might be a way of telling me she's going to talk to folk about what happened fifteen years ago, and whether Tóla really is a liar. Good luck to her. Be like getting blood out of a stone. If they've kept a secret all this time, they're hardly going to open up now.

"Tell the other fellows down there I'll drop in and see them sometime," I say. "When the build's finished. And ride safe."

"Look after yourself, big man."

"You too, Lady."

She doesn't take my hand this time. Just looks at me, and I look back, and then she turns away and she's gone.

At least I saw her, I tell myself as we get back to work on the heartwood house. At least she came here. And even if Bonehead didn't say any of the things he wanted to say, maybe there was no need to. Her and me, often enough we don't need words. Though words can mean a lot. *Strength in his hands,* I think. *Truth in his eyes. Love in his heart. Honor in his spirit.*

And I wonder if a tiny baby, so new it hardly knows what world it's come into, can listen to a lullaby and remember it deep down. I wonder if that baby, years later when she's a girl of fifteen, can speak the words without knowing where she got them from. If she's got a drop or two of fey blood, maybe she can. I wonder if there was only ever one baby girl at Wolf Glen.

29

BLACKTHORN

"I hope Cara is well," said Gormán as we rode down to Longwater. "Is she recovered from her ordeal?"

"An experience like that must make its mark on a person," I said. "Especially a young person. But yes, she is well. Happier now than when she first came to Winterfalls."

"We miss her."

"She misses you," I said. "She speaks very fondly of you, Gormán; as if you were family. You taught her wood carving, didn't you? She's remarkably skillful." When he glanced across at me, I added, "We let her borrow Grim's tools. It was obvious from the first that she knew what she was doing." Should I take a risk, step into the dangerous territory of old secrets? "Gormán, there's something I'd like to ask you."

"Yes?"

"What is the old tale about a heartwood house? Where did Master Tóla get the idea from?"

"Why would you want to know that, Mistress Blackthorn?"

"I'm intrigued. As a wise woman I know a lot of tales, and I'm always interested in hearing more. I've never come across a heartwood house before."

"I don't know where he got the story. From a druid, perhaps. A heartwood house is considered lucky. Each type of wood contributes a particular blessing. Oak for strength and endurance. Beech for ancient knowledge. Fir for clarity. Blackthorn for facing reversals with determination. And so on." There was good humor in his smile. Had the situation been different, I could have liked this man.

"You sound half druid yourself, Gormán."

"I'm a forester. A forester knows trees."

"Cara's favorite tree at Winterfalls is an ancient yew."

"I know the one," said Gormán. "New growth and old side by side. The younger wood glowing pink when the sun catches it. A remarkable tree. Its spirit born again, one might say."

Half druid, indeed. "What blessing would yew bring to the heartwood house?" I asked.

He hesitated before responding. "An understanding of the past. The wisdom to learn from what has come before. Some would say rebirth."

It struck me that this would be a very useful lesson for Tóla to learn. But I did not say so. "Are you sure you don't know any more of the old story?"

"I'm sure of one thing, Mistress Blackthorn. I've told you as much as I have leave to tell."

We rode on farther, down the track toward the lake. Clouds shaded the sun. I'd best not take too long visiting folk or I might be riding home in the rain with the light fading. Or spending another night in Longwater.

"Cara loves birds, doesn't she?" I asked, trying for a casual tone.

Gormán took his time in replying. After a while he said, "Or birds love her. It's been thus since she was a small child, running about the yard with a flock of chickens at her heels. I could wish those times back, Mistress Blackthorn. They were blessedly uncomplicated."

"Life has a habit of getting complicated, and often not in ways we would choose."

"Indeed. Mistress Blackthorn . . ."

"Go on."

"Please tell Cara I asked after her. Let her know that I hope all's well with her, and that I look forward to her return home."

"Why don't you ride on to Winterfalls with me and tell her yourself?"

"I wish I could, but my duties require a quick inspection of some goods in Longwater followed by a swift return to Wolf Glen. I hope the folk down there can provide you with an escort for the remainder of your ride."

"They'll offer; I'm certain." How was it the man was so friendly and courteous, yet had not told me a single useful thing? Was I asking the wrong questions? "You must have known Cara since she was a babe in arms."

"In fact, Cara was not born at Wolf Glen, but at the home of her mother's kinsfolk in the south."

"Oh? Why was that?"

"Mistress Suanach was not in robust health. It was considered wiser; her folk had a physician whom they trusted."

It was another part of the story that felt a little odd. "But she died anyway."

"Only much later, after they returned home. I remember the day they came back; little Cara sitting up in the saddle in front of her mother, proud as proud. When she was lifted down she staggered across the stable yard on her own feet, pointing at those chickens. Her first word was *bird*. Her second was *tree*."

I tried not to let my surprise show. There was an obvious question, but if I asked it, he might realize he had revealed a little too much. I chose another one. "Cara's mother died not long after that, didn't she?"

"A fever. It carried her away almost overnight. A terrible time. Master Tóla was out of his mind with grief. He loved his wife above anything. Cara's safety became all-important to him. As it still is. Not only to him but to all of us. The master's actions may seem odd to you, Mistress Black-thorn, but every decision is made in Cara's best interests."

I held my tongue, though there was plenty I could have said. Sending her to Winterfalls without explanation, that first time, had led to her running away and almost being lost forever. If not for her own resourcefulness and Ripple's tracking skills, she might now be in the Otherworld or worse. "I'll give her your message, and I'm sure she'll be glad to hear it. I know that she misses you very much. And the forest. That's where she feels most at home."

"And she must be missing her father."

"Him too." Though, in my opinion, he didn't deserve it. "Ah, I see the lake. We must be almost there. Does that side path lead to a cottage? The place where that man used to live, the one who is working with Grim and the other builders?"

"What do you know about that?" His tone was suddenly sharp, and I was reminded that he was a big, strong man, whose hands would be weapons in themselves.

"The day Cara went missing, Grim and I were both in Longwater. Grim must have told you. I was assisting with a difficult childbirth and he had escorted me there. I sent him off to gather herbs, and he happened to meet that man, Bardán, at the old hut."

"The folk at Longwater talked to you about the wild man? About the time when he lived there?"

"The folk at Longwater had very little to say on the subject. Their attention was elsewhere, with one of their own in danger of dying along with her unborn babe. We were all working hard. I know not to gossip, Gormán. So does Grim."

"You seem unduly interested in our situation. I don't understand why that would be."

"No? I've been placed more or less in charge of Cara. I like the girl. She's interesting. A puzzle. She's also sad and confused, and I wish I could help her more." Should I push this a little further? Risk getting myself in trouble with Tóla all over again? In view of what Gormán had already let slip, it might be worth trying. "She is keeping herself busy. She's undertaken a kind of mission."

"A mission? What do you mean?"

"She wants to find the story of the heartwood house," I said as we rode down to level ground and the last approach to Longwater settlement. The lake was slate gray under the clouds; a few swans floated there, ghost pale against the water. "She's looking for it in the prince's books. Hoping it might explain the situation."

"Tell her to stop." Gormán drew his horse to a halt; mine came to a stand beside it. "Tell her to stop looking. This is best left alone. Master Tóla would say the same. Let Cara continue down that path and she'll stir up something nobody would want. Believe me."

"I won't ask you to explain that. I've had some doubts about her project too. But it is keeping her occupied. Giving her less time to brood about the injustice of her situation. As she sees it," I added hastily. "I can't order her to stop. It's for her father to do that, if he doesn't want her finding out the truth. But, Gormán, this is not some sweetly biddable young woman. Cara loves her father. She wants to please him. But she's no longer a child, and she has good cause to want the truth. Tóla might order her to stop looking now, and she might do as she's told. But sooner or later she'll try again. If there's some kind of secret, sooner or later she'll find it."

There was a long silence then. Long enough to bother me. The horses didn't move; we didn't move; it felt as if time stood still for a while. Then Gormán said, "You and Grim. Fond of each other, are you?"

"That's none of your business!" My voice was a snarl. I felt myself flush.

"And this is none of yours, Mistress Blackthorn. You and your friend should step back from this now. Grim with his questions and you with your . . . encouragement of Cara. Go any further and you will put several folk in danger. Yourselves included."

I could think of nothing to say.

"I'm entirely serious," Gormán said. "If you value Grim's safety, if you value your own, stop meddling now."

30

CARA

She hadn't intended to go back to the library. A whole morning spent poring over those manuscripts was more than enough. But she'd left her warm shawl there and it was getting cold outside. There might be rain. As she walked toward the library, Cara thought of the trees sucking up moisture, breathing the damp air, stretching and easing themselves in the slow way they had. It would be interesting to be a tree. A long, gradual sort of life, with many visitors. A tree could observe the passing of time in a way no man or woman ever could. A tree could see generations of birds and squirrels and humankind be born and live and die; it could see wars fought; it could see flood and fire and disease ravage the countryside. It could see saplings grow from its own seed, ready to take its place when it finally succumbed to age and decay or the ax of the forester.

Oh, she missed Gormán! His wise words, his little jokes, his sideways smile, as if he and she shared secrets nobody else knew. It was so long since she'd seen him. That night didn't count, the night he'd helped rescue her. By the time she'd started to get over her shock, she'd been all tucked up in bed with Aunt Della fussing over her. And the next morning, when she'd asked if she could say good-bye, Father had said no. Just like that. Which meant there was something really odd going on, not just what Father had said about the workers, but something else.

Cara pushed open the library door. She took a step inside and stopped in her tracks. The three men who were standing by the table turned to stare at her. Three of *those* men, the Swan Island warriors.

"Oh," she whispered, backing away. "Sorry."

"Wait," said a male voice behind her.

Cara froze.

"You were going in, weren't you?" It was the young one, Cúan. He stepped around her and motioned forward. "We'd like a word, anyway."

A birch in a spring storm must feel like this, Cara thought. Trembling all through. As if the wind might topple her. But a birch has roots in the ground, strong roots. They held her steady. She walked forward. If she tried hard enough, maybe she could make her voice work.

"Sit down," said one of the others, the man who looked like a hawk. "My name is Ségán."

"Art," said a broad-shouldered, dark-bearded man.

"I'm Caolchú." This one looked friendly enough, with an amiable face and a shock of wheaten-fair hair. A warrior, though; his muscles were like knotted ropes.

"And you know my name," Cúan said. "No need to be alarmed."

"I just . . ." Her voice was a timid mouse's, a secret vole's, a spider's, a wren's. She cleared her throat. "I just wanted my shawl." What were they doing here?

"Please," said Ségán. "Be seated. We have a few questions for you."

"I can't . . . I have to . . ." She moved forward anyway and sat on the bench he was indicating. Seated, it might be easier to hide the shivering. *Be like Blackthorn,* she told herself. *Be brave. Be strong.*

Ségán sat down opposite her. "You've been spending your mornings here with Mistress Blackthorn; is that right?"

That one was easy. A nod was enough.

"Doing what, exactly?"

Cara could hear Mistress Blackthorn answering, *None of your business!* But the words wouldn't come out at all. Not those words. Not any words, now. The walls felt very close suddenly. She could hear the beating of her own heart. She shook her head.

"Tell us, Cara." The man called Art was standing behind Ségán with his brawny arms folded. Caolchú was turning the pages of a book, not looking at her. If that was supposed to reassure her, it wasn't working. Cúan was over by the door now. On guard? Against what?

What is this, an inquisition? Blackthorn would say. Or, *Since when did fighting men have an interest in scholarship?* Or, *I refuse to say a word without witnesses present.* Cara opened her mouth. Tried to speak.

"This might be more successful if you let Cara write her answers down for us," Cúan suggested.

Ségán frowned. "Fetch some materials, Caolchú."

Cara breathed. This would be over soon, whatever it was. Quill, ink pot and scrap of parchment were duly set in front of her.

"Is she unable to talk?" Ségán was looking at Cúan. Asking the question over her head, as if she were not there. Or as if she were a half-wit.

"She can talk. But not always easily."

"This will be slow. Never mind, I'll keep the questions simple."

Wonderful. He did think she was a half-wit. Maybe she could scribble all over the page, or make a drawing of a tree. Or a row of little men with patterns on their faces.

"Write down what work you've been doing in the library, all these mornings."

Reading books of old tales, she wrote. Then drew a tiny book, open. That made her feel calmer. No need to tell him any more than exactly what he asked for.

"Has Mistress Blackthorn been doing the same work?"

She helps me sometimes. She drew Mistress Blackthorn, chin in hand, frowning over a great tome. Looked up to see Art, Caolchú and Cúan watching with grins on their faces. Ségán looked as grim and intent as before.

"Has Mistress Blackthorn spoken to you about the past, before she came to Winterfalls?"

Cara realized she had stopped shivering; the drawing had helped. You couldn't do a good drawing with shaky hands. "No," she said.

"She speaks," said Ségán, his eyes fixed on her face. "Are you quite sure about that, Cara?"

Yes, she wrote.

"This belongs to Mistress Blackthorn, doesn't it?" He nodded to one of the others, who came forward and put a little book down on the table. Cara felt her heart lurch. Mistress Blackthorn's notebook. Her wise woman book. Her secret book. How had these men come by it? Why hadn't Blackthorn taken it with her?

Yes, she wrote. She wished she was brave enough to write, *and it's private.*

Ségán opened the notebook. A marker had been placed between the pages, quite far through. Cara spotted a drawing, some kind of plant, and on the opposite page the wise woman's script, smaller than usual as if to fit as much there as she could. He held it open before her. "Is this her writing?"

Cara pushed it away. *A wise woman's book is secret,* she wrote.

Ségán passed the notebook back to the other man. "I only need to be sure this is Mistress Blackthorn's own account," he said. "Does she write in this book while the two of you are in the library?"

Cara didn't like his searching eyes. That look was like the one Father used when he was disappointed in her. When she had failed to be the perfect daughter he expected her to be. She didn't like his tone of voice. What business was it of his what Mistress Blackthorn was writing or where? "That's her personal notebook." Being angry seemed to help the words come out. "Where she writes down useful things about her work. Remedies, drawings of herbs, potions. She doesn't do that here. But sometimes she writes . . . notes." Cara would have had to be blind not to notice those loose pages filled with small, neat writing. She would have had to be stupid not to see how Blackthorn hid them somewhere different every night. But unlike these bullies, she knew when something was none of her business.

"Notes. Where?"

"Just on . . . pages. Parchment."

"And where are those pages now, Cara?"

Nothing in the world could have persuaded her to tell him. Without a doubt, Mistress Blackthorn would expect her to keep it secret. But she couldn't stop her eyes from going to the shelves, stacked full of books. It was only for a moment, but Ségán saw it.

"Here in the library?"

"I don't know where they are." Not quite a lie; they were here somewhere, but she didn't know exactly where.

"Mistress Blackthorn is your friend, isn't she?"

Cara nodded.

"Telling me anything you know about this will be in her best interests. We mean her no harm."

"She only went to Longwater. She'll be back before supper time. Why don't you ask her yourself?" All those words, and with him staring at her. Blackthorn would be proud of her.

"You know where those notes are, don't you? Show me."

"I . . . I . . ." Curse it! *No,* she wrote. The pen wanted to write, *Stop it! You're scaring me!* but she made it draw a little picture of an owl instead, and beside it, *May I go now please?*

"Just one more—" Ségán began.

The door flew open and with a shrill barking the white terrier, Bramble, came hurtling in, closely followed by a furious Mhairi. "What is this?" Flidais's maidservant demanded. "Four of you questioning one young girl, and all behind closed doors with not another woman in sight! What would Lady Flidais think? You should be ashamed of yourselves! Come, Cara. Whatever this was, it's finished. Bramble, stop that noise!"

31

BARÐÁN

Night. Dark night. The moon hiding away. Scared to show her face. What might she see? Murderers and thieves, beatings and killings and blood, so much blood . . . Dáire, her sweet face peaceful, sleeping her last long sleep. Sleeping in a sea of blood, the sheet dyed violent red. He had thought he might die of grief. Would have made an end of himself. But there had been Brígh. Tiny, struggling, crying those wrenching sobs. Bloody herself, until he cleaned her and swaddled her and carried her down to Longwater, looking for help. They came up and helped him bury Dáire. They would have taken Brígh from him. Said he was out of his mind with sorrow, which he was, then. Said he couldn't cope on his own, told him the babe was too small for goat's milk, told him she'd have a better home with them, told him all sorts of things. It's coming back now, in the dark, while not far off Grim stands on his hands and hauls himself up on ropes and does what he does to hold off his own demons.

They were right about one thing. He couldn't be father and mother to Brígh and earn a living as well. But he wouldn't give his child to Dáire's kinsfolk. Once they had her, they'd make her theirs forever. They would not let Bardán be her father. They'd never approved of Dáire marrying a man like him. If he let them take his child, if he let them raise her, Brígh would be lost to him forever.

So he had reasoned, not that there'd been much reason about that brutal time, when Dáire's burial rite had turned into a screaming argument and he'd been accused of all manner of crimes, lies every one of them. Brígh had screamed too, in someone else's arms, and he'd wrenched his daughter away and hurt her doing it, making her cry as if mortally wounded. He had ordered them all away. Then he'd put his child on his back, and taken his tools, and walked to Wolf Glen. Thrown himself on Master Tóla's mercy, offering work in return for a place to stay and someone to look after his child. Shown Tóla what he could do, his skills, his special touches with wood. And Tóla had hired him to build the heartwood house.

They got a woman in to feed Brígh. He remembers that. No need for goat's milk. He worked long days. Not that he didn't want to do a good job. He was grateful. Brígh was safe, warm, secure. And not being turned against him. How could he not be glad of that? But he was sad to see his baby only for a little each day, in the evenings, when often as not she was already tucked up in her cradle fast asleep. He'd sit by her awhile, singing the song his mother had sung to him long ago. *Feather bright and feather fine, none shall harm this child of mine.* But they did. Someone did. Someone took her out into the forest and left her there, and she died. Not him. He wouldn't have done that. He couldn't have done it. Not to Brígh. Not to his precious baby girl. It was someone else, some evildoer, the fey perhaps. But the fey wouldn't have left her in the oak roots. They would have taken her for their own. Instead of taking him, they would have taken his daughter. The fey were like a hungry fire. They were like the drowning sea. You could feed them and feed them, but they were never satisfied.

"You awake, brother?" Grim has stopped doing his exercises; the voice in the darkness comes from his pallet.

"Awake. Thinking. Remembering. Might be truth. Might only be hopes and wishes."

"Got a question for you."

"Mm?"

"You know that rhyme you sing sometimes, the one about the birds? *Feather bright and feather fine*, that one?"

In the night, without seeing, without speaking, they've been thinking of the same thing. "My mother would sing it," he says. "When I was dropping off to sleep. To keep me safe." That feeling, that warm, good feeling—how precious it had been. He had sworn to love Brígh the way he had been loved. He had promised her, had promised Dáire with tears choking his voice, that he would protect her. "I used to sing it to my baby. Only I must have done it wrong. Because she wasn't safe, she was hurt, she was killed." Sobs well up. He puts his fists against his mouth to hold them in.

"Sorry, brother." Here's Grim, moving over to sit beside him, putting an arm around his shoulders. And here's Ripple, creeping in on the other side to lay her head in his lap. "Didn't mean to upset you. Only, I was wondering if you could sing it to me again, the whole thing through. Or tell me the words."

"Why?"

"You know my friend. Blackthorn. You saw her today. She loves old rhymes and songs and stories. I told her about your song, your lullaby. She said she'd like to hear it."

"Breaking the rules again. The master's rules."

"Blackthorn and me don't worry much about other folk's rules."

Can he bear to sing the song? He thinks of Brígh in his arms, the slight soft weight of her, the wispy nut-brown hair, the shadowed lids closed over her lovely eyes. The tiny fingers curled around one of his. The creamy skin, the perfect small ears. His daughter. His only treasure. He wonders if the Red Giant might have kept his baby son if he'd had the right lullaby. He wonders, for a moment, if singing the song now might bring Brígh back. *"Starling, woodcock, owl on wing,"* he whispers. *"Nightjar, chiffchaff, bunting sing, goldcrest, warbler, thrush and jay, redpoll, siskin darting by . . ."* He goes through the whole song. Then Grim asks him to say it again. Up above, the owl hoots, maybe joining in, maybe talking to another owl out in the wood somewhere.

"Your mother liked birds, did she?" Grim asks.

Bardán's stroking Ripple. Her ears are soft. Her head's heavy on his knees, as if she's gone to sleep. "How did you know that?" he asks.

"Just wondered. With the rhyme and all."

"Birds would follow her around. She'd sit out in the sun with her embroidery and they'd perch close, all kinds together. She put them in her pictures."

Grim goes quiet. He goes quiet for a long time. Bardán sits quiet too, thinking of his mother. Wishing her embroideries still hung bright and perfect on the walls of that little house. One of them was all birds. Every bird from the song: starling, woodcock, owl and the rest. And some that were not in the song. *Every birdling in the wood,* she had told him when he asked. You can't afford to forget even the smallest of wrens. He hadn't known it at the time, but she'd been talking about the heartwood house.

"Bardán?"

"Mm?"

"How well did you know his wife? Tóla's wife? Suanach, was that her name?"

"Hardly saw her. I was working. She didn't come out much."

"What was she like?"

He tries to remember. A little, wispy woman who hardly ever smiled. When she had come out of the house, Tóla had shepherded her around. Watched every step as though she might break if he took his eyes away. Bardán gets a sudden picture of her holding a child, with a shaft of sunlight coming through a window and lighting up both their faces. "She was fond of Brígh," he says. "Used to call her love, sweetheart, precious. She was fussy. Never satisfied—that's what the nursemaid used to say. Mistress would undo the swaddling and wrap the baby up all over again. Thought she was the only one who could do it just right." It's coming back, more of the past, more of that time. "She didn't like me coming into the house to say good night. Said it disturbed Brígh. That made me angry. Only I couldn't be angry. Had to swallow it down. I had nowhere else to go."

"Holy Mother of God," murmurs Grim. There's another silence.

Then he says, "Suanach's own daughter must have been born around the same time as your Brígh, though."

What is he talking about? What daughter? "There was a boy. The nursemaid's child. And Brígh. Enough milk for two."

"But the master's daughter, Cara—she's fifteen now, nearly sixteen. She'd have been here. Or expected."

"Why are you asking this?"

"Just tell me, Bardán. If you can."

"They had no children. Don't think she was expecting one. Little, tiny woman—it would have showed. And nobody spoke of it. Must have been born later. Long after. After I . . . after that night, when I ran and fell and lost myself."

"Must have been," says Grim. "Come to think of it, someone did say the master's wife went away to give birth. Went to her kinsfolk."

"I didn't kill my baby," Bardán says. He's sure of it now. "I didn't do it, Grim. She was safe in the house that night. Tucked up in bed. Mistress wouldn't let me in to see her. Not the first time she'd done that. Said Brígh was fast asleep and wouldn't know if I was there or not, so it didn't matter. I said *I'd* know, and she got angry, and then the master came and sent me back to my quarters. Gormán made supper. Some sort of stew, full of spices. And then . . . later . . ." Something bad. Something dark and terrible. A pain so crippling he thought his head would split apart, and his bowels turning to water, and things pursuing him, monsters and demons and creatures all spiky teeth and rending claws and screaming voices that made his whole body shudder. Running from them, running through the forest. Rough hands grabbing him, dragging him, pulling him down. Falling, falling . . .

"Later what?" asks Grim.

"Nothing." He moves away from Ripple, away from Grim. Curls in on himself, arms up over his head, eyes squeezed shut. Willing that night away. The night he lost her. The night he lost himself.

32

BLACKTHORN

"I have a question for you, Ide. I'm not sure you'll be prepared to answer."

"You can try me."

I had finished my examination of Fann and her baby son, and had pronounced both to be in good health. I'd planned to pass on the instructions for my healing salve to Ide, but I didn't seem to have my notebook with me. Stupid not to check before I left the prince's house. Could I have been careless enough to leave it in the library? I'd have to retrieve it as soon as I got back. For now, it was good to sit with Ide and enjoy a brew while Fann and the child slept. "It's about Bardán, who used to live in that cottage on the hillside a long while ago. And his wife, and their child."

"And why wouldn't I want to answer a question about them?"

"Because someone paid you to keep your mouth shut? Or threatened dire consequences if you spoke out?"

Ide looked at me, brows lifted, smile crooked. "Why the interest in them? Dáire's long gone, and the fellow . . . He was never one of us. Not even when he lived among us. Folk tolerated him. He was a fine craftsman. But he never belonged."

I liked and respected this woman. She was wise, practical, a plain speaker. Even so, I must tread carefully. Reveal too much of what I knew about Bardán and the past, and I might get Grim in trouble. I'd just been warned off, after all. *Don't meddle.* "I don't think I mentioned that I'm staying on Prince Oran's holding while he and Lady Flidais are away," I said. "And so is Master Tóla's daughter, Cara. She and I have become quite close."

"I don't see the connection, Mistress Blackthorn."

"No?"

"No. Maybe if you ask the question, I may understand you better."

"That day when I first came here, when Fann was in labor, someone mentioned a kinswoman having been a wet nurse. In Tóla's household. At around the time when Bardán was first employed there. I think it was Osgar who spoke of that. His aunt, was it? That would make her your sister."

"That's no secret. My brother's wife, Luíseach, was feeding her infant son then; she had enough milk for the girl as well. Luíseach wasn't in that household long. Three turnings of the moon at most."

"Does she still live here in the settlement? Could I speak to her about that time?"

"You could, I suppose. She's still here, though her house is a bit of a ride away. If I were you, I wouldn't. It might be seen as unusual curiosity. If that got to the wrong ears, you might find yourself in trouble. And so might Luíseach."

My good deed in seeing Fann's baby boy born safe and well had evidently won me a high degree of trust. If, as I suspected, Tóla had been paying the folk of Longwater to keep quiet about the past, they risked a great deal in speaking to me about that time. "I don't want to get anyone in trouble," I said. "That includes Cara, who is intent on finding out the truth about her father and that place he's hired Bardán and Grim to construct for him. If there is an unsavory secret behind all that, I'd sooner Cara didn't get hurt stumbling across it."

"You didn't ask for my opinion, Mistress Blackthorn, but I'll give it. The truth will hurt that girl no matter how she discovers it. She's safe; she's healthy; she has a father who'll give her the world if he can. Why not leave things be?"

"Because it wouldn't be right," I said.

I made my way around the top of the lake, then along a broad track that ran between grazing fields. I was out of the Wolf Glen forest here and my horse seemed happier with the open country. The sheep had well-grown lambs at foot; here and there farmworkers moved animals between enclosures or checked on the stock. There was the same evidence of prosperity and good management that could be seen in Longwater settlement.

Ide had suggested I take Osgar with me, but I'd said no. The fewer folk who were party to this, the fewer I could get in trouble. As I rode I considered how I might best broach the subject of what had happened at Wolf Glen all those years ago. From what I'd heard, Tóla's wife went away from Wolf Glen so early in her pregnancy that she was not visibly with child, and did not bring baby Cara home until she was old enough to sit up in the saddle and toddle across the yard in pursuit of chickens. There'd have been no need for a local wet nurse, since a child who could walk would be able to drink goat's milk. Indeed, she'd be eating porridge or a mash of vegetables. It seemed Luíseach was hired to feed a different infant: Bardán's baby, Brígh.

Who had told me that story first? Osgar? I thought he'd meant his aunt was wet nurse to Cara. Ide had not contradicted me when I'd implied that. But I must have been wrong. The story, as folk knew it, was odd but possible. Bardán had been hired to build the heartwood house; part of his payment was good care for his motherless baby daughter, and that included the services of a wet nurse. He stayed only three turnings of the moon, then he ran off with his daughter and abandoned her in the forest, where she died that same night. Bardán fell down a hole into the Otherworld, where he remained for fifteen years, returning with his wits scrambled and his memory gone. A strange story but possible. And Suanach, finding herself with child at around the time baby Brígh was in her household, left home and traveled to stay with her kinsfolk, where about two seasons later she gave birth to Cara. Whom she did not bring home until the child was at least nine turnings of the moon old. Even then Cara must have been an early walker. That part did not surprise me; she'd probably been climbing trees not long after. But why had Suanach waited so long to come home? Had she still been frail, unwell? She'd died quite soon after her return, when her child was less than a year old. Had she been afraid of her husband? Was Tóla an abuser of women? The master had loved his wife. He loved his daughter. But then, love could take curious paths.

I toyed with the possibility that Bardán and Suanach had been lovers; that baby Cara had been Suanach's daughter but not Tóla's. That would certainly account for Tóla's hatred of the wild man. It might account for Suanach's choice to leave Wolf Glen so early in her pregnancy, perhaps as soon as she had suspected she was with child. It might even be connected with Bardán's flight through the woods and his fall to another world. The piece that did not fit in that particular puzzle was Brígh. Nobody denied that Brígh had existed. She had been born, her mother had died and been buried, her father had taken her to Wolf Glen. And she'd been abandoned in the woods. Or she hadn't. Had Bardán fathered two little girls, one destined to die alone in the chill of the forest, and the other to grow up as a rich man's daughter? Or had there only ever been one child? If Brígh and Cara were one and the same, if the willowy girl who talked to trees and crafted little creatures from wood was the daughter of the wild man, the master builder, then some truly appalling lies had been told. Lies that had broken hearts and destroyed lives. Lies that had severed the sacred bond between father and child. The damage those lies had done was surely beyond mending.

Maybe Gormán was right. Maybe I should let this go. Maybe I should trust that Cara would not find the story of the heartwood house, or that if she did, it would not lead her to the truth. But then, if the tale held no enlightenment, why had Gormán reacted so strongly to the news that Cara was searching for it? There must be something revealing in it, some insight. I did wonder how an ancient tale of magic could shine any light on what had happened here. This was a human story, not one of those grand accounts of gods and monsters. It was a story in which the threads of truth had become hopelessly tangled with what might be, with what could be, with what one person believed and another discounted. Bardán and Suanach? I didn't think so. Tóla would have killed him. He might have killed her too. A man like him wouldn't be able to bear such a blow to his pride; that kind of man believed he had a natural entitlement. In that, Tóla was like Mathuin of Laois: both would ride roughshod over others to get what they believed should be theirs.

I rode on. The farm buildings were in sight now; this was a well-maintained holding. There were horses grazing in an enclosure, their coats glossy under a watery sunlight, their manes neatly plaited. The drystone walls dividing the fields were in perfect order. Smoke rose in a lazy plume from the chimney of the dwelling house; somebody was at home.

Maybe I'd let my thoughts lead me too far down the path of the unlikeliest story, the most unpalatable truth. I knew very little about Suanach. I did not know if she'd been the kind of woman to cuckold her husband. Maybe she had lain with Bardán. Maybe his grief over the loss of his wife had addled his good judgment. But even if Tóla had forgiven Suanach, a man like him wouldn't accept that child. He'd never go along with the pretense that she was his own flesh and blood. Bardán had been considered odd even then, with his half-fey mother and his Otherworld-raised father. Tóla recognizing that man's daughter as his sole heir? That really was impossible.

And yet, and yet . . . there was Cara. Cara shinning up trees to perch high above the ground, surrounded by birds; Cara as unhappy at Winterfalls as a wild creature caged; Cara telling stories to trees and hearing their answers; Cara standing barefoot in Dreamer's Pool, so perfectly still she might have been part of the forest, part of the wild. Cara echoing the words of a lullaby that could only have been sung to her by Bardán. When I had first met her, I had not seen anything of the fey in her. Now, I wondered that I had missed it. Unlikely as it seemed, I'd wager half of Grim's bag of silver that she was Bardán's daughter.

Now here I was at the farmhouse, and here was a young man coming to greet me and take the horse. I explained that I had come to visit Mistress Luíseach and thanked him when he offered to tend to my mount. Being the only healer in the district did have its advantages. Few doors were closed to me, even when I arrived uninvited.

Luíseach was some years Ide's junior, a broad-faced, no-nonsense person who welcomed me into her kitchen without hesitation and got on with her baking while we talked. I invented a story about wanting to visit every household in Longwater so I'd know who had chronic ailments or old injuries that were likely to keep needing my attention. Luíseach listened and kneaded her dough. Her young assistant made a brew, set the cups on the table, then, at a nod from her mistress, left us.

"Help yourself, Mistress Blackthorn. I'll let mine cool awhile. I must shape these bannocks and set them to rise again. The fellows will be hungry when they come in. Old injuries, you say? What sort of thing?"

It was a good opening. I told her about Bardán's hands and how I had made a salve especially for him. "Not that I can cure a condition like his," I said. "He has hands like an old man's, and I don't imagine he's so very old—around my own age, perhaps."

"He'd be three-and-thirty at most," Luíseach said. "They married young. Him and Dáire. Too young, her kinsfolk said. They'd have liked her to wait for a better husband, one who was more like the young men of the settlement. But Dáire was a strong-minded girl. Some would have said willful."

"Did you think she was willful?"

"She was a fine girl, Mistress Blackthorn. Nothing wrong with knowing your own mind. She was full of hopes for the future, and whatever folk might think of the fellow she married, she was good for him. Brought him out of himself; made him smile. But she died birthing her daughter, as I'm sure you will have heard. A sad loss. Made even sadder by the way they all set to squabbling over the child, with the earth barely settled on her grave. But you don't want to hear that sorrowful story." She covered her tray of perfectly uniform bannocks with a clean cloth and set it on a bench near the fire. "I'll just go and wash my hands."

There was a scullery area out back. While she was splashing there and I was thinking hard, the young man came in.

"Horse is enjoying a rest and a drink, Mistress," he said. "Fine mare, that."

"She's one of Prince Oran's. My purse doesn't stretch to a creature of that quality."

"You're Mistress Blackthorn, aren't you? The healer?"

"How did you know?" The lad was young, sixteen at the most. And he had a familiar look about him. "Oh. You must be Mistress Luíseach's son. Osgar's cousin."

"I'm Fedach, yes. Pleased to make your acquaintance."

"Likewise." Someone had taught this young man excellent manners. If my son had lived, perhaps he would have been like this, forthright but courteous, full of goodwill. Healthy and strong. With an effort, I forced Brennan back into the locked corner of my heart, which was his keeping place. "Do you breed horses here?"

It seemed they did, and Fedach was keen to tell me about it. I nodded and smiled and tried to ask intelligent questions until Luíseach returned, wiping her hands on her apron.

"What are you doing in here, son?" she asked. There was such love and pride in her tone that it did not seem like a criticism.

"I came in to tell Mistress Blackthorn her horse was being well looked after."

"And stayed to pass the time of day, from the sound of it. Aren't you supposed to be helping your father? Mistress Blackthorn's come down from Wolf Glen and she's still got to ride all the way to Winterfalls. She doesn't have time to listen to your horse talk."

"What are you baking?" Fedach asked with a grin. "It smells good."

"Not ready yet," said his mother. "Off with you, now. I'll see you later."

On the threshold, Fedach hesitated. "Do you know the girl from the big house?" he asked me. "Up at Wolf Glen?"

I got in before Luíseach could speak. "Cara? I know her quite well," I said. "She and I are staying in Prince Oran's household at present. Why do you ask?"

"That's—" Luíseach began, but was interrupted by a man's voice, calling her name from out back somewhere. Muttering something under her breath, she got up and went out.

"Cara's like someone from an old tale, isn't she?" Fedach said. He leaned closer, his eyes bright, his tone confidential. "Like a lovely wildwood creature. She's the one I'm going to marry, Mistress Blackthorn. Someday. If she'll have me. That's a secret, though. Don't tell my mother."

"I wouldn't dream of it, Fedach. Does Cara know about this?" It seemed unlikely; as far as I could recall, she had never mentioned this charming young man. Sadly, a farmer's son was unlikely to meet Tóla's requirements for a future son-in-law.

"Oh, no. We've hardly spoken to each other. Her father doesn't let her out much. But I've seen her at the lake, with Gormán, once or twice. Had a word or two. When it's the right time, I'll ask her. And she'll say yes. I know it deep down, Mistress Blackthorn."

His shining, hopeful eyes made me sad. "Whatever lies in your future, I hope you will be happy, Fedach," I said. "And I hope the same for Cara."

I waited, hands curled around my empty cup, while Fedach took his leave of his mother and went back out to the horses. I waited while Luíseach made another brew.

"That sorrowful story you mentioned," I said. "I would be interested to hear a little more. Am I right in thinking Master Tóla hired you as wet nurse for Bardán's daughter, not long after that fine son of yours was born?"

Luíseach was standing opposite me, hands twisted through her apron. "That's right," she said. "I had enough milk for two. My son and . . . the girl."

"Who went up to Wolf Glen with her father. And never came back." The baby who'd been abandoned in the forest. The baby who had died alone and cold, in the night. If that story was true.

"She was an odd little thing." Luíseach was staring off into the distance now, remembering. "Long and spindly, all legs and arms. I fed her, yes. But the one who was always walking around with her and holding her and singing to her was Mistress Suanach. Calling her pet names: my precious, my sweet, heart's dearest. Didn't like anyone else tending to the girl."

"She must have been heartbroken when the baby died."

"We never heard how she felt. One day I was wet nurse in that household; the next day the baby girl was missing; the day after that they told me she was dead and I was packed off back to Longwater with a purse of silver for my trouble. Mistress Suanach went away to stay with her kinsfolk that very same day, or so the story went."

"To come back later with her own child."

Luíseach nodded.

Now the most awkward question; I hoped she would not tell me to mind my own business. "She was away a good while, wasn't she?"

Luíseach gave me a very direct look. "Poor thing wasn't a mother long. My son was born in the autumn. By the next autumn Mistress Suanach was dead. An ague, they said."

Morrigan's britches. So Cara could not have been Suanach's natural daughter. "Before Cara was a year old," I murmured.

"As you say."

"It's . . . a very sad story."

"It is, Mistress Blackthorn. And you did not hear it from me, or from anyone in this household."

"Understood. Your son is a fine young man, Luíseach. You've raised him well."

"I have a good husband. He's shown Fedach what a man should be."

Curse it, what were these sudden tears? I turned my face away, but not before she saw.

"I'm sorry, Mistress Blackthorn. Have I upset you?"

"It's nothing." I wiped my eyes on my sleeve. "I should be on my way. You must have work to get on with."

"Nothing that can't wait. Ide told me about you. How you birthed Fann's child when everyone thought she would die and the boy with her. And she told us about Grim. A fine man, she said. A good man."

"He is. But we're not—we are friends, he and I. Thrown together by chance." The words sounded like a betrayal. The tone I attempted, light and inconsequential, made a mockery of the truth.

"When you have a man like that, you should hold on to him," Luíseach said quietly. "Such a man is rare. Worth his weight in gold, and more."

I wiped my face again. "Not so easy," I said, wishing I had the strength to get up and walk out before I waded in too deep. "Give your heart to someone, and you spend your life in fear of losing them. In terror of seeing them hurt."

Luíseach stared at me, her sweet features creased with worry. "You're the kind that takes on other folk's burdens," she said. "That's what Ide said, and I see it in you. Don't load yourself up too heavy. Even the strongest heart has a breaking point."

If Grim were here right now, I thought, he would bear half the load for me. If he were here, I could lean on him. And when he was in trouble, I would take my turn as the strong one. I didn't want him to be at Wolf Glen. I wanted him home. "I should go," I said, getting up. "Thank you for talking so frankly, Luíseach. Don't worry—you didn't tell me anything about Cara or any other baby. Wise women are good at keeping secrets."

"What worries me," Luíseach said, "is what happens when this particular secret does come out. That girl looks like she'd break easily. Looks like a puff of wind would carry her off. My boy's fond of her, though he doesn't want me to know it."

"You'd be surprised," I said. "Underneath, Cara's as strong as an oak."

. . .

As I rode back to Winterfalls, taking the shorter way, sudden rain came pelting down, whip-hard. The noise was deafening. I did not know I had company until the two riders loomed up, one on either side of me. My horse shied in fright and I nearly came off. One of them dismounted and reached for the mare's reins. I whipped my knife from my belt and pointed it in his general direction. It was raining so hard I couldn't see his face clearly.

"Lay a hand on me and I'll cut off your fingers!" I snarled. My whole body was shaking; my heart was jumping about. "I mean it! I'll do it! Don't doubt me!" Mathuin's lackeys. They had to be. Who else would be out here waiting for me? They were here to make me talk. To force information out of me. Those bastards were expert at that. They would throw me back in that vile place and torture me until I broke all over again. They'd wring every scrap of dignity from me. Just like last time. Only it wouldn't happen. I'd kill them first. Or I'd take the knife to my own wrists.

"Mistress Blackthorn!" The man was shouting to be heard over the downpour. "Let us escort you back to Winterfalls."

"Let go of my horse!" I screamed. "Get out of my way!" Escort, hah! I'd need to be stupid to believe that.

The other one was off his horse now and grabbing for the knife. I struggled to control the panicking mare as I slashed out in defense, snarling an oath. Then, so quick I hardly knew what had happened, the first man had hold of the mare's reins and the other had twisted the knife out of my hand. Bile rose to my mouth.

"It's a choice, Mistress Blackthorn," said the man with the knife. "You can keep on fighting us, so we have to tie your wrists and take you under guard. Or you can see sense and ride along with us. Ségán wants you escorted wherever you go from now on. Our orders are to bring you safely back."

Wait a moment. Ségán wants? I narrowed my eyes, trying to get a better look at them through the downpour. Made myself draw a slow breath; did not like the way it shuddered in my chest. Yes, they were familiar. Swan Island men, from Winterfalls. Why had they set on me with such violence?

"You scared me," I said. "What business is it of Ségán's or anyone else's where I go or what I do?" They could still be in Mathuin's pay. I had doubted them from the first time I saw them. I'd never understood why they were in the district.

"He'll explain that back at Winterfalls," said one of them. I guessed it was the man called Caolchú, though I wasn't sure. The other one was probably Art, the tallest of them.

"Why don't you explain it right here and now? You could be taking me anywhere."

"Our orders are to bring you back. And to keep you safe. What has to be said is best said behind closed doors."

"Behind closed doors where nobody can see or hear what's going on." Winterfalls? I didn't think so. If not all the way to Mathuin's hell-hole, they'd take me to someplace just like it. I tried to keep my breathing steady. Tried thinking of Grim, but that didn't help. I saw him in the lockup with me, staring out through the bars, a big, shaggy-bearded man with sad eyes. Calling me Lady when everyone else had a foul name for me. Talking to me softly amid the screaming and shouting and the begging for mercy. "At least have the guts to tell me the truth," I said. "Who really sent you? Where are you really taking me?"

Art had stuck my knife in his belt. Caolchú was putting a leading rein on the mare. Short of leaping off and attempting to outrun two fit warriors, I had few choices. It was one of those moments when I'd have welcomed a sudden appearance by Conmael, who doubtless had the ability to turn men into toads whenever he liked. Unfortunately my small facility in hearth magic did not stretch so far.

"We mean you no harm, Mistress Blackthorn. Please believe that." Caolchú checked the leading rein, then mounted his own horse. "Our purpose is to make sure you get back to Winterfalls safely, no more—I promise. When we get there Ségán will talk to you. The matter is confidential. I cannot discuss it here."

"I'm not talking to anyone without a witness. Someone impartial." Why would they think I needed an escort to get home safely? Why bother riding out in the rain when they could simply have waited until I reached Winterfalls? This made no sense.

"It's not for me to say yes or no to that. You can ask Ségán." He pulled his hood up. If anything, the rain was getting heavier. Both of us were shouting to be heard above it. "We'll move on now. He wants us back as soon as possible." A pause. Then, "You're safe with us, Mistress Blackthorn. You have my word on that. And the word of an Island man is always good."

Ségán was waiting in the library. I stepped through the doorway, my clothing dripping onto Fíona's immaculate floor, and saw in an instant what was on the table before him. My notes. My precious, secret testament. Cara had told him. She had seen where I'd hidden them, and she had betrayed me.

"Sit down, Mistress Blackthorn." The hawklike features were calm; the tone was even. He motioned to the bench opposite his. "Caolchú, you might have allowed Mistress Blackthorn to change her wet clothing first. Take her cloak, please, and send someone to fetch a warm shawl."

Caolchú left; the door closed behind him. Which left four people in the library: Ségán seated at the table, and me, and two other men—Cúan and Earc—standing at a slight distance. They appeared to be on guard.

"Do sit down," Ségán said again. "You've had a long ride."

"I want a witness," I said, not moving. "Someone impartial. Aedan. Or one of Prince Oran's men-at-arms."

"The matter is extremely confidential." Ségán waved his hand across the closely written leaves of my document. "I'm certain Prince Oran would not want even his trusted steward or his reliable guards to become aware of it before he is ready to tell them. Such knowledge could endanger them. I give you my word that I mean you no harm. I will not ask you to leave the safety of this household. What I will ask, indeed insist upon, is that anytime you choose to do so, you take one of us with you."

I could have protested that the calls on a healer's time and expertise did not fit a neat pattern; that women in childbirth or folk with grave illnesses did not want armed men on their doorsteps. I could have raised a dozen other objections. But right now that did not seem of pressing importance. "I'm not answering any questions until you tell me, at the very least, what you and your men are doing here. I know the official story, that you're augmenting the household guard because so many of the men-at-arms went to court with the prince. But household guards don't haul the local wise woman in for questioning. They don't stop her on her travels and drag her back home like some miscreant."

"As I understand it," Ségán said, "you were the one who drew a knife and threatened to chop off Caolchú's fingers. And weren't you heading back here anyway?"

Caolchú must have delivered that information in the time it had taken me to get off the mare, shivering and cramped, and follow Art to the library. "I believed I was under attack," I said. "What was I supposed to do, collapse in a trembling heap?"

Briefly, Ségán smiled. "If this document is a true account, Mistress Blackthorn, then that is the last thing I would expect of you. My men were anticipating that you would recognize them. Your response was . . . surprising."

"If you've read those pages, it shouldn't surprise you in the least," I snapped. "Besides, it was raining hard. I could barely see a thing. Now, tell me what's going on."

"We are indeed here to augment the household guard."

"And?"

He leaned back in his chair; appeared to relax just a little. "Let me explain something to you. Swan Island men have several strings to their bows. We train warriors who come to us. Train them in skills they cannot learn from their own masters-at-arms. Train them to a level unlikely to be achieved elsewhere. Occasionally, we undertake missions. Most leaders have their own fighting forces and need not look beyond them. But sometimes there comes a need for special services. Unusual ways of solving problems. Skills beyond those possessed even by the most elite of men-at-arms. Where a leader faces a difficulty and the only way to overcome that difficulty involves breaking established codes of conduct—breaking the rules, if you like—then that leader may call on us. The community on Swan Island was founded by a man commonly regarded at that time as an outlaw. A man who cared little for convention, but who believed in justice and fairness. In all we do, we continue to adhere to those principles."

My mind was working hard. "You're telling me Prince Oran is prepared to break the rules? To break the law?"

"You know already that we are in the district at Prince Oran's invitation. I cannot answer further than that."

My heart was beating fast. My palms were clammy. "Not good enough," I said. "I understand that some matters are strategic and must be kept confidential. But at the very least you can explain to me why you sent two men to convey me back here, and scare me witless in the process, when I was heading home anyway. I'm not saying anything about that document on the table until you tell me that."

"Very well. There was an earlier attempt on your life, from a certain quarter. My men happened to be close at hand and took the individual into custody. He was questioned. The information he provided led us to believe there was a link between yourself and . . . Prince Oran's enemy."

"Wait a moment . . ." My mind was racing. An attempt on my life? When? "You don't mean—do you mean that day in Dreamer's Wood, when Cúan brought my assistant home? Emer said she saw a sort of scuffle, but—you mean that was one of Mathuin's spies?"

"We won't speak of the details," Ségán said. "But yes, that was the occasion. A person was sent to silence you. Very fortunately, at the time, my men were in the area and dealt with the attempt swiftly."

My stomach felt hollow. "What happened to the man?"

"He won't be troubling you any further."

"But that was some while ago. Why are you suddenly taking steps to protect me now? I could have been killed ten times over since then."

A slow smile spread over Ségán's aquiline features. "Not with my men at Winterfalls, Mistress Blackthorn. Our role here extends to regular patrols of the district. What that man revealed suggested you might have information of value. Of such value, indeed, that you required immediate protection. We have been watching over you, to the extent that your work makes it possible to do so covertly."

"That doesn't fully explain today's episode, Ségán."

"Until today, we had not realized you were writing this document. Its existence, along with certain developments that I am not at liberty to tell you, changes the situation considerably."

"Not at liberty to tell me. But it's my document. Which it appears you have read without my permission."

"Entirely justified, under the circumstances. Is this a true account, Mistress Blackthorn? Correct in every detail?"

I'd have to tell him. I'd have to risk it. "It's a true account of what happened, yes. In saying so, I'm trusting you with my life, Ségán. If the man named in that document knew it existed, he would work even harder to hunt me down, and this time he'd make sure he silenced me for good. Even with your men in the district."

"Which is why, from now on, we want you to take a personal guard—one of us—whenever you leave the safety of this household."

Could this be what it seemed to be? "Ségán. Might this document be . . . useful? In the work you are doing for Prince Oran?"

"It might. It might be still more useful if the writer were present to back up her account in person."

Oh, gods! Was this the chance, the one chance I had dreamed of?

"I must put something to you before we go any further, Mistress Blackthorn."

I waited. He had answered my question, in a manner of speaking. I owed him an answer in return.

"If Prince Oran knew the contents of this account," Ségán said, "he would have told me about it. I must assume, therefore, that although you have been living and working in the district that lies under his authority for some considerable time, you chose not to divulge these important details to him. Why?"

"You must have at least a little imagination, Ségán. You must have seen what conflict can do to a person. You must know how grief and loss and abuse can wear a person down; make them less than they once were. When we first came here I did not know the prince. My experience of men in authority had not been good; as a result I mistrusted all of them. It took time to realize Prince Oran was a good man, just and fair. By then, I . . . I had become settled here. My friend too. I was afraid to confess the truth about our past. Afraid we would lose our home and our livelihood."

"And yet, you say you know Prince Oran is just and fair."

"Fear does strange things to a person. I'm not proud to admit that I held this back. But I would have told him. I would have told both of them, Oran and Flidais. In time."

"We're running out of time. When they return, either you tell them or I do. It's important, Mistress Blackthorn."

Oh, gods. I wished so much that I had told Oran long ago. Now, even if I did so willingly, it would look as if I had confessed only under pressure. "Will you let me tell him first? I would very much prefer that."

"Provided that occurs as early as possible, yes. I consider that the better way. He'll need to know your written account exists, since it is rich in exactly the kind of detail that stands up well under scrutiny— names, dates, precise and factual descriptions of events. You should have been a lawman, Mistress Blackthorn."

"If you knew me better, you would realize what a laughable idea that is." A shiver ran through me.

"You have more questions, no doubt," Ségán said gravely. "Please remember that this conversation is in strictest confidence. Not one word to anyone—you understand? I don't believe I need to repeat that to you, Mistress Blackthorn. Your enemy—who is also the enemy of Prince

Oran and his wife—is a powerful man, and we know he has a long reach. As for how your statement might be used, any discussion of that must wait for the prince's return." I made to interrupt, but he silenced me with a raised hand. "I understand he will be back within a few days. Believe me, I am not authorized to give you further information. Nor do I have all the details myself yet."

A knock at the library door. Cúan went to open it and came back with a shawl, which I wrapped around my shoulders. The warmth was welcome. I reminded myself to be careful. It was an old trick, using kindness to make folk relax and give away secrets. I believed Ségán. But maybe I believed him because I wanted to—because he seemed to be offering the long-dreamed-of chance to bring my enemy to justice. How that could happen, I had no idea. But he had said the Island men worked outside the rules.

"I want to believe you," I said. "But I'm cautious. With good reason." I glanced at the pages. "What happens to my document now?"

"We will find a hiding place more secure than the one you used."

"How can I be sure you won't send it straight to Mathuin of Laois? How can I know you won't send a pigeon to give him the news within a day?"

Ségán sighed. "Mistress Blackthorn, I do not know how to reassure you. Tell me, do you trust Prince Oran?"

"Yes." Oran was a young man of high ideals, ideals he put into action every day in looking after his household and the folk of the district. "But you might have lied to him."

"He hired us, Mistress Blackthorn. We're working for him. And he will soon be back here with more information for us." He indicated the pages on the table. "Now, do you need to write anything further, or is this account complete?"

"It's complete, more or less. I should go over it, check everything. If I have time."

Grim, I thought. What if Grim came back? What if I had reason to go up to Wolf Glen within those few days? I couldn't not tell Grim.

Especially if this turned out to be what I thought it might be. And what about Conmael? "Ségán?"

"Yes, Mistress Blackthorn?"

"There's a man mentioned in those papers. My friend, who came north with me."

"Safe at Wolf Glen, working—is that right?"

He knew everything. "He's there at present. What you said about keeping this secret—he should know. About what is planned. What might be planned."

"Safer, for now, if he does not know. When Prince Oran returns, you may ask him about it. Now, I'd better let you go. Do not forget what I said. Not a word to anyone. Not even the most trusted members of the household. And if you need to go anywhere outside the walls, speak to me and I will arrange an escort. Anywhere, Mistress Blackthorn—you understand? Even a short trip to the settlement or back to your own house. What we have here is not only invaluable, it puts you at considerable risk."

"Really?" My voice cracked. Now surely he was telling lies. "Crimes against ordinary folk, folk without a voice, folk without the means to stand up for themselves, weighing anything at all alongside the invasion of another man's territory and the sacking of his household?"

"In a council of the usual kind this might bear relatively little weight. But we are not speaking of such a council. Will you entrust these pages to me until tomorrow, Mistress Blackthorn? In the morning you and I should sit down with them and go through everything in detail. And then we will find a safer hiding place."

Morrigan's curse. I must have blanched, because he said, "Cúan, take Mistress Blackthorn to the kitchen, will you, and ask Brid to find her some food and drink."

"I believe I'm still capable of walking along the hallway and getting my own food," I said, rising to my feet and finding the room was indeed swirling around me in a distinctly odd fashion. "And I don't think you said anything about needing an escort inside the house."

"You're white as a sheet, Mistress Blackthorn." Cúan was beside me, offering an arm to steady me. "Let me help you, please."

Rather than make a liar of myself by fainting away, I took his arm and let him escort me out. I sat quietly before the kitchen fire for a while, drank some ale and ate a wedge of mutton pie, then returned to the farm cottage I was sharing with Cara. I wasn't entirely happy to leave my testament with Ségán. But if the Island men were all he had claimed, perhaps it would be safest in their custody.

33

CARA

Mistress Blackthorn came in looking pale and tired. But bright-eyed all the same. As if something had changed; something big. Maybe she'd been to see Grim. Maybe she'd even seen Father, and Cara could ask if he was well.

She'd been lying on her shelf bed, thinking of home. She sat up, and Blackthorn started. "Oh. You're here," the wise woman said. Her voice was cold and so, now, was her face. Cold and furious.

"What's wrong?" Cara tried to ask, only the words wouldn't come out, not properly, and Blackthorn was too angry to hear anyway. Cara got up and wrapped her shawl around herself, tightly.

Mistress Blackthorn didn't say anything else. Only went to the storage chest and got out some clothes. The ones she was wearing were wet. It would be right to offer help. To build up their little fire. To make a brew. But Cara's feet were putting down roots.

Blackthorn slammed the lid shut.

"Mistress Blackthorn?" Cara whispered.

She might as well not have been there. Blackthorn didn't even bother to go out back, just stripped off all her clothes and dropped them on the floor. There were scars on her body, old ones. As if she'd been beaten badly. *Don't stare, Cara,* came the voice of Aunt Della, and Cara looked down at the floor instead. She thought about her aunt, because right now that felt safer than thinking about why Blackthorn was so angry. She thought of all those years Aunt Della had spent caring for her. What sort of life would her aunt have had if she had not come to help them after Cara's mother died? Cara had never thought about this before, and now that felt rather shameful. Maybe Aunt Della would have married and had children of her own. Or maybe she would have done something quite different. Been an independent woman with her own household. Become a master of some craft. Bred dogs or sheep or pigs. Instead, she had given her life to Cara.

Mistress Blackthorn was dressed now, warm in gown and shawl and soft slippers, with her hair making a bright, tangled halo around her face. She still looked stony as she took her wet garments out back. Cara made herself move; filled the kettle from the bucket of clean water and set it on the fire. Fetched two cups and some herbs for a brew. Chamomile and lavender were what Blackthorn used when someone was upset.

The wise woman sat down by the fire. Not relaxed. Tight in the body and dour in the face. She didn't say a word until the brew was made and Cara had passed her a cup. Then she spoke at last. "You told them."

"W-wha . . .?" Cara's voice ran away like a rabbit before the fox.

"You told them about my document. Ségán and his men. You told them where I'd hidden it."

"I—" That look on her face, as if Cara were the lowest scum she'd ever seen in her life. It was a look to freeze a person's insides. Her voice was hard as iron. Cara wanted to say, *That isn't fair.* She wanted to say, *I'm sorry,* even though whatever had happened with the Island men was not her fault. She hadn't told them. She'd done her best to explain that the notebook was private and so was any other writing Mistress Blackthorn might have been doing. But she was scared now, scared of her trusted friend, and that was so terrible she couldn't speak a single word. She made a sort of gesture, trying to explain that she would talk if she could.

"As it happens," Blackthorn said, studying the cup in her hands, "the Island men appear to be allies rather than enemies. But this could have led to disaster, Cara. It could have been the end for me and for Grim if that document had got into the wrong hands. As it is, it seems there is no lasting harm done, though this has put me in a very awkward position with Prince Oran. What I cannot forgive is your betrayal of my trust."

It was too much. She was supposed to be a friend. She *had* been a friend. And she was wrong to accuse Cara, quite wrong! All she'd done was tell those men Blackthorn had been writing her own notes, and she'd tried hard not to do even that. Besides, Blackthorn had never actually said her document was secret. And Cara had always looked away when she hid it.

Blackthorn had her eyes on Cara again. She made her own gesture, as if she were writing. Ah. The wax tablet. When a person couldn't speak, they could always write. And, fortunately, both tablet and stylus were here in their quarters.

Cara fetched them and wrote: *I did not betray a secret. I told Ségán you'd been making notes, but only when he pressed me for answers. I never said where they were or what they were. I didn't know that myself. Please don't be angry. It makes my chest hurt. It makes my words go away.*

For a long while, then, Mistress Blackthorn sat staring into the flames or studying her cup as if it were the most fascinating thing in the world. Cara sat too, thinking how often she had got things wrong. Why couldn't she do something good, like discovering the heartwood house story hidden away in some obscure place? Then Mistress Blackthorn would tell her how clever she was, how good at solving puzzles.

"Tell me what happened, Cara," Blackthorn said now, sounding tired and sad. "I'm not angry anymore. I didn't mean to scare you. I believe I've misjudged you, and if that is so, I'm sorry. Take it slowly and don't leave anything out. If you need to write, write."

Cara tried to speak. She still couldn't get the words out. But she didn't want to write this; she needed to say it out loud. She pointed to her cup, which was still half full.

"A good idea," said Mistress Blackthorn. "Let's have this first, then talk. Oh, I have something to show you. I went up to Wolf Glen today.

Had a word with Grim." Her face softened as she said this; thinking of him changed her. "And with your father."

"Oh! How is Father? Is he well?" Cara spoke aloud without even thinking.

Mistress Blackthorn gave her a funny look. "He looked well enough, though he didn't have much time for me. I asked for the materials for a talisman and he sent your aunt to find them. She brought these. You can tell me if they're suitable."

She must have laid the little items on her bed while she was changing her clothes. Now she fetched them and put them on the table near Cara.

"That is from a tunic Father used to wear when highborn folk visited us," Cara said, picking up the scrap of dark blue silken fabric. "It got so worn-out that Aunt Della couldn't mend it anymore, and he was sad. It was his favorite. This is hers. Aunt Della's." She remembered the woven edging, twisted wool of green and brown, on a cloak her aunt used to wear. "This one . . . I don't recognize it. Was it my mother's?" This piece looked older than the others, the cloth so worn it was almost in holes. It would have been delicate even when new: a summer fabric in soft rose.

"That's what your aunt said. I didn't ask her what the garment was. A shift, maybe. I wish I knew how the dyer obtained that color. How about that one?" Blackthorn pointed to the strip of leather that lay beside the other tokens.

Cara felt a smile spread across her face. "Gormán?"

"Correct." Blackthorn did not smile back at her. She wasn't angry anymore. But she wasn't happy either. What had happened with her manuscript had really upset her. If this had been someone else, Cara would have said it had frightened her. But Mistress Blackthorn wasn't scared of anything.

"Did you see Grim?" Cara asked.

"I saw him, yes. Not for as long as I'd have liked. Your father doesn't give his workers much time off. And I visited some other people. In Longwater."

"That woman with the baby."

"Fann, yes, and her mother, and some other folk." A silence, as if she was thinking hard. "Cara?"

"What?"

"Do you know a young man called Fedach? A farmer's son, from a place near Longwater?"

"You mean that boy with the . . ." There was only one farmer's son Cara had ever spoken to in Longwater, and she remembered him well. But she didn't know his name. Maybe he'd told her what it was, that first day when he'd come over to talk to her while Gormán was busy on the loading jetty. But if he had, she'd forgotten.

"With the what? Sweet smile? Nice manners? Bright eyes?"

Cara could feel a blush rising. Ridiculous. She hardly knew the boy. "What about him?"

"I visited the household where he lives. Met his mother. He mentioned you."

"What did he say?"

Now Blackthorn did smile, a nice smile that lit up her face. "Only good things, Cara. He thinks a great deal of you. Did you know he once lived at Wolf Glen for a while?"

"No! When?"

"Let's make another brew first; then I'll tell you about it."

She made a point of showing Cara the right proportions for chamomile and lavender. "You could add a pinch of mint if you'd like," she said. "It livens up the flavor and helps give folk heart."

Cara wondered who needed heart most, herself or Mistress Blackthorn. "But at bedtime, skip the mint?"

"Correct. I'll make a herbalist of you yet."

"That's for Emer," Cara said. "While she's being a wise woman, I suppose I'll be at Wolf Glen, being a sort of farmer. Unless Father makes me marry someone who doesn't want to live there."

"However your life unfolds," Blackthorn said after a bit, "I hope you will be happy, Cara. Now, let's sit down, and I'll tell you something about this lad, Fedach. Who *will* one day be a farmer and a horse breeder like his own father, provided his life takes a straight path."

"I hardly know him," she said a bit too quickly. "I've only met him twice."

"You made a big impression, then."

"I did?"

"You did."

"How could he have lived at Wolf Glen without my knowing? He's only about the same age as me."

"He was a tiny baby. His mother went there as a wet nurse. Your parents hired her."

"But . . ." Cara tried to work it out. Tried to remember what she'd been told about her mother and the brief time when the two of them had both been alive. "I don't think that can be right," she said. "How long does a baby need a wet nurse? When do they start eating real food?"

Mistress Blackthorn smiled. "There's nothing more real than mother's milk. A baby lives on that alone for maybe six turnings of the moon. Most women go on feeding their infants far longer, but at that age they can start on what you call real food as well, thin porridge and suchlike. And they can drink goat's milk."

"Then the story must be wrong. I wasn't born at Wolf Glen. My mother went away to her kinsfolk for the birth. We didn't come home until I was getting on for a year old. So I couldn't have been nursed along with Fedach."

"Cara." Blackthorn's voice had gone really serious. Something bad was coming; Cara knew it. Some kind of secret, and not a nice one about a boy thinking kindly of her.

"What?"

"I have something to tell you. I wasn't going to. Not yet, anyway. But I'm growing sick of lies and secrets and pretense. Especially after what's happened today, with Ségán's men and the wretched document. I misjudged you before. I treated you like a child. But you're a grown woman now, and you need to hear this."

What could she be talking about? "All right," Cara said.

"Before I start," said Blackthorn, "I want you to remember what I said about possibly getting other folk into trouble. Your father has made it very clear, for a long time now, that he doesn't want his personal business spread abroad. He's kept some other folk's business secret too. As you've worked out for yourself, there's something about the story of your first year that doesn't add up. I don't have the whole answer to that, but I do have some of it. If you decide to pursue it further, you'll need to tread carefully. A number of folk could be in serious trouble over it, including me and Grim."

"And Fedach?" Cara's voice was fading away. She cleared her throat and tried again. "And his mother?"

"His mother, certainly, since I made a guess at the truth after speaking with her. Probably not Fedach, since this was long ago." Blackthorn took a deep breath, as if she needed to pluck up courage before she could say whatever it was. "Cara, it's to do with building the heartwood house."

"So, what is it? What do you need to tell me?" Her heart was thumping.

"There was another baby. You know already that Bardán was hired by your father to build the heartwood house, the first time. He was a widower with an infant daughter. Fedach's mother came up from Longwater to feed that child as well as her own."

"Oh. So it wasn't me after all."

"It was Bardán's daughter. But there's another story. A story in which, after only three turnings of the moon, that little girl died. Suanach was by then with child herself, though not visibly so, and she chose to travel away to her kinsfolk for the pregnancy and confinement, returning home with her baby girl after, by my reckoning, about six turnings of the moon. Your mother died within a season of coming back to Wolf Glen."

Your father's a liar, a liar, a liar. "Wait," Cara said, frantically trying to add it all up and failing. "But—no, but—"

"If that were true," Blackthorn said, and the gentle tone of her voice scared Cara, "the story about Suanach going away to give birth, I mean, you would have been a tiny babe in arms when you came home. And you might indeed have needed a wet nurse. But I've heard, from someone who was present at the time, that on the day you arrived home you were starting to walk. That suggests to me a child getting on for a year old."

"No." What was Mistress Blackthorn saying, that Cara was not her parents' daughter at all? That she had been switched with the builder's daughter? "You mean that wild man? You're saying *he* is my father? That can't be true!" She grasped at a possible lifeline. "Anyway, didn't that baby die?"

"That's how the story goes, yes. They say he took her from the house and went out into the forest and abandoned her. But the only people who ever saw her body were your father and Gormán. I'm sorry, Cara. This is a lot for you to take in."

Ah. It was all right after all. "Gormán wouldn't tell a lie," Cara said. "If he said that baby died, it must be true. And my father wouldn't lie." *Your whole life is a lie.* "Why would he?"

"Only he could tell you that. I could put forward a theory, but it's best if I don't. In a matter as sensitive as this we need to stick to facts. Cara, experience has taught me that people do strange things for love, and these are two men who love you dearly. Both your father and Gormán want the best for you. They want to keep you safe, and perhaps shielding you from this story is part of that. You are Master Tóla's only child and heir to a considerable holding. You have wealth, security, a good future ahead. You have people who care about you. Many folk would say it was foolish to risk that."

Cara felt sick. She couldn't take it all in. This had to be wrong. She knew she was her father's daughter; she just knew it. *You're a pretender, pretender, pretender.* "If this was right, I wouldn't—the forest, the trees—I couldn't—"

Blackthorn came over to sit beside her. She put her arm around Cara's shoulders. "You need time to think about all this," she said. "It's for you to choose what to do about it after that. You may decide to ignore the whole thing. You may discount it as wild speculation. I'm sure that's what your father would want. He would be angry if he knew I had discovered this, and even more furious if he knew I had passed it on to you."

"He could get you in trouble. He might have you and Grim sent away." Mistress Blackthorn had taken a big risk telling her the story. She had trusted her with it, knowing how dangerous it might be. Even after what had happened with the secret document.

"I doubt he has the authority to do that, though he might attempt to influence Prince Oran on the matter," Blackthorn said. "Don't let that part of it bother you. It's the least of my worries right now."

"The thing with the document . . . those men . . . Are you in serious trouble, Mistress Blackthorn?"

"Let's just say that matter is very pressing for both me and Grim. But extremely private, Cara. Not to be mentioned anywhere."

Cara nodded. Her thoughts were whirling about, trying to add up the passing of time between her mother's leaving Wolf Glen and coming back, trying not to remember the look in the wild man's eyes that day when he spotted her up in the tree. "I can't be his daughter," she said. "I can't be. He's a sort of . . . He . . ." She fell silent. What was it Gormán had said to the wild man that day, while she was being ushered quickly away? *In the name of all the gods. You're alive.*

"Bardán and his wife lived in Longwater, up on the hill. He worked as a builder long before your father hired him. His wife had kinsfolk in the district. But . . . his mother was half fey. And his father was raised in the Otherworld, though he was human."

"How do you know so much? Who told you that? And why didn't you tell me before?"

"That part of the story is not a secret. It's well-known in Longwater."

"But . . . he's crazy."

"He's different," said Blackthorn. She didn't need to add, *and so are you.*

Then there was a long silence. A long, long silence. Outside it was getting dark; it must be supper time, and they were supposed to go over to the main house for it. Over there everyone would be getting on with their own business. It made no difference to them that Cara's world had been turned upside down. Father. Gormán. Wolf Glen and the forest. If this was true, none of it was hers. None of it. *Your whole life is a lie.*

"When you showed me your talisman," Blackthorn said quietly, "you gave me a list of birds, for the feathers you'd used. I believe that list of birds may be part of a lullaby Bardán learned from his mother. The song was a charm of protection he used to sing to his baby daughter. He would visit her in the evenings, after his day's work was done. *Feather bright and feather fine, none shall harm this child of mine.*"

Cara felt hot tears spilling down her cheeks.

"Bardán is still at Wolf Glen," Blackthorn said. "Wild, yes, but a man who can feel love and grief and pain like any other man. He's the way he is because on the night his daughter was said to have died out in the forest, he fell down a hole and ended up in the Otherworld, and the fey kept him for fifteen years. That's why the heartwood house was not finished. When Bardán came back his mind was scrambled; he had forgotten a great deal of the past. When he looked at you, perhaps he was reminded of his wife or of his mother—who knows? Grim has befriended him; been his protector, as far as he could. And Grim shares my suspicions about the official story of what happened that night and afterward. Here." She handed Cara a clean handkerchief. Cara wiped her eyes and blew her nose.

"Cara."

"What?"

"This calls for cool heads. You should give yourself thinking time. By all means, keep looking for the heartwood house story in the library. Whether it can cast further light on this, I don't know. Consider what I've told you, and decide whether you want to talk to your father about it. If you don't, I will respect that choice, as I said. But don't forget your other father, who loves you just as dearly. It seems he has been very badly treated. Grievously lied to. If you decide to do nothing, he will never know that his daughter survived. And . . . I think Grim would find it hard to keep the truth from him."

"I don't know what to do. I don't know what to believe." She wanted it to be back before this happened, when all she'd had to worry about was Aunt Della fussing about muddy skirts and leaves in her hair. But everything Blackthorn said was making the bizarre story truer. He—the wild man—had fallen down that hole, that same one, she knew it was, and he hadn't had the birds to help him, and those fey creatures had taken him, stolen him away, and kept him for fifteen years. Nearly the whole of her life. That was truly terrible. "Why are they so wicked, Mistress Blackthorn? The fey, the Fair Folk? In the tales, they're noble and good."

"I suppose they are like us. Some good, some bad. Some downright evil." Blackthorn got up and stretched. "We should go to supper. I don't suppose you feel like eating, but a hot meal will be good for you. What I was saying before, Cara—promise me, please, that if you decide to go and talk to your father, you'll tell me first. You should take me with you, and we'll have to take one of the Island men as a guard, perhaps two."

"Why them?"

"Ségán's new rules for me." Blackthorn grimaced. "But it's common sense; if you confront him with this, your father will be . . . unhappy. It's best if you speak to him in my presence and probably Grim's as well. Promise, please."

"I promise." Cara could just imagine it: herself and Father opposite each another in his council chamber, and the room full with Blackthorn and Grim and two guards. Maybe the wild man would be there too. The man who might be her real father, the man with the sad, crazy eyes. She would open her mouth to speak and the words would dance away like sparks from a fire, leaving her mute and helpless.

34

GRIM

Happy to see Blackthorn. Wish it had been longer. Tóla made sure she left quick. What I said once, about this place being a den of wolves—nothing's changed my mind on that. Gormán's as bad as the master. Rushed her off before we had time to talk properly, didn't he? Nice enough fellow, but he's in Tóla's pocket, does what he's told. Might have a few secrets of his own that he doesn't want coming out. My guess is, the master's got some sort of hold on him.

After what she said—Blackthorn, I mean—I'm half minded to tell Bardán the truth. If it is the truth. If Cara's his daughter, it's cruel to keep it secret. I mean, he's been thinking his child is dead. Worse, he's been thinking it's his fault. All those years. If she's still alive and well, how can I not tell him? Thing is, though, telling him would be like touching a flame to a stack of straw. It'd be the blowup of all blowups. That'd be the kind of shocking news that stayed with you for life, like a scar. The girl's only fifteen. Wouldn't want to do that to her. Be worse if she found out later, though. What if it came out after she married and had children of her own? Or worse, just before she married? She might be all set to wed some young man she liked, and when he found out she wasn't Tóla's daughter he'd say, sorry, changed my mind. Couldn't inherit then, could she? But what's Bardán got to offer her? Some folk would say love was enough. Sounds good. But a girl of that age wants a home and security. She wants a future. Bardán can't work. He can't earn a living; he can't support a daughter. She'd be the one supporting him.

Late afternoon, rain comes pissing down and I call a halt for the day, tell the crew to head off home. Put covers on where we can and hope for dry weather tomorrow. The build's going well. Another reason not to say anything to Bardán. Fact is, I miss Blackthorn. I miss the cottage. I miss working for the folk down around Winterfalls. But mostly Blackthorn. It was good seeing her. Nearly shed tears when she had to go. And I'm tired. Nights, I sleep mostly catnaps. In between, I'm awake, on alert—can't help myself. Keep my body strong with the exercises. Wish I could fall asleep quick and stay asleep long, but it doesn't work that way. Every little sound startles me: a mouse in the thatch, a door creaking in the wind, the trees blowing about outside, the rain drumming on the roof. And when I'm awake I'm thinking of the past, seeing the bad things. Faces of the dead and the lost. Twisted, broken bodies. If I'm asleep, I dream, and it's the same. I dream of Mathuin and the lockup. I dream that Blackthorn's a prisoner and I'm chained up and I can't help her. I see the folk I care about being tortured and killed. Over and over again.

Means I'm often snappish with tiredness. In the day, if the fellows are taking a break from work, I'll sometimes sit down to eat and fall asleep right where I am. Catch Gormán looking at me once or twice. Don't know what I'm supposed to say.

Anyway, today it's too wet to work any longer, so I head for the living quarters to stir up the fire and make a brew. Hoping Blackthorn got safely down to Winterfalls. Hoping she's back in the prince's house, dry and warm. I'll have a wash, change my own clothes, help with the cooking. Leave the heartwood house to think about itself for a while. Supper, then an early night. Wouldn't hurt any of us.

Doesn't work out that way. I'm halfway out of my wet clothes when a serving man raps on the door. Master Tóla wants to see me down at the big house. Rain still pelting down out there, but the fellow says it can't wait. I throw on some dry things, cloak over the top. Head out after him. What can be so urgent? Hope something hasn't happened to Blackthorn. Hope she hasn't had an accident on the way home. Can't help seeing her lying in the rain somewhere with a broken leg or a broken head.

By the time we get to the big house and go indoors I'm wound up tight and in no mood to talk to Tóla, not calmly anyway. The fellow takes me to the council chamber, knocks on the door, then goes off and leaves me. Tóla calls out something, which I hope is, *Come in*, and I do.

The master's got a couple of men in the chamber with him, fellows I've seen working around the farm. No idea why they're here. The two of them are standing near Tóla, sort of an embarrassed look about them. They're big men, one nearly as tall as me, the other one a bit smaller.

"You asked to see me." I come in. Door shuts behind me.

"Grim." Tóla's got cold eyes at the best of times. Wintry now. Only time I've seen a soft look on his face was that night we brought Cara home, and it wasn't there for long. Bit sad when you think about it.

I wait. Remind myself that I did help save his daughter's life. And I'm building his wretched heartwood house. Can't wait till the day I put the last touches on that nine-course thatched roof. Happy day, that'll be. Wish I'd never agreed to this.

Tóla moves his hand in a sort of shooing gesture and the two men move away. One stands by each door. Looks like he's using them as guards. Can't see a weapon on either of them. Doesn't mean they don't have any.

"Your friend went down to Longwater after her visit here," Tóla says.

I want to say, *Speak ill of her and I'll get angry quick as quick. And if I get angry, it takes more than a jumped-up landholder and a couple of farmhands to hold me back.* I try to breathe slow. Don't let the red rise up in me. "Mistress Blackthorn, you mean. Her work takes her all over. She went to visit a woman called Fann. The one that gave birth not so long ago."

"Mistress Blackthorn's activities are of some concern to me. It's come to my notice that she visited two households today. The woman you mention lives in one of them. The other, I'm given to understand, does not currently house any person in need of a healer's services."

"You got someone following her around, then?" Should shut my big mouth, maybe. But the man's annoying me. What business is it of his where Blackthorn goes or what she does? And how am I supposed to know anyway, seeing as he hardly gave us time to say a word to each other?

"Why would I do such a thing, Grim?"

"You tell me. I've got no idea who she visits down there. That's her work, and right now, building your heartwood house is my work."

"What did you say to her earlier? What did you talk about?"

Anger's bubbling up, getting near the surface. "This and that," I say, trying to stay calm. "Nothing much." Couldn't say what I wanted, could I? With everyone so close there was no privacy at all. Why's he asking, anyway?

"I hope that is true," Tóla says. Jaw's tight, eyes cold. "When you took on this job, you agreed to my conditions. No gossip. No spreading of tales, whether you believe them to be truth or wild rumor. No talking about my daughter."

I can't help myself. "That'd be the daughter Gormán and me rescued out in the forest that night, yes? The one we saved from down that hole?"

"Watch your words!" He's losing his temper now, and I'm holding on to mine, just. "I have not forgotten that you brought Cara home. I gave you thanks at the time, along with an appropriate reward. I'm aware that your friend visited Wolf Glen today only because certain items had to be fetched for a . . ."

"A luck charm," I say. "Yes, she told me."

Tóla scowls. Looks like he doesn't want anyone knowing about anything. Not without his personal say-so. "Then she should learn to keep her mouth shut," he says. "That's nobody's business but mine."

"And your daughter's," I say, quiet-like. I want to say, *if she really is your daughter,* and I come a hairbreadth from doing it, but I hold the words back.

"Are you deaf? Don't speak of her!" He's on his feet now, fists balled. The two farm lads take a step closer. Eyes on me. Looking more nervous than anything, like they'd rather run away than try to fight me. Fair enough. If I was them, I'd be feeling the same.

"Maybe what you should be doing is talking *to* Cara," I say. "Lot of secrets in this place. Don't speak of this. Don't speak of that. I've done what you wanted so far. Not because I need the work. Not because I want your bags of silver. I've stayed because I don't like seeing a man mistreated. I don't like seeing a man who's addled in his wits and can't use his hands left to look after himself in a cold, leaky old hut. I don't like seeing a man kept on for his skills but treated like dirt—"

"Shut your mouth!"

Tóla's arm comes up as if he's going to smack me in the face. I grab his wrist hard, push him away. The two lads move a bit closer, look at each other, look at me. I glare and growl, and they back off. What now?

"Take your hands off me," Tóla says. Sounds like a king talking to the lowest scullery boy.

The way I'm holding him, I could snap his wrist without much effort. Give him a taste of how it feels not to have the use of your hand. "Send your boys out and I will," I say. "You won't want them to hear what I've got to say. They can wait outside the door."

"Go!" says Tóla, and they do, quick. I let go of his arm, and he rubs his wrist with the other hand. "You should lose your job right now," he says. "How dare you lay hands on me?"

"Thing is," I say, "if it looks like a man's going to take a swing at me, I like to stop him *before* he does it, not after. And I'm quick for a big man. Isn't that why I got the job? Build the house and keep your wild man in order?"

Tóla's at a bit of a loss. Not sure what to say, from the looks of it. Fiddling with the things on the table, not meeting my eye. "This should not have come to blows," he says. "I need you for the job, yes. I expected you to guard him, and you have done that. I did not expect you to appoint yourself his champion. I did not expect Mistress Blackthorn to stick her nose into my business. She's been seeking out information, hasn't she? Information she might pass on to my daughter."

"I can't answer that. Seeing as you don't want me to mention Cara."

He makes an impatient, angry noise. Sweeps his hand across the table, fist clenched. Knocks a cup, an ink pot and some sheets of parchment to the floor. "Don't try to be clever," he snarls. "It doesn't suit you."

Next thing he'll call me Bonehead and I'll really snap. *Breathe,* I tell myself.

"What is it you have to say? What is so particularly private? Spit it out."

Wishing I hadn't said that bit now. Trouble, this is. Trouble for everyone. "I promised to stay and see the job finished," I say. "Agreed to the conditions, yes—no days off for rainy weather, no going home until it's done. Hard conditions, when a man can't enjoy a visit for long enough to draw a breath or two before his friend's whisked away again. But I said I'd do it and I'll do it. One thing, though. Any harm comes to Mistress Blackthorn, one ill deed, one bad word, and I'm off like a dog after a rabbit. You can keep your payment. I don't know who she visited today and I don't much care. She's a healer. Goes everywhere. Sees everyone who needs her. You think that's suspicious, you're out of your mind."

He doesn't say a word. Can't tell what he's thinking.

"I'm a good worker," I say. "I get the job done. I give respect where it's deserved. I can't respect a man who lifts a hand against his workers for no good reason. I can't respect a man who ties up a troubled soul and throws him in a dark cellar, or a man who—"

"Enough. Spare me the catalog of misdemeanors. Say whatever it is you want to say."

"You won't like it."

"I'm sure I won't." He folds his arms, taps his foot.

"Got no daughter, myself. Never had one. But if I did, I'd want her to grow up kind and honest and good-hearted. I'd want her to learn that it's always best to tell the truth. I'd want her to understand that you can't build your life on lies and secrets. That's all I've got to say."

There's a long silence. Then he says, "Get out!" And it's terrible. Angry and sad both. So even though I despise the man, I feel sorry for him.

I'm opening the door when he says, "Stop."

I halt with my back to him, like a well-trained dog.

"You're in deep water, Grim, deeper than a man like you can possibly understand. I don't know what you and that woman of yours think you've discovered, but if she's been spinning wild stories to my daughter, she'll pay a heavy price, and if you—"

It'd be so easy to put my hands around his neck and squeeze hard. There'd be a count of five in it, before he went limp. I make myself breathe. I don't turn around. "Got my breaking point," I say, trying to sound calm. "And that's Blackthorn. Maybe you didn't understand, before. You threaten her, you deal with me. And you'd want to do better than those two lads for bodyguards if that happens. Don't say her name again, *Master* Tóla. Don't even think of it."

"This is over," he says, cold as cold. "No word of this discussion, here or anywhere, understand? I don't want to have to warn you again."

"Right," I say. Mustn't understand how easy I could kill him. Or how angry I get when folk insult Blackthorn. Or why. Well, he wouldn't know that. Nobody does but her and me and Mathuin's thugs.

"I need the job finished," he says. Voice is shaking a bit. Maybe I scared him. "I must have the heartwood house completed. Until that is done, we will be plagued by ill fortune. When the house stands true and perfect in every detail, I will be all too glad to part ways with you. Now go."

I leave without another word. The two lads are outside the door; they move back to let me pass. I bid them good night.

Walking back up to the barn in the rain, I wonder why he wouldn't just get rid of me. There's got to be someone else who could take the lead with the build. I just insulted the master, laid hands on him, more or less told him he was a liar. So maybe he's keeping me not because I'm a good worker, and not because I can watch over Bardán, but because I know too much. Maybe I should turn round and head for Winterfalls right now, even if it's night and rainy and I'd be leaving Bardán on his own. But I'm tired, and there's a light up in the quarters and a meal waiting. And if I left him without a protector, I'd be making a liar of myself. Said I'd teach my own daughter to be kind, didn't I? Kind and honest and good-hearted. And the way to teach a little one is to show her how it's done. Leaving the wild man, running away, that wouldn't be kind or good-hearted. So I head straight on to the barn. Calmer now. Thinking of a baby girl, not Tóla's daughter or Bardán's, but mine. The one I might have, someday. I can see her, crouched down beside me in the garden. I'm showing her which ones are the weeds. She finds a worm; squeals with excitement. Big smile on her face; little hands all muddy. Hair like a bright flame.

35

BLACKTHORN

"I'm astonished," Prince Oran said, "that you believed this information might somehow discredit you in my eyes or in my wife's. I know from experience that you are courageous and trustworthy. The story you've just told me only strengthens that opinion. It appalls and horrifies me. Sadly, I imagine that there might be many such accounts from folk under Mathuin's rule, were those people not afraid to speak out. I know Flidais would agree with me if she were here. You could have told us this much earlier without any fear. Indeed, that knowledge would have aided our planning."

It had been hard getting the truth out. Telling the tale in all its ugliness had been like peeling off a layer of skin. At least Oran had not expected me to do it before a large audience. There were only four of us in the council chamber: the prince, his indispensable companion Donagan, Ségán and me. And while I could have wished the Island men's leader not to be present, the fact that he knew my story already made it easier to speak. Still, I felt as exhausted as if I had run a long race. When Donagan poured me a fresh cup of mead and passed it over, the cup shook in my hands. "I'm glad now that I wrote it all down. It felt like a risk. But from what Ségán said, it can be used in some way. Can you tell me what is planned?" My stomach was tying itself in knots, waiting.

Oran glanced at Ségán.

"We can give you limited information," the warrior said. "There is an enterprise planned, yes. One of which I know you will approve. Secrecy is essential to its success. You'll have to take a great deal on trust."

"Almost everything, from the sound of it. If you're using my testimony, you could at least tell me where and for what purpose. I'm good at keeping secrets."

"That a woman does not break under torture does not mean she can afford to risk capture a second time," Ségán said, sending a chill through me. "We want you alive and well to provide this evidence in person. That will be far stronger than offering the written account alone. It could be discounted as a fabrication."

My heart pounded. I thought I might faint. "So you are bringing him to justice? And you're giving me the chance to speak? Where? When?"

They exchanged glances again, as if to say, *How much can we tell her?* The wait was unbearable. "Please," I said. "Please tell me this is happening at last."

Oran was looking especially solemn. "You will have the opportunity to speak, yes," he said, making my heart lurch. "And soon. You may not know much about the Island men, what they do, the kinds of tasks they are called upon to perform. What we plan lies well outside the accepted rules for bringing a miscreant to justice, especially when that miscreant is a person in high authority. This mission will remain secret even after the goal is accomplished. The fewer people who know the details, the better the likelihood of success. And the safer for all involved."

I tried to take this in. A raid? An assassination? But that wouldn't require testimony. And while I would shed no tears if Mathuin were killed, his death alone would not satisfy me. Nor, I was sure, would it be enough for his other victims. He needed to be brought to account for his crimes. Brought to account, if not publicly, then at least before his peers.

"There should be justice," I said, picking my words with care. "Not only justice done, but justice seen to be done." What about the High King? He was hardly likely to sanction a secret mission that broke all kinds of rules.

"All those who should know, do know," Oran said. His mouth was set unusually grim; his eyes made me think of a winter sky. "All those who should be consulted have been consulted and have given their approval."

"Morrigan's britches," I murmured, making Donagan smile. Unthinkable. The High King knew about this, whatever it was. I wondered if the Island men might have magic on their side. A druid to advise them. Someone like me, only a lot more powerful.

"Mistress Blackthorn," Ségán said, "you'll need to travel. And it will be at short notice. We're taking certain precautions in order not to draw any attention. There will be no massing of folk, no riding in numbers. You'll go with one of our men, perhaps two. And soon. That means we need you in this house, ready to depart, unless there is a life-or-death call for your healing services in the immediate district of Winterfalls. Make sure you go no further. The timing is tight; we've kept it that way for a reason."

"I see." What question could I ask that he might be prepared to answer? What was most important? "Grim," I said. "He must come with me. You know why. You've read the document." Conmael was another matter; I would think that problem through when I was on my own. One thing I knew: no vow, no promise, no threat of dire consequences was going to stop me this time.

"Would Grim also be prepared to testify?" Ségán asked.

"You'd have to ask him. I don't think he would want to speak before an . . . assembly. But he would want to be present. And . . . it would be easier for me to do this if he was there."

"I concur. Grim should be part of this," Oran said. "It should be simple enough to arrange. I understand he's still working up at Wolf Glen. He'd best come back here until it's time. How soon can we get a message to him?"

"I'll send someone," Ségán said. "We'll get a message there in sufficient time for him to ride with you, Mistress Blackthorn."

The mission, the longed-for chance had driven Cara and her problem right out of my head. Now they returned, and with them Bardán and the whole difficulty at Wolf Glen. "You might need to word it carefully," I said. "Make sure Grim knows it's vital for him to come back straightaway."

All of them were staring at me now, as if I were talking nonsense.

"Would not a message that you needed him here be sufficient?" Oran asked, brows lifted.

"Usually, yes." Before Wolf Glen, before the wild man, such a message would have troubled Grim so much that he would have leaped on a horse and galloped all the way back. Or run all the way, if there had been no horse. But now . . . "He's promised to stay up there night and day until the job is finished," I said. "If he knew what this is about, he would come, certainly. But you can't tell him. I understand why. Couldn't I go to Wolf Glen with an escort and talk to him?"

"No," the three men said together.

"I'll word the message precisely," Ségán said. "My messenger will take a spare horse and ask Grim to ride back with him."

It was already late in the day. Prince Oran had arrived home in midafternoon, with a small number of Swan Island men and Donagan. Flidais and little Aolú had not come with him; they were staying at court. For their own safety, I assumed. I felt for Flidais. She went everywhere with Oran; it would be hard for her, knowing he was going into danger. And she would be party to the secret, I was sure. Not only were she and Oran close, but Mathuin was her father's enemy. It was not his crimes against folk like me that had sparked this venture, but his armed attack on Lord Cadhan. Though it seemed both Oran and Ségán believed my account would make a difference. If I'd been readier to trust, if I hadn't let my old fear stop me from telling Oran my story, maybe this venture could have happened far sooner.

"Master Tóla won't be pleased if Grim walks off the job," I said.

And Bardán would be on his own again, just when I had told Cara she might be his daughter.

"The message should bear my signature," said the prince. "Master Tóla can be as displeased as he likes, but if he has any common sense, he won't refuse a direct request from me."

"Am I allowed to know how long we might be away? I will need to tell Emer, my assistant. There's nobody else to do my job while I'm gone."

"Not long," Ségán said. "The journey there requires an overnight stop and a change of horses. You may be away for as few as four or five days. Master Tóla will surely be content to grant Grim leave for such a short period. Not that these things are ever entirely predictable. Something as simple as an unseasonal storm can cause a delay. We've built in a little time, but not much. That's why it's vital that you be ready to go when we give the word. We're waiting for a signal before we move. I can't tell you more."

"I understand. What do I tell Emer?"

"You can leave that to me, Mistress Blackthorn," he said. "We'll inform her after you depart. Does Emer need a key to enter your cottage? Any particular instructions?"

My heart sank. Emer was very young; what if there was a terrible fire, or an injury requiring an amputation, or . . . I must not dwell on what might go wrong. The folk of Winterfalls settlement were practical. Emer's brother, Fraoch the smith, was a big strong man who could hold a limb still or wield a bone saw if he had to. And Emer was not only a sensible girl, she was studious in her own way and already quite skilled. She would cope. "Could you tell her that if she encounters anything she can't deal with alone, she can send for help here? Donagan, will you be staying?"

Donagan did not answer. But Oran said, "Emer can certainly come here anytime she needs help. Aedan will send for one of the court healers if necessary."

"Thank you." It was going to be hard to keep this to myself. The secret would be written all over me, in my eyes, on my face, in the way I conducted myself. Cara would see instantly that something had happened. "I will need to go over to Dreamer's Wood and collect a few items from the cottage. Prepare things for Emer even though I can't tell her about this. I will take one of the men with me, if someone can be spared."

"Let me know when you want to go," Ségán said. "I suggest getting it done tomorrow."

"You'll have a lot to think about," Oran said, giving me a smile. "I don't think we need keep you any longer now. And I know you require no further reminders to maintain absolute secrecy. Outside these four walls, act on the assumption that anyone could pass on what they hear to the wrong ears. Within the walls, take any concerns straight to Ségán."

"I understand. I have one more question before I go."

"Yes?"

"What happens to my written testimony? Do I bring it with me?" It had been stored in a locked chest in the women's quarters. I had the only key around my neck.

"Far safer if you and your document travel separately," Ségán said, turning me cold again. "I will arrange for it to be safely transported where it needs to go. You might give me the key now."

Slipping the cord over my head, passing the key to him felt like something from a bad dream. I understood why this was necessary. But the thought of what might go wrong made me feel sick.

"Thank you, Mistress Blackthorn," Ségán said gravely. "I understand why it might be hard for you to trust. But you can trust us."

As I walked back across the garden to the quarters I was sharing with Cara, I tried to compose myself. I tried to arrange my face in a peaceful expression. I made myself breathe in a slow pattern. But my heart was still racing, my palms were clammy, and my thoughts were whirling. What if I had to leave tomorrow, as soon as I'd fetched what I needed from the cottage? What if they insisted on going before Grim got back? What if I still couldn't summon Conmael, and we were traveling over the border, and I was breaking my promise twice over? And how could I even try to summon him if I couldn't go to Dreamer's Wood without one of the Island men dogging my steps?

I was sure Cara would read the truth all over me the moment I stepped in the door. But she wasn't there. For a moment I stood frozen, thinking she might have broken her own promise and rushed off to Wolf Glen, evading guards and servants. She hadn't spoken of Bardán or the past since I'd talked to her yesterday. I'd been away most of today, visiting my regular folk, old people with wheezy chests or aching joints, young women expecting babies, a man with a broken leg that was still mending. I'd ridden over to the neighboring settlement of Silverlake to pull a rotting tooth from a man's mouth, a job for which I could have done with Grim's assistance, though Cúan, who'd been my escort for the day, proved an able helper. I'd come home to find that Prince Oran was back, and had asked to see him urgently. I hadn't seen Cara since breakfast time.

If she'd decided to bolt, she might have been gone all day. Could she possibly have left on her own and unseen, again? Under the very eyes of Ségán's men? Gods, why hadn't I thought to check on her at some point during the day? I should at the very least have asked Mhairi or Fíona where she was. I should have thought of it as soon as I came home. Oran's return had put that right out of my selfish head.

But no. I was panicking for no good reason. The lamp was burning, the cottage was warm, the fire was banked up under a blanket of ash. She'd been here, and not so very long ago. And now I saw, beside the lamp, the wax tablet with its covers open and something written there. *The druid is here and he knows the story. I want to talk to him on my own. If I am very late, I will sleep in the women's quarters so I don't disturb you coming in. Cara.*

Disturb me? Hah! I had enough churning around in my head to ensure I wouldn't sleep a wink. And how late was she likely to be anyway? It would hardly take half the night to tell an old tale. I'd have liked to go and listen; not only would it be a welcome diversion from Mathuin, but I was curious about the story. Still, the message was clear. *I want to talk to him on my own.* At least, this way, I was spared from having to pretend to Cara that nothing was bothering me. As for Master Oisin, maybe I could speak to him in the morning. Before I went over to Dreamer's Wood. Before I made one last attempt to summon Conmael.

All this time, I thought as I took off my shoes. All this time, and now, suddenly, it was happening. Two days' ride at most, and surely it had to be south. That meant somewhere near the border with Ulaid. Perhaps still in Dalriada, perhaps not. But I'd be breaking my vow anyway, because I'd promised Conmael I wouldn't seek out Mathuin. The oddest part of it was, if the hearing or council was only two days' travel away, it most certainly couldn't be in Laigin. Nor could it be at Tara, under the eye of the High King. We weren't going to confront Mathuin on his home ground. So he must be coming to us.

36

CARA

The druid, Master Oisin, was not lodged in the men's quarters but in one of the farm cottages, like her and Blackthorn. Once Cara got the first words out, she saw the kind look on his face and had no trouble asking if he knew the tale about the heartwood house. He did, and when Cara asked if he would tell it to her straightaway, in private, he said yes, of course.

She told Mhairi she was going to bed. Master Oisin said he would walk over to the cottages with her. But they both went to his lodging. If someone happened to see her, Cara would say she was seeking spiritual counseling. Aunt Della would have thought it more proper for Mistress Blackthorn to be present, no doubt. But Cara didn't want anyone else to hear. The story might be anything. She needed to do this on her own, with nobody watching her. She could pass on the tale to Mistress Blackthorn in the morning, when she'd had time to think about it. Time to cry without anyone knowing, if it came to that. Except this druid, who would not judge her.

Master Oisin kindled the fire that was laid ready on his little hearth. He was so quick and tidy that she did not offer to help. He filled a kettle and put it on to heat.

"There now," he said. "Shall I tell the tale straightaway, and we can have a brew when it's finished?"

"Mm," Cara murmured, nervous now.

"Could you tell me, perhaps, why this is of such intense interest?"

"My father is building a heartwood house. Or rather, he's having someone build it for him. It seems very important to him. So important he's . . . he's behaving oddly. He did try to have it done once before, when I was a baby. And it didn't get finished. My mother died soon after, and my father thinks if he'd built the heartwood house earlier, she would have lived."

"Oh," said Master Oisin softly. "That is sad, my dear. How hard for you to bear. Your father knows this old tale, then. Have you not asked him to tell it?"

"I don't think he really knows it, not properly. Only that the heartwood house brings good luck if it's made the right way. He doesn't talk about it. At least, not to me. It makes him too sad. And now that it's being built again, he's sent me away."

"If he does not know the tale, how can he know the right way to build?"

"There's a . . . a man who does know. A man who's telling the builders what to do."

"I see."

How could he see, if he did not know Bardán's story? Part of her wanted to tell him everything. Druids were wise. They knew about the fey. They knew all the old lore. They even had uncanny powers. But she should hear the story first. It might have nothing to do with the strange way Father was acting, or with Blackthorn's theories. "Will you tell it now, please?"

"The tale is very old and has several names. The variant best known to me goes like this: There was once a wealthy man whose lands were broad and whose cattle were sleek. A river flowed between his fields, with a bridge of worked stone across it. Under this bridge there lived a monster. Not the troublesome kind of monster that frightens good folk about their daily business and eats prize cattle and makes fires and floods to amuse itself. This was a quiet creature, content to stay in the concealment of the bridge by day, coming out to bathe in the river water at twilight and to spend the moonlight hours conversing with wild birds and eating the grasses that grew along the banks.

"Not to say that folk did not fear the monster, for she was bigger than the most formidable bull in the herd, with skin like a toad's and a face only a mother could think beautiful. Folk did not cross the bridge after dusk unless they had pressing business, and if they did so, they blocked their ears and kept their eyes straight ahead. For the monster liked to sing. She had a little one, you see, and she'd sing to it as the two of them swam in the river.

"Now the man I was speaking of had many worldly blessings, but there was one thing he lacked: a child of his own."

It's only a coincidence, Cara told herself. *This is an ancient tale. It can't have anything to do with me or Father. It can't.*

"It happened that the wealthy man was walking over the bridge one night, having been out on an errand and delayed in his return. And he caught the sound of singing from down below, singing and splashing as the monster bathed her little one. The words of that song made him stop in his tracks to listen. *Build it, build it, stone on stone, stone on stone on stone,* the creature sang. *Strong as faith, strong as love, strong as living bone.* She went on to describe a house with a roof of nine couples, a house built from every timber in the wood. A heartwood house. A magical house. Every tree would impart a particular blessing on the one who built it. Rowan for protection from evil spirits. Oak for strength of both body and mind. Fir for clear-sightedness. And so on. Every blessing a man could possibly want for himself and his family was contained in the heartwood house. Including the blessing the wealthy man most desired at that time in his life: fertility, represented by the elder.

"He listened in silence, and in silence he walked on, leaving the monster bathing her child, still singing. *Stone on stone on stone.* The next day he came to the bridge with armed men, while the creature was sleeping, and he stole away her child."

Tears brimmed from Cara's eyes. There was nothing to say. Maybe her heart would break right here and now, split apart in her chest so she fell down dead. That might be a good thing, a merciful thing.

"My dear child, what is wrong?"

"Nothing," she whispered. "Please tell me the rest."

But Master Oisin got up to make the brew, and would not go on with the tale until she had drunk some of it. He gave her a cloth to wipe away the tears. It would have been easier to stop crying if he had not been so kind.

"I'm all right now," she said, though surely she'd never be all right, not after this. "Please go on."

"If you're sure, my dear."

"I'm sure."

"The monster made her way to the man's house, ponderous out of the water, leaving a trail of slime across the fields and scaring the cattle. She howled outside his door. She screamed outside his window. But he would not give back her child. Not unless she built for him a heartwood house like the one in the song. Stone on stone on stone. Nine couples. Every timber in the wood. A house that would shower him and his with blessings. When it was done, he told the creature, when it was perfect in every detail, he would return her baby."

"Cruel," Cara whispered, trying to picture the creature that lived under the bridge, and finding she could only think of Bardán, the wild man, the monster to her father's rich man. "Cruel and selfish."

"And, as it turned out, misguided," said Master Oisin. The firelight flickered over his calm features, his silver-gray hair, his hands curved around the earthenware cup. "The creature built him the house. Cut the timber herself, with her teeth. Laid the stone. Hammered in the uprights. Heaved up the roof beams; she was strong. All the time weeping for her child, who would be frightened and lonely in a house of strangers, with no river to swim in and no mother to sing to him. Would they remember to keep his skin damp so he did not come out in blisters? Would they tickle his belly and make him laugh in delight? Would they be kind to him? She built and built, and the heartwood house grew and grew. Folk from all around came to stare at her as she worked. But they kept a safe distance away. Those teeth were formidable. They did not know that she used them mostly to pull up grass and chew it fine, so her little one could eat it without choking. What were they feeding him? The man did not listen when she tried to ask him. He was deaf to all but what he chose to hear.

"In time the heartwood house was finished, and the creature came to the wealthy man's door to tell him so. He went to inspect the place. It was indeed a splendid sight, standing tall and fair in his home field, the thatch golden in the sun, the timbers fine and strong, the stone well-shaped. He could find no fault in it. So he had his steward bring the child—a slimy, puling thing that his servants had loathed to touch, an abomination that had wailed all night and lain curled in a tight ball all day—and gave it back to its mother."

"She held her little one close as she made her way to the river. Not saying a word. Not until she was under the bridge again, and soothing his poor blistered skin with cool water and kisses. Not until she had fed him and rocked him and comforted him, and he, worn out by crying, had fallen into a hiccupping half-sleep.

"When it was twilight she ventured out, and bathed her son tenderly, and sang a new song. A farmhand coming home late happened to hear it, and so strange a song was it that he remembered every word. *Every tree in the house, every tree but the ivy, the poplar and the crooked yew. Every tree in the cruel man's house but the ivy, the poplar and the crooked yew.*

"The farmhand had no idea what it meant, but it sounded interesting, so the next day he told a friend, and that friend told his friend, and in time the words the creature had sung came back to the wealthy man. And he raged to hear them, for this could mean only one thing. The creature had tricked him. She had not used every timber in the wood after all. She had left out ivy, poplar and crooked yew. He asked a druid what that might mean. The druid told him that by omitting those three, the creature had denied him and his heirs the vital blessings of self-knowledge, protection against illness and safe passage to the next life. Even if he might now father a child, without those three, neither he nor his line would have a sure future.

"The wealthy man was enraged. He would kill the monster. He would chain her up and lock her away. No, he would take the child again, and he would make the wretched creature finish the job properly. He summoned his men, armed them with pitchforks and scythes, and marched down to the river, cursing all the way. Where was the monster?

"They looked under the bridge. They hunted all along the river-banks, this way, that way. But the creature was nowhere to be found. She had swum away before dawn with her little one clinging to her back. She had gone to find a new home, far from the habitations of men. And search as the wealthy man might, he never found her, not in all his living days."

"And the heartwood house was never finished." Cara's voice was a little thread. She couldn't seem to catch her breath.

"It was never finished. The rich man tried to add pieces of the three missing timbers, but somehow they could never be made to fit. There was magic in the making of it, of course. And a man like him has no magic."

"At least the creature escaped," Cara said. "At least she got her child back and found a safe place for the two of them." What did this tale mean? It felt as if it was about her and her father and Bardán. But how could it be? She wanted to go away and hide. She wanted to be up in the yew tree, with her eyes closed against the world, leaning against the strong trunk and thinking of nothing at all. But she had to ask. Had to make herself ask. "Master Oisin?"

"Yes, Cara?"

"These old tales . . . Can the things in them sometimes happen again? Not exactly the same, of course, but . . . very much the same?"

"If this were your story, Cara, who would you be?"

"The monster's child." Her voice shook. Deep down, she knew it was true. Even though it would mean Gormán had lied, and her father had lied, and something cruel and terrible had happened.

"Ah, the monster. But she was only a monster in the eyes of those who did not understand the strange and different. The tale makes it clear she was a loving mother, a skilled and hard worker, a gentle creature who fed only on grasses, a singer, a poet, a student of lore. All of those things."

Cara was shivering; she edged closer to the fire. "But folk wouldn't see that," she said. "They'd only see the big teeth and the scaly body and the slime. They'd judge straightaway that she was dangerous."

"It is often thus, sadly. Have you known such a person, Cara? One who is so different that folk feel fear and loathing rather than compassion?"

Cara remembered that day when she'd been up in the guardian oak and the wild man had come. She had looked down into his mad eyes and been frozen with terror. It would have been so easy to climb down, to smile, to ask if he was all right. "Yes," she said. "And I think he might be my father. My real father."

The druid fell silent. For a long time he sat staring into the flames, so long that Cara wished she could take back the words, that she could go on pretending it wasn't true. "How can it be," she asked, "that an ancient tale like that can be so close to my story, or at least the one Mistress Blackthorn thinks may be the truth about me and my family? Is that magic?"

Master Oisin smiled. "A tale has as many forms and variations as it has tellers over the years. Mine was only one version of this story about the wealthy man and the monster. The heartwood house possesses a deep natural magic; there is no doubt of that. One would imagine the skills required to build such a house could be learned only in the Otherworld. Do you think your father knew that when he hired his builder?"

"I don't want to think about it. But I have to. I have to talk to my father. The man I always believed was my father. Only . . . if I do, and if Mistress Blackthorn is right, it would be . . . it would break his heart. He would get angry. He might do something terrible." Like the man in the story, who would have killed the creature if he could have found her. Only this was worse. In the story, the wealthy man had never pretended the baby was his. He hadn't decided to keep the child and tell lies about it. "I don't want it to be true. I don't want to lose my father and my home and my whole future. But I have to know."

"Dear child. This seems daunting indeed, and you are very young. Do not rush to action. Take time to consider. Talk to Mistress Blackthorn again; she is wise and brave." He seemed to consider for a little, then added, "You see this as a loss. But it is not so much a loss as a choice. Two paths lie before you. One is the path you always believed would be yours: a broad, straight way, a path of security and advantage, a path with few challenges or surprises. Safe, predictable, comfortable. The other is a path of many twists and turns, of darkness and light, of difficulty and reward, a path on which you would be forever learning."

Cara stared at him. "How can you know all that? You don't know anything about me."

"The flames tell me much. They tell me that you too are somewhat strange and different. You might turn that difference to the good, Cara."

There was a question she must make herself ask. Another to which, really, she would rather not know the answer. "Can you tell if I have . . . if I have fey blood? Like the man who is building the heartwood house?"

"Have you reason to believe so? Other than the possibility that he is your real father?"

How much should she tell him? Would a druid keep a secret, the same as a wise woman? "There was a time . . . I heard voices, out in the forest, and they led me to a . . . a hole in the ground. I fell down, and there were things there, creatures, only I couldn't see them. They told me my father was a liar. They said my whole life was a lie. It was . . . it was the scariest thing that's ever happened to me. Except this. Except finding out it might be true."

"Dear child. And how did you escape?"

"I found the tree roots, oak roots, and held on. I knew the oak would keep me safe. The trees are my friends. They have been since I was very small. And after a while a dog found me, and two men let down a rope, and I climbed out. There were some birds too. A crow and some others. They kept those . . . those things . . . away while I was climbing up. They . . . the fey beings . . . wanted me to stay. They would have made me stay. Like he did. The builder. They kept him for fifteen years." She was crying again, the tears flowing with the words. "From not long after his child was born, right through until the start of this spring."

Master Oisín had an odd expression on his face. She could tell he didn't think she was just making it up. He looked at her with . . . wonder.

"Birds do follow me around," Cara said, dabbing her cheeks with the cloth. "They come close. Especially when I'm up in a tree. Closer than they would for most folk."

"I think you have answered your own question, my dear. What a remarkable tale. Stranger far than the one I told."

Cara thought of Wolf Glen, her father, Gormán. Gormán had lied to her. That was the hardest part to believe. She thought of the wild man and how he had looked at her so hungrily. "I'm scared to go there and talk to him. My father. Both of them. But I have to. I have to know. Why my parents did it, how they did it. How could my father even think of such a thing?"

"That, only he can tell you. Cara, do not forget what I said before. Take your time over this. And do not go alone. Take a friend with you. A witness and protector. Ask Mistress Blackthorn if she will go, with her friend Grim. I would be your companion myself, but sadly, I am here for one night only, then must travel on."

"Grim is at Wolf Glen already. The wild man—the builder—has crippled hands; he's telling Grim what to do, and Grim is building the heartwood house."

"Then you have a friend in place."

"I don't really know Grim. Only from Mistress Blackthorn. I met him just once. His dog found me that night. He helped save me."

"A fine man, strong in body and spirit. A man who will stand by folk in trouble. Between them, he and Mistress Blackthorn would keep you safe."

"Safe," Cara echoed, wondering if he meant she needed protecting from her own father. What about Aunt Della? Did she know all about this? Had she too told lies from the first? "Maybe it's not true," she said. "Maybe it's all some sort of misunderstanding." Knowing as she spoke that it wasn't. The hollow, sick feeling in her belly seemed to confirm it.

"Remember the two paths. Be strong, child. Do what you know to be right."

They sat there a while longer, not talking. Then Master Oisin offered to escort Cara over to her sleeping quarters, but she said there was no need—it was not far and she would like to be on her own for a little.

She hadn't really thought about what would come next, but once she was outside under the open sky, dark though it was, she knew she could not sleep indoors, not tonight, not after hearing that story. The only place she wanted to be was high in the yew tree, cradled safely in its branches and sheltered by its canopy. Nobody would miss her. Mhairi would assume she was with Blackthorn. And she'd told Blackthorn she'd be in the women's quarters. As for guards, there were some about, despite the late hour, and there were still lamps lit in the main house and—a surprise—over in the stables. Maybe someone was traveling tomorrow. Not Master Oisin, who walked everywhere, but someone who would be riding.

It was easy enough to reach the tree. She took off her shoes and walked barefoot, and her feet found the way in the dark. When a guard seemed to be moving in her general direction, she whispered, *Don't see me*, and imagined herself to be invisible, just a part of the night and the wind and the grasses whispering their own secrets. Whether it was real magic or just luck, she didn't know, but the guard passed by as if she were not there. Once under the shelter of the big yew she hauled herself up, settled in her favorite spot, wrapped her cloak around herself and tried to do what the druid had suggested: consider the two paths ahead of her so she could do what was right. Master Oisin had seemed to think she was a brave person like Blackthorn, a person who could make hard decisions. But this was worse than hard. Losing your father, your home, your whole life up till now, having that all ripped away was like dying. And it hurt. Having a knife stuck in her belly and twisted around might feel something like this. She wouldn't sleep. Couldn't. Maybe she should have woken Blackthorn and told her the story. But that wouldn't have been fair.

She leaned her cheek against the yew. Closed her eyes. *I have something to tell you,* she said in the voice only a tree could hear. *A strange story. There was once a rich man, and on his land there was a bridge . . .*

37

BLACKTHORN

My sleep had been fitful at best. The moment I'd dropped off I'd been trapped in my familiar nightmares: Mathuin laughing, the torture chamber and the lockup, my family burning. I'd woken drenched in cold sweat with my heart hammering. I'd built up the fire. Made brew after brew until I was awash. Paced the floor of the small cottage until my legs ached. I'd conducted long conversations with Grim and invented his replies, trying to calm my restless thoughts.

Dawn came at last, as welcome to me as air to a drowning woman. With it came Cara, looking pale and disheveled. Wherever she'd slept, I was pretty sure it hadn't been the women's quarters.

"Brew?" I suggested, deciding not to ask questions. She was here; she was safe. That was all that mattered.

"What?" She hadn't heard me. She was in some other place, not here in front of me.

"Sit down, Cara." Gods, she was freezing cold. I steered her to the fire. Found a blanket and passed it to her. She didn't speak until I had the brew half made.

"Master Oisin told me the story. About the monster's child and the heartwood house."

"Ah. And was it what you were expecting?" Whatever she'd heard had shaken her badly. A monster's child?

"It was bad. So bad I have to go up there, to Wolf Glen, and talk to my father. Today, if you're not too busy."

I opened my mouth to tell her I couldn't go with her, but I swallowed the words. I passed her a steaming cup. "Drink some of this, then tell me the story, if you will."

It came out quickly, almost too quickly for me to follow. The monster, the child held hostage, the blessings conveyed by the different timbers, the creature's vengeance. The sting in the tail. The story did not exactly parallel Cara's own situation. But it was close. Uncannily close. There was no human mother in Master Oisin's tale. In Cara's, it seemed to me Suanach might be the key.

"So I have to go. I have to talk to him. To both of them, if I can."

"Your father and . . .?"

"My two fathers," Cara said. "Can you come today? Master Oisin said I should take someone with me, and I don't want anyone else coming, not a guard or Mhairi, and the sooner I do this, the braver I can pretend to be. If you're with me, I might be able to get words out. The right words. I don't know what they are yet." When I did not reply straightaway, she said, "Master Oisin would have come if he could, but he's traveling on today. And I want you."

I set down my cup on the table. My own worries crowded back into my mind. "I'm sorry, Cara. I can't come with you. Not today, and not for quite a few days ahead."

"But . . . why?"

Did she have to look at me like that, as if I was her best friend and had turned against her for no good reason? "I can't tell you why. I'm sorry, but that's the way it is. I may need to travel at very short notice. That's all I can say."

"Travel where?"

I just looked at her. Felt myself getting angry. Made myself breathe slowly. To her, this was every bit as important as Mathuin's fate was to me. "You have a choice," I said. "Take someone else with you, or wait until I can come. Nothing's going to change up at Wolf Glen if you leave this for a short while. You are safe here in the prince's house. Speaking to your father about this will be opening a box of trouble."

"But I have to—"

"I understand that. If I were in your shoes, I'd be wanting to rush up there and get it done. But remember, whatever results from this, it's going to hurt someone. It may well change your whole life. You need to have me with you, and a guard as well."

"Grim's there."

"Grim can't deal with this on his own." Grim wouldn't be there until he and I got back from Prince Oran's secret mission. But I couldn't tell Cara that. "Besides, he's working for your father. That will place him in quite a difficult situation when the truth comes out. He's broken your father's rules by telling me about this, and I've disregarded warnings from both Master Tóla and your friend Gormán."

"Gormán? You spoke to Gormán? What did he say?"

I regretted mentioning the forester. Cara was fond of him. Trusted him. That had been evident for a while. The affection was mutual; he had spoken of her as if she were his own daughter or granddaughter. And he knew about this. He must know. "Not much, Cara. He told me not to talk to the folk at Longwater about what happened in the past. And I went straight ahead and did just that."

She was silent a moment, clutching her cup with white-knuckled hands. Then she said, "How can I wait? How can I do nothing for days and days?"

I've waited years, I wanted to say. *Endless, soul-destroying years.* "The time will pass quickly enough," I said. "Keep busy. Occupy yourself. And use your common sense. Doing this on your own would be foolish, even if you could get out of here without someone stopping you. Have you forgotten what happened last time? Whatever lies in wait down that hole is still there. And elsewhere at Wolf Glen, no doubt. The fey might welcome another chance to turn you off your path."

She turned tear-damp eyes on me in reproach. "I can't believe you just said that. I can't believe you tried to frighten me out of going."

Wretched girl! Every part of me was on edge. The desire to throw something, hard, was rising fast. *Grim, come home. I need you.* "If you're not frightened," I said, "you have an inflated idea of your own abilities. Please do as I ask. Don't go to Wolf Glen until I can come with you. And don't ask questions about why I can't rush off and do your bidding at a snap of the fingers. That matter is confidential. You're not to mention it to anyone, understand?"

In response she got up, dabbing her eyes, and headed for the door.

"Where are you going?" My voice was sharp, angry. I drew a breath and tried again. "Cara. I'm doing my best to help."

"I wanted you to come. I was relying on you. There's nobody else I can ask." She had her back to me. The tone was that of a child betrayed.

"And I will come. I've told you that. But not yet. I'm sorry, but this other matter is of pressing importance. It's not something I can set aside. Cara, the world will not come to an end because you waited a few more days."

Cara muttered something and went out, slamming the door behind her. And it came to me that when she confronted Master Tóla with the truth, the world she knew would indeed come to an end. One way or another, her life would be changed forever.

Anger filled me. I was furious that the world was so unfair; disgusted with myself for dismissing Cara's concerns; enraged by my own need to have Grim back home, as if I were some drooping creature who could not take so much as one step on her own. "A pox on it all!" I snarled, casting around for something to hurl at the wall, something that would make a lot of noise. My cup. The iron poker. The hedgehog Grim had carved for me. I stilled; drew a shaky breath. Heard Grim's voice in my mind, clear as clear. *Curse and shout all you want. Don't mind me. Only, not your house, is it? Be better not to make a mess.*

I picked up the hedgehog, held it on my palm, looked it in the eye. It gazed beadily back at me. I reminded myself that Grim would be getting a message from Ségán, possibly today. He might be home by supper time. If I could tell Cara to wait several days before undertaking the most important task of her whole life, I could surely control my temper until then. "Right," I muttered. "Take your own advice. Keep busy. Occupy yourself. Wash your face, go to the privy, have breakfast. Talk to Master Oisin if he's still here. Ask for an escort. Go over to Dreamer's Wood and get things ready for Emer. Try to summon Conmael. So what if you can't stop thinking about Mathuin? Just keep on putting one foot in front of the other. Or you really will become that pathetic weakling who can't pull herself together and act on her own. Some wise woman you'll be then."

38

GRIM

Day after Tóla threatens me, I'm half minded to walk off the job, Bardán or no Bardán. I don't like a bully, and that's what the man is. Playing God, telling us all what to do and how to do it, making us dance to his tune. And that big secret, that big pack of lies weighing heavy on him. No wonder he's a touch short-tempered. He needs to tell his girl the truth. He needs to put things right. Wasting time and money on the build, trying to buy good luck for himself instead of facing things the way they are. He should forget about luck and try a bit of honesty.

That's not the only thing making me want to go home. I'm worried about Blackthorn now. Who did she talk to down at Longwater? What did she find out and what's she going to do about it? Don't want her falling foul of Tóla. Not that I can stop her if she's got the bit between her teeth, but if I was there, I could warn her. Tell her to be careful. I could be around if she did get in trouble. Stupid, maybe. She'd tell me she can look after herself. But I still want to go home.

I don't do it. The rain clears. Bardán's ready. The Longwater crew's here. Waiting for me to run through the day's work. Word comes that a farmer's got the straw for the thatching. Bringing it in on a cart as soon as the weather looks set fine for a few days. I hate to take on a job and not get it done properly. So I work all through the day, and by late afternoon the place is looking good. A little touch or two and we'll be ready to start thatching. I talk to Gormán about ladders and he says he'll look out a few, and if they're not long enough, he'll knock together a new one for us. I ask the crew if anyone doesn't mind heights, and who's helped with thatching before, and a couple of the lads say yes to both. All good. Only, underneath, I'm worried still. It's not just Blackthorn. It's Bardán. The truth's eating away at me. If I don't tell him what I know, what Blackthorn thinks might be the real story, aren't I just as bad as Tóla? How can I not tell him his long-lost daughter is alive and well? I should tell him even if it opens a bag of trouble. I should. If I was in his shoes, I'd want to be told. Can it wait till the heartwood house is finished, thatch and all? I'm thinking no, it can't. Wish I could talk to Blackthorn again first, though. Find out if she knows any more. Ask her if we should tell them both at once, Bardán and the girl. Once they know, there's going to be a big storm, and nobody's going to walk through it without getting hurt.

I'm tired after the day's work. Always tired now. Never as much sleep as I want. I can see myself getting home after this is all done and sleeping for days and days, like someone in an old tale. Supper time, my eyes won't stay open. Spring's heading into summer and the dark doesn't come till late, but I head off to bed as soon as I've helped Conn wash the dishes. Ripple's happy to come with me, doesn't care if it's night or day as long as she's got company.

Expecting the usual sort of night, lying awake, getting up, going through my exercises, trying not to think about bad things, listening to Bardán breathing and Ripple snoring in her sleep. But tonight's different. Head hits the pillow and I'm fast asleep.

Slammer's got her by the hair. Hands tied behind her back. She tries to fight but he forces her down on her knees. Everyone's yelling, cursing, me loudest of all. We know what's coming. Seen it before. *Let her go! Take your filthy hands off her!* But he pushes her head down, shoves her face in the bucket. Water would be bad enough. This isn't water.

I smash my fists into the bars till they're raw and bloody. Counting how long she's under, how long before she has to take a breath. One . . . two . . . three . . . The others go quiet. Me, I'm still yelling. My whole body's shouting. *You filthy scum! I'll rip your head from your body! Get her out, you vermin. Get her out now!* But I'm locked in. I can't reach her. I can't save her.

He lets her up. She gasps and splutters, face streaming with the vile stuff from the slop bucket, and then he pushes her back in again. One . . . two . . . three . . . four . . . I stop yelling. *You're strong,* I whisper. *You can do this. Hold your breath, Lady.* I hold mine. Hold it till my chest's aching. He lets her up. She chokes, wheezes, fights to suck in air. "Filthy slut!" says Slammer, and pushes her straight back down. *No!* Got tears running all down my face. *No! Get her out!* I belt my head against the bars till I nearly pass out. *Get her out, Slammer, you piece of shit!* Ten . . . eleven . . . twelve . . . He gets her out. Lays her on the floor. Picks up the bucket and pours the slops in her face. A roar comes out of me like thunder. Like the noise of the end of the world. *Lady!* Feels like I'm crying blood. *Lady!*

Someone puts a hand on my shoulder. I jump as if I've been hit. *Get your filthy hands off me or I'll—*

"Grim. Wake up."

She's dead. She's gone. I'll rip that man limb from limb. I'll—

"Wake up, brother. It's me, Bardán. Grim, open your eyes. Take a breath. That's the man. You're here. You're safe."

Ripple's tongue, warm and wet, licking my hand. Moonlight shows me her silvery fur, her bright eyes. Bardán's worried face. I try to breathe. Try to stop sobbing. Morrigan's curse. Never been so pleased to wake up.

Someone's thumping on the wall, calling out from next door. "Shut it, will you?"

"Breathe now," says Bardán. "Take your time. You're safe. You're back."

"Shit," I wheeze. "Oh, shit. What was I . . .?"

Bardán sits down beside me. Ripple on the other side. "You were somewhere bad," Bardán says. "Take it slowly, Grim. You're all right now."

"She . . . she . . ." Can't put the words together. I can still see it: Slammer, the bucket, her lying there. "Lady . . . Blackthorn . . . she was . . ." I lurch to my feet, stagger to the door, in the dark, blunder through Gormán and Conn's sleeping quarters. Make it outside, just. Everything comes up, gushes out of me in a foul-smelling flood. I go on retching and dribbling long after my gut's just a big empty ache.

Lamplight behind me in the quarters. Sound of voices, talking quiet. Ripple's come out. Sniffing around what I've spewed up. I tell her to leave it and she backs off.

"Making a brew." Bardán's in the doorway behind me. "You all done?"

Kettle's on the fire. Gormán and Conn are awake—no surprise. Bardán sits me down. Conn finds a spare blanket, puts it around my shoulders. Ripple pads back inside and lies across my feet. Gormán makes the brew. One thing I know. I'm not going back in there to lie on my bed in the dark.

"Nightmare," I say. "Get them sometimes. Sorry I woke you." Can't stop thinking of Blackthorn. Why did I dream that? Is she in trouble?

"Not much of a sleeper, are you?" That's Gormán, giving me a funny look. What he means is, I've kept them awake other nights too. Only they haven't said anything.

"Be going home soon," I say. "Out of your hair."

"Not so very soon, surely," says Gormán. "With the thatching still to do."

"A couple of the fellows will help me." I feel like telling him the truth. That I can't wait to get out of this place. But I don't. Might need to ask if I can go down and see Blackthorn, though. Set my mind at rest. But that's not for Gormán to say yes or no to. "Shouldn't take too long. I hope."

I catch Bardán smiling when I say that. One of his odd smiles, like he knows something nobody else knows. Have to ask him why. Hoping there isn't something odd about the thatching, something he hasn't told me. But now's not the time. Conn's yawning and Gormán's finishing his brew. It's the middle of the night. I don't want to ask for a lantern. Don't want to look weak.

"We need a light through there," Bardán says to Gormán. "The lantern, the one with a cover."

"With all that straw around? What do you want to do, burn us to a crisp?"

I fight down the memory of a man tortured by burning, a man who took too long to die, while all of us listened and sang songs behind our prison bars. I push away the story Blackthorn told me about her husband and her little son. I struggle to keep the half-cup of brew from coming straight up again.

"We'll put it up on the shelf," says Bardán. "It's that or we sleep in here on the floor."

Gormán doesn't look happy. Doesn't care to have the wild man telling him what to do. But we get the lantern. Turns the sleeping quarters into a shadowy in-between place. But not quite dark, though Gormán's shut the door on us. Still, the nightmares hang close, and Bardán sees it.

"You all right, Grim?"

"Have to be, won't I? Got work to do."

"You can't keep going with no sleep."

Ripple snuggles up close. Worried. Dogs know. If I sent Ripple to Blackthorn, would she go? Would she understand what I wanted? And could I manage without her?

"Need to get myself sorted," I say, talking to myself. "Get this finished. Go home." Bardán doesn't speak. But he's sitting up, like he plans to keep me company. The two of us awake together. "Bardán?"

"Mm?"

"Thanks, brother."

He doesn't say anything. Me, I'm sitting there, still shaky and sick. Still wanting Blackthorn. But thinking now. Thinking a way through the shadows. Remembering what she wrote. *Truth in his eyes. Love in his heart. Honor in his spirit.* If I can believe in that, I know what I have to do.

"You're a kind man," I tell him. "A good soul."

Bardán makes a sound, halfway between a laugh and a sob. As if he thinks that notion is ridiculous.

"Thing is," I say, keeping my voice low, since I don't want Gormán hammering on the wall again or coming in to listen, "there's being so beaten down and broken that you've got nothing left to give. Not even the weakest little glow of kindness. I've been there. You've been there. And so has Blackthorn. But it only feels that way. Go deep enough and you find that last little bit of warmth, still there, hiding away. A person might think they're a wreck, a ruin, with the road crumbling away in front of them." I see myself at St. Olcan's, crawling through the mud, crying my eyes out. I see Blackthorn and me looking at each other through the bars, across the gap between the cells. I remember the day our house burned down, and Blackthorn back in the past, screaming for her man and her baby. "But you can make your own road. And you can find the good inside. You just did."

Bardán says nothing, just reaches out to stroke Ripple. She sighs in her sleep.

"Bardán," I say.

"Mm?"

"I've got something to tell you. It's about your daughter."

39

BLACKTHORN

"Today," Ségán said. "As soon as you can be packed and ready. Take only what you can stow in your saddlebags. You'll have one night sleeping in the open, but at your destination there will be a house to stay in. Your escort will provide food. Bring your own water skin. Dress for riding. You do have time for breakfast first, but make it quick."

"Today," I echoed. It was impossible to keep the dismay from my voice. He'd warned me to be ready to leave at short notice, but . . . already?

"I did make it clear—"

"I know that." Now I sounded snappish. I reminded myself that I'd been waiting years for this opportunity. Only . . . "What about Grim?" I asked.

"If Grim is not here in time, we'll be going without him."

Breathe, Blackthorn. "So the message was taken to Wolf Glen? He is coming?"

"The message was delivered, yes, but not to Grim in person. He was away at the time. The best our man could do was extract a promise that Grim would be given the message as soon as he returned."

My heart sank. "Away where?"

"That I do not know. But we must leave this morning, Mistress Blackthorn, or there's a risk that you won't reach your destination in time. Your escort is waiting for you at your cottage over by Dreamer's Wood."

This felt wrong, even though he'd told me to expect short notice. "If you are so expert at planning this kind of thing, why leave it so late to go?"

"Not your concern. I think I mentioned the need for secrecy. You are the last to leave from here. Others are already on their way. We want no undue attention. As for the timing, it was necessary to wait for a certain . . . confirmation . . . before we could begin to move. This is a complex mission. Pack quickly."

"Ségán."

"Yes?"

I heard the impatience in his voice. It set me on edge. "I need Grim to come with me. It's important."

"We can't wait for him."

"What is the very latest I could leave and still get there in time for the . . . and still get there in time? I know there's an overnight stop. It doesn't get dark until quite late at this time of year. Surely it wouldn't matter if we reached that stop a little later than planned."

"Grim may be waiting at the cottage when you get there. The message was clear enough."

"Answer the question, will you?"

Ségán's eyes widened a little. I had managed to surprise him. Perhaps he was accustomed to being obeyed without challenge.

"Don't lie to me," I said. "If it can wait a bit longer, tell me. I don't want to leave Grim behind."

"If I had not believed it best that you leave immediately, I would not have demanded that. If you delay, you allow greater opportunity for someone to notice that you are traveling and to wonder where. For someone to decide he will prevent you from reaching your destination. And there would be no allowance whatsoever for problems on the way, ordinary problems such as a horse going lame or a sudden storm. I explained this before."

"I know. And I recall you mentioning an allowance of that nature. How much allowance, exactly?"

"Mistress Blackthorn, if every leader let his team change the rules of the mission as the mood took them, nobody would ever accomplish anything."

"Please." It hurt to get that out. I failed to sound at all conciliatory. "This discussion is wasting valuable time. As no doubt you're aware."

"We might wait until later in the morning, yes. If you did not leave by midday, you would be unlikely to reach the place in time. We want you there, Mistress Blackthorn."

And I wanted to be there. I wanted it so much that if I had to leave without Grim, I would. Grim would want me to go. I was quite sure of that. "Grim would be a useful addition to my escort," I said. It was a good argument. "He's . . . a man of formidable presence."

Ségán surprised me by smiling. "I have heard as much. Very well, you may wait for him. But I want you away before midday whether he's here or not. And I want you packed and over at the cottage as soon as you can be. Best if you wait there. Don't offer any explanations; just go. One of the men will walk over with you and carry your bag."

"If it's to be such a small bag, I expect I can manage it myself. Anything else really would draw attention. Thank you, Ségán. I'll go and pack now."

What did a person pack to face her worst fears? To confront her vilest enemy? To stand up before the man who had burned her loved ones alive, robbed her of her faith in humankind and in the gods, treated her like dirt beneath his boot sole? If I could have packed courage, tenacity, belief in myself, I would have done so. As it was, I took one change of clothing, a handkerchief, a water skin, a small selection of dried herbs in sealed packets, and a handful of coppers in a drawstring bag. I put in the little wooden hedgehog. I added a comb. Best that I did not face Mathuin looking like the disheveled wreck I had become in his lockup. Gods, I could hardly believe this was happening.

I fetched out my notebook and opened it at the page where I had copied Grim's words. *All fight on the outside, all goodness within. She walks her own path.* "Come home," I whispered. "Come home in time. Please." Then, annoyed with my own foolishness, I wrapped the notebook in my red kerchief and added it to the bag. It would all have to be unpacked at the cottage and stowed again in the saddlebags. I hoped Ségán knew that I was not an expert rider and would get me a steady horse.

Cara was not at breakfast, which worried me a little, but I did not ask anyone if they had seen her. Instead I sat staring into my bowl—my stomach was churning with nerves and I ate little—then left as soon as I possibly could. The earlier I got over to Dreamer's Wood, the readier I would be to leave when Grim arrived.

Cara hadn't been the only one missing from the meal. Neither Oran nor Donagan had been present, though nobody had remarked on their absence. Gone at first light, probably, intending to stop for the night somewhere much closer to the final destination. There was no sign of Master Oisin. Could he also be part of this mission? I found myself hoping he would be at this hearing or council. His calm presence would be reassuring. It seemed to me some of the Island men were gone too. No sign of Lonán or Art. Caolchú was also missing. They would be with the prince. Oran was taking a risk with this, whatever the nature of it might be. Playing outside the rules. Even with the High King's blessing, that might turn perilous for him and for his father. I hoped they had not underestimated Mathuin.

40

CARA

The sky was a clear pale color, not quite gray or green or blue, but holding something of each. Threads of mist wreathed the boles of the trees. The birds that had joined her as she walked up through the forest were quiet now. The crow flew from post to stump to low branch, keeping its bright eye on her all the way. The siskin rode on her left shoulder and the tiny wren perched on her head. The pricking of its little claws was somehow reassuring. Without the three of them, perhaps she would have strayed again, been led off course and into that dark hole or another place like it. She'd been tempted to use the main track but could not risk it.

Getting away had been oddly easy. Although she'd left at dawn, there had already been folk about. Guards patrolling. Lights in the house, perhaps the cook and her assistants starting up their fires. But nobody had noticed Cara slipping across the garden and the farmland and the open space between the trees to climb over the gate and walk away from the prince's holding. She wasn't sure how she had managed it. All she had done was think of an oak tree, how even when the branches and the foliage were whipped to confusion by a winter gale, the trunk stood strong and still. As she'd moved, she had held the inside of herself as still as that tree. She had thought of other quiet things, a shadow on snow, the tiny footprints of a vole, the wings of an eagle, gliding. An egg in a nest. The breath of a spider, spinning magic.

She'd wondered, moving on through the forest, whether she had worked a magic of her own. Made herself invisible. The old Cara, Cara-Before, would have known that was impossible. But Cara-Now might be able to do all kinds of things. Cara-Now was a completely different girl. She had a drop or two of fey in her blood.

And now she was here. The house lay low and quiet within its green shield of beeches, holding its secrets close. Cara shivered, pulling her cloak more tightly around her. The weight of this was heavy on her shoulders. What she had to do. What she had to say. The words she had to find, even if her father's heart broke right before her eyes. If she did manage to say them, what about afterward? What was meant to happen?

The leaves stirred in a breath of cool wind. The crow spoke at last, a sound that might have meant anything. It brought the druid's words back to Cara. *Two paths lie before you.* He'd said one was broad and straight, without surprises. That would be the path of turning around right now and walking back to Winterfalls. The path of doing as her father bid her. Of not facing up to the truth. And the other one was the path of twists and turns, of challenges and surprises. The path of confronting her father with the past and dealing with the consequences. Being brave, like Blackthorn. Being strong, like Grim. Being wise, like Master Oisin. Being honest even if it hurt so much she could hardly breathe.

"Forward," she whispered. And with the three birds for company, she walked toward the house.

There was a familiar horse in the yard, loosely tethered. Father's gray, Willow. He must be planning to ride out somewhere. He wasn't heading out to look for *her*, was he? No, that couldn't be it. How would anyone here know she'd even left Winterfalls?

What now? The door stood open. Should she just walk in? He might bundle her onto Willow and take her straight back to the prince's house.

The crow spoke again. *"Kraaa."* It had settled on the post where the horse was tethered. Willow regarded the bird with nervous eyes.

"All right," murmured Cara. "You'll be here if I need you. I understand." What a crow could do, she wasn't sure. But the presence of the birds made her feel a little less alone. "You little ones had best not come inside with me. Fly off. Go, find a safe perch!"

Siskin and wren flew to settle on the thatch above the door. And now there came voices from inside the house. The voices of two men, rising fast, interrupting each other, talking over each other. One was her father's.

"Out!" he shouted, and she heard an inner door crashing open. Something smashed on the floor. "Get out of my sight now! This is Grim's doing, him and that woman of his, the two of them sticking their noses in other folk's business, spinning lies! Where is he?"

Cara stood frozen, caught between the wish to be brave and the urge to flee before he saw her. She could run. She could hide herself the way she had before. She could get all the way back to Winterfalls and her father need never know.

And then there he was, in the doorway. The wild man, Bardán. Her other father. "Brígh," he said in a hoarse whisper. In that one word were shock and love and tears and joy, all rolled up together. He still looked like some creature of the woods, more leaf, twig and bark than man. He still stank. But his eyes were warm—how had she not seen that before? And the smile that now curved his mouth was the smile of a man who has expected nothing and has been granted a miracle.

Cara opened her mouth to say something. She thought of the words she should have spoken that other time, when she'd been up in the oak. *You are welcome here, traveler. I offer you the hospitality of this house.* But all she could think of was, "Is that my name? Brígh?"

The wild man stepped out of the doorway and into the courtyard. Tears were spilling from his eyes; he fumbled to wipe them away and she saw how hurt his hands were, so crippled that he would never be a builder again.

"Oh, your poor hands," Cara said, stepping closer.

A great sob burst out of Bardán's mouth. He held out his arms to her.

This is the test, Cara thought. *This is the choice, one road or the other.* But before she could take the step, forward or backward, her father was storming out of the house with a pair of brawny serving men behind him. "I said get out!" The look on his face paralyzed her. The fury in his voice stole away her words in an instant. She stood, mute, as the servants grabbed Bardán's arms and hauled him away.

No! Cara formed the word with her lips, but no sound came out. *No! Don't hurt him! I know the old story. I know what happened when I was born!* Her words fell away like spilled water. Where were they taking him?

Halfway across the yard, Bardán wrenched free of one keeper for long enough to turn and glower at Tóla. His laugh was as strange as his sob, a high, mocking sound more like the call of a creature than human laughter. "So much for your heartwood house, rich man!" he shouted. "So much for your dreams! It'll never be finished, not in a hundred years! Don't know your tales very well, do you? Ask a druid. Ask that friend of Grim's, the one who worked out the truth about your trickery!"

"Stop." Tóla walked past Cara as if she were not there. He halted two paces from Bardán, lifted his hand and delivered a blow that made the other man's head snap to the side. And another blow, to the other cheek. "Not one more word." And to the serving men, "Take him away. Lock him up. And Grim with him. This is unconscionable."

The crow flew to Cara's shoulder. The wren and siskin followed.

"The thatch," said the wild man, his voice unsteady now. Red marks flowered on his cheeks and jaw. "One feather from every kind of bird in the forest. Given willingly. Without that, the house brings no luck at all. You'll never do it. Nobody could. How would you find them all?" He was not looking at Tóla now, but straight at Cara. *"Weave a charm for luck and good, every birdling in the wood . . ."*

"Oh, gods," Cara said. Now she was the one with tears spilling. Her chest ached. Maybe her heart was breaking. Or maybe it was mending. "You really are my father."

"I said take him away!" Tóla roared to his men. "And send Gormán here at once! No, I will find him myself."

"Don't," whispered Cara as they dragged Bardán out of the court-yard. "Don't hurt him."

But Tóla did not hear, or did not choose to hear. "Cara!" He was trembling with fury. His hands were tight fists. His face was livid with rage. "Get inside! Now!"

"You lied to me," she breathed, backing away. "All my life, you lied to me."

"Do as I say! And be quick about it! This is all a monstrous mistake, and I blame that poxy wise woman for filling your head with nonsense. Now go indoors. I'll deal with you later."

Cara backed farther away, until she felt the warmth of Willow's shoulder against her body. *I'll deal with you.* As if she were the one who had done something wrong. *Lock him up.* For the crime of finding his daughter after fifteen years. For telling the truth.

"Now, Cara!"

"*Kraaa.*"

She turned her head. The crow had hopped to the post, and with its beak had unhooked Willow's reins.

"Cara!" Tóla was striding toward her; in a moment he would lay hands on her. Her own father. The man who had made himself her father. "Cara, don't be foolish!"

She put her foot in the stirrup and pulled herself up onto Willow's back. *I am the silence at the heart of an oak. I am a still pond. I am a feather on the breeze. I am a shadow, passing unseen.* She touched her heels to the horse's flanks and rode away, not looking back. The crow flew ahead.

"Cara?" Tóla's voice, confused, startled. "Where are you?" As if she really had become invisible. Then, "Cara!" A furious shout. "Get back here this instant! How dare you play tricks on your father?"

"You are not my father," Cara whispered, riding on. She guided Willow into the forest and away down a side path, where the cloak of leaves would shield them. She leaned forward on the horse's neck and murmured in her ear. "Quick as you can! Run like the wind!"

Willow ran. Cara held on. She'd thought she could be brave. She'd thought she could speak out. But he'd been so angry, shouting, cold-eyed, yelling at her as if he hated her. He'd hurt Bardán and he would hurt him again. His loathing had been written all over him. He was going to lock Grim up too. She'd thought she could do this on her own, and now she'd messed the whole thing up, and her real father was in danger, and if she wanted to save him, she had to go for help. *Brígh,* he'd said with his whole heart in his eyes. So that was her true name. "Brígh," she murmured, trying it out. "Brígh the brave. Brígh the bold. Brígh the beautiful." It was a good name. She'd better start earning it. "Good girl, Willow," she said, ducking her head as they passed under some low-growing foliage. "Don't stumble. Don't fall. Carry me all the way to Dreamer's Wood. And pray that Blackthorn will help me this time."

41

BLACKTHORN

"Mistress Blackthorn?"

A pox on it! Just when I was starting to feel a very slight tingle of the uncanny, as if finally Conmael might be thinking of putting in an appearance, Cionnaola had to break into my half trance and banish in an instant any chance of bringing my fey mentor here. It had been hard enough to get the Island man's permission to be out of his sight for more than a few moments. Even as I'd settled cross-legged by the pool and begun the sequence of slow breathing that was required, I'd been aware of him just up the rise, standing behind some oaks. Keeping watch. Guarding me against possible abduction, even here, a stone's throw from the prince's house. My protectors were taking no chances.

I should have been glad. Glad that they were giving my testimony such weight. Glad that they were taking it, and me, seriously. And I *was* glad. Get this over and I would be free of the most monstrous burden I had ever borne. Get it done and I would know that in a world where so many people were cruel and selfish and downright evil, justice was still possible. Only . . . I did not want to go without Conmael's blessing. Odd, that. I had so much resented his taking control of my life, making rules for my behavior, thinking he knew what was best for me. I'd only agreed to that because I'd had no choice. It had been say yes or die. Time after time since then, I'd come within a hairbreadth of breaking those rules. I had broken them over and over in thought, if not in deed. So why did this matter so much? It wasn't even the threat he'd made, the penalty he'd said he would impose if I did break my promise. What he'd said he would do was impossible, unless he had the power to make time go backward. Besides, deep down, Conmael was on my side. He might well agree that I should go. It was that, more than anything, that made me want to see him first. Which didn't make much sense. But there it was. Whatever I might think of his interference, Conmael had saved my life. I owed him honesty.

"Mistress Blackthorn, we must leave soon."

No chance of bringing Conmael here now. I couldn't feel the least spark of the uncanny. Not even here, on the shore of the most eldritch body of water I knew. Had something happened to him? Was some reversal preventing him from coming back? Grim had joked about my going to the Otherworld to find Conmael. I almost wished I could.

I rose to my feet and made my way around Dreamer's Pool to the higher ground where Cionnaola was waiting. "What about Grim?" I asked.

"If we don't leave very soon, we won't reach the place in time. You agreed to leave before midday. That is already stretching things. We don't want to push the horses beyond their endurance."

I fell into step beside him as we walked back to the cottage. I willed Grim to be home. I told myself, stupidly, that if I saw exactly three of something on the way back—blue flowers, white stones, birch trees, small clouds in the sky—he would be there by the time the cottage came in sight. But I didn't, and he wasn't. I almost cried. There had been a clear picture in my mind of how it would be, his horse tied up by the steps, his familiar figure in the doorway, almost filling it, his eyes brightening as he saw me, the sweet smile lighting up his plain features. "Brew?" he'd say, and in that one word would be wrapped up everything that our friendship was. But the only man there was Cúan, my other minder, adjusting the harness on the mare they had brought for me to ride. The other two horses were cropping grass beside the vegetable patch. Ready to go.

"We should be off," Cúan said, glancing at the sky. "Cutting it fine as it is."

"I'm sorry," said Cionnaola. "But we can't wait for Grim any longer."

A wave washed over me, disappointment, sorrow, anger too, that they had timed this so tightly. But the fact was, they had already waited most of the morning at my request. And most likely the planning for this mission had not been the work of either of these two, but of Ségán or of some leader above him. Who knew? Maybe even Prince Oran or his father, the king of Dalriada.

"All right," I said, feeling like a betrayer. "If we have to go, we should go. I will leave a note for Grim." I couldn't go without doing that.

"No," Cionnaola and Cúan said together. "You must leave no record of where you have gone or for what purpose," Cionnaola went on. "You understand why, I am sure."

"What if he comes just after we've left and doesn't know where I am? After getting a note that he's needed urgently?" He would be beside himself with worry.

"Prince Oran's folk will deal with that if and when it happens. Best close up the cottage now, and we'll be on our—ah. Perhaps Grim has reached us in time after all." For there was the unmistakable sound of hoofbeats coming our way, fast. Not from the prince's holdings, but from the other direction. From Wolf Glen.

The horse came into view, a fine gray galloping at full tilt, and on its back not Grim but a much slighter figure with a cloud of brown hair streaming out behind her. A crow flew alongside. Cara. Cara looking as if she had demons on her heels. Cara so white and shocked that I forgot to be disappointed that she was not Grim. She managed to halt the sweating mare and half jumped, half fell from the saddle next to us.

"Father—I went—he hit my father—I think he might do something—something terrible—he said, he said—you have to come—" She had her hands on my shoulders, gripping hard. She was wild-eyed, shaking.

"Slow down, Cara. Take a breath."

"Mistress Blackthorn," Cúan said. "We—"

"Wait!" Too sharp. I made myself speak more calmly. "I'll keep this as quick as I can—I promise."

The men did mutter a little, but they turned their attention to the distressed mare, and I drew Cara inside, made her sit down, bade her wait until she had her breath back before telling her story.

"I'm guessing that you rode up to Wolf Glen on your own, ignoring what I'd told you, and spoke to your father," I said. "And that he was angry, so you turned around and rode back again. Yes?"

She didn't speak now, just stared at me.

"If I sound a little short, it's because I was just about to leave, and I have no time to spare. Now tell me what's happened. Calmly and clearly."

To her credit, she gathered herself and got the story out, even though Cionnaola came to stand in the doorway when she was halfway through, all but tapping his foot with impatience. It seemed she had walked into a scene between Tóla and Bardán; the implication was that Bardán had learned the truth, and that meant Grim must have told him. And now, Cara said on a sob, Bardán was being locked up and so was Grim, and she thought her father—Tóla, that was—might hurt them, hurt them badly, because he had been beside himself with rage. He had hit Bardán. And he had shouted at her.

"How did you get away?"

"I . . ." She glanced at Cionnaola, then lowered her voice. "I . . . sort of made myself invisible. I think. At any rate, just for a little, Father couldn't seem to see me. I took his horse—the crow helped me—and I rode here as fast as I could. I should have done something. I should have helped them. Only I wasn't brave enough. If he hurts them, it'll be my fault."

"Not at all." There was a frozen thing inside me, lodged in my chest. "You may have been foolish to go up there on your own, but you showed good judgment in leaving while you could. And we'll help. You need someone to go back with you, a couple of men-at-arms and someone else from the prince's household. But not me, Cara. I can't come. I'm already late for . . . for where I need to go." Oh, gods, Grim. Grim, who had not responded to an urgent request to come home. Grim, who would always come when I really needed him. "Cara, did you actually see Grim?"

She shook her head. "I think he may be in trouble. Mistress Blackthorn, you have to come with me!"

Cionnaola folded his arms. Jerked his head at me as if to say, *Now*.

"Two of the Swan Island men are here. One can take you over to the prince's house and find you an escort, then catch us up." I glanced at Cionnaola.

"If it's quick," he said.

"I never even had a chance to talk to him," Cara said in a wisp of a voice. "Not properly. But he is my father. I know it. He said *Brígh*, like he'd found the best thing in the world. And he said—he said, about the thatch, he said—"

"Cara, you need to go with Cúan. Now."

"But . . . Grim." Cara turned her big eyes right on me. "Grim's in trouble. How can you not come with me?"

Morrigan's curse! I tried to think sensibly; tried to ignore the terrible ache in my chest. "Grim probably isn't even there. A message went up for him yesterday, and they told the messenger he was away."

"He is there." Cara's flat tone chilled me. "My father said—Tóla said—he said, *Lock him up. And Grim with him.*"

Dear God! This was going to break my heart.

"Mistress Blackthorn," Cionnaola said, "please. Others are waiting for us."

Cara would be perfectly safe with guards to protect her. Someone from the prince's household could take her up to Wolf Glen and sort things out. Grim was a big, strong man. He could look after himself; he didn't need rescuing. Besides, he would want me to testify. He knew how badly I needed to do it. I had to go. I had been waiting years for this.

"Cara," I began.

There was a sound of barking outside, and Cúan exclaiming, "Dagda's mercy!"

It was Ripple. Ripple, on the point of collapse, her chest heaving, her legs wobbling, her tongue hanging out. Ripple, with cuts and scratches all over her body, as if she had run a terrible race. Ripple, trying to tell us something, though her voice was less of a bark now and more of a labored rasp.

Cara found a dish and filled it with water. Ripple lapped a little, then collapsed beside the bowl. For all her exhaustion, she could not relax, but kept lifting her head, listening for something.

"She's run all the way," Cara said. "There's something really wrong." She looked up at me from where she was crouched by the dog. "Mistress Blackthorn, I'm scared my father might . . . might kill someone."

I stood completely still. Took a breath. Felt the world go quiet around me. Ripple had run herself to the very end of her strength. She would die for Grim, if it came to that. And Grim would give his life to protect me. I knew it as I knew the patterns of sun and moon. I knew it as I knew spring brought new life to the stark, bare trees of winter. I knew it as I knew even the bitterest, angriest, most wounded woman in all Erin could learn to love again.

"I'm sorry," I said to Cionnaola. "I can't come. I must go to Wolf Glen with Cara, and I must go now."

Perhaps he'd seen it coming; he didn't try to argue the point, only raised his brows. If it had been Ségán, it might have been a different story.

"Only," I said, "Cara needs a fresh horse, and we need an armed escort. And we must go right now. The other way, through Longwater, because it's quicker. I'll understand if you have to ride off immediately for . . . the place you were taking me to. Only, if you would come with us, it would save a lot of time." This felt quite unreal. I couldn't believe I was doing it. I couldn't believe I had made this choice. But I knew it was right. Ségán had my written testimony. And I could still go later, if one of the men would take me. I would be too late to stand up and speak, but I could find out what was happening with Mathuin. I could at least be witness to the aftermath.

"A moment," Cionnaola said, and went out to confer with Cúan. I could have hugged him for not getting angry with me; for not pressing the point. For not bullying me.

"We should take Ripple," Cara said. "We might need her."

Exhausted as she was, Ripple was up on her feet again now, wobbling, making little whining sounds, pawing at my leg and at Cara's. Trying to make us understand.

"She was the one who found me when I fell down into that place," Cara said. "If—if he's—I think we should take her."

That made two men, two women and a biggish, exhausted dog. And only three fresh horses. "The Island men are supposed to be good at this kind of thing," I said. "We might leave it to them."

They were indeed good at it. The ride to Longwater took us back through Winterfalls settlement, where we left Cara's tired horse at the stables behind the brewery and borrowed two more mounts. Ripple shared Cionnaola's horse; the tall warrior with his long twists of hair seemed a good match for the leggy hound, who rode draped across the saddle in front of him. I borrowed a rope leash, stowing it in my saddlebag. Cúan led the spare horse.

In Longwater, folk came out to ask questions, for which we had little time. We learned that the local workers who had been helping Grim with the building had been told to take the day off. No reason had been given. I spotted the farmer's son, Fedach, at the back of the group; he gazed only at Cara. She was wound up tight, her face pinched and pale, her shoulders hunched as she rode. But when Fedach flashed her a grin, she managed a watery smile in return. A good boy, that one. He would be beneath consideration as a future husband for Tóla's daughter. But for Bardán's daughter, the son of a successful horse breeder would be an excellent match. I found myself hoping for them; hoping they would be blessed with time and peace to learn what it was they truly wanted.

Several of the Longwater men offered to come with us—we had told them only that there might be some kind of trouble up at Wolf Glen—but Cionnaola said no. We rode on. Past the path that led to Bardán's old cottage, where baby Brígh had been born. On through the woods. The crow was still with us, close but never too close, keeping watch over

Cara. Maybe it had appointed itself some sort of guardian. Maybe it was an Otherworld creature. In the company of the two men, I did not ask her. I limited my conversation to "Are you all right?" To which she replied, "Yes," though she wasn't, of course. Who would be? As for me, my belly was a churning mess, my body was all jangling nerves, and my thoughts were racing as fast as my heart. When we got there, I could not expect Cionnaola and Cúan to take the lead. I would have to do it. What to say? How to start? And in the background, Mathuin. I'd had the opportunity, and I'd let it go. If my absence led to a finding of innocent, I would never forgive myself.

We were not yet in sight of Tóla's house when the increasingly restless Ripple made a sudden leap from the horse's back, landed in a tumble of limbs, collected herself, then charged ahead, baying.

"Ripple!" I yelled, wishing I had Grim's deep voice. "Stop!"

Cúan stuck his fingers in his mouth and delivered a piercing whistle. Remarkably, the dog pulled herself to a halt and came back, obedient as always, to stand beside my horse. Her whole body was quivering.

"So much for an approach by stealth," commented Cionnaola. "If that was what you were planning."

"I don't think there's a plan," I said. "Cara's in charge. What should we do, Cara?"

"Ride straight to the house. When I tried to speak to my father before, he cut me off. I need to tell him what I know. I want him to give me the true story. But he'll be angry. Not only with me, Mistress Blackthorn, but with you too."

I grimaced. "I can cope with that. I don't imagine Master Tóla would physically threaten either of us, but I suppose he might try to remove you from my bad influence. You two," I looked at the Island men, "should make sure that doesn't happen. This may have been Cara's home for the last fifteen-odd years, but I doubt she'll be staying here."

"And I want to talk to my other father," Cara said. "My real father. I want to know if he's safe. After this, he might not want to stay here either. But I don't think he's got anywhere to go."

"We'll face that problem when we come to it," I said. *Let Grim be all right. Let him be safe.*

There was no sign of activity at the barn, though Ripple clearly wanted to go there. I leashed her. Then we rode on down to the big house and waited in the courtyard while a serving man went to tell Tóla we were there. But it was not the master who came out. Instead, in the doorway stood Tóla's sister, Mistress Della.

"Cara!" she exclaimed. "What is going on? Who are these people?" Her gaze went from guard to guard, finally lighting on me. "Why have you come here?"

"Aunt Della, I . . ." Cara seemed suddenly struck dumb.

"Good day to you, Mistress," I said, lifting my chin and straightening my shoulders. "I'm not sure if you know this, but Cara came here earlier today wanting to speak to her father. He frightened her away. So she's brought . . . reinforcements. These men are from Prince Oran's household. Could you tell Master Tóla we're here, please?"

The woman had gone white. "I heard a—disturbance, in the morning. But I did not realize—Cara, is this true? Were you involved?"

Cara opened her mouth and closed it again without a sound. Cionnaola spoke for her. "Mistress, this is quite true. And we are in haste. Where is Master Tóla?" His hand made the slightest of movements toward the weapon at his belt.

"Are you threatening me?" Mistress Della was no shrinking violet. I almost expected her to add, *young man.*

"I don't threaten women," said Cionnaola mildly. "Fetch Master Tóla, please. And Grim, if he's here."

"Grim," Mistress Della echoed. "Why Grim?"

Because we think he may be in trouble. "He's needed urgently at Winterfalls," I said. "The prince sent a message. When Grim didn't arrive, we were concerned."

"I imagine he's at work, up by the barn."

"There's no sign of life there," I said. "And the men from Longwater said they were told not to come to work today."

"Perhaps Master Tóla can explain," said Cionnaola. Something in his quiet tone made my flesh come up in goose bumps. "Fetch him now, will you?"

"Wait. Please." Mistress Della, plainly shaken, vanished back into the house. The door closed behind her.

When Tóla came out, after a considerable wait, he had two serving men with him, one bearing a makeshift club, the other a pitchfork. In the moment when he stood in the doorway, he looked not at the formidable Island men or at me but straight at Cara, and there was such sorrow in his eyes that I felt some sympathy for the man, despite the terrible lies he had told. Despite the heinous offense of stealing another man's child.

It was only a moment. Then he stepped forward, glaring at me. "You are no longer welcome on my land, Mistress Blackthorn. I don't know why these armed men are here, but I want them gone immediately, and you with them. As for my daughter, I remind you that she is only fifteen years old and is under my governance. Cara, go indoors immediately." Cúan was holding our horses; Cionnaola stood unmoving beside Cara. Behind Tóla in the doorway, his sister was silent.

"I think not," Cionnaola said. "Not until you have answered the young lady's questions. I believe Mistress Blackthorn may have her own questions for you. Grim should have come to Winterfalls yesterday, when he got our message. Where is he?"

"I don't believe anyone agreed to answer *your* questions, fellow." Tóla's voice was icy. "Do you not understand a simple command? Get off my land. Now." His servants stood awkwardly on either side of him. Their desire to be somewhere else was plain.

"Brother," said Mistress Della from behind Tóla, making him start. "Whatever this is, it's best conducted indoors, not standing out here in the open."

"Don't give me orders, woman!" He turned on her, and she took two steps backward, almost tripping on her skirt. Cionnaola moved, to do what, I was not sure, and I laid a hand on his arm. Then, like an eldritch shadow, a dark bird flew across the courtyard, passing over Cionnaola's shoulder to alight on Cara's. She flinched at the crow's sudden weight, then drew herself up, squaring her slight frame.

"My questions can be asked here," she said. "But I want Gormán present, and Grim. Where are they? And where is Bardán? I would never have believed you would strike a defenseless man, but I saw that this morning. I would never have believed you would speak to Aunt Della like that. But then, I always believed you were my father."

I was speechless, and so was Tóla. Cara. Cara, who had been so intimidated by both Tóla and his sister that she had lost her voice in their presence. Cara, who had often seemed young for her age. Cara, speaking with power and purpose. But then, she was not Cara anymore. She was Brígh. Stolen from her father; taken away to live a lie, while he was lost to the Otherworld. Oh gods . . . "Grim," I said, failing to sound in the least calm. "Where is Grim?"

Tóla relaxed his pose; his tone became conciliatory. He did not look at me or Cara, but at Cionnaola, man to man. "This is all some sort of misunderstanding," he said. "A silly error, compounded by sheer fancy. My daughter should come inside, and you men should escort Mistress Blackthorn home to Winterfalls. Had Cara not fallen under her influence, there would have been no such foolish talk."

"If no lies have been told," I said, and now there was iron in my voice, "then you should have no trouble telling Cara the whole story, Master Tóla. About the wild man, Bardán, who came to work for you, building the heartwood house fifteen or more years ago with the fey knowledge he had from his father. And the baby girl he brought with him to Wolf Glen, his motherless daughter, who disappeared when her father suddenly downed tools and walked away. A baby girl who reappeared many moons later with a different name, a name your wife had given her. Cara. Beloved. A pet name, like sweetheart and poppet and the other endearments I'm told your wife lavished on baby Brígh. Tell us about the mysterious disappearance of Bardán. Explain why the story doesn't add up."

"That's enough—"

"Let Mistress Blackthorn speak," said Cionnaola. "And then we will hear your side of this tale."

"It's none of your—"

"Silence," said Cionnaola in a quiet voice that demanded instant obedience. Master Tóla fell silent. "I do not know you, and nor does Cúan here. But on the basis of what I have heard and seen today, I believe that if you do not tell your daughter the truth, you may lose her."

Tóla went scarlet. "How dare you threaten me?"

"You would be a fool not to take this opportunity to tell your version of the story. The true story, whatever that might be."

"Gormán should speak too," Cara said.

Ripple was barking again; pulling so hard on the leash that Cúan was struggling to hold her. "But first," I said, "we want proof that Grim and Bardán are safe and well. We need to see them."

"Why would they not be safe and well?"

"You ordered your men to lock them up," Cara said. "I heard you. You hit my father. You hurt him."

Tóla flinched. Her blow had struck true. "I am your father," he said.

"Then prove it." Cara's voice was steady. "If you've told no lies, you have nothing to worry about. Tell the story of the baby that was supposed to have died out in the woods. Tell the story of the baby my mother—your wife—brought home with her, who was already old enough to walk by herself. Tell me why I've never been the kind of daughter you really wanted, one who likes sitting quietly indoors and making polite conversation, not climbing trees and talking to birds. Tell me why the wild man recognized me the moment he first set eyes on me, even though he didn't know who I was back then. Tell me the truth."

"Cara, this is foolishness. You are the daughter of a wealthy household; you may not realize what a life of privilege you have led. I have provided you with an abundance of opportunities. You have been raised with love and kindness. I have seen to it that all your needs were met. You have a secure future ahead of you. It would be sheer folly to throw that away."

It was close to an admission, and it left Cara lost for words. It was her aunt who spoke. "Brother, are you saying this wild tale of Mistress Blackthorn's is true? That Cara is not your daughter but another man's child? How could that possibly be?" Unspoken, but clear in her tone, was *How could you not tell me?* She had not been here from the start; she had only come to Wolf Glen after Suanach had died, when Cara would have been close on a year old. As for seeing to it that all Cara's needs were met, I imagined Mistress Della's role in that had been substantial. Tóla had all but forgotten her.

"Cara is my daughter. Mine. The rest is foolishness, and I will not waste time on it."

"Father," said Cara softly, "are you afraid that if you tell me the truth I will walk away and never come back? Because one thing is certain. If you have lied about this, you are not fit to be my father, and I will turn my back on Wolf Glen forever."

Cionnaola put a hand on her shoulder briefly, as if to salute her courage.

"What is this nonsense? You're fifteen years old. Where would you go? Without me you have no resources, no home, no safety. You'd last a few days at most before you came running back. This is a young girl's folly, no more."

"Brother." Mistress Della's voice was cold and clear. "I am no young girl, and I too want to hear this story from your lips." She looked across at Cara. "You'll always have a home with me, child. If you need it."

"What are you talking about?" Tóla blustered. "What home?"

"You are not my only living kinsman, Tóla. There are several households where Cara and I would be welcome."

He opened his mouth and closed it again. For the moment, she had silenced him.

"Grim," I reminded him. "Bardán. Where are they?"

"Gone," Tóla said. "Walked away this morning without explanation."

"Bollocks," said Cúan. "If Grim had left here, he would have come down to Winterfalls. What about the urgent message?"

"I know nothing of any message."

"Now that really is a lie," Cúan said. "The fellow who brought it up here told me he'd passed it on to you in person, and you'd promised Grim would be told."

"Where is he?" Something terrible had happened; I knew it. Grim wouldn't just walk off.

Tóla folded his arms. "Who knows? Don't look so surprised, Mistress Blackthorn. Grim was employed here not only as a builder but also as the wild man's keeper. We know how unreliable Bardán is. Didn't he walk off the job once before? And Grim has taken his duties all too seriously. I imagine he followed Bardán, out of concern the wild man might . . . might injure himself. Or wander off the path and into . . . well, who knows? Wolf Glen is an odd place."

My jaw was clenched so tight it hurt. He would go on lying; he would go on denying the truth until it was too late. We had already wasted precious time. But I had no idea where to start looking.

"Mistress Blackthorn?" Cúan had released the horses, which stood by calmly. He had his hand on Ripple's collar and was looking at me in question.

I had been stupid. "Untie the leash," I said. "Let her go."

Set free, Ripple bolted in the direction of the barn. Grim must be there, surely. And still alive. Or was it only that it was the last place the dog had seen him? Tóla began a protest about folk wandering uninvited all over his land, but it was not his permission I needed. "Cara?"

"We'd best all go," she said.

"You'll find nothing there," Tóla said. "I have nothing to hide." Which was, I suspected, the biggest lie of all.

We rode; nobody needed to spell out that it was best to keep the horses close in case we had to leave in a hurry. Ripple's barking rang out ahead of us, a cry of urgent purpose. We dismounted in the yard next to the barn, close by the place where I had spoken to Grim on the day of my last visit. Where we had, for a brief moment, held each other's hand. Why hadn't I said something to him while I still could? Why had I pushed him away, over and over?

No sign of any grooms. Cúan tethered the horses. I glanced back down toward the house; Tóla and his sister were walking up after us, the two of them conducting what looked like a fierce argument. The men who'd been acting as bodyguards had been joined by several more. "Trouble," I murmured to Cionnaola, pointing.

"Nothing we can't handle. Where's that dog?"

A door stood open at the end of the barn, and Ripple had disappeared inside. The foresters' living quarters, Grim had said. And now here was Gormán, coming out to investigate. A smell of cooking wafted past. Mushrooms?

"Gormán." Cara's voice was strangled, difficult.

"Cara!" The burly woodsman had turned pale. "This is no place for you. Let me—"

"I found the story of the heartwood house," Cara said. "A story about a man who stole a child. I know my father lied to me. I want you to tell me the truth about what happened when I was a baby. But my real father needs to be here. And Grim. Where are they?"

For a moment Gormán was speechless. Inside, it sounded as if Ripple was knocking things over. The barking rose to a frenzy. "They're not here," Gormán said.

"That's a lie." I strode toward the open door, and the woodsman grabbed me by the arm. He was strong; maybe a match even for an Island man.

"Don't touch her!" Cara cried, and almost instantly the two warriors were there beside me, Cúan applying a hold on Gormán's arm that made him release me quickly, gasping, and Cionnaola moving up to the doorway. I did not see him draw his knife, but it was in his hand as he took a stance just outside the entry.

"We'll be wanting to have a look around," he said easily. "Seems there might be something amiss. Why don't I just stand here and keep folk out for a bit? Cúan will go in with you, Mistress Blackthorn."

"Gormán." Cara's voice could hardly be heard over Ripple's now. "I didn't think you would ever lie to me. It would help very much if you would tell the truth now."

But Gormán had seen Tóla coming, and he stood silent, his eyes on Cara. His face was painful to look upon, all love and regret and farewell.

We went in: Cara, Cúan and I. Gormán had been cooking. A covered pot was on the fire, and various spoons, knives and ingredients lay on the table. Field mushrooms, chopped. And right next to them, a small pile of something very similar in appearance, but most definitely not the same. My blood ran cold. No time to question Gormán now. "Cionnaola," I said over my shoulder, "make sure nobody touches what's on the table. The same with whatever's in that cook pot."

"Understood, Mistress Blackthorn."

Ripple had upset some long poles that must have been standing against the wall, and they had dislodged baskets and boxes as they fell, blocking an inner doorway. The dog was in danger of hurting herself with her wild efforts to get through. She was making so much noise I could not tell if there was any sound from the other side.

"Can you quiet her?" Cúan asked.

"Ripple, here!" Thank the gods for such a good dog. She came to stand by me, panting, whining. "Ripple, hush. Down."

Cúan dealt with the fallen objects swiftly and methodically. When they were piled up out of the way, he set his shoulder to the inner door. "Step aside, Mistress Blackthorn."

The inner door crashed open on the shadowy space of the main barn area. Stalls for cattle, empty now. Items hanging from pegs on the walls. Shelves holding neatly stacked supplies. A cleared area close by the door, with two straw pallets and folded blankets. Ripple ran past Cúan and began a search, sniffing everywhere.

"That's Grim's cloak," I said. "And those are his boots."

Cúan was looking farther in. It was darkish. The prevailing smells were of dung and hay.

"Get away from there!" came Tóla's shout from outside. "How dare you bar me from my own property!"

"Easy now, Master Tóla." Cionnaola might have been facing nothing more troublesome than a persistent fly on a hot day. "We're just taking a look, that's all. If you've told us the truth, you've got nothing to worry about."

Ripple moved into the darker area, between the cattle stalls. Cúan bent to pick up something from the floor. He brought it back to the door to look at it in better light. A length of wood, heavy-looking. Stained red at one end. "Don't want to worry you," he said quietly, "but I think that's blood. And there are marks on the floor in there. There's been some kind of struggle. But where could they be?"

Out in the forest, thrown down a deep hole to disappear forever. Oh gods, I would never forgive myself for being so slow. How could I have said no to Cara when she first asked me to come with her? Ripple was making a different sound now, a high-pitched squealing cry that made my flesh crawl. Grim was not out in the forest, barefoot and without his cloak. He was here. But silent. Silent as death.

"There's a sort of cellar," Cara said. "Where they store vegetables and things. I'll show you."

More noise from outside. Surely that was a bigger crowd than could be made up solely of Tóla's own household, even with his farmworkers. "A cellar," I echoed as she led us to the far end of the barn. Grim hated the dark. He only got through the nights by staying awake and keeping his body moving. Being locked up in some underground place would surely break him. *I'm here. I'm here, Grim. Hold on.*

"Over here," said Cara. "There's a trapdoor—see?"

Was I imagining the dark stains on the floor? If that was blood, there was a lot of it.

"Might be a flesh wound," said keen-eyed Cúan. "Stand back now." He squatted down and heaved the trapdoor open.

42

GRIM

Can't talk. Can't swallow. Wretched gag's too tight. Wrists and ankles tied. Same as they did with Bardán the first time. Two of us down here together. Want to help him, but there's not much I can do. Hard to move where I want to. Sitting against the wall now, next to him, touching so he knows I'm here. Thirsty. That's going to get bad. Trying not to be sick. Choke on vomit, it's all over. Waiting. Waiting for Ripple. Waiting for Blackthorn to come. Saying the words in my head, like I used to in Mathuin's lockup. *In loco pascuæ . . . ibi me collocavit . . . super aquam refectionis . . . educavit me . . .* Try to see those peaceful fields, the still waters. I say the part about walking in the shadow of death, and God being there beside me. If he's in here now, he's keeping pretty quiet.

Wish I could speak out loud, help Bardán. Wish I could tell him to say his own words over, keep the demons away. I'm guessing it'd be that verse about the birds. *Every birdling in the wood . . .* and the part that makes it a charm, a sort of spell. *Feather bright and feather fine, none shall harm this child of mine.*

I pray too. Funny, that, when I've given up on God, more or less. I pray that they won't drag us out and kill us. I pray that we don't die down here in the dark, slowly. I pray that Bardán won't go crazy. I pray that I won't fall to pieces like I did before. I pray that I'll see Blackthorn again. But those aren't prayers, they're more like wishes. So I say I'm sorry for all the things I've got wrong. The times I wasn't brave enough, the times I hurt people, the times I made bad choices. And I say to God, if it's my time to go, it's my time. As long as Blackthorn's safe, I'm all right with that. But Bardán deserves another chance. He's just found out his daughter's still alive. He's had his hope woken up. He needs to get out, live his life. Make up for those fifteen years he lost. Wish he hadn't gone down there on his own to front up to Tóla. I should've gone with him even though he said no. Don't know what happened at the house. He went off, and I was having my breakfast, miles away thinking about Blackthorn and how much I wanted to go home. Feeling sorry for myself. And suddenly there were four fellows trying to grab hold of me. One of which was Gormán. Not fighters, but they were armed and I wasn't. So I tried to calm them down, talk them out of it. Stupid me. Hard blow to the head knocked me out cold. When I woke up I was in the dark, trussed up like a bird for roasting. And right next to me was Bardán.

Blood on my face. Head throbbing a bit. Can't tell if Bardán's hurt. Can't see a poxy thing down here. Only knew it was him from the smell. Got to stay awake. Drop off and I'll be out of my mind before you can snap your fingers. Dreaming the bad things and waking up to the dark. I'd be a gibbering wreck.

What's Tóla got over Gormán, to keep him dancing to the one tune? I know Gormán's a good man underneath. Maybe Tóla's told him he'll be sent away if he doesn't obey orders. Never get to see Cara again. Could be that. Like a grandfather to the girl, Gormán is. Friends since she was a little thing.

Hard to breathe in here. Head's muzzy, hurting too. *Don't go to sleep, Grim. Wait. Only wait.* Can't hear anything from up there. If folk were looking for us, would we hear them? They can't be going to leave us down here. Would they do that? Leave us and walk away?

Shit. Maybe they would. Not much of a way to die. More I think about it, the harder it is to breathe. Is Bardán still breathing? I give a sort of grunt, which is the only sound I can make with the gag on, and he grunts back at me. Funny, how happy that makes me. *Not alone. I'm not alone.*

I'm thinking about hope. Thinking it's like a candle. New and bright at first, strong and steady. Then the draft creeps in, and the candle burns down, and it's not so strong anymore. Flickering. Wavering. Struggling. Holding on as long as it can. Or hope's like a song. A lullaby you'd sing to a new baby. *None shall harm this child of mine.* A promise you'll keep your child safe. Or it's like reaching out for someone's hand, holding it in yours. It's seeing the beauty in things. A thrush singing. Children splashing in a stream. A dog's faithful eyes. Blackthorn's red hair. Her own flame, that she carried through the living hell of Mathuin's lockup. That's hope. For Bardán here, I'm guessing hope is his daughter. Now he knows, that'll get him through.

Holy Mother of God! I hear Ripple. Ripple barking up top, loud enough so we can hear it down under in the black. Means she went where I told her to and help's come. If it was them, Tóla and Gormán, they'd have shut that noise up fast. Wolves, the two of them. No mercy. But she's still barking, and now someone's tramping around up there. The trapdoor creaks open, and Ripple's voice is joy and pride and hope all rolled into one.

43

CARA

They brought the men out from the root cellar. There was blood all down Grim's face from a cut on his head. Bardán was pale as a ghost and shaking. And her father—Tóla—was still telling lies. The two of them had been locked in to cool off, he said, because Bardán had flung wild accusations at him and physically attacked him, and Grim had got involved as well. They would have been let out in due course, when they'd had time to learn their lesson. As for the rest of it, it was a fanciful story with no substance at all. He told Cara, again, that her rightful place was with him, her father, at Wolf Glen. And none of it was anyone else's business.

Maybe he thought they would all just go away. Even the five men from Longwater who had ridden over despite Cionnaola saying he didn't need them. Didn't Tóla realize those men had seen Bardán and Grim brought out of the barn? Did he really still believe life could go back to what it had been? It seemed so. It seemed he was in a world of his own, for he went on protesting while Aunt Della sent serving folk away to fetch clean water and salves and bandages, and Mistress Blackthorn washed and bandaged Grim's wound, then sat on the ground with his head in her lap and said absolutely nothing for a while. Tóla went on talking as Aunt Della herself wiped Bardán's face and held a cup of water for him to drink. Cara waited and listened as Tóla talked himself to a stop while telling them nothing. Then she stepped forward to speak, finding her voice with no trouble at all, even with all those people looking on. Her new voice: Brígh's voice.

"It's time for you to tell the true story, Father," she said, wondering if this might be the last time she called him that. "The whole story, from when Bardán came to Wolf Glen with his baby girl. Don't lie this time. I see a man here who was nursed alongside Bardán's daughter, in our— in your house." The young man, Fedach, had come up from Longwater with the others. Cara was glad he had done that. She liked the steady look of him. He was a man who would surely never tell lies. "You said that little girl died," she went on. "You said Bardán ran off with her into the forest and abandoned her to her fate. And then, after two seasons away, your wife came home with her own baby, though nobody had known she was with child when she left just after Bardán vanished. Her own baby: Cara, daughter of the house. Except that baby could already walk. She could sit upright on a horse. She was getting on for one year old. I was that baby. Not your daughter, or my moth—your wife's. Bardán's child, Brígh. If you did not steal me, if you did not lie to him, what happened?"

It seemed for a little that Tóla was not going to answer. The folk watching whispered among themselves while he stood tight-lipped, apart from everyone else. The men who had been acting as guards had melted away into the crowd; he was alone.

"Must this matter be aired here, in front of all these folk?" he asked. "Let us observe some small measure of propriety. A meeting behind closed doors, down at the house."

"That won't suit anyone but yourself," said Cionnaola, who still stood in the doorway, blocking entry. "It appears you've incarcerated these two men on dubious grounds. That matter will be referred to Prince Oran, to be discussed at his next open council." When Tóla made to speak, the Island man went on. "I'm not finished. Your actions in that instance are for Prince Oran and his advisers to deal with. The other matter, the question of this young lady's identity and the strange events surrounding her first year, might better be discussed in private, yes. But I don't believe that will satisfy anyone present here. In particular, it will not satisfy Cara. And she deserves the truth. She's waited fifteen years for it."

"We're well beyond the point where any of this can be kept secret, Master Tóla," Mistress Blackthorn said.

"What you suggested . . . It is partly true, Cara," Tóla said. A sigh went through the crowd. Cara held herself calm and still. She would do her best not to cry anymore. "But you are my daughter and my dear wife's daughter in everything but blood," he went on. "That man, the man who fathered you . . . he's out of his wits. He was unreliable from the first. He cared nothing for you. Couldn't cope with you. Didn't want you." A sound of outrage came from Bardán. Aunt Della hushed him, murmuring something about letting the story be told. "From the moment he passed you into our care, he showed no interest at all in you," Tóla said. "He was already known as a lone wolf, tainted by the fey blood of his mother. Such a man is not cut out to be a husband or father. He failed at both."

Grim started to say something, and Blackthorn put her fingers against his lips to silence him.

"As for what happened when you were an infant, it was more or less as folk know already. One night he took you from the cradle and ran off into the woods. He was seen leaving, but we could not track him down. We found you, almost too late, wrapped up and left between the roots of an oak tree. A tiny babe, cold, hungry, weak. But alive."

"Then you lied," said one of the Longwater men. "The story went out that the child was dead. You said she'd been attacked and mauled by wild beasts, the body so damaged it was best her kinsfolk did not see it."

"I acted for the child's protection," said Tóla. "Her mother was dead. Her father had run off. Even if he returned, he could offer her nothing. He had no home and no future. He could not provide for her. As our daughter, as the daughter of Wolf Glen, she would live a life of security and comfort. She would be cared for. She would be loved. Don't tell me that was the wrong choice."

"She had family," the Longwater man said. "Folk who would have taken her in. But you told them she was dead."

"And when folk saw young Cara, later," said one of the others, "and remarked that she looked a lot like Bardán's mother, you paid them to keep quiet. That's what folk say, anyway."

"Rubbish," said Tóla. "Vicious rumors and poisonous lies. Besides, who'd be old enough to remember Bardán's mother?"

"One or two folk."

"How could you say I was dead?" That was terrible. It was so cruel Cara could hardly believe it. "My kinsfolk, my mother's people in Longwater—of course they would have wanted me."

"You misjudge village folk, my dear."

"Don't call me your dear!"

He flinched, but went on. "They didn't want you. Your fey blood was seen as unlucky. And Bardán was never one of them. Never had been. He too had the taint of the Otherworld about him."

"But you still wanted him to build the heartwood house."

"He was the only one who could. The only one with the knack of it. I had no choice."

"You used him!" Cara could not stop her voice from rising. Her real father was sitting over there on the steps, gazing at her without a word, while Tóla spoke of him as if he were an outcast, a nothing. As if he were not even a real person. "You used him and you stole from him! Just like the rich man in the heartwood house story! Only in that tale, the mother got her child back while it was still small. My father would never have got me back. If Mistress Blackthorn hadn't worked it out, you never would have told anyone."

"I say again, I had no choice. Besides, I believed Bardán was dead."

"There's always a choice, Master Tóla." Mistress Blackthorn was on her feet now. Behind her, Grim was also standing, a little unsteady, but very stern in his gaze. "Good or evil. Lies or truth. I don't believe what you just told us is the true story. Not all of it, anyway."

"What more do you want, witch?" Tóla's voice was a snarl. "A groveling apology? Recompense in gold pieces? I did what was right! I acted out of love for my wife and the infant! How dare you, a childless, unwed woman, accuse me of ill intent?"

"You foul-mouthed scum!" Grim made to lunge forward, but Blackthorn laid a hand on his arm, and he halted at her touch.

"Gormán," said Tóla, "confirm my account of events for Mistress Blackthorn, will you?"

Gormán had been standing in the shadows by the barn wall, keeping very quiet. Cara willed him to say that he had not known, that he had been misled, that if he had been aware of the truth, he would have taken no part in it.

"And while you are doing so," put in Mistress Blackthorn, "you might tell us what you were planning to do with those toadstools that are standing ready on your table in there. They're screamers; did you realize? One mouthful would be sufficient to send a man raving mad. Two would kill him. It seems to me screamers might have played a part in this story before."

Cara heard Grim draw in his breath. She realized she had sunk her teeth into her lip so hard it was bleeding.

"Toadstools? What are you talking about?" Tóla had his legs apart and his arms folded. He looked as if he was defying the world. "Gormán, it seems Mistress Blackthorn doubts the credibility of my story. Sadly, my daughter is so much under the witch's influence that she too cannot believe it. You were there. You were there from the first. Speak up!"

Gormán's face was all shadows and lines, as if he'd suddenly turned very old. Cara felt a pain in her chest, looking at him. Her friend. Her dear friend, the one person she'd always been able to go to, to talk to, to say anything to and know she would be heard. She had done this to him. She had brought that terrible look to his face by being discontent. By wanting answers. She knew before he opened his mouth that he was not going to say what Tóla wanted.

"Mistress Della," Gormán said, "and Cara. My words will cause both of you pain, and for that I am truly sorry. But they must be said.

Cara, you have been as dear to me as a daughter. Anything I have done, I have done out of love for you and in the belief that I was acting in your best interest."

"Now wait—" began Tóla, outraged, then fell silent as Cúan stepped up beside him, his hand on his knife hilt. Several of the Longwater men had closed in around him. Fedach was among them, looking very serious.

"Some of Master Tóla's account is true," Gormán said, sounding like a ghost of himself. "Master Tóla hired Bardán to build the heart-wood house, having learned that such a building brings many blessings on a family. Bardán's wife had died, he had a newborn daughter, and his terms of employment included the child being looked after in Tóla's household. A wet nurse came from Longwater; her son stands among you now. She fed both infants. But . . . it was Mistress Suanach who loved the baby girl, who cared for her and sang to her and spent every waking hour with her. She wanted to do everything for the child herself." He looked at Tóla. "Mistress Suanach and Master Tóla had no children of their own, though they had been wed some years then. It was . . . Mistress Suanach was . . ."

"How dare you!"

"Let him speak, Master Tóla." Cionnaola was calm. "Best that it all comes out. Your wife is no longer here; this cannot hurt her now."

"Her need for a child was gnawing away at her," Gormán said. "When the little girl came into the household, it was as if Suanach had suddenly been granted a miracle. Within a matter of days she was treating the baby as her own. Then believing Brígh *was* her own. If that sounds strange, well, it was. But it was good to see her happy at last; it was a long time since she'd smiled so much. That made Master Tóla happy too."

"By all the gods," murmured Aunt Della. "I had no idea. No idea in the world."

"Bardán used to go over to the big house every day after work to see his daughter. Hold her, talk to her, sing her a lullaby. But Mistress Suanach didn't like him anywhere near the baby. She started making rules, shutting him out. Bardán spoke to Master Tóla about it. Said he wouldn't keep on with the building if he couldn't have time with his child too. Said he'd walk away and get help from his wife's kinsfolk instead.

"Master Tóla didn't want that. He wanted the heartwood house. He believed it would keep his family safe, healthy and prosperous for generations to come. He thought that in time it might grant them a child of their own. And only Bardán knew how to build it. But Master Tóla wanted his wife to stay happy and content, the way she'd been since the baby came. He feared that if Bardán took the child away, Suanach would become . . . unhinged. She was always . . . she was delicate in her temperament. Frail of body and fragile of mind. He truly feared the consequences of Bardán's leaving. So he came to me with a proposition." Gormán's voice faltered. "I am ashamed to tell you this. Bitterly ashamed."

Nobody spoke. Even the crow, perched now on the roof of the barn and picking insects from the thatch, held back harsh comment.

"Tóla suggested a way he could keep his builder and secure the baby for Suanach. It involved . . ." He looked at Mistress Blackthorn.

"Screamers," Blackthorn said. "Not in sufficient dose to kill the man, since he was needed for the building. But enough to muddle his memory. Enough to confuse him. Am I right?"

"Sweet Jesus!" exclaimed Grim. "That night when he ran away into the forest—you're saying—"

"Monsters." Bardán himself spoke. "Chasing me, sharp claws, spiky tails, running, running in the dark. All around me. Running, running. Falling. Down, down . . ."

"It's all right, brother," Grim said, moving to lay a hand on Bardán's shoulder. "You're safe now. You're back. And she's alive. What they said—you didn't do it. You never hurt your baby."

Gormán grimaced. "Screamers, yes. Mistress Blackthorn is a herbalist, and understands these things. But I got it wrong. We had intended to give him only sufficient of the toadstools to induce a waking nightmare. We would have locked him in somewhere safe until a reasonable time had passed. When he was recovered, we would have broken the terrible news that while in the grip of some ailment of the mind he had snatched his daughter and run off into the woods with her. That we had found him lying unconscious, and that much later we had discovered the baby dead. That because of injuries inflicted by wild creatures, we had buried her where she lay."

"But you gave him too much," Blackthorn said.

"We gave him too much, and he did run off into the woods. We tried to find him. Without him, the heartwood house could not be finished. But search as we might, we never did track him down."

"Falling," muttered Bardán. "Down, down . . ."

Cara felt sick. "He fell down that hole. Into that place. The same place I would have been in if I had . . ." She made herself meet Gormán's eye. Gormán, whom she had loved since she was one year old. Whom this crushing pain in her heart told her she still loved. "Tell me you didn't know where he was," she said. "Or you." She looked at Tóla. "Tell me you didn't just leave him there and walk away."

"I didn't know," Gormán said. "I swear it, Cara. But . . ."

Cara waited.

"I did know that place existed. The deep hole in the ground, a spot with certain stories attached to it. I could have searched there and I chose not to. It seemed to me the whole idea of the heartwood house was cursed. It seemed those who touched it fell into strife. I thought it was fortunate Bardán was gone. The baby would be safe and happy and so would Suanach. If she was content, Tóla would be content."

"So you wove a web of lies to cover what you had done," said Mistress Blackthorn. "You and he."

"Suanach went away that night, taking the baby with her. The story we had planned to tell Bardán was put about the district: that he had run mad and abandoned his child to her death. At that stage folk did not ask awkward questions, though the wet nurse was distressed. Later, as you know, Suanach returned home with little Cara. The story was that she had given birth in the home of her kinsfolk and waited a while to return because of her precarious state of health. She died not long after coming home. That is all I have to say, save this. I have worked at Wolf Glen since I was fourteen years old, first for Master Tóla's father and then for him. I came here without home or family. Master Tóla has provided me with a home and work that I loved. I have been blessed to share every step of Cara's growing up. She is a fine young woman; any father would be proud of such a daughter. I have been loyal to Master Tóla. There have been times when I have questioned his intentions. When I have challenged his decisions. Never more so than in this matter. But he had it in his power to send me away. To snatch from me, in a moment, everything that made my life worth living. To gain my obedience, he had only to remind me of that. I will regret my weakness until the day I die." His voice shook, and he put a hand up to his eyes as if to shield his expression. Then he gathered himself, but his face was as bleak as a winter tree. "I will stand up at Prince Oran's district council. I will tell the truth and face whatever penalty the prince determines. As for Wolf Glen, I can stay here no longer. My service to you is ended, Master Tóla. You must find yourself a new forester."

Cara wondered how many times a heart could be broken and still go on beating. She wondered if even Brígh the Brave might not have enough courage for this.

"Prince Oran, I imagine, will take into consideration the fact that you have given a full account of yourself now," Blackthorn said. "Or have you? Am I wrong in thinking those ingredients laid out on the table in there were designed for a very particular purpose? One would think that having used screamers before with such unfortunate results, you would have thought twice about trying the same trick again."

"Master Tóla asked me to gather them." Gormán's voice was very quiet; the crowd hushed to catch his words. "Cook them into a stew, as I had done before. He feared you, Mistress Blackthorn. He feared Grim almost more, since Grim has both an inquiring mind and great physical strength. Bardán came to Master Tóla this morning to reveal that he knew Cara was his daughter. He could only have learned that from Grim. Master Tóla was desperate, I imagine, to stop the story from getting out; what he feared most of all was losing you, Cara. He did not tell me precisely what he planned, only asked me to prepare the stew. He asked for a full cup of screamers. I assume both men were to be . . . eliminated."

Cara could not take it in. He was saying—he was saying—no, he couldn't mean that.

"Wait a bit," said Cionnaola. "Isn't Bardán still needed to build the heartwood house?"

"Hah!" A derisive sound from Tóla.

Cold crept deep into Cara's bones. Maybe she wasn't Brave Brígh after all. *I'll always be afraid of him,* she realized. *And I'll always love him. I'll always love them both. Even after this.*

"The heartwood house will never be finished," Tóla went on. "He came down to see me this morning—him, that godforsaken apology for a man—and told me there was a part to the tale he hadn't divulged before. About the thatch. It's impossible to do."

"Feather bright and feather fine," said the wild man in his thick, awkward voice.

"None shall harm this child of mine," said Cara, looking at Bardán. "That's the song, isn't it? The lullaby you used to sing me." The chill in her bones retreated. "That's about the heartwood house too."

"Thatch of straw and feathers," Bardán said. "One feather from every kind of bird in the wood. Given willingly. Starling, woodcock, owl. Nightjar, chiffchaff, bunting. Goldcrest, warbler, thrush, jay. And many, many more."

"Crow, wren, siskin," said Cara, glancing up at the barn roof. "You need them all or the heartwood house loses its magic."

"That bastard never meant it to work," Tóla said. "He tricked me. It was all lies from the first."

"In the old tale," said Blackthorn, "a rich man steals a creature's child and makes her work for him to earn it back. She builds him a heartwood house. Only she tricks him. The story I heard says nothing about feathers in the thatch. In the version the druid told Cara, the creature leaves out certain kinds of wood, and that robs the family of certain blessings."

"Put in every kind of timber, didn't we?" Grim said, looking at Bardán with brows up. "Don't think we forgot any."

Bardán gave a strange smile. "There's the stone. Stone on stone on stone. Then the wood; every tree. Then the thatch. Nine courses."

"You told me all that. But you didn't mention feathers," said Grim.

"Maybe he didn't," Blackthorn said. "And maybe that was on purpose, to punish Tóla. Though Bardán cannot have understood the importance of that. Not fully. Not back then. His wits were scattered; his memory was unreliable. As for the feathers, a tale changes from one teller to the next. Sometimes this story may have a monster and sometimes a human mother. Sometimes the trick is with the wood, sometimes with the feathers."

"And sometimes the creature gets the child back," Cara said. "But sometimes the child is taken and kept, and brought up as another man's daughter."

"He lied," said Tóla. "Bardán lied. He promised he would build my heartwood house, every part just so. But that, with the thatch—it simply isn't possible. He could never do it, not in a thousand years. Nobody could do it."

"You're wrong," said Cara. "I could." And she saw a smile creep over Bardán's wild face, a smile that warmed her deep within.

"What nonsense—" began Tóla.

"Oh, she certainly could," said Mistress Blackthorn. "Not the thatching itself; she'd need someone with the right skills for that. But collecting the feathers—that, Brígh could do quite easily. Have you not noticed how the birds come to her? How they stay close and watch over her? Have you not noticed that the girl you raised as your daughter has some remarkable gifts?"

"Only," put in Fedach, "it wouldn't work the way Master Tóla wanted, would it? Keeping Cara—Brígh—safe, I mean. Bestowing blessings on her. Master Tóla's the landholder. He's the one who asked for it to be built. But Brígh's not his kin. She's not his daughter."

"Enough!" Tóla was shouting. "Enough of this! Clear off my land, all of you! Get yourselves and your horses out of here and don't come back. Mistress Blackthorn, if you set foot over my border again, I won't answer for the consequences. Grim, your services are no longer required.

And don't expect any further payment. I don't take kindly to folk who stick their noses where they're not wanted. The two of you have caused ruin here, utter ruin. You have destroyed my daughter's life and mine—"

"Stop!" Cara said, hardly recognizing herself. "That's enough. These are good people. They've helped me at great cost to themselves. They helped me uncover the truth, and isn't truth always better than lies? I'm going away now, with my father. Somewhere, I don't know where, but I can't stay here, and I can't be your daughter. You have given me some good things. Safety. A home. An education. An inheritance. But none of that counts when it's built on lies. I need to learn who I am all over again. That's what I'm going to do." She moved over to Bardán—to her father— and slipped her hand through his arm. He did smell bad up close. When they got to wherever they were going, she'd need to persuade him to take a bath.

"He has nothing to offer you." Tóla's voice was stone cold now. "Nothing but poverty, grief and madness."

There was a little silence. Then Bardán said, "Daughter, I offer love. I offer craft—my hands are not good for it now, but I will teach you all I know. I offer wisdom, born from sorrow. I offer tales. I offer truth."

Cara felt tears spilling down her cheeks. Her father was crying too. "I accept your fine gifts, Father," she said.

Tóla was about to speak, but Aunt Della forestalled him. "Brother, you are not yourself. Go back to the house. Go now. I will deal with this. You two, accompany him." She gestured to a pair of serving men. "Stay with him until I return."

Tóla drew a ragged breath. Took a step one way, the other way, as if he hardly knew what he was doing. "You can't do this, Cara," he said in a whisper. "You're only fifteen. Any lawman would say—"

"I'm sure Prince Oran will have an opinion," Blackthorn said. "Of course, he will hear the whole story before the open council. Including your personal account, Master Tóla. Perhaps Brígh's as well. Shall we conclude this as Mistress Della so sensibly suggests?"

He wouldn't go. It made Cara want to cry all over again. There was still a part of her that wanted to run to him, put her arms around him, say she was sorry she had made him so sad. But she didn't do any of those things. Her true father was here, right beside her. She could feel his warmth. His smile made her feel safer than she'd ever felt before, even though she had no idea where she would sleep tonight or what would happen tomorrow. So she stayed by Bardán and watched as the Swan Island men took Tóla between them, as if he were a miscreant, and walked him down to the house with the serving folk following behind like sheep. She wondered if she would ever see him again.

Mistress Blackthorn asked Grim to look at the toadstools; she asked Aunt Della too. So that there would be witnesses to speak up at the council, if needed, she said. Cara tried not to think about that. Tried not to think of Tóla and Gormán facing charges of . . . all sorts of things. Stealing a child. Telling lies. Poisoning. But her mind was full of a terrible realization. If she had not come to Wolf Glen today, Grim and Bardán might both be dead, their bodies neatly disposed of, and the truth might never have come out.

Mistress Blackthorn consigned the toadstools to the fire, then washed her hands three times over. "Where did Gormán go?" she asked, looking around.

He had gone away while Tóla was arguing; while the rest of them were listening. Cara had seen him walk off into the forest just as he was, without cloak or bag or water skin. But she had not mentioned it to anyone. "He gave his word he'd be back for the prince's council," she said. But she doubted he would keep that promise. Her heart told her she would never see him again.

Cionnaola and Cúan returned, and Cara remembered that when she had burst in on them at Dreamer's Wood they had been about to set out on a journey. Mistress Blackthorn too. It was late afternoon now; if they were going, they should go. She could not ask Mistress Blackthorn for any more help. That would be unfair.

"Cara?" Aunt Della was beside her, pale but perfectly composed.

"My name is Brígh now."

"Brígh. It will take time to get used to that. The folk from Longwater have offered you and—and your father a place to stay. They've got room for you."

Brígh looked at her father. "What do you think? We can't stay here."

"The house," Bardán said. "At Longwater. Our house."

"Needs fixing up before you can live in it," said one of the Longwater men. "We could get it done in a few days. Mend the roof, clean things up a bit. You can stay at our place until it's done. Me and Luíseach and our son here. If it suits you."

The son was Fedach. Which meant that if she stayed there, she would meet the woman who had nursed her when she was an infant. "Is that all right?" she asked Bardán. "Only, if we're staying with other folk, you'll need to have a wash. Cut your hair. Put on clean clothes."

"I made a promise. That I wouldn't, until I got back what Tóla had stolen from me. I couldn't remember what it was then. Only that it was what I held most dear in the world. My precious thing. My hope and joy, my smiles and tears."

"That must have been a hard promise to keep," Brígh said, wishing she could stop crying.

"I got used to it. Got used to being the wild man. But not anymore. I will wash myself clean. A new man."

"A new life," Brígh said. "The best one we can make, yes?"

"It is already the best," said Bardán.

Brígh said good-bye and thank you to Mistress Blackthorn. Bardán hugged Grim, who looked pale under the bandage Mistress Blackthorn had wrapped around his head. The wise woman said she would come to Longwater as soon as she was home from her journey. It was plain to Brígh that Blackthorn had other things on her mind; she kept looking at Grim, then looking down toward the house.

Aunt Della embraced Brígh and offered a home for the future, again.

"You are very kind, Aunt," Brígh said. "But I must be with my father; I only just found him. I've tried your patience badly over the years. I'm sorry for that. I'm sorry you had to spend all that time looking after me instead of living your own life. What will you do now?"

"I will leave Wolf Glen," Aunt Della said. "But not before I set my brother's household to rights after this disturbance. And someone must ensure he prepares himself for Prince Oran's council. I will be here some while longer. May I visit you in Longwater, Cara? Brígh?"

"Of course. But . . . I cannot see *him* again. Not so soon."

"I understand, child. I will explain that a visit would do his case no good. For the longer term, you and he will have to reach an agreement of some kind if you are to be living in Longwater, so close."

"Thank you, Aunt Della. And good luck."

"Ride safely, my Cara. I will miss you, child."

"And I will miss you," Brígh surprised herself by saying. "Who will remind me to sit up straight and wear the right shoes?"

"I expect you'll manage."

44

BLACKTHORN

"I have something to tell you," I said. "Something important. But it'll have to be quite quick."

"Go on, then."

We were seated a little apart, waiting for Cionnaola and Cúan. Ripple was leaning against Grim, her muzzle on his knee. Someone had brought a blanket, which Grim had around his shoulders. Someone else had brought a water skin, but neither of us had touched it. The toadstools had been a close thing.

I told Grim about Mathuin. A gathering so secret nobody could say a word about it. A council that was unofficial, but that had the High King's approval. A hearing at which Mathuin would, in effect, be tried in secret by his peers. At least, that was my understanding. I told him about my document, already on its way to that hearing. All this I passed on in a whisper. There was no need to tell Grim how important it was to me to give my evidence in person. He had the same passion for justice written on his heart.

"Morrigan's britches," said Grim. "So why aren't you looking happy?"

"I missed my chance to go. It's too late now."

"Missed it? Why?" Grim sounded bewildered.

"I gave it up. So I could come to Wolf Glen today."

"You what?"

"You heard what I said. That was the choice, ride off for the hearing this morning or answer Brígh's call for help. And as you see, I came here."

Grim looked stunned. "Brígh could have got help from Winterfalls. You knew that. Wouldn't have taken much longer. What stopped you from going? Conmael?"

"There was the minor matter of you being in all kinds of trouble. I knew how bad it was when Ripple turned up half dead from exhaustion. And Brígh said she thought Tóla might kill you."

Grim stared at me. There was no reading his expression now. "You're saying you—nah."

"I'm saying I what?"

"You gave up the chance to put that wretch behind bars at long last because of *me*?"

"That's it, more or less," I said, not looking at him.

"Holy Mother of God."

"I've never known anyone to mix oaths the way you do, big man," I said. "We have missed our chance, yes; I'd already made them wait all morning in the hope that you would turn up in time, and then Brígh rode in just as we were leaving. I did send my written testimony. I'd like to go there anyway, so we can witness whatever comes from the hearing. I think I can persuade the Island men to take us as planned, even though it's so late. Only you're hardly in a fit state to ride."

"Pity we can't turn back time," Grim said. "Wasn't that what Conmael threatened if you broke his rules? To put you back in the lockup, everything just the same as it was when we first clapped eyes on each other?"

"You know Conmael's not here," I said. "I've tried and tried. He won't come."

"You might be doing it wrong."

"You're hardly an expert."

"I was thinking, though. Children, weren't you, when you knew each other? That's if he's who you think he is. Might not need a charm or incantation or anything like that. Maybe only something simple. Something the two of you did back then. Something that made him happy. If he was ever happy."

"I've tried every way I can think of to summon him. You know that!" I made myself take a breath. "Sorry. But I never did believe he could make time go backward. And I don't need his permission for anything now. It's too late for that."

Grim stared down at his hands. Frowning. "Might not be," he said. "Feels wrong that they'd have the hearing and you wouldn't be there to speak up. You could try to call Conmael. Try again, I mean. Do something different."

My sigh of exasperation was loud enough to turn the heads of the Longwater men, who were organizing themselves into two groups, one to walk with Brígh and her father, since Bardán's crippled hands meant he could not ride, the rest to go ahead with the horses and prepare the folk of the settlement for two unexpected additions to their number. They felt a duty, maybe; the need to make amends for their poor treatment of Bardán in the past. They were good folk at heart, even if, as it seemed, some of them had accepted Tóla's money to hold their tongues. They would look after Brígh and Bardán until they got on their feet. As for Tóla, Prince Oran would see justice done there.

"Not like you not to try," said Grim.

"All right, I will," I snapped. "But not here. And not in front of Cionnaola and Cúan either. It'll have to wait until we're back at Dreamer's Wood. And I doubt those two will be happy about yet another delay."

He didn't say anything. I remembered that he had spent hours trussed up in the dark, not knowing what came next. That he had a head wound and had lost quite a lot of blood. That I was expecting him to get on a horse and ride off to some unknown place without any kind of rest first. "I'll tell them you need a meal and a bath before we go on."

"Mm-hm."

"What?"

"Might be nighttime before we get going."

"It might. That's why we need Conmael. Look, those two are on their way back. Let's go, big man. One step at a time, yes?"

"Lady."

"You know I don't like you calling me that. What?"

"Thanks for saving me. Thanks for . . . I still can't get my head around it."

"Don't try," I said. "It's what we do, isn't it? Save each other?"

45

BARDÁN

As they make their way to Longwater, he hears his mother's voice, singing: *Feather bright and feather fine, none shall harm this child of mine.* And here is his child, safe. Walking beside him. Returned to him. His girl, his own Brígh. On her face he sees his wife's sweet smile. In her voice he hears his wife's kindness. But his daughter is strong, too; as strong as a fine young oak. He remembers her half hidden in a dapple of green leaves and golden light. How could he not have known her instantly?

The world is so full of wonder. Sorrow has blinded him to that, but now he sees clear. The sun on still water. A baby's tiny hands, a miracle. The flight of a bird. A friend's touch in the dark. Kind words and gentleness. Truth, and a pathway forward. He is mended. His child has come home, and he is whole again.

46

GRIM

Too much to think about. Bardán and his daughter. Gormán going off into the woods like that. Like he wasn't ever coming back. That eats at me. Wish I could go after him, find him before he does himself some mischief. Tell him that even if good men do bad things sometimes, there's a way back. But that forest's big and he knows it inside out. If he wants to lose himself, nobody's ever going to find him.

And Blackthorn, riding beside me now wrapped up in her own thoughts. Blackthorn choosing not to go to this hearing. Can't get my head around that. Got the chance to face up to Mathuin in a proper council at last, and she said no to it. That's the only thing she's cared about since we got out of that place. Vengeance for her family. Justice for all the folk Mathuin's hurt over the years. It's been the only thing keeping her going. And this time it would've been easy. No need to ride all the way to Laois. Guards to go with her, everything arranged. But she said no. Because of me.

Don't know what to think about that. Don't know where to start. So I think about Conmael instead, what might bring him when we need him. What might've held him back from coming. I think about it all the way down to Dreamer's Wood and home.

"Got an idea," I say to Blackthorn. Cúan's looking after the horses. Cionnaola's drawing water from the well. They've said we can still go with them to this place, even though it's too late for Blackthorn to speak. Place is so secret nobody'll say where it is, only it's a couple of days' ride. I'm tired. Head hurts. Other bits of me not doing so well either, after being cramped up so long. Long soak in a hot bath, then rest—that's what I want. Don't say so, though.

"What?" says Blackthorn.

"When you think of Conmael, what do you think of?"

"I don't know what you mean."

"Pretend I've never seen him. Paint a picture for me."

"Tall, pale, dark-haired, noble-looking. Obviously fey. Usually wearing a sweeping cloak and a lot of silver rings. Looks forbidding. Arrogant. Most of the time."

She's said what I expected her to say. "I think that might be the trouble," I tell her. "I think you might have hurt his feelings."

"The fey don't have feelings to hurt," Blackthorn says. "Especially not him."

"Brought up by a human mother, wasn't he? Some of that might have rubbed off on him. Made him different. Different from what he was born as."

"Then he'd be an outsider in his own world as well as the human world. That's terrible. But now you say it, of course he has feelings. Or had them. The other children used to taunt him because he was odd-looking. Calling him changeling. He hated it. He shrank from it. Wouldn't fight back. They kept on and on at it until I made them stop."

"Explains why he's helped you. You were his protector. His friend. His only friend."

"He's repaid any debt a hundred times over by saving us from Mathuin's lockup. He owes me absolutely nothing."

She still doesn't understand. "Explains why he helped you, yes. And why he made you promise to follow his rules. He wanted you to be that old Blackthorn again. The one who stood up for what was right. The one who saw him as a real boy. The one who took time to listen."

Blackthorn's starting to look cross. "How does that help?"

"Not sure. Don't know much about charms and spells. You're the wise woman. What we want is a spell to bring Conmael here. He can come here anytime he wants—he's fey. But he doesn't come. He might be upset. He might've been waiting all this time for you to remember he's Cully. Thinking you never will. Thinking that didn't matter to you like it did to him. Being friends, that's a big thing for some folk. One good friend can change your whole life. He might have given up coming to visit you because he's . . . sad."

"Conmael?" Blackthorn's brows go up. "Hardly."

"Not Conmael, maybe. But Cully, yes. Lonely little boy, bullied by everyone, living on the outskirts, never had a friend to stick up for him. Then along you came. Brave. Sure of yourself. Strong. Ready to take on the world. He must've been . . . dazzled."

"Her hands are strong as a warrior's," Blackthorn says. Gives a crooked smile, as if she doesn't believe it.

My heart does a bit of a jump. "You saw that, then," I say. Feels like a long time since I wrote those words for her.

"I copied it into my notebook. There are times when I need to remind myself I'm supposed to be brave." After a bit, she adds, "I liked what you wrote."

"I liked what you wrote." I feel myself blushing. Fool of a man. "Didn't copy it down. Got it in my head. Thought of it when Bardán and I were . . . in there."

"Good," Blackthorn says. She's blushing too. "Now, Conmael. You're saying think of him as he was back then, a lonely little boy in need of a friend, and he might appear?"

"Worth a try. What did the two of you do together? Play games? Tell stories?"

Cionnaola comes out of the cottage. "Fire's lit. Water's heating," he says. "Cúan will get some food ready." He doesn't need to say, *It's getting late and if we don't go soon, we'll be riding in the dark.*

"Thank you," says Blackthorn. "Just one thing. I need some herbs from the wood, to wash Grim's head wound. They grow not far in.

Grim can come with me; no need for you or Cúan to trouble your-selves."

I get to my feet. Try to look as if there's nothing wrong with me. But Cionnaola's an Island man. Doesn't miss much. "Grim's not fit to fight off a stray terrier right now," he says. "If you're going out of sight of the cottage, you take one of us."

Blackthorn swears under her breath. Know how she feels. What if she tries this and it works, and Conmael suddenly appears, and this fellow sticks a knife into him, thinking he's an enemy?

"Cionnaola," she says, keeping her voice calm, "you know I'm a wise woman. Sometimes we have to do things that are . . . a little unusual. If you insist on coming with us, you must respect a couple of rules. Don't approach without my say-so, whatever happens. And don't bring iron weaponry."

Feel a bit sorry for the man. She's made the two of them wait nearly a whole day, so they couldn't carry out their mission, which was get-ting her to this council at the right time to say her bit. She's got them heating bathwater and cooking a meal. And now she's saying they can't protect her the way they're supposed to do. "Should be all right," I say to Cionnaola. "Knows what she's doing."

We go into the wood. Right down to the spot where the bank of Dreamer's Pool dips and flattens out. Weather's cleared up. Sunlight creeping through the trees. Dragonflies busy over the water. Frogs hav-ing a talk. Blackthorn wanders around a bit, picking up stones and a few sticks. Then sits down cross-legged on the shore. Asks me to wait a short way off, in plain sight. Cionnaola's on the high part of the bank, across the pool. He can see us, but folk passing by wouldn't easily see him. Human folk, that is.

"Right," says Blackthorn. "We used to play a game called Hop-the-Frog. I'll try that. Cionnaola's going to think I've gone mad. And if this works, he's going to get the surprise of his life." She brushes her hand over the ground in front of her so there's a patch of flat bare earth. Puts her stones in two piles, one in front of her, one where another player might sit, opposite. Sets two short sticks next to each pile. Then shuts her eyes and does nothing at all. That's what it looks like, anyway. I wait. Maybe she's calling him without speaking out loud. Maybe she's just getting in the right mood.

"I'll go first, Cully," she says all of a sudden. Eyes open now, but not seeing me. Looking into the past. "Ready? *Hop, frog, hop, frog, out of your den. Hop across the top of the pond and hop right back again.*" While she's chanting the rhyme, she's flicking a stone out of her heap, not touching it but using the sticks. Flicks it once, flicks it again, and the stone sails through the air and onto the other heap. Where it settles. But not for long. It wobbles, flicks itself down to the ground, then hurtles across the cleared space and lands on Blackthorn's stones. Can't see Cully, but it looks like he's playing.

"Your turn," says Blackthorn. Voice shaking a bit.

He's there, sitting cross-legged opposite her. Reaches to flick a stone from his own pile to hers. Falls a bit short, half a handspan from Blackthorn's heap. She gathers it in with her two sticks. *"Mine to keep, Froggie weep,"* she says, and looks over at him.

Cionnaola's seen him. Comes striding down the path. I put up a hand, palm out, and he stops where he is. Fair enough to be a bit alarmed. Not a little boy sitting there, but a tall man in a black cloak, dark hair tied back with a cord, silver rings glinting on his long fingers. Take one look at his face and you'd know he was fey. Even if you'd never seen one of them before. You can tell he's different. You can tell he's dangerous. Looks the way Blackthorn said, arrogant, forbidding. He's always like that, even when he's being helpful.

The two of them put their sticks down.

"I was right, then," Blackthorn says. "About where we had met before and why you've helped me."

"I had thought the memory lost to you forever." His voice is like the cloak, dark and soft. Sort of voice that could draw a person in deep if they weren't careful.

"The memory wasn't lost. Only . . . you're so different now. It was hard to imagine the Cully of my childhood becoming . . . this." She goes quiet, thinking. "I have a favor to ask. A big one. Probably undeserved. Only I want to ask questions too. All kinds of questions. But there isn't much time."

"I have been gone some while," Conmael says. Solemn as an owl. Not so haughty now. "I owe you a few answers."

Blackthorn doesn't ask, *Where have you been?* She doesn't ask, *Why didn't you come when I called you?* She doesn't even tell him about Mathuin, at least not yet. "Back then, I never thought you might be a real changeling," she says. "I should have known."

"You were young. How could you have known?"

"Does that mean . . ." Blackthorn's thinking twice about asking, I can see. "Does it mean a human child was left in the Otherworld? In your place? Raised among the fey? That's what happens in the tales."

"It is sometimes so, yes." Conmael's tone was cautious.

"Only sometimes?"

"To be raised, to be offered a different life—that is a gift of sorts. Not every human child taken by my kind meets such a benign fate. Some are simply . . . cast aside. Or worse. I will spare you the details. You already have sufficient material for a lifetime of bad dreams."

"So it's not because someone in the fey world wants a human child for their own?"

"That may occasionally be so. Your kind breeds easily; mine does not. But more often such an action is taken as a punishment."

Blackthorn laid her stones in a neat circle, not looking at Conmael. "A punishment for whom?" she asked.

"For one of your kind who has offended one of mine. Torched an ancient site; cut down a hawthorn; walked where he or she should not. Or it might be a punishment for one of my kind."

"But how could—oh."

The look in Blackthorn's face tells me what she's thinking. Every-one knows changeling tales. There's the human mother who goes to the cradle and gets a nasty surprise. She's settled her rosy, perfect little one to sleep, and now there's a wizened thing like an old wrinkly turnip looking up at her. Crying a cry that could never come out of a human baby's mouth. But that's only half the picture.

"Two mothers grieving," says Blackthorn. "Two fathers inconsolable. And two children, in effect, lost forever."

Conmael bows his head. Meaning yes. But that isn't right. He's not lost, is he? Looks to be doing well for himself. Dresses like a nobleman, can move around by magic, got a few supporters we've seen over the years. Casts some pretty good spells, like the one that made the roof of Mathuin's lockup fall in. Though he could have managed that better, not killed a bunch of folk doing it. One thing doesn't fit: the way he interferes in Blackthorn's business. In the tales, the fey don't care about anyone. It's not in their nature. But he cares about her.

"You went back," Blackthorn says. "Did you . . . Did you find them?"

"A tale for another day," says Conmael. Doesn't want to talk about it—that's plain as plain. Too painful. Would be, wouldn't it? "Suffice it to say that cruelty and kindness exist in both worlds. There are folk who love unwisely; folk whose burning need for vengeance blinds them to common sense. Folk eaten up by jealousy, such as the woman who pronounced the curse you encountered at Bann. Folk with a mad lust for power, caring little who falls by the wayside. And folk who do their small best to mend, to heal, to make peace. Those, too, who have in us both good and bad. Who must work hard every day to keep our hearts steady and our minds in balance."

Blackthorn doesn't say anything. Just looks at him.

"And in that, I have long believed we should help each another," says Conmael. "Did you mention a favor?"

Blackthorn takes a big breath. "The promise I made you," she begins. "The seven years. Is there a chance you might reconsider? There is an opportunity. Or there was. An opportunity to testify against Mathuin of Laois at a council of his peers. A secret council."

"Was," says Conmael. "Not is?"

She explains. About the attack on Flidais's parents, and the king's council at Cahercorcan, and the Swan Island men. About this meeting being so secret she had to go at the last moment, and how she ended up saying no. Conmael's still as stone, listening. A bad thought comes into my head. If he says he'll do it, if he turns back time so she can get there to testify, that'll leave me trussed up in Tóla's root cellar bleeding all over the floor. Waiting to be fed screamers and die. Hope she's thought of that.

"I tried to call you," Blackthorn says. "All different ways. Over and over. When they told me about this, I wanted to go with your blessing, not to break the rules."

"Not to risk my meddling with time? But is that not what you are about to ask for now?"

"I'm hoping you will release me from my promise, Conmael. Not all of it, but the part about not seeking out Mathuin. He is coming north. Or, more likely, being brought north. I can't tell you if the place is in Dalriada or over the border. But the hearing is properly organized, even if it's not quite being done by the rules. The High King has given it his blessing." She's keeping her voice down. Remembering she's been told not to talk about it.

"Let me understand this fully. After turning down this opportunity, the one you have craved for so long, in order to save your friend here"—he gives me a nod—"you wish me to take you back to this morning so you can make the other choice? Condemn him to his fate?"

"Of course not! If I found myself back there, I would make the same choice again."

"Tell me why."

"Mistress Blackthorn!" Cionnaola calls from up on the higher path, keeping it as quiet as he can. "Time's passing."

"Tell me why," Conmael says again. Sounds as if her answer might be pretty important.

"Speaking out against Mathuin," she says, "helping bring him to justice—not long ago I would have thought nothing could possibly be more important. And it is important. I still want to do it. Need to. But not if it means losing Grim. That would be too high a price to pay. We're a team. If I go to this hearing, I need him to come with me. And if I don't go, I need him anyway. To walk along beside me. To be there.

To stop me from . . . losing myself." She runs out of words. And me, I'm thinking I might cry, right here in front of Conmael and Cionnaola.

"So, in a human mind," Conmael says, calm as calm, "the welfare of a friend weighs more than a greater cause such as the removal of a tyrant? Is not that decision somewhat selfish?"

"I don't care a rat's balls if it's selfish!" Blackthorn's angry now. Got a fierce look I know well. "And it's one particular human mind I'm talking about, mine. I'm not making some grand philosophical statement on behalf of all humankind! Don't imagine it was an easy choice. Don't ever think it didn't hurt. Mathuin burned my husband and son alive. Not going to testify in person felt like betraying them. But in the end I didn't hesitate. If your friend's in deep trouble, you save him. He's saved me more times than I can count. He's stood by me through everything. Even when I was a bitter, cantankerous creature unfit for anyone's company." She stops to suck in a breath. She's crying too, messily now, with her nose running. "Maybe I should mention that my written testimony has gone south under armed guard, and that if I'm not there, someone will read it out at the hearing. I have faith that there's sufficient evidence for Mathuin to be found guilty without my being there in person. I don't believe Prince Oran or the king of Dalriada or the High King would have sanctioned this venture if it didn't have a strong chance of success."

"So you need not go," says Conmael, still perfectly calm.

"I do need to go," Blackthorn says. "Not for the greater cause. But for me. For Grim. For the poor souls who shared that lockup with us day after miserable day and night after endless night. For the women who were brave enough to ask me for help. Who trusted me with their stories."

Not sure if I should speak or keep my big mouth shut. I take the risk. "Thing is," I say, "that *is* the greater cause. Isn't it? All those tales put together. Tales from prisoners and downtrodden women and ordinary working folk. Like a lot of threads, frayed and weak they might be, woven into something big and strong and beautiful. And powerful."

"A tapestry of justice," says Conmael, and gives me a proper smile.

"Now seems the right time for me to tell you that I am already aware of the meeting, or council, that lies before you." He means Blackthorn, not me. "You have not seen me for some while; that is true. But I never ceased to watch over you, my friend. Many parties have been working to make this thing happen, and happen both safely and secretly."

"You knew about it?" Blackthorn's shocked. "But waited until it was too late for us to get there?"

"Look on what has occurred as a test. As events fell out, you were provided with an opportunity to demonstrate that you had learned the hard lesson I set you. For a long while you allowed your quest for vengeance to govern you. It came close to consuming the woman you had been—a person of great strength, sound judgment and remarkable compassion. Oh, you had good cause," Conmael adds quickly, like he's expecting me or Blackthorn to interrupt. "To want justice—that cannot be a bad thing. But to let your want eat away at your heart . . . that would have been to pass victory into the hands of your enemy.

"I watched and waited. I saw you come close to failing. I saw you on the brink of giving up hope. I watched you stumble and fall and pick yourself up again. When you were too worn-out to rise, I saw your friend lift you up. I saw you learn, and I hoped. Today you made a choice. That woman I knew before, the one full of bitterness and hate, would not have set aside her chance for vengeance in order to help a friend. Not even to save his life."

He smiles, and it's a nice open one. Takes away that distant look. "This lesson has been hard for you to learn. At times it has cost you dear. Never more so than in the final choosing. But Grim is here, and safe. And your chance to bring Mathuin of Laois to justice still lies before you."

Blackthorn's been getting twitchier as he makes his speech, with more time passing. "In a way, yes," she says now. "But we can't get there when we were meant to. Unless . . . unless you really can turn back time, and do it without harming Grim."

"Ah," says Conmael. "As it happens, I can assist you. I would not meddle with time. Such charms are perilous indeed. But I can provide you with a different way to travel. The journey will be a great deal quicker. There are paths we may take, paths unfamiliar to humankind. It will be perfectly safe if you are with me. Provided your formidable guards can tell me where this council is to be held, I can ensure you arrive at the agreed hour. Both of you. Your guards as well, since I understand they are under orders to bring you there safely."

Blackthorn looks surprised. I'm the same. "So you are releasing me from the promise?" she asks. "Even though I haven't held to it for seven years yet?"

"I am releasing you, my friend. I trust you will use your abilities only for good. That you will aid those who need you. That you will walk forward in hope. Now, let us seize this opportunity to deal with Mathuin of Laois once and for all."

"I hardly know what to say." Blackthorn sounds tired to the bone. Great pair we'll be, standing up in a council and all yawns. Been a long, long day. And it's not finished yet. But Bonehead can't help asking another question.

"You know before. When she called you back with that sticks-and-stones game. Did that work a charm to bring you out, like she hoped? Or was it what you said, you were waiting and watching and you appeared because it was the right time? Because that choice was coming, that test?" Hope I'm making some sense. Head's throbbing a bit. A lie-down would be good.

Conmael gives me his nice smile again. "Both," he says. "Both together."

"It seems a lot, still," says Blackthorn, "in return for the small favor I did you."

"It may seem small to you," Conmael says. "To an outcast boy, alone in a strange world, what you offered was a matchless gift. You treated me not with the ridicule, suspicion, or downright fear I was accustomed to, but with acceptance. You listened. And you defended me. You saved a part of me that would otherwise have died. It gladdens me to see you on a path of light at last—a path where your talents may be used as they should be. You have a good companion to walk beside you in this world.

You might consider me as another such. I walk between worlds. I will watch over you from both of them."

There've been times when I didn't trust Conmael an inch. Times when he annoyed the shit out of me. Comes to me now that he's given Blackthorn her own matchless gift. In his tricky fey way, he's given her back her life twice over.

47

BLACKTHORN

I expected the Island men to argue the point or to refuse outright. Why would any reasonable person believe we could travel by some uncanny path and be at our destination in time? Why would they trust our safety to someone who'd popped up out of nowhere and was obviously not human? But Cionnaola simply looked Conmael up and down—my fey friend was waiting at a distance, out of earshot—and asked me if I was sure he could be trusted. That was fair enough, since Conmael would have to be told our secret destination. All Cúan asked was whether the journey would be safe for the horses. Then Cionnaola said, "Prince Oran trusts your judgment, Mistress Blackthorn. If you can vouch for your friend there, and if you believe this will be safe, we will try it." I must have gaped at him, for he went on, "We are trained to deal with the unexpected. To weigh the odds and to make decisions quickly. Our original orders were to get you to the hearing on time and safely. If accepting this person's help will allow that to happen, I won't refuse."

There was time for Grim to wash and change his clothes, and for all of us to have a quick meal, though I was too nervous to eat much. Conmael sat down with us and shared the food, which felt odd. At one point Cionnaola took him aside and they had a brief conversation in lowered voices, I assumed to discuss exactly where we were going.

"What about Ripple?" I asked Grim. The dog was lying prone before the fire, snoring gently.

"We can't leave her behind," Grim said. "Might be best if she goes up on the horse again, with me this time. Feeling a bit odd about this myself. Worse for a dog. You can't explain to them. You can't tell them they're safe and it'll be over soon."

"Hope it is over soon, or you'll be falling asleep while you ride."

Grim smiled. "Doubt that. When we get there, maybe. Depending."

"I can't believe this is happening at last. I'm scared I'll wake up and it'll all be a dream."

Grim reached up to touch the fresh bandage I had wrapped around his head. "It's real enough," he said. "Sore head and all. Hope they're all right. Bardán and his girl. Big change for both of them. Be hard for a while."

"Brígh's stronger than she looks. And those are good folk over in Longwater. If Tóla leaves them alone, they might do very well. Though with Bardán's hands the way they are, it could be hard for him to earn a living."

We both looked over at Conmael.

"He could help," Grim said. "Couldn't he? Remember how those fey folk at Bann mended me? Had to be magic, it was so quick. And they were only little folk."

"He could, I expect. But I don't plan to ask him for any more favors right now. I feel as if I've been very lucky. Later, maybe. Depending on how this goes."

"It'll go fine," Grim said, putting his hand over mine on the table. "Breathe deep. Stand tall. Speak the truth. You're good at that."

Even for me, a wise woman, the journey was confronting. We rode out, the five of us and Ripple, along the path through Dreamer's Wood, as if we were heading to Winterfalls settlement, barely a mile away and surely in the wrong direction. Conmael was in the lead, astride a long-legged black horse that had mysteriously added itself to our number while we were indoors eating. I came next, with Cúan beside me. Then Grim with Ripple. Cionnaola rode at the end. Day had given way to the long twilight that marks the approach of summer; the time when nothing is quite what it seems. We came to the spot where Dreamer's Wood opened to farmland. But now there were no fields, only a pair of strange trees clad in leaves of blue and silver, leaning toward each other to form an archway over the path—a path that had turned unfamiliar. A new way, shadowy and strange, leading forward through a long tunnel formed by many such trees, so dense in foliage that there was no seeing what lay behind them. A secret way.

Conmael drew his horse to a halt. "It will not take long," he said. "Stay calm. Best if you do not speak until I tell you it is safe to do so. If you hear voices, disregard them. Keep the rider in front of you always in sight. Come, then."

We moved forward through the portal—I had no doubt this was such an entry place—and along the tree tunnel, which did not follow a straight line but curved one way and the other so we could never see far ahead. The trees were of a kind I did not know. In form they were something like willows, but no willow ever had such leaves. One side of each was as bright as moonlight on water. The other was like the sky on a warm summer day. Beautiful indeed; they invited the eye. I fixed my gaze on Conmael and rode forward.

Now there were pale fruits half hidden in the foliage, glowing as if each held an inner light. Or—surely that one had eyes. Not fruits at all, but creatures. Or some uncanny blend of the two. Little sounds came, hissing, humming, almost-words. *Look straight ahead, Blackthorn,* I reminded myself. Behind me, Ripple was whining. My horse twitched her ears, tossed her head. I stroked her neck in reassurance but held my silence. Conmael's mount didn't miss a step. Perhaps it was accustomed to this kind of thing.

This way, whispered the voices. *Oh, this way lies wisdom beyond that of the most accomplished human healer. The knowledge to mend the most broken of bodies, to soothe the most tormented of minds. What might you accomplish, if you would only learn from us? Come, turn, look upon us!*

I wondered what they were saying to Grim. How would they try to tempt him? With the spiritual life that had been snatched from him on one terrible day of blood and death? With promises of a lovely young wife and a brood of little ones? Grim would make a wonderful father, strong, sure, gentle. If not for me, he might have found that wife by now and been settling in to that kind of life. But then, I thought, if not for me, Grim would be still in Mathuin's lockup, if anyone could have survived it that long. More likely he'd be dead. If not for the need to save me, Conmael would have left that vile place alone, and none of the poor souls incarcerated there would have been freed. The more a person thought about such things, the harder it became to untangle right and wrong.

"Not far now," Conmael called quietly, as if to reassure us that all was well, voices or no voices.

What has your life to offer you? The voices were trying again. *Weary, aging, bitter creature that you are? Here you can be young again. You can be beautiful. You can be powerful. Get down from your horse. Step between the trees. What have you to lose?*

I made myself breathe slowly. Swallowed the quick anger that welled in me. Held back the words. To those who loved me, I was beautiful. To Cass, in whose arms I had slept safe at night through the too-short years of our marriage; to Brennan, whom I had fed from my own body. To Holly, my first mentor, who had given me the love my parents could not give. And to Grim, who did not care if I was weary, aging or bitter. Grim who was riding behind me, and who was most likely fighting his own tormenting voices.

I reminded myself that I was a wise woman, whatever these fey creatures might think of my skills. I had brought my own magic with me. Now I reached down to the saddlebag, awkwardly, and drew out the item I had packed at the top, within easy reach. With the reins in one hand, I tucked the red kerchief into my belt. It just needed to be secure and visible. Right. My link with the human world; with friends who cared about one another; with goodness and strength and . . . well, with love. No matter what those creatures were whispering in Grim's ears, if he could see the red kerchief, he would not be drawn off the path. As for the Island men, I thought they would hold to their mission whatever happened. The wheedling voices would be no match for such disciplined individuals.

We had not gone much farther when Conmael said, "We are here," and rode out of the tree tunnel into a clearing full of sunshine. Not evening. Not nighttime. Bright morning. And surely not the Otherworld, for the trees were apples, plums, peaches, their last blossoms turning to the first green fruit. Some ordinary-looking goats were foraging beneath them, but scattered in surprise at our sudden appearance. When I looked behind me, I could see no eldritch trees, no opening, no portal. Only the orchard and the goats and, behind them, a neat drystone wall.

"Sweet Jesus save us," said Grim.

"That was . . . a new experience," said Cionnaola. He glanced at the sky; took a look at the tree shadows across the grass. "What day is it?"

Conmael dismounted. "I thought it best that you arrive at the time you were expected," he said calmly. "That way you do not attract questions. This is the morning you told me the hearing was to take place. Early. You will have time to rest a little and prepare yourselves." His gaze met mine in a kind of salute. I saw pride there, and affection, and a recognition of the bond between us. I saw that he believed in me.

"Thank you," I said simply. He appeared to have turned time not backward but forward. From what he'd said, we had lost a whole day coming through that portal. More than a day, since it was morning now. That was a formidable power to wield. I would never understand how he chose when to use it and when to stand by and watch humankind repeat the same old errors.

"It's nothing," said Conmael. Then, to Cionnaola, "Go that way, through the gate, and you will find some of your men watching for your arrival. And you will no longer require my assistance."

"Are you leaving?"

"What about going back?"

Grim and I spoke at the same time. He had dismounted and lifted Ripple down to the ground. She relieved herself copiously, then headed off toward the goats, which were gathered by the wall in a nervous-looking clump. A word from Grim stopped Ripple's attempt to herd them.

Conmael smiled at us. "The slow way will be best for the journey home," he said. "Time to reflect. You will need that, however this falls out. I will be present during the hearing. How could I not stand by you at such a time? You may see me, but I will not make myself obtrusive. You will find it is a very small gathering. Small and select. Farewell for now, Saorla." He put his hands on my shoulders and, to my great surprise, bent to kiss me on the brow. The touch of his lips was cool. It felt odd but strangely right to hear him use that name, the one I thought I had left behind me. "Go armed with your formidable courage, your passion for truth and your strength of heart. Farewell, Grim. Stand by her as always. Would that everyone had such a friend as you." He turned and led his horse away before we could say another word. As he moved into the shadow under the trees, he and the animal became part of it. Within a count of five there was nobody to be seen.

It was indeed a small gathering, if you didn't count the considerable number of Island men in attendance—they were everywhere. I had not realized their number was so great. The place was a grand house with a stone-walled courtyard and a little tower. A nobleman's house. But I did not know if we were in Dalriada or one of the neighboring regions, perhaps Ulaid, and nobody was saying whose home had been provided for the purpose. Certainly there were no household guards visible, only the Island men with their distinctive facial markings and their air of calm competence.

Grim and I, with Ripple, were taken through a massive kitchen into a small adjoining chamber where we were allowed to sit and rest. There were armed guards at the door. After a while Prince Oran appeared, a welcome sight, and sat down with us to go through what would happen.

I expected him to be surprised to see us, then remembered we had arrived more or less exactly when expected. Oran had Donagan with him. It came to me that Donagan was the prince's Grim—not that there could ever be another Grim, but he was close. Donagan stood by Oran in bad times and good. He provided the voice of common sense when it was needed. He coped calmly with whatever happened. He smoothed the way. And when he had to, he delivered hard truths. The prince was lucky to have such a friend.

"We're at the home of a local leader," the prince said, indicating to the guards that the door should be closed. "In effect we have borrowed this place in order to provide appropriate security for the hearing. Whatever happens here, the intention is that no element of this will become public knowledge. Hence, our hiring of the Swan Island men, who specialize in this kind of thing. Now, the hearing itself. Don't be overwhelmed by those you see there. We have two kings in attendance, one of them my father. Five senior chieftains. Flidais's father, Lord Cadhan, is here, as it was Mathuin's offense against him that sparked action at last. We have two senior lawmen present, neither of them from Laigin. A representative from the High King is with us. And we have two trusted scribes. You are the only woman present, Blackthorn." Oran glanced at me. "You must speak for all his female victims. You will do so eloquently, I know. Just take it one step at a time and keep calm."

I swallowed, wondering if my heart might give out from beating so hard. "Who has come here with Mathuin?" I asked. "Has he brought his own lawmen? Retainers? Supporters?" That was the usual practice at a legal hearing. Last time I had faced Mathuin in public, I had been shamed and vilified. The memory welled up in me, sharp and painful; my whole body shrank from it.

"It's all right," Grim murmured, putting a hand over mine on the table.

"Lord Mathuin has the services of one of our lawmen," Prince Oran said coolly, as if this were not a point on which he might be challenged. "Let it never be said that he was unrepresented at the hearing.

Apart from that, he is alone. He was conveyed here covertly by the Island men."

"If—if he is found guilty, how will you—"

"Now is not the time for that conversation. When the hearing is over, I may be at liberty to give you more information. Only remember that what happens here does not go beyond these four walls. I have included you because I want your testimony to be heard. And because I trust you—the two of you—not to speak of this afterward. Not to anyone. I need to be quite sure you understand that."

I could have asked questions. Even with my limited knowledge of the law, I understood that the hearing was not being conducted in the accepted manner. On the other hand, two kings would be present and the High King himself had approved the proceedings, if unofficially. If Mathuin was found guilty, what would the penalty be and who would carry it out? And how could they stop him from speaking out about this secret trial? It sounded as if the Island men had abducted him, something of a feat in view of the heavy presence of guards he took with him everywhere. Say the penalty was exile. I knew Mathuin. He would be eaten up by the need to punish those who had wronged him. That was how he would see it. Even if they sent him far, far away, he would reach out his destructive hand and wreak utter havoc. I would be one of his accusers today. I might spend the rest of my life looking over my shoulder. Too scared to relax for a moment. Too scared to let others close lest they be destroyed as Cass and Brennan had been destroyed. That meant I could never have a family again. I should not even have a friend. But here Grim was, risking everything with me. Expecting me to be brave. They all expected me to be brave. But my mind was full of Mathuin. Mathuin hurling abuse at me, Mathuin taunting me, Mathuin ordering his henchmen to light the fire . . . I was not brave. I was a quaking mass of terror.

"We should go in now," Donagan said quietly. "Are you ready, Mistress Blackthorn?"

"Now." My voice was a choked gasp. "Right now?"

"If you can manage," said the prince. "I don't believe the hearing will take long. After that you will have time to rest."

Now. Right now I had to go through that door and into another chamber and face up to Mathuin. Look right into his eyes. See his vile face. Hear his mocking voice. I would be like Brígh in the face of Master Tóla, unable to get a word out.

Grim rose to his feet, a big bear of a man. Not looking worried. Looking calm and solemn and as if he had never doubted I could do this. "Better leave Ripple here," he said. "Ripple, stay." The dog settled on the floor, obedient as ever. Grim held out a hand and I took it. "I'll keep right by you," he said. "Might be hard not to spit in that scum's face, but I know the rules. Just go through it one part at a time. Good to get it over with, mm?"

I stood. Found that my legs would support me, just. I took the red kerchief out of my belt and tied it around my neck, bringing a smile to Grim's face. I thought of all the women I was speaking for, women with no voices, women hurt and downtrodden and abused, women struggling to go on living their lives after what Mathuin had done to them. I thought of Strangler and Dribbles, Poxy and Frog Spawn and the other broken men who'd shared our time in the lockup. I thought of the prisoner who had been tortured with hot iron and had taken too long to die. I remembered how we had sung songs and told tales all night, until with the dawn he'd fallen silent.

"All right," I said, finding my voice. "I'm ready."

It was a gathering that might have struck a far bolder speaker dumb. The chamber was similar to Prince Oran's large council room, with a raised section at one end holding a long table with three rather grand oak chairs behind it. To one side was a writing table where the two scribes sat, their materials before them. The main part of the room was bare of furniture; it seemed those gathered would remain standing, which suggested a short hearing indeed. A number of men stood in small groups, talking quietly among themselves. All were dressed very plainly, in clothing more suited to farmers or craftsmen or scholars than to the kings and chieftains they were.

I recognized Oran's father, Ruairi of Dalriada, but not the tall, gray-bearded man he was speaking to. Cúan, who had come to stand beside me and Grim, whispered, "Lorcan of Mide. And the fair-haired man is the High King's representative, a senior councilor. Over there, chieftains from Ulaid and Tirconnell, Laigin and Connacht. And the man in blue"—he indicated a handsome individual of about five-and-forty, his dark curls frosted with gray—"is Lady Flidais's father, Lord Cadhan."

No wonder they wanted to keep this quiet. It had the potential to cause a storm of unrest. Perhaps to unseat the High King, should his involvement reach the wrong ears. And what about Mathuin's family? He had grown sons.

There were Island men at every entry, silent and watchful. No doubt they ringed the outside of the house as well. It must have been quite a feat to get everyone here without arousing suspicion. And Mathuin—how had they done that? And where was he?

I had wondered which of them would lead the proceedings. Somewhat to my surprise, it was Prince Oran who went up to the platform and took the central position, with a black-robed lawman on either side. Donagan moved to stand behind the prince. Everyone hushed.

"My lords, learned men of the law, honored friends, I thank you all for your attendance and for your discretion," Oran said. "We will conduct these proceedings as quickly and efficiently as we can, to allow you to leave at the times arranged. Remember that the hospitality of this house is available to you and to your personal attendants until it is your hour to depart. If there are any questions about the practical arrangements, our guards are able to assist you. Let us begin. Bring in the accused man."

Mathuin of Laois came in with a Swan Island man on either side and his hands tied behind his back. He was white with rage, his eyes wild, his jaw clenched tight. A muscle twitched at his temple. *Don't collapse and die,* I thought, cold at the sight of him. *Not just yet. Not before you hear every last word I have to say.*

It seemed Mathuin did not want anyone but himself to speak. He launched into a tirade of protests. Everything was unacceptable. That he had been snatched from his horse while out hunting. That he had been brought all the way to some godforsaken place under guard without any explanation whatsoever. That an upstart prince appeared to be in charge. That I was present—he spotted me quickly, which was perhaps unsurprising given my red hair and the fact that I was the only woman in the room. That he seemed to be facing some kind of covert trial, when he had committed no offense. The absence of a lawman of his own choice. The absence of the High King. He shouted until Prince Oran offered him a choice: hold his tongue or be tried in absentia, with no chance to speak up for himself and no lawman to represent him. He was quieter after that, but if looks could have killed, we'd all have been struck dead on the spot.

One of the prince's lawmen, Master Saran, read out a long list of offenses, starting with the forcible seizing of Lord Cadhan's home and holdings, with great loss of life, and the consequent driving of Lord Cadhan and his wife out of Laigin to seek sanctuary. The dispute leading up to this was over a particular parcel of land which had long been part of Cadhan's holding. It would be shown that Mathuin had no rightful claim to it either now or in the historical record. There followed numerous other offenses of a kind more familiar to me. The lawman, in dispassionate tones, outlined the activities of the band of thugs who constituted Mathuin's personal guards. The rape and assault of local women, with intimidation used to stop them from speaking up afterward. The beatings and killings of folk who dared to challenge their chieftain's decisions. The incarceration of prisoners in conditions so vile it was a wonder any at all survived the experience. The propensity of Mathuin himself for taking advantage of women whenever he chose, often condemning them to being thrown out by their husbands or parents afterward, especially if they were carrying one of his by-blows. The resulting poverty, despair and, in more than one instance, suicide.

"As to personal testimony," Master Saran said, "Lord Cadhan is here to give his account of the offense against himself and his family. The nature of this hearing precludes most of the other injured parties from being present today. But Mistress Blackthorn is here. She can speak not only for herself but for a significant number of others. Mistress Blackthorn has provided a detailed written account of numerous acts carried out in the accused man's home territory of Laois; testimony gathered from victims who were readier to speak to her, a wise woman, than they would have been to present themselves before a council, formal or informal. This document has been considered by Prince Oran, by myself and by my learned colleague here. Would that every witness might provide such a meticulous account."

"Lies!" Mathuin was almost spitting with fury. "Vile untruths! That woman is a meddler! She's nobody. She's a filthy, flea-ridden slut!"

I felt Grim draw a breath beside me, then check himself. The second lawman said to Mathuin, "It is in your best interest to remain quiet, my lord, until it is time to offer a defense."

"Mistress Blackthorn will speak on the matters covered in her document," said Prince Oran. "I can vouch for her honesty. She has lived and worked within my holding at Winterfalls for some time and is of exemplary character. My father will also confirm her to be trustworthy." He glanced at King Ruairi, who nodded. I was more than a little surprised. I had met Oran's father during our rather uncomfortable stay at court, but I doubted I'd made much impression on him. The prince must have had a word in his ear. As for *exemplary character* . . . if only they knew.

Lord Cadhan spoke first. I stood between Grim and Cúan and listened as he described how it had unfolded: the festering dispute over a parcel of land that had never been Mathuin's; Mathuin's expectation that he would be granted Flidais's hand in marriage, his first wife having died, and his fury when Flidais traveled north to wed Oran; Mathuin leading his men-at-arms to take Cadhan's holdings by force; the blood and carnage; the flight to safety; and Cadhan's bitter regret that he had not stayed to fight to the end but had been persuaded to leave with his wife while he still could. He gave his account calmly. It was only when he spoke of that last flight and those left behind that his voice cracked and broke.

Lorcan of Mide asked a question about any previous conversation or correspondence between Mathuin and Cadhan over the disputed territory. There had been demands from the one and courteously worded refusals from the other. One of the chieftains asked about the status of Cadhan's seized property under the law, and the second lawman, Master Bress, clarified the situation.

I was trying to listen and concentrate. Doing my best to stay calm, knowing that with every moment that passed, every measured speech, every furious interjection by Mathuin, I was one step closer to having to speak. With my heart going like a drum and my skin all cold sweat, I'd be lucky if I could put two words together. My head was muzzy; there were spots in front of my eyes.

And here was Cúan with a stool, setting it by me, helping me sit down.

"Is all well, Mistress Blackthorn?" asked Oran. With so few folk in the chamber, he could see me clearly.

I couldn't answer. I worked on breathing; on not fainting. Grim crouched down beside me, eyes anxious. Someone put a cup in my hand and I took a gulp. It was watered mead and tasted vile. But I did feel better. I felt much better, especially when I looked up and saw Conmael standing on the other side of the chamber, under a tapestry of strange beasts cavorting in a forest. He was leaning against the wall. His arms were crossed; his pose was nonchalant. He didn't need to say a thing. Wouldn't, anyway, since it was quite plain nobody else could see him except perhaps Grim, who followed my gaze, then turned his eyes quickly away. Conmael nodded gravely. His face told me what he wanted to say. *You are strong. You are good. You are wise. You can do this. See? I'm not worried in the slightest.*

"I'm fine now," I said. "Thank you, my lord."

"A long journey for you," said the prince. "Learned colleagues, might we allow Mistress Blackthorn to give her testimony first? The accused man could answer to all the charges at the end, both Lord Cadhan's matter and the others."

After a murmured consultation, the lawmen agreed that yes, this was acceptable to them provided Lord Cadhan agreed. Lord Cadhan said he had no objection.

"If this is the way you conduct a hearing," said Mathuin, "then God help any man who wants justice from you. You ask him if it's acceptable. What about me? Does my legal representative make decisions without consulting me?"

"You prefer Mistress Blackthorn to wait, unwell as she is, until Lord Cadhan's matter is fully resolved? You wish to speak on that matter now?" Oran's tone was icy. He was a young man and looked every bit the scholar, soft and kindly. I knew from experience how deceptive that could be.

"Let the slut have her moment," Mathuin said, eyeing me in a way that made my flesh crawl. "She's waited long enough for it. Let her tell her pack of lies. Every so-called wise woman's got her two coppers' worth of magic tricks. She might be good for a few moments' entertainment. That's all she was worth in the lockup. Or so my men said when they'd finished with her."

I felt Grim tense; felt the rage in him. "No," I murmured. "No, Grim. Don't let him do this." I could see how it might be: my friend hurling himself forward, using his size and strength to cast aside anyone in his way, be it king or prince or chieftain, and fastening his hands around Mathuin's throat to make an end of the man. Thereby robbing me of the chance to testify and ensuring justice would never be done. We would not be free of this until the day we died.

Grim was quivering with fury. His grip on my hand hurt. It told me he was using all his strength to keep still and hold his tongue.

"Good," I said in a whisper. "I have to speak. You know that."

He gasped in a breath. Nodded.

"I prefer to do so without broken fingers."

He slackened his grip. Then lifted my hand and touched it to his lips. "Sorry," he whispered. "Go on, Lady. Do it for all of us."

Oran beckoned me forward. Asked me if I preferred to be seated while I gave my account. I said no. Mathuin was there, standing between his guards. I was here, no more than four strides away. I would face him on equal ground. I drew one long, steady breath.

"My name is Blackthorn. I am a wise woman and healer," I said. There was Grim, watching me with burning eyes. There was Conmael, cool as ever. Cionnaola stood by the rear door. Cúan was a couple of paces from me, watching Mathuin with a look that said, *Make one move, friend. Just try it.* Kings and chieftains stood quiet and attentive, waiting. "But once my name was Saorla," I went on, my voice strong and sure now, "and I was wife to a scribe and scholar named Cass, dwelling in the region of Laois . . ."

48

I t was over. The whole grueling account. I had wept as I told of the fire that took Cass and Brennan from me, and the cruel hands of Mathuin's men, holding me back as the screams of my dear ones tore me apart. My voice had shaken with rage as I told of that year of hell in the lockup. When I told the tales of the abused women, I had spoken calmly, holding Mathuin's gaze. Hoping to see some flicker of remorse, some small sign of understanding there. But there was nothing. We were scum. He was a chieftain. He could treat us any way he pleased. He was entitled.

For a little, after I finished, the chamber was completely silent. Perhaps Mathuin understood that another outburst would lose him the right to respond.

"Thank you, Mistress Blackthorn," said Oran. "You may step down. I commend your courage. That cannot have been easy."

"Wait a moment." Mathuin spoke now. "Don't I get the right to question her? What kind of joke is this?"

"You will have the opportunity to speak," Oran said. "And to ask questions. A limited number of questions. It may be wiser if Master

Bress speaks on your behalf. I will give you a little time to confer with him now." He turned to me again. "Step down, Mistress Blackthorn."

I did as I was told. My legs got me as far as the stool, where I sat, shivering. The last time Mathuin had questioned me, I had been publicly mocked and humiliated. I had been scorned and spat upon and worse. And then I'd been thrown into the lockup. I did not want questions now. I had told the truth, and it had hurt more than anyone could understand. I had been brave. Somewhere, deep down, I felt proud that I had spoken up. But I did not want to go back there. I did not want to go back to that day when Mathuin had made me the lowest of the low, when he had stripped away the last of my dignity, when he had shown me that sometimes all a person's courage is not enough.

"You did fine." Grim was crouched beside me again, holding the cup. "Take a sip or two. Should steady you a bit. Nearly over."

I took the cup, but it shook so violently in my hand that Grim took it back. He held it for me while I drank. "I don't think I can . . ." I whispered.

"Do it together, right?" said Grim. "Team, aren't we?"

I attempted a smile. Up by the long table Master Bress was speaking to Mathuin in hushed tones. Trying to convince him, perhaps, that it might be better if he did not ask his own questions. And failing, since Master Bress now turned toward the prince and said, "Lord Mathuin wishes to question Mistress Blackthorn himself, my lord, as in the matters she has raised it is only her word against his. I believe that should be allowed. I have advised him to moderate his language."

It felt like a bad dream. I stood up, moved forward again. Grim walked beside me.

"Bonehead!" exclaimed Mathuin, as if he had not noticed my companion before. "You useless lump of horseshit, you're still alive!"

"If that's your idea of moderating your language," said Oran, "you'll be out of here before I can count to ten. If you have questions, ask them. With at least a modicum of courtesy."

"I only need to ask one. *Mistress* Blackthorn." Mathuin made the title into an insult, and I cringed despite myself. "You know you've told a pack of lies, just as you did when you stormed into my council chamber back in Laois and accused me of all manner of foul things. Quite an imagination, you have. That's about all you do have. You may have provided a testimony, setting out names and times and more disgusting details than any man would have the stomach for. But where are your witnesses? You haven't produced a single one. That makes these proceedings a total sham. A nonsense. A waste of everyone's time. No accusation will stick on the word of one person alone. Especially if that person is of dubious character, and a woman."

Grim took a deep breath. I waited for him to shout a furious response. But he spoke quietly, not to Mathuin but to Prince Oran. "I'm a witness, my lord. Not to all of it. But that time in the lockup, I was there. What she saw, I saw. Folk beaten and abused. Folk tortured to death. Men smashing themselves against the walls because they couldn't go on. Guards ordering folk to hurt one another. Folk doing it so they wouldn't get hurt worse. Some prisoners in there hadn't done anything wrong. Like her. Blackthorn. Stood up for people with no voice, that's all she did. Spoke out against that man you see there. Risked her own neck doing it. Should be more like her. Me, I stopped that man's thugs from beating a lad to death. So Mathuin threw me in the lockup. Doesn't like folk to challenge him. Doesn't like folk to speak up. I'm speaking up today. Never been good with words. Not like her. But I know how to tell the truth."

It felt as if everyone in the chamber let out a breath.

"Thank you, Grim," said Prince Oran. "Mistress Blackthorn, do you wish to speak further?"

"Everything Grim said is true. Both of us have told only the truth. I have nothing more to say, except that I trust this assembly to see justice done."

"Thank you, Mistress Blackthorn. You and Grim may leave the chamber now if you wish, and wait in the other room. Master Saran? Master Bress? Do you concur that the question Lord Mathuin posed has been adequately answered?"

The lawmen nodded. No need for discussion.

"Very well. Master Bress, does Lord Mathuin wish to question Lord Cadhan on the other matter? Or will you speak for him?"

We allowed Cúan to usher us out of the chamber. If I heard one more word of poison from Mathuin, I thought I might be sick. And I did not want to be sick in front of such an august gathering. In the smaller chamber, Cúan stayed with us while another of the Island men went off to fetch a platter of oatcakes and a jug of ale. The ale was welcome. The food, I could not touch.

"Better eat something," said Grim. "You still look shaky."

"I didn't say thank you."

"To me? No need. It's what we do, isn't it?"

"Stand up for each other?" *Save each other over and over again.*

"Mm-hm. Didn't think I'd be saying anything. Not in front of kings and chieftains and the like. But it felt good. It felt right, for the fellows who didn't make it out of that place. And the ones who got out but never . . ." He stumbled over the words. "The ones who saw the open sky and then died. Strangler. Poxy. Dribbles. Poor bastards."

He'd never told me the full story, and I didn't ask for it now. Whatever had happened, it had wounded him deep. Another scar to bear.

"How long do you think they will be, Cúan?" I asked.

"I don't suppose they will debate it long. Determining the penalty might take a while."

I remembered with some horror that in another case, when a young woman had been abducted and abused, Prince Oran had asked Grim and me to join the discussion of an appropriate penalty. I wanted no part of it this time. There was too much hate in me. I had seen in Mathuin's face that he could not change; that he had no will to become a better man, no understanding of what that meant. I did not want him exiled, for an exile can break a promise and return covertly. I did not want him banished for a term, perhaps to some monastic island. A man like him would break the rules without a moment's hesitation. I did not want him working off his debt, even in the farthest corner of Erin. He would be walking the same ground as I was. He would find a way back. I wanted him gone. I wanted him dead. And for a wise woman to think such a thought was deeply wrong. Was not my craft to mend the broken, heal the wounded, cure the sick?

"Funny," observed Grim. "Remember that wretch Branoc? Thought I recalled the prince saying something then about unofficial execution."

He was reading my mind again. "Not a remark Prince Oran would want shared," I said, glancing at Cúan. "Who will make the decision?"

"I believe all those present in the council will discuss the matter and reach a conclusion by consensus. That will include determination of the penalty if the accused man is found guilty."

We waited, and waited some more. Tight-strung though I was, I could feel myself dropping off to sleep. If we had not traveled Conmael's way, this would have been the middle of the night. Without thinking about it too hard, I leaned my head on Grim's shoulder and closed my eyes.

A knock at the door. I started, sitting upright. I might have been asleep for a moment or an hour. "Sorry," I murmured vaguely as the door opened to admit a number of men. Donagan, Prince Oran and the two lawmen, Cionnaola, followed by . . . Now I was wide-awake. Followed by Conmael. Cúan shut the door behind them. I rose to my feet. Beside me, Grim did the same. He was stifling a yawn. Perhaps we had both been asleep.

"Be seated, please," said the prince. "There's a matter I wish to discuss with you, Mistress Blackthorn, and with Grim, since you are both injured parties in this case. The hearing is concluded but for delivery of the determination and the penalty. Because of the need to keep the conduct of this secret, I asked those present to give me their decisions and their reasoning in private, one at a time. We are unanimous in finding Lord Mathuin guilty on all charges. As for the penalty, that has caused us some difficulty. We have the means to make him disappear. Permanently." He glanced at Cionnaola. "But that could give rise to awkward questions. The man has family, lands, influence. Besides, it might not serve justice well. It might, in effect, be too easy an ending for him, and too difficult for those of us left behind. Exile would seem more appropriate."

"He would come back," I said in a croaking whisper, then cleared my throat and tried again. "Anger would bring him back from the end of the world. We would never be free of him."

"Man's got a couple of grown-up sons," said Grim. "Way I see it, they'll step in and be just like him. Same thing all over again."

"Lord Mathuin will forfeit his entire holding," said Master Saran. "It will be passed into the stewardship of the High King for disposition elsewhere. The land is lost to Mathuin's heirs. If we could banish his sons along with him, be sure we would do so. But that lies beyond even the widest interpretation of the law."

"Lord Cadhan's holding at Cloud Hill will be restored to him," Oran said. "Sadly, there can be no restoring the lives lost in that raid."

I was trying not to look at Conmael, who stood quietly beside Cionnaola. What in the name of the gods was he doing in here?

"Mistress Blackthorn," said the prince, "we had not realized that your friend Lord Conmael of Underhill was to be part of these proceedings. I have been advised that he rode here with you, under the protection of my guards, but chose not to be involved in the hearing itself. He has, however, offered a solution to the current difficulty. That solution fits the requirements of the law. And by its nature it will be somewhat easier to keep from public knowledge."

So they could see him now. *Lord Conmael of Underhill.* It had an impressive ring. Only Prince Oran, I thought, could be approached by one of the fey under such circumstances and be prepared to listen and take notice. I'd bet a bag of silver that every other man of standing present for the hearing would have called the guards to throw the interloper out. But Oran knew about magic. He knew about the fey. So did Donagan. We had shared a very odd experience with them not long after we first came to Winterfalls, an episode all of us had kept secret. Oran was a man who loved ancient tales, a man who was open to the strange and uncanny. To most folk, the fey existed only in those tales; they were either a product of the imagination or something from the distant past, long dead and gone. As for Cúan and Cionnaola, they had traveled here by Conmael's path. His presence would be no great shock to them. They had probably been the means of his gaining the prince's ear.

"Will you explain, my lord?" I spoke to Conmael direct, using the title he'd given himself for the occasion. Or maybe he really was Lord of Underhill, who knew?

"You know what I am, Mistress Blackthorn." His voice was full of authority, as if he stood so far above any human king or prince that there could be no comparison. This was not arrogance. It was an acceptance of what he was. As if, in knowing him as Cully, I had given him back his true self. "I have the power to exile your offending chieftain not only beyond the borders of Erin, but beyond the borders of the human world. I can take him to a place from which there can be no returning home. The choice is not mine to make; I play no part in the workings of human law. I understand exile to be an appropriate penalty for these offenses. I know, perhaps better than most, what an impact exiling Lord Mathuin anywhere within your own world would have on his victims. They would be forever fearful of his return. Forever living in dread. So I offer to do this for you. I will take him away, and you will never see him again. Within my world, he will be appropriately punished."

"Holy Mother of God," murmured Grim.

It wasn't hard to imagine what that punishment might be like. I only had to think of Bardán, a master craftsman with scattered wits and ruined hands. Brígh in that hole, beset by tormenting voices. It would be worse than the lockup. Far worse. It might go on and on until Mathuin died of it. I felt as if my veins had turned to ice.

"Mistress Blackthorn?"

Prince Oran had said something and I'd missed it. "I'm sorry, what was that?"

"Lord Conmael is genuine in his wish to help us. His offer may be a little difficult to explain to the others, but I will word it carefully. It may be best, Lord Conmael, if you are not present when the verdict and penalty are delivered."

"Could just say, exile to a far-off land," suggested Grim. "For life. Under the supervision of Lord Conmael."

Oran smiled. "Nicely put," he said. "Mistress Blackthorn, I need only your approval for this. The penalty is severe, though perhaps not quite as severe as you might have wished."

Maybe not. The Island men were entirely capable of performing an unofficial execution. A swift killing, an equally swift disposal of the body in some lonely corner of the land. But then, Conmael offered an exile from which there really would be no return. An exile in which Mathuin would endure a punishment such as his victims had endured, should Conmael decide that. And from the look on his face, I suspected he might. In the stinking hell of the lockup, we'd believed our torment would not end until the day we died. Mathuin would learn the weight of that burden. "You have my approval," I said. "And I thank Lord Conmael for offering this."

"Very well," said the prince. "We will proceed."

It was quick, after that. The prince and his lawmen went out to speak to the assembled nobles, and then we were called in to join them. Conmael did not come with us. The guards brought Mathuin in again, silent now. He still had his wrists bound.

I had wondered why it was Prince Oran who'd led this from start to finish; why his father, the king of Dalriada, or the still more influential King Lorcan of Mide had not been asked to speak or to deliver the verdict. But it was obvious now. There were the plain clothes they all wore, the sort of garments a farmer might put on for feast days. There was the fact that none of them had said much, despite their status as leaders. It was to limit the risk and preserve the secret—a secret that went right up to the High King.

We stood at the back, beside the guards. Now that it had come to this, now that it was almost over, I felt no sense of triumph, no joy, no vindication. Instead, I felt tired and confused and a little sad. The wrongs Mathuin had done, or had caused to be done, could not be put right. I was glad he would be gone from the human realm. But this was not the only man in Erin to misuse power, to trample on those he believed to be lesser beings, to grab what he wanted and care nothing for the consequences. This was not the only man—or woman—to let entitlement blind him to a knowledge of good and evil. And if I was everything Grim and Conmael and Prince Oran believed me to be, I'd be fighting that until the day I died.

"Mathuin of Laois." As Oran spoke, I did not see the young man of four-and-twenty but a leader who would one day be king of Dalriada, and likely a very fine one. I hoped his father, looking on in silence, was proud of him. "With due attention to the evidence brought forward, this hearing has determined you guilty on all charges. For the unprovoked assault on Lord Cadhan's household, the loss of life, the damage to property and your consequent seizure of his lands, we pronounce this penalty. You are henceforth stripped of your chieftaincy. Your lands are forfeit to the custodianship of the High King, who will distribute them as he sees fit. Your heirs will have no future claim to title or land. Lord Cadhan's property is restored to him from this day forward. Any attempt by you or yours to dispute this decision, or to take up arms in order to retain or reclaim land or goods, will result in severe consequences."

Mathuin said not a word. His face showed no feelings at all. Had he expected this, or something like it? If so, his earlier performance had been remarkable. Perhaps he was so shocked he was beyond a response. Or maybe he had anticipated something worse.

"For your offenses against Mistress Blackthorn and against the many other innocent victims whose tales she has told today, Grim included, the penalty is exile for life."

Mathuin opened his mouth to say something. Now, for the first time, Oran's words seemed to have sunk in.

"Do not speak," warned Master Bress.

"You will be delivered forthwith into the custody of Lord Conmael of Underhill, who will convey you to the place of exile. It is far from here. I do not imagine we will meet again, Mathuin of Laois."

"Now wait a moment—" Mathuin began.

"These proceedings are concluded." Oran's quiet voice cut through the protest like a knife through soft butter. "I thank you all for your attendance and cooperation."

"Guards," said Donagan, "take the prisoner out. Lord Conmael is waiting."

"Underhill?" Mathuin was talking now, all the way to the door and out. "Where in God's name is Underhill? This is a travesty! You'll never get away with . . ." He was gone.

With a speed born of the Island men's rigorous training, the kings and chieftains were escorted away, each at his appointed time and with his appointed guards. By dusk on the day of the hearing, only Grim and I and a small complement of warriors were left. Oran and Donagan, with two guards, had been the last to depart. Oran had suggested we ride with them, but the Island men had thought that unwise.

"The fewer who travel together, the less the likelihood of attracting notice," Cionnaola said.

There was no need to ask whether traveling in twos and threes meant one was more likely to be overcome by thieves or other miscreants along the way. The presence of an Island man meant any such attack would be both brief and unsuccessful.

So now we were rattling around the big house like forgotten peas left to dry up in the pod. I wanted to go home. But it was late, it was getting dark and there was no Conmael to make it happen with uncanny speed. I had not seen him again after the sentence was delivered. He had taken custody of Mathuin, and before I'd had a chance to say farewell and thank you, the two of them had gone.

"Longish ride home," Grim observed, as we sat in the warmth of the kitchen while Cúan did some rudimentary cooking. "Sleep first would be good. Don't you think?"

"It would be sensible. I think we may have been awake for two days and a night. Or even more. That doesn't stop me wanting to get on a horse and ride for home right now."

"The plan is to leave in the morning, before the residents of this house return," Cúan said. "Ride tired and you risk making foolish mistakes."

"I was joking," I said. "I think."

"Best not think too much," Grim said. "Eat, sleep. New day tomorrow."

We ate. My appetite had returned, and Cúan's dish of eggs and cheese went down well. Then Art, another of the Island men I knew from Winterfalls, showed us to a rather grand bedchamber, lit by a number of shielded candles. There was a bed so generously proportioned that a whole family could have slept there. One bed.

I was too tired to protest, and Grim had nothing to say. Our spare clothing lay neatly folded atop a storage chest; someone had unpacked our bags for us. My head was swimming with weariness. This wasn't the first time someone had assumed we were the kind of couple that shared a bed. And, the fact was, we'd been undressing and washing and sleeping at close quarters for the last year or two. Though, through the haze of exhaustion, I did sense this was a little different.

"If you want, I'll sleep on the floor," Grim said, bending to take off his boots. Ripple had settled herself on a mat of woven rushes.

"Don't be silly. That bed's big enough for five or six people. Even people your size. Just turn your back while I take off my gown, will you? Gods, I feel as if I haven't slept for days."

The bed was soft, the blankets warm. There were pillows stuffed with what felt like goose feathers. "Imagine sleeping in something like this every night," I said as I climbed in. "Feels wrong, somehow." Though it felt good too. Especially when his weight settled on the other side of the mattress. It felt oddly right. "Good night, Grim," I said. "Thank you for standing by me today."

"Sweet dreams."

I was walking through that tree tunnel again, alone this time, with the strange leaves whispering around me. The tunnel branched to left and right. "Choose," said a voice, though I could not see who spoke. "Will it be the hermit's way or the warrior's way?" Before I could take another step, I was awake in the night, with three candles burned down to guttering stubs and the other gone dark. And I was acutely aware that even though the bed was big enough for five or six, Grim and I had both ended up in the middle. My head was resting on his shoulder. His arm was around me. The rest of me was pressed up against his side and, somewhat to my astonishment, I found myself reaching out a hand to lay it over his heart. The warrior's way meant being prepared to take risks.

"Grim? Are you awake?"

"Mm-hm." His hand came over mine. "Had a good sleep, though. Best in a while. Should do this more often."

"Shh," I said, moving my leg to hook it over his. "Don't say anything, mm?"

There was no need to speak. Our hands, our mouths, our bodies spoke for us more eloquently than any words. I had not thought I would ever be ready for this. I had believed my body was too hurt, my heart shut too tight ever to enjoy the act of love again. But I had known tonight, as soon as I woke, that I'd been wrong. With this man, it would be all right. He knew me. He knew my past. He had seen me at my worst, filthy, abused, degraded. And still he had called me Lady.

For such a big man, Grim was the gentlest of lovers, the most considerate, waiting always for me to be ready, waiting for the little signs, accommodating my smaller frame, harnessing his own desire until he knew I was satisfied. When it was over we fell asleep in each other's arms. The dying candles set shadows dancing across the walls.

When I woke next morning I was alone in the big bed. Half-awake, I thought, *That was the best sleep I ever had.* Then I became aware of certain aches in my body, good ones, and a general sense of well-being. And then I remembered, and thought, *What have I done?*

I packed up. Had breakfast. Helped Cúan wash the dishes while Cionnaola and Grim saddled the horses. Then we rode home. In the company of the Island men, Grim and I did not speak a word about what had happened between us. It seemed to me the longer we stayed silent, the harder it was going to be to find the right words when we did talk about it.

The journey was long enough to require an overnight stop, and for this we camped in a secluded spot near a small wood. Grim and I slept on opposite sides of the fire, wrapped in our own thoughts. The next day, in the late afternoon, we reached the cottage, said farewell and thank you to Cúan and Cionnaola, and watched them head off to the prince's house with the horses. We were home.

"Brew?" asked Grim. "I'll get some firewood in."

"Mm. Give me your things. I'll put them away."

A little later, the fire was glowing, Ripple was settled in her favorite spot and our cups were steaming on the table.

"You all right?" asked Grim. "Been a bit quiet."

"I didn't mean that to happen." The words spilled out, ill considered. "What happened that night. I didn't mean to change things between us."

"Mm-hm. Felt like a good change to me."

"It was good. Only . . . you and me, the way things are—were—I didn't want to spoil that. To make it . . . complicated. Didn't want to get too close, not that close anyway, because . . . well, you know."

He waited a little, then said, "I don't know. Tell me."

"Because if you love someone, you set them up to be used against you. You make them a target for your enemies. And if you lose them, it breaks you. There, I've said it."

"So," said Grim carefully, "that was only once? Back to being just friends?"

"No. Yes. I don't know. And that makes me angry. And that isn't fair. I think you may be too good for me—that's the truth."

"Me?" he said. "Nah. That's rubbish. If you want it to be just friends, all right. Only . . . seems to me your argument's got a great big hole in it."

"Oh? And what's that?"

"Remember what happened at Wolf Glen? You setting aside the mission you'd been living for since the lockup so you could rush up there and save me? You know I'd do the same for you any day. So maybe it's too late for that argument. Don't you think?"

And of course, he was right. Even before that night, what was between us had been far more than simple friendship. It had already grown into the kind of bond I had thought never to form again. Unless I decided to turn my back on him and walk away, or send him into his own exile and break both our hearts, we were a pair forever. And if that was so, there seemed no reason not to enjoy everything that pairing had to offer.

"Oh, gods," I said, putting my hands up to my face.

"You laughing or crying?" His voice was gentle.

"Both," I said. "This is going to take a bit of getting used to." I brought my hands down and surveyed the interior of our house, cozy, modest, smallish, and rather full, what with the two narrow shelf beds, the hearth, the dog, the table and benches, the shelves holding the paraphernalia of my craft. "We could do with a bigger bed. Only where would we put it?"

"Ah," said Grim, smiling. "Had a thought about that. You know that silver I earned up at Wolf Glen? I was thinking of making a change here, building on another room. For your work. If you wanted it. Thought I'd earn the funds first and then ask you. There'll be no more from Tóla—that's plain. But there's enough for the materials, and I can do the work. What do you think?"

"I think yes. Especially if you can make a bed too."

"Won't be grand like that one we slept in. But big, yes—I can do that. And comfortable."

"Good," I said. "Meanwhile we'll have to make do with one of these. Could be a squeeze. But I'm sure we'll manage."

His grin was like a flash of sunlight on a dark day. It made my breath catch.

"You know," I said, "that it won't all be easy going from here on. Trouble will keep finding us. Puzzles and traps and enemies, uncanny problems and worldly ones too. It's the nature of things. We'll always have battles to fight. We'll always need to take risks and put ourselves in danger. Someone asked me if I wanted the hermit's path or the warrior's path. I think ours is the warrior's path. Even though we seem to be . . . settling down."

"I'll go on any path you want," Grim said. "Might give you a push sometimes, keep you walking straight. But whatever happens, I'll be right there beside you. Rain or shine. Shadows or light. Step for step. Always."

acknowledgments

The seed idea for *Den of Wolves* was a traditional tale from western Scotland, "Big MacVurich and the Monster." I first came across the story in a small book, *The Celtic Tree Oracle* by Liz and Colin Murray (St. Martin's Press, 1988), that accompanied a wonderful set of divination cards. The tale captured my imagination from the first. The Murrays' source was Alexander Carmichael's collection *Carmina Gadelica: Hymns and Incantations*, a scholarly and comprehensive collection of lore from the Highlands and islands of Scotland. A one-volume English edition of *Carmina Gadelica* was published by Floris Books in 1992. The tale told by the druid Oisin in *Den of Wolves* is my own version, and the only one to use the term "heartwood house." In the best storytelling tradition, it takes the bones of the existing versions and adds new flesh.

My thanks go to everyone who helped bring this book to fruition. The editorial staff at Pan Macmillan (Australia) and Penguin Random House (USA) provided their usual blend of support, professionalism and flexibility. A big thank-you to Claire Craig, Brianne Tunnicliffe and Rebecca Hamilton in Sydney, and to Anne Sowards and Rebecca Brewer in New York. A small crew of trusted family and friends helped me with brainstorming and beta reading. Heartfelt thanks to Elly, Godric, Tamara and Gaye for their bright ideas, their honest and perceptive feedback and their precious time.

Thank you to my agent, Russell Galen, for his calm and reasoned advice and his astute decisions.

Last, thank you, readers, for loving Blackthorn and Grim as much as I do, and for allowing me to continue doing what I most enjoy: sharing stories with you, helping you over rough patches, keeping you entertained and taking you on a journey.